MY DARLING ARROW

ST. MARY'S REBELS
BOOK 1

SAFFRON A. KENT

Cover Art by Najla Qamber Designs
Cover Model: Jon Herrmann
Editing by Leanne Rabesa
Proofreading by Virginia Tesi Carey

May 2023 Edition

Published in the United States of America

OTHER BOOKS BY SAFFRON A. KENT

ST. MARY'S REBELS

Bad Boy Blues (SMR book 0.5)

My Darling Arrow (SMR book 1)

The Wild Mustang & The Dancing Fairy (SMR book 1.5)

A Gorgeous Villain (SMR book 2)

These Thorn Kisses (SMR book 3)

Hey, Mister Marshall (SMR book 4)

The Hatesick Diaries (SMR book 5)

BLURB

Darling Arrow,

I shouldn't be writing this.

It's not as if I'm ever going to send you this letter, and there are a million reasons why.

First of all, I was sent to this reform school as a punishment for a petty, *totally* inconsequential crime. Not to ogle the principal's hot son around the campus.

Second of all, you're a giant jerk. You're arrogant and moody and so cold. Sometimes I think I shouldn't even like you.

But strangely your coldness sets me on fire.

The way your athletic body moves on the soccer field, and the way your powerful thighs sprawl across that motorcycle of yours, make me go inappropriately breathless.

But that's not the worst part.

The worst part is that you, Arrow Carlisle, are not only the principal's hot son.

You also happen to be the love of my sister's life.

And I *really* shouldn't be thinking about my sister's boyfriend, or rather fiancé (I overheard a conversation about the ring that I shouldn't have).

Now if I can only stop writing you these meaningless letters that I'll never send and you'll never read...

Never yours,
Salem

NOTE: This book is a standalone and DOES NOT contain cheating.

For every girl who has secretly loved a boy and written him love letters at midnight.

And of course, for the not-so-secret love of my life, my husband.

READER'S EXTRAS

Official Spotify playlist
Pinterest Boards
Arrow & Salem
St. Mary's school for Troubled Teenagers

AUTHOR'S NOTE

The regular Major League Soccer (MLS) season ends in October. However, for the purpose of this story, this timeline has been tweaked.

Unrequited Love:

When the one you love doesn't love you back.

Doomed Love:

A type of unrequited love; when the one you love is in love with someone else.

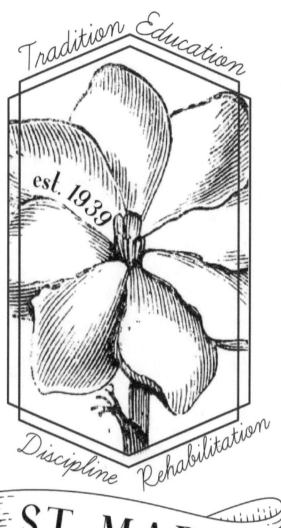

Tradition Education

est. 1939

Discipline Rehabilitation

ST. MARY'S

SCHOOL

FOR TROUBLED TEENS

ST. MARY'S GUIDE
to Lip Lovin'
for One and All:

FOR GIRLS DOOMED IN LOVE
Teenage Decay

Dream Broken Darling   I Jinx U   Drip Drip Gasoline

Good Bad Girl   Sweet Little Sweetheart   Golden Eyed Queen

FOR GIRLS BETRAYED IN LOVE

Heartbreak Juju   Crazy-Hearted Loner   Moon-Eyed Wasteland

Queen of the Bards   Sex and Candy   Train Wreck Princess

FOR GIRLS WHO DREAM

Red Addict   Pink and Shameless   Cherry Picker

Lollipop Lover   Pinky Winky Promises

FOR GIRLS WHO LOVE TROUBLE
Troubled Sweetheart

Handmade Heaven   Cute Corruption   Young and on Fire

God of a Girl   Purple Witchcraft   Wild Child Bad Child

FOR GIRLS WHO FALL FOR THE BAD

Desert Rose   She-Desperado   Watermelon Sugar

Dangerous Woman   Pink Lemonade   Glitter Glitter Baby

CHAPTER ONE

S ome girls are born perfect.

They have perfect hair, perfect eyes, perfect skin.

They have perfect grades and high ambitions. They're popular and admired. They're adored and revered. And loved.

I'm not one of them.

That's the first thing to know about me: I'm not perfect.

I have flaws. Many, many flaws.

I don't have perfect grades. I don't have high ambitions.

I don't get why the sum of all the angles of a triangle *has* to be one hundred and eighty or the world will collapse. Or why when we talk about the heart, we reduce it to a muscular organ with four chambers that's sole purpose is to pump blood through the body.

I'm far from being popular and I've got something called witchy eyes.

Or at least, I call them that.

They're golden in color and they arch up at the corners, making them look sort of catty, witchy. Which is super poetic because I've got a witchy name too.

Salem.

Salem Salinger, and the second thing to know about me is that along with witchy eyes and a witchy name, I've got a witchy heart as well.

Meaning, my heart has secrets.

In fact, my heart is swollen with secrets. Many, many secrets like my many, many flaws. And that is why I did what I did.

The thing that landed me here.

The little, inconsequential crime that got me sent to St. Mary's School for Troubled Teenagers – an all-girls reform school.

Only they don't call it a reform school anymore.

It's not the 50s or the 60s. These days, schools like this are called therapeutic school. Because they believe in therapy. And restoration and reformation. They believe in teaching us to be productive members of society.

Who's *us*?

We're the bad and hopeless girls.

We're the girls who break rules and love rebellion. We don't like school or classes. So we keep getting into trouble with our classmates and teachers. Sometimes we get expelled multiple times from multiple schools until our parents or guardians are forced to take drastic actions.

Some of us break the law too, which technically I did.

I mean, there were a couple of cops involved. They didn't handcuff me or anything but I had to ride in their squad car and go to the police station. But there were no charges pressed. Instead, I was sent to St. Mary's.

I've been here almost a week and I'm already behind. In assignments, I mean.

God, the assignments and homework.

They're very strict about that here.

So I really shouldn't be falling asleep in class if I want to catch up.

But it's Friday afternoon and it's trigonometry and it's not as if I'm magically going to understand everything to do with triangles and tangents by paying attention in the last fifteen minutes of the class anyway.

Honestly, I don't think anyone is paying attention even though everyone is quiet and facing the blackboard.

There are probably fifteen other girls besides me in this small beige-painted concrete and cement classroom where I sit in the back.

We're all slumped over the hard, wooden desks, with our chins in our hands.

We all have tight braids either flowing down our backs or draped over our shoulders, tied at the end with a mustard-colored ribbon. We all wear a starched white blouse and a mustard-yellow skirt that touches the tops of our knees. Except I have a black chunky sweater on because I'm a sunshine girl and the inside of St. Mary's feels like winter.

We pair our uniforms with knee-length white socks and polished black Mary Janes.

Our notebooks are lying open in front of us and our butts are planted in chairs as hard and wooden as the desks.

From time to time, we squirm and adjust ourselves in our seats because I'm guessing the wood is digging into our asses.

At least, it's digging into mine.

So it should be really hard to fall asleep, right? Or daydream.

But I'm doing both until I hear a sound.

Psst...

It's coming from my right. Slowly I turn to find my neighbor, over in the adjacent row, trying to get my attention.

It's a girl I've seen before.

Around campus, in the cafeteria and in the dorm building where every student who goes to St. Mary's stays, but I've never talked to her.

Because no one talks to me here.

I've actually tried very hard to get them to talk to me or even smile at me or just wave their hand at me by waving mine but I haven't been successful. I can't even get my roommate, Elanor, to say hi to me.

So I don't know what this girl, my neighbor with blonde hair, wants from me. But as soon as our eyes meet, she motions her head toward something.

Biting my lip, I look at what she's pointing at.

It's a piece of paper.

It's sitting at the edge of my desk, folded over twice to make a little square.

For a second, I can't comprehend what a piece of paper is doing on my desk. Confused, I look up from it and focus back on the girl. She widens her eyes at me and gestures at it with her chin again.

What the...

Oh.

Oh!

I finally get it. It's a note.

She's passing me a note and she wants me to open it.

Got it.

Immediately, I go to grab it but stop, my hand suspended in midair. I look up and see that the teacher, Mrs. Miller, is busy solving a weird-looking equation on the board. So I'm safe there.

But why is this girl writing me a note?

Doesn't she know that I'm the most hated girl at St. Mary's right now?

I'm the principal's ward.

Yeah, the principal of St. Mary's School for Troubled Teenagers, Leah Carlisle, is my guardian. She's *been* my guardian for eight years now, ever since I was ten.

And somehow because of that I'm enemy number one around campus.

So far in the week that I've been here, people have glared at me, tried to trip me in the cafeteria, accidentally-on-purpose bumped into me in the dorm hallways and locked me in the bathroom.

From what I can gather, the students think I'm a spy, and if they talk to me and reveal their secrets, I might go to Leah and rat them out. And teachers think that since I'm her ward, I'll be given special treatment.

So it's natural for me to debate whether or not I should open the note.

But then I hear my neighbor's whispered words. "Open it."

I swivel my gaze at her and she says those words again, or rather mouths them, *open it*, before giving me a big smile.

A big and brilliant smile.

It's the smile that does it.

Someone is *smiling* at me.

A girl at St. Mary's – my new reform/therapeutic school – is smiling at me and I didn't even have to do anything to get that smile.

So fuck it.

My hand resumes its journey and practically snatches the note off the desk. I bring it down to my lap and open it.

It's boring, huh? I get it. Miller is a snooze-fest. But don't let her catch you falling asleep. She loves to take away student privileges.

Ah, the infamous privileges.

This whole reform/therapeutic school system runs on a little thing called student privileges, which you earn by following the rules.

So here's the whole concept: when we're sent to St. Mary's, they take away everything that we've so far taken for granted in our old, corrupt and rebellious lives.

First of all, there is no personal technology allowed. Meaning no cell phones or laptops or iPads or whatever. Everything that we use has to be school-issued and it is heavily monitored. If you want to use the internet, you go to the computer lab and use the computer there, for an allotted number of hours. If you want to talk to someone on the phone, you do it using the school phone, again only during an allotted time period.

Second, if you want to go off campus, you need a permission slip from a teacher and you can only go out during an allotted time.

Now if you're good – your grades are okay and you've been doing your home-work and participating in activities – you get the privilege of using the computer longer than everyone else or you can go out twice a week and stay out longer and so on.

And who keeps track of things like this? The guidance counselor assigned to you that you meet with every week.

But all of this is useless to me.

Because I just started here and so I have a four-week ban on any privileges. Meaning I can't go out no matter what. My computer usage is one hour per day and I can't make any outgoing calls; I can only receive calls on Saturdays.

If at the end of the four-week period, my guidance counselor, who just happens to be Mrs. Miller, thinks I'm fit to be rewarded for my rule-following and hard-working ways, I might get to go out or use the computer for more than an hour.

So I write a little note of my own:

Thanks for the heads up. But since I'm on the four-week grace period, I basically have no privileges.

I hand over the note to the girl and she grabs it like I'm handing her a lifeline. I guess she's as bored as me.

Quickly, she opens it and dives into writing a reply on a freshly torn piece of paper, which she hands me back a few minutes later:

Oh right! Sorry! I completely forgot that you're a newb. But Miller has been known to deduct privileges in advance. She's a biatch. Pardon my language.

I'm Calliope, by the way. But everyone calls me Callie. I'm sorry about all the stuff some of the girls are putting you through. I do gotta ask though: Is Principal Carlisle really your guardian? And are you really not a spy?

I have to smile at her note.

There's no malice there. Not after the way I feel her looking at me with so much eagerness.

So I reply, *Gotcha. No sleeping in Miller's class. She's actually my assigned guidance counselor too. So not looking forward to that meeting next week.*

Yes, Principal Carlisle is really my guardian. My mom and her were childhood friends. She died when I was ten so me and my older sister were sent to live with her. And no, I'm really not a spy. I'm just like the rest of you guys.

Also, you're the first person to smile at me in this place. So thanks again.

I pass the note back to her and like before, she jumps at it and devours it quickly. As soon as she's done, she writes back.

You're welcome! I would've said hi sooner but I had to be a little careful since I so don't wanna get on the bad side of Principal Carlisle.

Yeah, I don't blame her. Leah can be a little intimidating with all her rules and punishments and lectures and ambitions. I mean, what else do you expect from the principal of a reform school?

I, myself, am totally afraid of her and I lived with her for eight years.

But I guess she's only intimidating to girls like us, who break the rules and are perpetually bad.

I write down my reply, feeling light for the first time in almost seven days.

It's okay. Principal Carlisle scares me too.

A second later, her reply comes.

Right?! She is scary. Like, she never smiles. By the way, if you sit with us in the cafeteria, we'll make sure no one will bother you.

I'm about to ask who 'us' is, when the bell rings and the day ends thankfully. Everyone dives down for their backpacks like they're diving in to save their lives, which could very well be true because God, this class was killing me.

I turn to Callie, the first girl to talk to me at St. Mary's, and say, "Thanks for having my back."

She smiles brightly. "Of course. I've been there. Miller is so fucking boring."

"Did I hear someone dissing Miller?"

This comes from a girl with black hair and glasses. She's got a husky voice and a mischievous face, and she's wiggling her eyebrows at us.

Callie rolls her eyes. "Poe here has a great aversion to Miller."

"Duh." Poe zips up her backpack and skips over to us. "She's evil. And my guidance counselor. So I'm super lucky." She turns to me then, curious. "I'm Poe, by the way, as Callie said. Poe Austen Blyton. My mom was an Austen fan. And a Poe fan. And that." She points to a third girl. "Is Bronwyn. Bronwyn Littleton. Isn't that the greatest name ever?"

The girl she's pointing at has the longest hair that I've ever seen. Like Rapunzel. Her light brown braid goes down to her ass but when she looks at Poe and shakes her head in a very indulgent and patient manner, I completely forget about the length of her hair and marvel over her eyes.

Because her eyes are silver and so ethereal looking.

She slings her backpack over her shoulder and looks at me. "But people call me Wyn. Because I hate Bronwyn, which Poe already knows." She swings her gaze to Poe. "Doesn't she?"

Poe sticks her tongue out at her.

"It's okay," I say, chuckling at their antics. "I hate my name too. Salem. It sounds witchy."

Wyn smiles at me gently. "I like it."

Second smile of the day. I can't believe it.

This is turning out to be the best day ever.

"Can I ask you a question?" Poe jumps in but before I can answer either way, she continues, "Why would Principal Carlisle send her own ward to St. Mary's? I mean, she could very easily discipline you back at home, right?"

Well, I guess I spoke too quickly.

All my earlier lightness evaporates as Poe and Callie and Wyn look at me with curious gazes.

It's a genuine question.

Very, very genuine.

So I don't blame them for asking me that. In fact, I'm surprised it hasn't come up before. But then, these girls are the only ones who have talked to me at St. Mary's.

It's just that I'm a little conscious about my crime.

A lot conscious, okay?

It's not as if I do what I did everyday. But I had to do it.

I *had* to.

"Because I stole some money from Leah – Uh, Principal Carlisle – and sort of ran away," I say. "Or at least, I tried to. Before they caught me."

The cops.

I was at the bus station, ready to board and get out of this town once and for all when they caught up to me and brought me back.

I mean, I still don't understand how it all happened.

I was so careful while getting out of the house. It wasn't the first time I was sneaking out in the middle of the night anyway. I'm an expert, for God's sake. But somehow, Leah woke up and when she found me missing, along with my sunshine-yellow bike and one hundred and sixty-seven dollars from her wallet, she called the cops.

And since she'd had enough of my bad girl ways and she didn't want me to ruin my life any further, she sent me here.

To become good.

"I've been doing you and your mother a disservice. I should've been more strict with you and sent you here sooner. If I had, then none of this would be happening. So you're going to St. Mary's."

That's what Leah told me.

I could've refused. I'm eighteen now; turned eighteen a few weeks ago.

I could've just walked out but I didn't have any money. Whatever money I had, I used that to buy the bus ticket and the rest, Leah confiscated.

So here I am.

"But I was going to return the money," I continue. "I was going to get out of town and get a job and once I had enough savings, I was going to give the money back to her."

Which is all true.

I actually have a part-time job, or had one. At a restaurant in town where I worked as a waitress. But I'd just blown my savings and I really needed the cash. And I really, *really* needed to run away.

"Why were you running away?" Poe asks, her eyes wide.

Damn it.

I never should've let out that information. That I was running away.

My heart swells and pounds inside my rib cage.

My witchy heart with a thousand secrets.

"Uh, I... was..." I try to think of an acceptable lie.

Maybe I can tell them what I told Leah, that I hated this town and my old school and everything else so I was just hauling ass.

She bought it. I bet they'd buy it too.

But Wyn gives me an out. "It's okay. You don't have to explain."

Callie smiles. "Yeah, we all have our secrets."

"Yeah." Poe nods, putting her hands up. "Sorry if I came on a little too strong there. It's one of my weaknesses. I talk too much. And I always ask too many questions."

Just like that the tension breaks and I can breathe easily.

Thank God.

I just met them. These are the first people to actually be friendly and talk to me in here. I don't want them to hate me too.

And they will if I tell them why I was running away.

If I tell them my secret.

"Okay," Callie chirps. "Let's go to dinner. And you can definitely sit with us, if you want."

Suddenly, Poe bursts into a series of gasps and actions. She looks at the clock hanging over the blackboard. "Oh my God, we have to go. Now. Forget dinner for a sec. I've got something to show you guys."

"Show us what?" Callie asks.

"Hello? What else? Eye candy." Poe wiggles her eyebrows again.

"Oh my God. Yes! I needed something nice the first week back to this hell-hole." Callie grins.

"I know. Apparently, there's a press conference that we should see. This girl from junior year tipped me off. We gotta go."

I'm confused. "What eye candy?"

At my question, Poe's eyes go wide again as she takes me in. Not only that, she gasps too before lunging for my arm.

"Oh my God. This is perfect." Then she turns to Callie and Wyn. "Isn't this perfect? She knows him!"

I have absolutely no idea what they're talking about. But Callie catches on and whips her eyes to me.

"Yes, she does," she breathes out to Poe before turning to me. "You do!"

"I do what?" I ask, now more confused than ever.

Wyn is shaking her head again in that indulgent manner of hers that I've seen before. "Leave her alone, guys. She doesn't know what you're talking about."

So Poe explains it to me. "You know him. You know the Principal's hot son. Our eye candy."

All right. I still don't know what they're talking about.

Principal's hot son.

Who the fuck…

Principal's hot son.

Him.

Oh my God.

The boy with sun-struck hair and summer blue eyes.

He's the principal's hot son now, isn't he?

He *is*.

Because I'm stupidly at St. Mary's and Leah Carlisle, along with being my guardian, is now my principal as well.

"You *lived* with him," Poe says. "You lived with a soccer superstar."

"Yes. The Blond Arrow," Callie tags on.

The Blond Arrow.

That's his soccer nickname.

That's what they call him, his fans, the critics, the sports people, whatever. They gave it to him when he debuted last season. When he free-kicked the ball from the center of the field and it went soaring through the air, past all the players and hit the net, right in the center.

Holy fuck, they're talking about Arrow.

My Arrow.

Before I can say anything though, Poe and Callie are dragging me out of the classroom with Wyn tailing behind and discussing how I can tell them everything there is to know about Arrow Carlisle, the celebrity athlete, because I lived with him before he went pro.

I'm not listening to them though.

I mean, I am, here and there but I'm mostly in... shock.

Which is stupid because I should've thought of this.

I should've known.

That he'd come up in conversations or that I'd hear his name in passing. It used to happen a lot, back in my old high school, *normal* high school.

He's pretty famous around these parts.

He's The Blond Arrow, the pro soccer player. Of course he's famous. And of course he'd be famous here as well, at a girl's reform/therapeutic school. His mom is the principal, isn't she?

So yeah, I should've expected this.

But somehow I didn't.

And now I'm here. In the third-floor bathroom.

Because Poe wants to show us something. A press conference, she said.

The reason we're in the third-floor bathroom is because it's always out of order so no one goes here. No one who's up to any good anyway and we fit the bill perfectly.

Because Poe has a cell phone in her hand, which *everyone* knows is super duper forbidden, here at St. Mary's. If we get caught, we will probably lose all our privileges and God only knows what else.

But Poe is hitting all the keys on her phone like she's done it a thousand times before and Callie and Wyn don't seem to care and I'm in such shock that I don't care either.

Especially not when the video Poe was trying to get loads and I'm staring directly at him.

His dirty blond, sun-struck hair is the first thing I see.

Maybe because it's shining under what looks to be a thousand overhead lights. Not to mention the flash of a thousand cameras that are all pointed toward him.

He's sitting on a podium with a bunch of other people whom I've seen many times before. I haven't met them personally, of course, but they always hover around him on events like this.

It's an MLS press conference.

There's that yellow and blue shiny logo of his team, LA Galaxy, fluttering behind him on a giant screen with a black and white soccer ball, and there's his coach with the shock of white hair, sitting beside him at the podium.

For a second, I get distracted by the moving strip at the bottom of the screen, displaying different headlines.

Emerging star of the LA Galaxy injured during practice; LA Galaxy to replace their midfielder superstar with a rookie; The Blond Arrow, hailed by critics and fans as the new David Beckham, to leave the season unfinished...

There's more of it, more headlines, the same thing said in a variety of ways.

The same thing being: he is injured. And that he can't play for the rest of the season.

But I don't understand...

I don't get it.

He was fine a week ago.

"So what does it mean for the team and the rest of the season?"

I'm still reeling from the headlines on the bottom when someone asks this question. Someone off screen, and of all people sitting at the long table with black mics in front of them, it's directed at him.

I know because he hears it.

He hears it and his jaw that I've always likened to a sharp and sculpted blade moves back and forth. It's very subtle and I don't even think that anyone notices, not in the commotion of events like this, but I do.

I do because I'm attuned to him.

And because it's such an... atypical reaction for him.

Arrow never moves his jaw back and forth. He never gets annoyed enough to do that.

He's patient.

He's patient and determined and level-headed. I've heard this about him a number of times, at the interviews, at the press conferences.

His calm is legendary.

"What it means – obviously – is that I won't be playing on the team for the rest of the season."

That increases the roar around him and the team coach leans forward and says, "What he means is that it's very unfortunate and no one could've seen it coming. But Rodriguez is an excellent wide midfielder and as hard as it will be to fill the shoes he's had to step into, we'll be making every effort to help him. As we will help Carlisle as much as we can with his recovery."

His blue eyes flash, then.

They go from a summery blue to stormy and wintry.

Again, it's so atypical that I notice it right away.

I not only notice it but I absorb the shock of it.

Because Jesus Christ, a week ago, when I was packing my bags to leave for St. Mary's, Leah and I, we watched his game together.

The soccer season is on and they were playing New York City FC. And okay, so they lost that game and as far as I know Arrow, it must have hurt him because he's very competitive.

But he's lost games before and he always comes back swinging.

He appeared fine at the press conference after. A little grim but fine. Also, he called the house to talk to Leah later that night – he always calls after every game of his – and well, I listened in – I always do.

The conversation was slightly critical on Leah's part because they'd lost but nothing out of the ordinary. No signs whatsoever that there was something wrong with him.

I was actually mourning the fact that I wouldn't get to watch him play all that much anymore because of the stupid TV rules at St. Mary's.

So I really don't get it.

What the fuck happened?

"Can you tell us how long you expect the recovery to take?"

Another question fired off screen and to him but this time, he isn't even paying attention to them. He has his head dipped down and he's looking at his fists on the table. He's practically glaring at them and God, I have a very bad feeling about this.

Very bad.

What's happening?

Why's he acting this way, when he's always been so professional and polite?

When the coach realizes that his player won't answer the question – he looks kinda shocked by Arrow's defiance too – he takes the reins. "It's a very typical meniscus tear. I'm glad it happened during practice and we were able to get help quickly. It's minor right now but we all know that knee injuries have a way of creeping up on you, especially if you play contact sports. So we want to take every precaution that we can so it doesn't turn into something major."

I swallow when Arrow still won't look up.

His posture has gone even tighter, as if he's repelling his coach's words. As if he's repelling everything that's going on around him.

"Will you be staying in LA for the duration of your recovery?"

For some reason, it feels like the pause after this question is longer and heavier. Or maybe it's my own anticipation of what the answer is.

My own anticipation to hear his voice, his rich, deep voice.

A voice that I dream about.

Leaning forward, he looks into one of the cameras and it feels like he's staring directly at me. "No. It's been kindly pointed out to me that I need to disappear for a while, go off the radar. So I can heal. Recover from the injury that frankly no one saw coming. And well, I agree. So I'll be going east..." He trails off before his words become curt and clipped. "Back to my hometown, St. Mary's."

What?

No, no, no.

He didn't say St. Mary's, did he?

He didn't say he's coming back.

No, he didn't.

He couldn't have.

Because he can't come back. I don't *want* him to come back.

I don't.

I want him to stay far, far away.

He was the reason I was running away that night. He was the reason I stole that money and I was going to go somewhere before they caught me and stuck me inside a cage.

So he can't come back when he was the one I was running away from.

My Arrow, the guy I'm in love with.

My sister's boyfriend.

CHAPTER TWO

A rrow.

It's a crazy name, isn't it?

I always thought so.

Crazy and unique and completely his.

I can't imagine anyone else having that name. I can't imagine anyone else *owning* that name like he does.

He wears it.

In every part of his sculpted face and his sleek body.

From his arched and arrogant-looking eyebrows to his high cheekbones.

God, his cheekbones.

They're so sharp and yet so gracefully made that they almost cast a shadow on his jaw. His very angular and slanting jaw.

And then there's his body.

It's not bulky or massive but muscled and trim. Tanned from running under the sun. Athletic. Built for speed and precision on the soccer field.

Actually, every part of him is built and designed with such careful precision. Like someone up there decided to take their time with him. They decided to sit down and pick up tools, hammers and chisels so they could sculpt him and chip away at him and make him stunning.

That's what he is.

Arrow Carlisle, the love of my life, is stunning.

Always has been, ever since he was fifteen and I was ten, and I saw him for the first time.

Even though it was eight years ago, I remember everything.

I can tell you that it was early morning and the sunlight was streaming through the window like laser beams. Everything was bathed in yellow in that room, the kitchen to be specific. Orange, even.

I was wedged between a china cabinet and the wall, sitting on the floor, my knees hugged to my chest. I had a blanket wrapped around myself and yet, I was cold.

So cold.

I'd made rounds of the entire house, trying to find a spot where I could find some warmth, but so far, I'd been unsuccessful.

But then, he burst through the kitchen door, all sweaty and panting.

I remember thinking that he was tall. And that when he moved through the space, the sunlight rippled. The rays cast tiny patterns on his tall form.

He made a beeline to the sink and turned on the tap. He threw water over his face, his neck, and he did it so violently, with such agitated gestures that a few drops landed on my cheek.

I flinched automatically, thinking that it would feel cold.

But it didn't.

The water that he touched with his hands, that landed on me, did not feel cold at all. In fact, it made me feel warm.

His whole presence made me feel warm.

Like he was the sun or something.

My sun.

After he was done with washing his face, he bent toward the fridge and took out a juice carton. He proceeded to gulp half of it before he realized someone was watching him.

He whipped his eyes over to me, where I was hiding, all crouched and trying to make myself into a ball to preserve the warmth in my body.

He frowned and I sort of smiled.

Because his eyes were blue. They made me think of summer and sunshine and melting in the grass while catching the sun.

"Don't tell my mom," he said, motioning to the juice carton. "She gets upset when people drink right out of the carton." And then he frowned even harder, taking me in completely. "Are you cold?"

I wanted to answer him. I wanted to tell him that his secret was safe with me. That I'd never tell on him in a million years for breaking his mom's rule.

And then I wanted to tell him that no, I wasn't cold.

That somehow, he made all the cold go away with his sun-struck hair and sweaty, tanned skin and summer-blue eyes.

I wish I had.

I really, really wish that I had said something. Because when the moment passed, I never got the chance to tell him.

Because in a split second, everything changed.

The whole course of my life.

And his, too.

Because just then my sister walked in, Sarah, and he turned to look at her and he never looked away.

He hasn't looked away from her since that moment.

So basically, in the last eight years that I've known him, he's only looked at me with his full focus that one time. Since then, his focus has been on my sister.

The love of *his* life.

I can't really say for sure if the moment in the kitchen was when I fell in love with him.

I mean, I was freaking cold and scared after my mom's death. We'd just moved into a new house, a new town. Before then we'd only heard about the Carlisles in passing. We'd never met them because my mom and Leah had always been busy with their careers.

And a boy strangely made me feel warm for the first time in weeks.

I'm pretty sure that meant falling in love in my ten-year-old brain.

But now that I'm older and I have more perspective, I'm not sure. Maybe it happened in the coming days.

When I'd see him come back from his run and dutifully pull out a glass from the cabinet and pour juice in it before drinking. Or when I'd see him cleaning up after himself after each meal, picking up his laundry, his soccer cleats, even though they had a maid who could do those things. Or when I'd see him fix things around the house – especially the heat one day – even though again, they could call a guy if they wanted to.

It made my heart race that even at the age of fifteen, he was the man of the house.

His dad died in a sudden plane crash when he was seven. And in the coming days, I found out that he took that very seriously, his dad's death, the responsibility that came with it, the fact that he wanted to walk in his father's shoes.

My own father had left my sister and my mother just after I was born because he couldn't handle responsibility. So this was all new to me.

I'd never met anyone like Arrow Carlisle before.

Someone who was so serious and determined and focused. Not only around the house but at his school too. On top of being a straight-A student, Arrow was also their soccer superstar.

Honestly though, it isn't surprising at all because A, Arrow's dad was a pro soccer player himself.

And B, Arrow would spend hours practicing at the school. He'd spend *hours* watching game tapes in his room, and sometimes I'd find him dribbling the ball in the backyard, practicing drills and exercising before a big game.

Soccer was and is his life. He was born into it.

So I don't know when I fell in love with him.

All I know is that when I was falling in love with Arrow, *he* was falling in love with someone else.

With my sister, Sarah.

And they are perfect for each other.

Perfect.

They're both the same age.

They are both good-looking and popular. Both of them have high ambitions and goals.

In fact, they're so perfect for each other, so devoted, that when Leah had objections about her son dating her ward, they did everything to convince her. Leah made rule after rule, gave them strict schedules and ultimatums about grades and hanging out together with their bedroom doors open, and they aced every test she put forth.

Again, not a surprise, they're both excellent test takers.

They even went to the same college. When Arrow got a scholarship for playing soccer at a college in California, Sarah made sure to end up at the same school. They even picked out an apartment off campus so they could live together.

And when Arrow graduated a semester early – no surprise there; he's a genius – and got picked the January of last year to go pro and play for the LA Galaxy, they continued their relationship long distance. Not only that, Sarah made sure to complete her degree in Public Relations and follow him to LA, a few months later.

Now, she works with the PR firm that represents Arrow's team.

See? They're perfect for each other.

Perfect. Perfect. Perfect.

They've conquered every obstacle in their path to get to this point where they have a nice, expensive apartment in LA. He plays the game he loves and she has a bright future in PR.

They belong together.

So where do *I* fit in?

What is my role here, other than being this evil, witchy girl who wants her older sister's boyfriend?

I don't think I have any role except to be the villain in their love story.

The girl who has violated all the codes.

The betrayer.

Who feels warm at the sight of her sister's boyfriend. Who shivers when he smirks. Whose heart fills with an immense joy when she sees him on TV, scoring a goal and who wants to fly over to him and hug him and tell him how wonderful he is.

How freaking amazing.

Some girls fall in love and a boy catches them. He waits for them at the bottom of the cliff with open arms.

And then there are other girls.

Girls like me.

We're the girls in love with the boys who belong to someone else. We're the girls in doomed love.

When girls like us fall, there's no one to catch us. Least of all that boy for whom we've taken the fall.

We're the girls with secrets and witchy hearts. We're the girls who listen to sad songs. Who slow dance to them with tears streaming down our faces, even as a smile lingers on our lips. Who cry in our pillows at night and who ride our sunshine-yellow bicycle along the empty, desolate, miserable places, where no one goes.

We're the girls who run away in the middle of the night.

Like I was doing.

Because I'd overheard a conversation between Leah and him. Well, only Leah's side of it, but I heard enough to understand that Arrow was getting ready to propose to Sarah. He'd bought a ring and everything.

That's when I decided to run.

Because they're getting married.

Married.

I mean, I always knew that they would. But something about the talk of a ring really shook me up.

Arrow was going to propose to my sister.

She would obviously say yes, and they'd have a wedding day. Kids and a family.

Like a voyeur, I've been there for every moment of their love story.

I've watched them fall in love. I've watched them *be* in love for years. I've watched them go out on dates, go to the prom together. I've watched them hanging out together in the backyard. I've heard them whisper and talk out in the hallway, just by my bedroom. I've watched them leave for California. I've watched them when they'd come to visit over the holidays.

I've watched it all like the worst sister in the world.

I've watched *him* like the worst sister in the world.

I've watched him, craved him, *loved* him in secret.

I'd been the witch long enough. I had to do the right thing and get my toxic presence out of their lives.

Before they got married.

Right that very second.

And that's why I stole that money and I was running away.

But I got caught and now, I'm stuck here.

Until another opportunity arises.

When it does, I'll take it. I'll steal again and I'll run again.

I'm not a thief but there are worse crimes than stealing money.

There's no way that I'm staying close to them any longer. And I'm definitely not attending their wedding.

Not at all.

Because aside from the fact that their wedding should be full of people whose hearts are pure, there's this other thing, this other urge in me.

A very strong urge.

A dangerous urge.

I got it the moment I heard the word 'ring.' I got it the moment it dawned on me that he was going to be hers.

Irrevocably hers.

Forever and ever.

It's an urge to burn down all my inhibitions of eight years and say: choose me.

Choose me, Arrow.

Pick me.

Yeah, that's what I was thinking the night I was running away. I was thinking about how badly I wanted to say those words to him.

How badly I wanted him for myself.

How badly I wanted my sister's boyfriend – soon to be fiancé – for myself.

And God, he's coming back now and he's *injured*.

All I can think about is seeing him in the flesh. Making sure that he's really okay and if I somehow get to do that, if I somehow get to see him again, who's to say I wouldn't act on that urge of mine?

Who's to say I wouldn't try to ruin their relationship?

I'm already in love with my sister's boyfriend. I'm already so corrupt and despicable. I'm already so hopelessly in love.

Who's to say I wouldn't take it one step further and try to steal him away from her?

So I need to stay away from him.

I need to control myself like I've done for the past eight years.

Which is why tonight, I'm breaking a big, huge rule of St. Mary's.

Because the alternative is that I sit in my dorm room and cook up scenarios about how to steal my sister's boyfriend.

This rule that I'm breaking though will definitely banish all my privileges.

But even the thought of that can't deter me – or Callie, Poe and Wyn – from doing what we're doing.

Sneaking out to a bar to go dancing.

It's a whole process, too.

You have to go to bed, wearing what you will for going out, so when the time comes to actually sneak out, you don't go around hunting for clothes and waking up your roommate.

Then you have to stack all your pillows under the blanket so even if your roommate does wake up at some point while you're away, she can see your dark silhouette and suspect nothing.

After that, you tiptoe out of the room at a specified time and slowly, carefully walk down the darkened hallway so as to not alert the 24/7 warden, who sits all the way in the front at reception with her TV going.

If someone does intercept you, you say you're going to the bathroom. Hence you can't wear anything too flashy so the lie looks convincing.

Once you've reached the end of your hallway, you take a left, and you come upon a heavy metal door with a red EXIT sign on it. That's where all your friends will be waiting for you.

That's where Poe, who's done this a million times in the past because she's been here since her sophomore year, will jiggle the latch in a precise manner that will get the door open. And Callie who's also done this a million times before because like Poe she's been here since sophomore year will usher me out into the night. Then Wyn, who's been here since her junior year, will carefully wedge a rock between the door and doorjamb so we can get back in easily.

Then, we'll run and fly through the massive expanse of green grounds that surround the campus to get to a very special spot on the brick fence. This spot has dents and gaps, big enough that we can rest our feet in and scale the wall to get to the other side.

And so, ten minutes after we've broken out of our dorm building, we're making our way through the woods, in the middle of which our reform school sits, to get to the highway.

Poe has already arranged for a cab through her phone when we were in the third-floor bathroom.

How did she pay for it though, the cab I mean? She also has a secret credit card that she stole before coming to St. Mary's, and if she uses it in a very limited capacity, charges sort of go unnoticed. Or at least they have so far.

And how are we going to get into a bar even though we're underage? That's Callie's department. She says that the bartender at this particular bar is a friend and he'll let us in as long as all we do is dancing and no drinking.

I don't care about that.

I don't want to drink. I don't want to dance either.

I'm not sneaking out for any of that.

I'm sneaking out because my heart is witchy and I have dangerous urges.

The bar that we're at is called Ballad of the Bards.

I've heard of it, actually. It's a bar famous for its love songs. Meaning they don't play the regular, dancing music. They play the music of the bards, the poets. The songs of sad love and misery.

I've always wanted to go here. It's at the border of the town of St. Mary's and another town called Bardstown. And since I was sorta happy to know that we were coming here, I even let them put lipstick on me, on the way over.

"Every girl deserves a little lip lovin'," said Poe, while painting my lips with Teenage Decay, which is a dark coral color.

It reminds me of the sun.

It reminds me of him.

With that on my lips, I feel like he's close.

He might as well be. The press conference was a couple of days ago. We, at St. Mary's School for Troubled Teenagers, move slower than the rest of the world.

Maybe he's already back.

Maybe he's in town right now.

And maybe...

Okay, stop thinking about him.

Stop.

But I don't think that's possible.

At all.

Because as soon as we enter the bar and glance around the industrial-looking space with low-hanging light bulbs, rough brick walls and metal beams, I catch sight of something.

A baseball cap.

It's too dark in here to tell the color of it.

But I don't need the light in order to do that. I know what color it is.

It's gray.

Like all the other things in his life – his workout sneakers, his soccer cleats, his sweaters, his sweatpants.

His t-shirts.

Yeah, he has a bunch of gray t-shirts.

In fact, I'm wearing one now, under my chunky sweater, his t-shirt that I stole.

It was a long time ago, back when he'd just moved to California for college. I went into his room and snooped and well, snitched a couple of his t-shirts that he'd left behind.

Anyway, the point is that he likes gray.

And that he's taken to wearing a baseball cap ever since he went pro, so as to have a bit of privacy in these parts where they worship soccer more than any other sport, and hence him.

So I know that baseball cap.

I know.

The bar is super crowded though, jam-packed with bodies and saturated with the smell of liquor and foggy smoke. So it's not as if I can see very clearly.

But my witchy heart tells me that it's him.

Even though it's impossible that it could be him.

Because he should be at home, with Sarah. I'm assuming she's back too since Arrow is here.

Sarah is always where Arrow is; they're inseparable.

Besides, bars are not his scene anyway. Anything that interferes with his practice and training is a definite no-no. Which means he very rarely drinks and never stays out partying.

But I have to see.

I have to confirm.

Callie is introducing us all to her friend who let us in, Will the bartender, but I murmur a distracted excuse and leave them. I'll explain everything later. Like, in five minutes when I'm back after confirming that it's really not him.

And then, I'm standing there.

I'm standing at a place – in the middle of the bar – where I have a clear view of the baseball cap and the one who's wearing it.

He's tucked away in a corner, the owner of the cap, partially hidden behind a bricked pillar.

Although tucked away is a misleading description.

He's too big and tall to be tucked away anywhere, much less in a makeshift corner of a bar.

In reality, he's bursting out of there, that nook, his shoulders specifically.

His *shoulders*.

My heart leaps at the sight of those shoulders. They are broad but not overly massive. They're sleek, and even through the layers of clothes they appear sculpted and muscular.

Like *his*.

But that's not the thing that gets me, no.

Not the shoulders that could only belong to him or the baseball cap that hides the good view of his face, it's the layers of clothing that he has on.

One layer specifically.

A vintage leather jacket.

It's black. Well, it's so old now that it's weathered and gray.

I *love* it.

I love how dashing it makes him look. How handsome. I love the vibe it gives off, dangerous and daredevil-ish.

And he wears it all the time when he rides his motorcycle.

Yeah, he has a motorcycle.

Despite all the ways that he is so careful and disciplined because of his sport, he rides a Ducati.

Or at least, he used to.

Back when he still lived in St. Mary's.

When he left it all behind after leaving for California though, I was devastated. I bet Sarah told him to. She never liked his bike and his jacket.

I cried for the Ducati he left in the garage, covered up with a white sheet. I cried for his vintage leather jacket that I never really knew what he did with. It wasn't in his closet – I checked.

So seeing it now, it hits me like a storm.

No, not like a storm.

The sight of that leather jacket explodes in my stomach and sends warmth rushing through my veins.

Warmth and coziness.

It's him.

It's my Arrow.

God, he's here.

Here.

I press a hand on my stomach as a breath escapes me and my lips tug up into a smile.

But my smile doesn't reach fruition.

My lips stop midway when I realize something.

I realize that his face is dipped.

It's dipped toward someone. A girl whose back is facing me.

For a second I think it's Sarah.

It *has* to be. Who else would it be, honestly?

But it's not her.

The girl Arrow is looking at isn't Sarah.

Because Sarah doesn't have blonde hair. Her hair is dark like mine. Only my hair is curly – wild and savage – and hers is straight and shiny. But we at least have the exact same shade.

And neither is Sarah that short.

I am that short, as short as the girl Arrow is looking at.

So short that his tall body has to bend in a little. Like it would if he were to look at me from that close a distance.

This girl is not Sarah.

This girl is someone else and when that someone else reaches up her bare arm and flutters her delicate-looking fingers over his square jaw, a jaw that is shadowed due to the low light in that nook of his and under the rim of his baseball cap, I freeze.

Then she goes ahead and moves her fingers back and forth on his jaw.

And... and I don't know what to do with myself.

All I know is that even though it's dark and all I can really see is the outline of their bodies, I know that she's scratching the invisible-to-me stubble on his face.

Which makes him smirk.

The smirk that I've been watching from afar for eight years now. The smirk that makes me go all breathless even when it's not directed at me.

Because his smirks and smiles are for Sarah.

So why's he giving it to someone else?

Someone who's clearly not my sister.

The love of his life.

The girl tries to touch it, that smirk. She tries to touch his smirking lips with her thumb, but Arrow grabs her wrist at the last second.

He stops her, leaving her thumb hovering at the edge.

But she isn't deterred.

She goes on her tiptoes, presses her body against his and murmurs something close to his lips.

As shocking as *that* is, it's even more shocking when Arrow says something back, and whatever he says makes the girl stretch her body further.

A second later, she's touching him with her lips.

And he's letting her.

A second later, my sister's boyfriend, the guy I've been in love with, is kissing her.

A random girl in a bar.

A girl who's not my sister.

CHAPTER THREE

I can't...

I can't believe that this is happening.

I can't believe that he's kissing someone else.

That I'm standing here, in this strange bar, with sad songs blasting overhead, *watching* him kiss someone who's not my sister.

I *refuse* to believe it.

I shake my head even.

If I keep shaking my head in denial, all of this will go away. I'll wake up from whatever nightmare this is.

But it doesn't go away. None of this goes away. In fact, he's kissing her harder now, like things are heating up.

They're heating up so much that even I can feel it.

Me.

The girl who's never been kissed.

Somehow through all the confusion and tingling on my own lips, I manage to take a step forward.

Then another and another. Until I'm walking toward them.

Until I reach them. I reach *him*.

Until I'm in that little corner as well.

It smells of booze. It smells of *him*, spice and vintage leather.

My favorite scent.

I'm so close to them and my presence is such an intrusion in their dark, private corner that the girl jerks apart from him, snapping her head in my direction.

As much as I want to see her and find out who she is, I'm watching Arrow.

I'm watching him detach himself from the girl, bit by bit.

Slowly, he lifts his face up and away from hers.

Then, he takes a moment to sigh, as if irritated, followed by turning his head to look in the direction where the interruption came from.

Even then, his detachment isn't complete.

He still has one of his hands wrapped around the back of her neck.

I glare at that hand. It looks big and bad and seductive.

Finally, he shifts his face, cocks his head in a way that the shadows from his baseball cap vanish and I can see him.

I can see his bright blue eyes.

Eyes that remind me of lazy summers and bike rides in the sunshine.

Only now they're dark.

They're almost navy and he glances at me with them.

"You."

Before I can respond to that though, he detaches himself completely from her, takes that big, bad, seductive hand off her neck and asks, with slight annoyance and surprise, "What the fuck are you doing here?"

Even though more important things are at stake here, *far* more important things, I still breathe out a sigh of relief when he moves away from the girl he was kissing.

But I can't be relieved, can I?

He was kissing a girl.

A girl who isn't my sister.

"What the fuck am I doing here?" I ask, frowning, stumbling over my words. "What the fuck are *you* doing here? Who is she? Where's my si –"

"Can you give us a minute?"

Arrow swallows up my words when he speaks and for a micro-second, I think he's speaking to me. But he's turned his head and his eyes are directed at the girl.

I finally glance at her as well.

She's drunk.

That's the first thing.

The second thing is that even though Arrow's moved away from her, she's still leaning into him.

It bothers me.

That she's still attached to my sister's boyfriend.

But I guess it's more for balance than anything else.

"Can we please go back to the kissing?" She giggles slightly, completely ignoring my presence and staring up at Arrow with dreamy, drunk eyes.

The word *kissing* makes me tighten everything on my body.

But before I can protest, Arrow speaks. "I think we've had enough of the kissing for tonight. You should go."

"But I thought we were having such a good time and you know..."

She trails off to run her hand down his chest, her fingers hooking around the locket he wears.

So he wears a locket, a silver thing he never parts with.

His dad gave it to him when he was six or something. And like his sun-struck hair and tanned skin, his locket shines in the sunlight. It shines with his sweat when he's had a workout, or he's played a really grueling game.

It was shining the day I saw him for the first time in that yellow/orange kitchen.

And I dig my nails in my palms when I see this girl toying with it.

"You're drunk," he tells her, disengaging himself from her.

"I'm not."

She hiccups then, proving herself a liar.

"I beg to differ."

"I'm –"

"That's why you thought we were having a good time." He leans a little closer to her, as if to impart a secret. "We weren't. So as I said, you should go."

She frowns, looking peeved. "But I –"

"Look," he sighs, the annoyed lines around his eyes getting deeper. "I'm flattered. Okay? It's always flattering when a girl throws herself at you. Even as drunk as you clearly are. But as I said to you before you attacked me with your mouth, I don't fuck drunk girls so you should go before I say something you might not like."

Hold on a second.

Just please... hold.

Did he say fuck?

Did he actually say fuck?

Before I can process *that,* the girl, who is so drunk that she can't stand upright, somehow gets her spine up. Her foggy eyes suddenly become really alert and sort of vicious. "And what exactly will you say if I don't leave?"

"If you don't leave, I'm going to have to tell you the truth."

"And what is the truth?"

Arrow's answer is to sigh again.

Like he doesn't wanna do it but he will. And he does.

"The truth is that you're drunk as fuck and maybe that's why your kissing is all tongue and no mouth. And it feels like I'm drowning in a pool of saliva. But I don't think that's the case. I don't think your kissing is all tongue and no mouth because you're drunk. I think you kiss that way even when you're sober and can actually *see* who you're kissing. And I think that's because you're kind of an over-doer, aren't you? Too much perfume. Too many moans. You like to go the extra mile and generally, I appreciate it, going the extra mile, doing the extra work. But I don't appreciate that when I'm choking on tongue."

He shrugs then, all casual like. "And that's why you should leave. Because if I tell you all that I think it might hurt your ego a little bit."

Silence follows his truth-telling speech.

Well, as much silence as you can get in a crowded bar.

The girl is the first to gather her senses. "I... What..." She looks at both of us in a wild, aggressive way. "You two deserve each other. Assholes."

Then she spins around and stomps away, leaving the two of us alone in that corner. Leaving me to bizarrely wonder why she thought we were together, him and I.

Is it because I came here to stop them? Is it because I look like a jealous girlfriend?

I'm not. The girlfriend, I mean. Or jealous even.

I am not. So totally not jealous.

What I am, though is flabbergasted and shocked and kind of speechless.

Because holy. Shit.

He said those things, didn't he?

Again, I can't believe it.

I can't believe that he said all that. I can't believe *anyone* would say all that. Let alone a guy I've known for eight years, who's nothing if not polite.

And patient. And calm and collected and holy *fuck*.

I can't...

"You can't follow a rule to save your life, can you?" he murmurs and finally, I whip my gaze over to him.

Until now, I was watching the girl disappear into the crowd because I didn't know what else to do.

Because this guy, this rude asshole, can't be Arrow.

The Arrow I know.

The Arrow *I* know wouldn't be leaning against the brick wall as if nothing happened. As if he didn't say all those horrible things to her.

"You shouldn't be here," he says in a rough, growly voice when I continue to remain silent.

"Why?" I burst out, my words bitter. "Because I witnessed you completely humiliating a girl just now?"

"I wasn't humiliating her," he replies, casually.

I think he even goes ahead and folds his arms across his chest. I can't be sure though because I'm staring at him, at his smooth, unbothered features, with an open mouth.

I have to actually press my hands on my heated face to try to calm down before I can say anything.

"Are you kidding me?" I screech. "You're kidding me, right? You were *such* an asshole to her."

"Huh. And here I thought I was being nice," he murmurs as if he's genuinely surprised.

"You've gone crazy, haven't you? That's the only explanation. Or maybe I'm going crazy. I don't know what just happened. You completely shattered her confidence. I don't think she'll be kissing anyone for the rest of her life."

"Well, I wouldn't be too sure about that."

"Excuse me?"

He tips his chin at something over my shoulder. "I don't think you need to worry about her confidence."

I turn to look at what he's talking about. Through the swaying bodies of people, I see the girl again.

And he's right. I don't need to worry about her confidence at all.

Because she's kissing again.

Only...

"Is she..." I squint my eyes to make sure. "Is she kissing a girl?"

From where I am it certainly looks like it. The drunk blonde girl is kissing another blonde girl and she's doing it in the exact same way as she was doing it to Arrow, all leaned into her body and neck tilted up.

I hear him shift behind my back. "And here I thought I was special." Then, "Although, it makes me wonder..."

I spin on my heels to face him again. "Wonder what?"

He cocks his head to the side. "If she's really that drunk or if I just drove her to lesbianism."

"You can't drive anyone to lesbianism. You can..."

"I can what?"

Bring them back.

That's what I was going to say, that he can convert a lesbian because he's so gorgeous in his leather jacket, his face bent down, his blue eyes shining. As if sexual orientation is a choice.

As if I'm not having a very surreal moment right now as I stare at him.

And my next words don't help the matter. "Sexual orientation isn't a choice. In case you didn't know. You can't drive people or convert them or change it on a whim. As if they don't have enough problems to deal with and you come in with your ignorance and careless remarks and..."

I trail off because what the fuck am I doing, and I swear I see the lines around his eyes crinkle but I can't be sure.

"Thanks for that. Very educating and enlightening," he drawls.

I glare at him.

I can't believe that I'm glaring at him but that's not the point.

The point is that there are more important things at stake here. Far more important things.

Far more.

So I bring my hands down to my sides. I even take in a deep breath and try to rein in my agitation.

"*Why,*" I begin with what I think is a calm tone, "did I just catch you kissing a girl at a bar who's not my sister?"

At this, his eyes go darker, even darker than before.

I think they've surpassed the shade of navy blue now and landed somewhere in the spectrum of black, making them look like bottomless pools.

An abyss.

"Because you are where you're not supposed to be," he replies with a ticking jaw.

"What does that mean?" I ask, trying to not look at it.

The jaw.

Trying not to count how many times he moves it back and forth or how sleek it looks, how much more beautiful and sharper than before, now that he's using it to display his annoyance.

"It means that this establishment that you find yourself in, either by accident or on purpose, is called a bar."

"And?"

"And in case *you* didn't know, no one under twenty-one is allowed in here. It's the law, unfortunately. So if I were you, I'd get out."

My spine goes up. "I'm not afraid of the law. I'm not going anywhere. Not until –"

"It also means," he cuts me off, "that you shouldn't even be out of your bed, let alone off campus."

And then he freezes me with that dark gaze of his, pins me down like a bird, letting my wings flutter and flap furiously now that I've been captured.

"Lights out at nine-thirty. Those are the rules, remember? So either you're breaking them, in your first week no less, or you're sleepwalking. For your sake, I hope it's the latter. Makes you look more sympathetic if you happen to get caught."

It takes me a moment to understand his meaning.

I don't know why because he couldn't be clearer. There are no more ways in which to explain the meaning of his words.

But still.

It takes me a few seconds to fully grasp it.

Maybe because I myself had forgotten that I go to St. Mary's now.

I myself had forgotten that I don't live in his house anymore, and that I'm not free to go wherever I want.

Does he know why I was sent to St. Mary's though?

I mean, not the real reason. *No one* knows the real reason, and no one will. But the other reasons, the stealing and the running away.

"Like I said, I'm not afraid of the law or the rules," I say, averting my eyes from him.

"Obviously."

I look back at him.

The way he says it confirms it all. The way he stares at me, with a knowing glint in his eyes, confirms it all too.

He knows. He knows what I did.

However I don't know why it comes as a surprise. There are a lot of ways he could've found out. His mother might have told him, or my sister.

Besides, this isn't the first time that I've been punished in front of him.

My bad behavior and my bad grades were the norm in the Carlisle family. There have been numerous occasions when Leah would lecture me about my lack of ambition, lack of good grades and extra-curricular activities, my lack of following the curfew, at the dinner table in front of the whole family.

Everyone knows that I'm not perfect.

That I'm the opposite of my sister and Arrow and Leah.

And even my mom, who was a college professor, when she was alive.

So it shouldn't really embarrass me. Besides, this isn't about me anyway.

This is about my sister, Sarah.

"Where's my sister?" I ask, swallowing down all my selfish emotions. "Where's Sarah?"

The mention of her name changes everything.

It changes the air, the light, the noises of the bar.

Sarah.

Like her name has so much power. Over him. Over me. Over the things around us.

"I'm guessing she's back in LA," he says in a soft voice.

But that's the only thing soft about him.

The rest of him is hard.

His shoulders, the sleek, sculpted things, are rigid. His eyes are harsh.

So are his cheekbones.

And it's so strange that I have my next question completely mapped out and planned.

It's on the tip of my tongue, but then he chooses that moment to adjust the rim of his baseball cap and I notice something about his knuckles.

They're swollen and cut up, the skin flayed and rolled into tiny curls, and the words on the cusp of escaping completely change. "What happened to your hand?"

My question sort of surprises him, I think. But only for a second. After that, his expression shutters.

That bruised fist of his becomes tight as he brings it down to his side.

"I punched a door," he says in a low voice.

"What?"

"Repeatedly."

"Why?"

"Because I was drunk and pissed off."

"Because you were drunk and pissed off?"

"Yeah. Apparently, I've got anger issues."

He's lying.

He doesn't drink. He doesn't get pissed off. And he absolutely does *not* have anger issues.

"No, you don't," I tell him. "You don't get drunk. You're not even drinking right now and you're in an establishment called a bar."

"If I get a drink, will you leave me alone?"

"And you absolutely do not have anger issues either," I say, ignoring him.

At my vehement answer, a surprising thing happens.

His lips twitch and I swear to God, my witchy heart jumps in my chest for making them.

"Well, then you should've been there," he says in an amused voice.

His amusement is making my heart pound faster. "Been where?"

"When my coach signed me up for anger management therapy."

"Your coach signed you up for anger management therapy?"

I know. I *know* I'm repeating most of his stuff. But honestly, I can't keep up.

Because it's the most bizarre thing I've heard in my entire life.

Arrow and anger management.

Arrow, punching a door. Arrow, kissing a strange girl at the bar.

What the *fuck* is happening?

"Yeah." He nods, his amusement still in place. "Your glowing endorsement could've saved me."

"Why did he sign you up for anger management therapy?" I ask, as if this question is the holy grail of all questions.

"Because I punched a door," he deadpans. "Aren't you paying attention?"

Before I can say anything to that, he leans toward me.

He not only leans but he sniffs me too.

I draw back a little. "What are you doing?"

Keeping himself hung over me, he rumbles, "Smelling you."

"Why?"

"To see if you're too drunk to have this conversation."

I open and close my mouth for a few seconds. "I'm not drunk. I don't drink."

Well, not a lot.

I mean, I have had a few drinks here and there, mostly with people back in my old high school.

"Is that right?"

I raise my chin. "Yes."

"Surprising. Given the fact that you don't care about rules." Then, "What about getting high?"

"W-What about it?"

"Do you like it?" He looks me up and down. "I'm sure a girl like you must enjoy something like that once in a while."

I swallow at the look in his eyes, at the fact that he's still looming over me. "No, okay? I don't do drugs either."

"So if you don't do drugs, as you said, and you don't drink, why the hell did you come here?"

To distract myself from dangerous thoughts. Of you...

"I came here to dance," I snap.

He sweeps his eyes all over me, taking in my messy, curly hair, my painted lips, my sweater and my cargo pants, before standing up straight. "Well then, by all means, don't let me keep you."

Finally, I shake my head.

Enough.

Enough.

I frown at him and another surprising thing happens. A *shocking* thing.

He smirks at me. At *me*.

After eight years.

After eight fucking years, I finally get what I've been wishing for. His smirk.

And my stupid fucking heart can't handle it. My stupid fucking heart swells and swells in my chest until it's aching, and I know it's a rather drastic reaction to a simple smirk, and people might call me crazy.

But they don't know.

They've never been in my position. They don't know what it feels like when a guy you've loved for eight years, who loves someone else, smirks at you, and his eyes shine because of it.

You lose your breath. You lose your sense. You lose all your goddamn goodness and almost tell him that you want him.

But somehow, I pull myself back.

Somehow, I dig my nails into my palms and remember that he's Sarah's *boyfriend* and I'm here for *her*.

And he's lying.

He's trying to distract me. That's what it is, isn't it?

He's playing with me and he's enjoying it.

So weird.

So glorious.

"You're trying to distract me," I accuse.

"It's not my fault that you're so easily distracted."

"And you're lying to me, aren't you?" I squint my eyes at him, trying to control my heart. "You're making this whole thing up. You didn't punch a door."

"Yeah? What did I punch then?"

"I don't know. Whatever it was, it wasn't a door." I stab a finger at him. "You're trying to distract me from the real question."

"And what's the real question?" he asks in a whispered, almost mocking voice.

"Where's my sister?" I snap out.

His eyes bore into mine then. And maybe it's the trick of dismal light or whatever, but his features glow, as if drawing attention to themselves.

Attention to how sharp and harsh they look.

How tight.

"Told you. She's probably back in LA."

"But that's impossible. You're injured and..." My eyes go wide and *something* makes me ask him, "You *are* injured, right?"

I look down at his feet.

He has a washed-out pair of blue jeans on. I stare at the spot where his knees are. As if I'll be able to tell if he's injured or not by staring at his jeans.

"I know that you tore your knee." I glance up to find him still looking at me with heavy, intense eyes that are wreaking havoc on my breaths. "That's why you came back, isn't it? You're not finishing out the season and you said you were going back home. I saw the press conference."

"You saw it."

I swallow, nodding. "Yeah. O-on TV."

I grimace slightly.

That's a lie, of course.

I saw it on a forbidden cell phone, but he doesn't need to know that. Somehow though, he already does and his smirk comes back.

And my breaths run away.

"So sneaking out in the middle of the night to go to a bar for dancing isn't your only crime. I'm not sure if sending you to a reform school was a good idea. You might be a worse influence on the girls who're already in trouble for being bad."

My embarrassment jacks up a thousand times and I mumble, "Hey, I'm not that bad."

He flicks his gaze all over me again and my lips part.

"I'm starting to get that," he murmurs. "You're worse."

It's not a compliment. I know that.

But the way he says it, and the way he's staring at me with eyes that possess a shade of blue that I've never seen on him, it feels like it.

It *feels* like a compliment.

But I can't focus on all of this.

"So?" I ask instead, keeping my control.

"So what?"

"Did you... you tore your knee, didn't you?"

"Why?"

"Because I..." I pause to gather my thoughts.

There are many ways I can answer this. Many, many, dangerous ways.

Because I love you and I need to know you're okay.

Because I love you and I want you to be safe.

Because I love you and I can't see you injured.

Because I love you...

But I decide to go with the safest, the only option that I have.

Looking into his new-colored eyes that are strangely watching me in the same way that I'm watching him, I say, "Because soccer is your life and I know that it must be awful for you that you can't finish out the season. It must hurt. It's hurting *me*..."

Damn it.

I shouldn't have said that.

That kinda slipped out, and obviously he catches it.

He catches it with both hands, his eyes narrowed and roving over my face. *Curious.*

"Why?" he asks again.

"Why what?" I stall, my heart in my throat, on my tongue even.

"Why is it hurting *you*?"

Great going, Salem.

Just fantastic.

We've been talking for ten minutes and I've already fucked up.

"Uh, because." I look at his glinting chain, the V of his gray t-shirt. "You're my sister's boyfriend. She loves you very much. Of course I'm hurting. I'm worried. For her and for you. And that's why I can't believe she's in LA when you're here. Besides, why *are* you here? Why aren't you resting that knee? Shouldn't you be like, recovering instead of bar hopping or whatever? And…" I swallow, looking up from his chain. "Kissing strange girls who're not your girlfriend."

At this, his jaw clenches again.

"For a girl who's just the little sister, it's very touching. That you're hurting and all. But I've got a doctor's note that says it's okay for me to bar hop and kiss strange girls. So you can relax."

His voice is cutting and sarcastic. It clearly means I should back down.

But I don't. There's no way that I can.

"You said that my sister was in LA. Why didn't she come with you? She would never leave you alone at a time like this."

He pushes his tongue into his cheek before saying, "Isn't this the first conversation we've had that's lasted more than a minute?"

"I…"

"It is, isn't it?" He lets out a mock sigh. "I think we should stop. Because I have to admit, I'm starting to miss that time."

The time he's referring to is the past eight years.

He's right.

This is the first conversation we've had that's lasted more than a minute. Because as an attempt to keep him safe from my witchy ways, I've always kept my distance from him. I've always kept my head down around him. I've never even made eye contact with him, I think.

So yeah, this is the very first time we're talking like this.

And when he takes a step back, ready to leave, I don't want him to go.

So I blurt out the stupidest question in the history of all questions.

The only question that I've been wanting to ask ever since I saw him.

The *real* question.

"Are you cheating on my sister?"

Oh God.

I said that. I really said that.

I used the c-word. I used the most horrific word that can't be true at all. There's no way, *no way*, it could be true.

It's crazy. It's insane.

It's impossible.

But then... But then why was he kissing another girl?

Why has he been distracting me?

Why has he been acting so fucking strange?

"No."

His answer is short and clipped.

And completely true.

I believe that. I can see the truth of it in his dark blue eyes, on his sharp angry features.

"Then why were you kissing her?" I ask with complete faith in his loyalty and complete confusion about the turn of events. "Why were you kissing someone who's not your girlfriend?"

"Because I don't have a girlfriend."

"What?"

"Your sister and I are not together anymore."

I think he punched me.

He did.

Because I feel jarred. I feel like I've been pushed out of my body and I've hit the wall behind me. The brick pillar that sort of makes this into a secluded corner.

Where I found him kissing a strange girl.

But he's leaving now. He's leaving this corner and walking away.

After punching me in the stomach with his words, he's leaving and I don't even have the energy to stop him.

To ask him what the fuck is he talking about?

Why would he say something like this?

My thoughts break when he stops and turns around to face me. "One last thing."

I look at him strangely, barely able to breathe.

"Don't ever let me catch you where you're not supposed to be. Because when a student breaks a rule, it's my obligation to report it to their assigned counselor. And I hear Mrs. Miller doesn't take kindly to rule-breakers."

My heart jumps. "What? How do you..."

"How do I know?" He shakes his head once, his lips tugging up on one side in a cold smile. "I'll give you a hint."

Then, his gaze drops low, lower, down to the ground.

Like a puppet, I follow the trail and realize he's looking at my feet.

My shoes.

Why would he be...

Oh.

Because my shoes are not really shoes. They're soccer cleats. Neon yellow and worn even though they're sort of new. I got them a few weeks back when my old ones got too weathered to use after only a month or so.

I burn through my soccer cleats pretty quickly, abnormally quickly.

Mostly because I play a lot of soccer – yes, I play soccer too but it's a story for another time. And because I wear them everywhere. They're not meant to be worn off the soccer field, but when have I ever listened to logic?

My new neon-yellow soccer cleats are the reason I didn't have enough money that night to run away, and so I had to resort to stealing. Because I'd blown my savings on buying a new pair.

Standing a few feet away from me, Arrow looks at them for a few seconds before lifting his beautiful eyes.

"Make sure you're not late for your soccer practice on Monday. Because like Mrs. Miller, your new coach doesn't like rule-breakers either. And you don't want to find out what happens when you break his rules."

CHAPTER FOUR

I don't call him by his name.

At least not in front of other people.

Because his name has a power over me. Like the name Sarah has a power over him.

Every time I say it out loud, I flinch. As if *Arrow* is an incantation from olden times. A dark spell. It pricks my lips and covers them in tiny delicious paper cuts.

A spell that bites at my tongue.

I only say it when I'm all alone in my room and no one is there to witness the small spasms of my body and hear the tiny gasps that escape me.

In public though, I usually refer to him as my sister's boyfriend or the love of my sister's life.

So I don't know what I'm going to call him now.

Because he's not with my sister anymore.

He's not my sister's boyfriend.

How's that possible?

How is this real life?

How am I supposed to cope with this?

So it's during the group activity that I decide to take a drastic step.

I've been thinking about it ever since last night, ever since we came back from the bar and I found my roommate sleeping soundly in her bed.

Anyway, I think I'm going to do it.

I'm going to take that drastic step or I'll go crazy.

I'm already going crazy during the group activity.

Which is gardening by the way.

Because it's Saturday and at St. Mary's, we plant gardenias on Saturdays.

It's in the school crest and it's there because gardenia represents purity and innocence. It has an inherent goodness to it. So it's basically an example for us girls. Bad girls, I mean.

To become good and leave behind our rule-breaking ways.

But that's not the only thing that gardenias represent.

"Secret love," Poe tells me while clipping dead leaves. "It also represents secret love."

"Yup. They just don't know it." Callie snickers, looking at the teachers loitering around, keeping an eye on us; Miller is one of them.

"Which is so weird." Wyn shrugs. "Because you can just Google it."

Secret love.

I'm growing secret love.

I could laugh at this.

I *should* laugh at this.

It's funny, isn't it? It's a joke.

The universe is kidding.

The girl in secret love is *growing* secret love.

How tragic and poetic and totally not funny at all. And somehow it gives me the strength to make the decision. "I wanna call my sister."

Because I need to know what happened.

I need to know what was so horrible that they would break up when they were on the verge of getting married.

I *need* to know.

But the thing is that I can't call my sister.

I don't have the privilege of making outgoing calls yet. But then, I have access to an illegal cell phone. Which its owner herself, Poe, reminds me about.

"You can totally use it," she tells me and Callie nods for emphasis.

Wyn nods too, in fact.

I think it's because they have sensed that something is up. Moody silences after the press conference video; disappearing in the bar and then returning with a pale, shocked face will tell people that. But like that day in the classroom when they gave me space and let me keep my secrets, they do the same now too. They don't ask questions.

So I find myself inside the third-floor bathroom, with Poe's illegal phone in my hands, while they stand guard at the door.

Tightening my chunky sweater around myself, I psych myself up to dial my sister's number.

I tell myself that I can do this.

I can call my sister.

I mean yes, we haven't talked in months and I don't usually call her or email her, except on her birthday and special occasions when I send her cards and gifts, because she doesn't like when I bother her.

But this is an emergency, right?

A breakup is an emergency and I wanna talk about it. I wanna ask her how she's doing.

I can ask her that, can't I?

She's my sister, for God's sake.

Even though we're different.

We're so, so different and she doesn't like me very much.

But I absolutely love her and admire her.

Like I loved and admired my mother, who was also very different from me. The only thing is that my mother – as exasperated as I made her – loved me back.

My mother was a highly educated college professor who brought up two daughters all on her own after her husband left her. Until her heart gave way and she died suddenly, leaving us to be raised by her closest friend whom she'd always been in touch with, Leah.

But my mother had been a planner and along with her updated will, she also left us both some money for college.

Sarah is very much like her, actually. Ambitious, driven, beautiful.

Back when we were kids, I idolized my sister.

I idolized her beauty, her straight shiny hair.

I'd follow her around with my toys in tow. I'd ask her to play with me, play with my dolls.

She was my big sister. She was my best friend by default.

Or she should've been.

But she never thought so. She always found me annoying, a nuisance. An overenthusiastic puppy, I think. Well, she described me as such to one of her friends because I wouldn't leave them alone.

That was super hurtful. I think I cried.

But when I grew up, I understood why.

Why Sarah never liked me. It's because she's perfect.

She's beautiful. She's a straight-A student. She is popular. She is obedient. She follows the rules. She's smart and intelligent. She's practical, unemotional. She has a great job.

Whereas me, I'm the opposite of that.

Even though I have freckles and my hair is savage and wild and my golden eyes are witchy, I look exactly like my sister.

But that's where the similarities end.

I never had a lot of friends. I can barely pass a subject, let alone score perfect As. I don't even think I'm going to college, let alone getting a great job. My only ambition right now is to run away and live somewhere else so I don't try to steal my sister's boyfriend.

Not to mention I don't even *want* to be perfect.

I don't want to be like her or all the perfect people out there. Perfection intimidates me. All the rules intimidate me.

All I've ever wanted is to be myself, however flawed and imperfect that may be.

And all I've ever wanted is for my imperfection to be somehow perfect for him.

For her boyfriend.

So yeah, why would she like me?

On top of being completely different from her, I'm secretly betraying her. Her hatred for me is totally warranted.

But this isn't about me and her and how different we are.

It's about him and her.

So I take a deep breath and dial the number that I've memorized because we're sisters. We should remember each other's numbers by heart. I'm pretty sure she doesn't think so but it's okay.

I chew on my thumb – which Sarah completely hates – as I wait for her to pick up.

Pick up, pick up, pick up.

A few rings later, I hear a click and her smooth, sophisticated voice. "Hello?"

A breath whooshes out of me.

It's my sister.

My *sister*.

My flesh and blood. My best friend. Or at least, I wish.

"Hello?" Sarah goes again. "Hello? Who is it?"

"Sarah?" I say in a hoarse voice before clearing my throat. "Uh, it's... it's Salem."

For a few seconds, she doesn't say anything.

But I know we're still connected; I can hear things in the background, white noise from wherever she is.

"Salem?"

Her voice is full of disbelief and I get that. I'm probably the last person, no *definitely* the last, she was expecting to hear from.

"Yes," I say into the phone. "It's me. Uh, hi."

I chew on my nail again after that lame greeting. Like things are normal. Like I call her every day and I live in the regular world instead of being at St. Mary's where they have a hundred pages worth of rules about making a simple phone call.

"Hold on a second," she says.

Then I hear her murmuring something to someone before I feel her walking. Her high heels click-clack on the floor that sounds tiled until the sounds around her fade and her voice comes out clearer. "How... Where are you calling from?"

"Uh, from a phone?" I say nervously, spitting out the cuticle that I'd accidentally chewed off my thumb.

Again, lame.

But God, she freaks me out. My sister freaks me out.

"Are you trying to be funny right now?" she snaps.

"No, I –"

"Oh God," she breathes as if to herself.

"What?"

"You're not at St. Mary's, are you? You ran away. You finally ran away."

That was a shock to her, what I did that night: trying to run away with one hundred and sixty-seven dollars.

"Do you have any idea what kind of position this puts me in? That woman is going to be my mother-in-law, Salem. I'm marrying into that family and my sister is stealing from them. How can you be so selfish? So freaking thoughtless. And after everything that Leah has done for us. Everything. You know what, I don't even care. I don't care what you do. I'm washing my hands of you."

I completely understood her anger. I did put her in a bad position, even though I was running away to keep her relationship safe from my witchy presence.

And I completely understand her shock now and that's why I jump to reassure her.

"No, no, no. I'm at St. Mary's, I swear. I'm *here*." I splay a hand on my chest for emphasis like she can see it, like she can see me standing here, inside this reject, dusty bathroom.

"Then, how the heck are you calling me?" Her voice becomes shrill.

"Look –"

"I know the rules, Salem. I had Leah email me the entire welcome packet. I *know* you're not allowed to call so think very carefully before you answer me."

All right, everyone. *This* is my sister.

She doesn't even go to St. Mary's and she's read the entire welcome packet. Whereas I never made it past the table of contents.

If there was any doubt in my mind – which there wasn't – that Arrow and my sister belong together, it would be banished at this very second.

This gives me the strength to push through.

"I know I'm not allowed to call. Not until I earn the privilege by showing up to classes and completing my homework assignments on time. I know the rules, Sarah."

She scoffs. "If you know the rules, then what's your excuse for being stupid and breaking them this time?"

I clench my teeth. "I wanted to talk to you."

"About what?"

"About..." *Arrow.* "Your boyfriend."

She doesn't respond to that but I don't get deterred. This is my only chance of finding out what the hell is going on.

"I know about the breakup, Sarah," I say with a slight tremble in my voice. "I know you're not together anymore. I –"

"How do you know?"

He told me.

And I still can't believe it.

"It doesn't matter," I say, clearing my throat. "I... What happened? Gosh. I'm sorry, Sarah. Are you okay?"

Another stretch of silence and I know I've said the wrong thing.

"Is that why you called me? To find out if I'm okay?" She sighs sharply. "You're... impossible. You steal money from Leah. The woman who was there for us. She doesn't press charges but takes pity on you and sends you to a school that might fix you, and you're breaking the rules again."

"I –"

"I'm fine, all right? It's a breakup. No one died. Anything else you want from me before I hang up?"

And I know she'll do it.

She'll hang up so I blurt out the rest of it. "Is it because of his injury?"

"What?"

"Your breakup."

I grimace after I say it but I've thought about it.

It can't be a coincidence, right?

I mean, he was fine up until a week ago. He was on track to win the MLS cup even though he'd lost a game. He was on track to propose to my sister even.

And then all of a sudden, he's injured and he's here without her.

They *have* to be connected.

Something happened there and I have to find out what.

I sigh. "Look, I saw the press conference, okay? I know he's sitting out the season. And I also know that you think I'm stupid and a bother and a hundred different things. But I know these two things are connected somehow. His injury and your breakup. I know it. So just tell me. Please. For once."

Even then, she doesn't say anything.

So I go for even more drastic measures. "If you don't tell me, then I'll have to break the rules and call you again. And I'll keep doing it until you cave and tell me."

A sharp exhale of breath. "You're such a..."

"Please, Sarah."

"He's not injured," she says finally.

"What?"

"What I'm about to tell you is very confidential. If you open your big mouth and tell this to someone else, I could lose my job, okay? And I'm not losing my job because my sister is a freaking psycho and a loser."

I'm used to her words by now, her derogatory, insulting words. But still they hit me in the chest and sting my eyes.

Even so, I force out, "I'm not going to tell anyone. Just tell me."

"It's a lie they made up, or my team made up. Something to tell the media."

"B-but why would they lie?"

"Because he got suspended. That's why."

"He got suspended?"

"Yeah, he beat someone up."

"Excuse me?"

She takes in another breath and lets it out. A long, deep sigh. "It was one of the assistant coaches. But they wanted to keep it out of the press so we decided to lie. He isn't taking time off to recover. He's kicked off the team. For the time being at least. Until he does his anger management therapy and the doctor clears him."

I punched a door...

I knew right away that he was lying when he said that. But... Why would he beat someone up?

Why would he beat an *assistant coach* up?

I ask the same question of my sister. "Why would he do that?"

When she doesn't reply fast enough, I almost scream into the phone, "Sarah? Why would he beat someone up? He isn't like that. Tell me what happened."

"We broke up, that's why," she says, snaps actually. "We broke up. We had an ugly argument about it. He was upset. The next day, he went into practice drunk and got into a fight with the first person he saw, which turned out to be Ben. That's what happened."

"He was u-upset?"

That's the first thing I ask. Again, it's lame and useless.

Of course he was upset.

He *is* upset.

He broke up with the love of his life, didn't he?

"I can't believe he beat someone up. He broke his nose, his jaw, four of his ribs. It took three men, *three* big muscular men, to pull A off Ben. I saw it all on the tape. I've never seen A like that, so furious. Ben was threatening to press charges."

Sarah has always called him A and I've always wondered why she'd choose to do that when she has every right to call him by his beautiful, unique name.

Arrow.

"But we managed to talk him down," she continues. "And we came up with this whole deal. No cops. No bad press. As long as A does his anger management therapy and stays away from LA for the next couple of months. That was the only way to save his place on the team."

A breath whooshes out of me.

Thank God for my publicist sister. Thank God that she saved him.

See? He *belongs* with my sister.

My brilliant, beautiful sister.

"Why did you break up?" I ask quietly then.

Maybe because she's scared that I'll bother her again with my phone calls but she answers me without arguing any further. "Why do people break up, Salem? We grew apart, okay? We started leading different lives. I don't know when but it happened. And yeah, we broke up."

I swallow down a lump of emotions but barely. "But can't you work on it? The distance, I mean. You love each other."

"Look, Salem, you asked and I told you. Let it go, all right? It's none of your business."

"No, wait. I..."

I taste something salty on my lips and that's when I realize I'm crying.

That's when I realize that I haven't swallowed down anything.

My emotions welled up in my eyes and are now falling down my cheeks as tears.

It's so silly that I'm crying because it's their relationship, their breakup.

But God, they've been together for years.

I've *seen* them together and my heart is breaking for them right now.

"I don't understand, Sarah. You *love* each other," I whisper, pressing the phone tightly to my ear. "That's the most important thing, isn't it? You love him and he loves you and so you guys can work through this. You guys can overcome this. Love has to be bigger than any problems that you guys have. Love has to be bigger than everything else."

Shouldn't it?

Love has to be bigger. It has to be.

Otherwise what's the point? What's the point of a girl falling and a boy catching her in his sleek, muscular arms?

Shouldn't she fight for those arms? Shouldn't *he* fight to keep her in his arms?

Shouldn't they put in everything they've got so they can stay together?

"Ugh, please. Can you spare me the bullshit? I don't even know where you get it from. Mom was never like this. *I* was never like this. I don't understand how you came to be this way. So weird and strange. Like an anomaly or something."

My tears fall harder even as I tell myself that this isn't the first time I'm hearing this. This isn't the first time Sarah has called me an anomaly or weird.

It makes sense even.

I'm the only one in our family who doesn't have any ambitions, who isn't good at anything and who doesn't like rules.

I *am* an anomaly.

But I didn't call her to talk about my various flaws. I called because I wanted to know why. To maybe make her understand that this can't be the end of her and Arrow.

"All I'm saying," I begin with a determined voice, "is that there might be a way to fix this. You can't give up on a relationship of eight years."

Suddenly, something occurs to me.

Something glorious and wonderful.

Something that should've been obvious but wasn't because so many things have happened in the past twenty-four hours that I didn't give it more than a passing thought.

He is my coach now.

My new soccer coach.

"Maybe I can help you," I blurt out to my sister. "Maybe I can do something about it. He's here now. He's my new soccer coach. Which means I'll see him all the time and I can fix this. I can get you guys back together."

My mind is racing with possibilities now – *racing*.

There's so much I can do. So many ideas I can come up with.

"Salem," my sister snaps and brings me out of my daydream. "You're not doing anything. You're not interfering, you understand me?"

"But –"

"No. Not a word out of you. Enough. You stay out of this. You stay out of my life. It's my breakup. It's my relationship. This has nothing to do with you. Do not meddle into things you don't understand. And please don't call me again, okay? Do not break any more rules, Salem. If Leah gets sick of you and kicks you out of that school and her house, I'm not taking you in. You're on your own, you understand me? So please, just follow the freaking rules and keep your nose out of my business. And for the love of God, stop wasting your time on soccer. There are girls out there who can make something out of it, but you're not one of them. Accept that and do something worthwhile for a change."

I write him letters.

I've probably written him thousands of them ever since I started, when I was ten.

Because I wanted to tell him so many things.

I wanted to *say* so many things to him. I wanted to answer the question he asked me in the kitchen. I wanted to promise him that his secret was safe with me.

But I never got the chance and so I resorted to other measures.

Since then, it has become my addiction.

Every night I write him a letter. I tell him about my day, about all the things I did, all the mundane details. Every night, I ask him about *his* day. About what *he* did, all the places he went, all the people he saw.

Every night, I talk to him like a friend.

Every night, I call him my darling.

My darling Arrow.

That's how I start my letters. Not 'Dear Arrow' or 'Arrow' or something conventional like that.

Because what I feel for him can only be expressed in certain words, in certain syllables and tones and rhythms. And 'darling' hits all the right notes.

Darling says he's adored and loved.

But he also makes me hurt. It says that he's both a delight to my heart and a needle to it.

Loving him is the most wonderful, most awful thing in the world.

Loving Arrow is my doom.

So he's not my dear, he's my darling.

Once I've written them, I put them inside an orange envelope, which I then put inside a shoebox that I hide under my bed.

Well, whatever bed I'm sleeping in, that is.

Back at Leah's place, I had them – the shoeboxes, quite a few of them now – under my twin bed.

The night I was running away, I was carrying them inside my backpack and my little suitcase. The shoeboxes full of letters and the t-shirts that I stole from him. I didn't want anything else other than those.

When I came to St. Mary's, I smuggled those boxes inside too.

Tonight, after talking to my sister, I sit in my bed, while Elanor snores away in hers, close to the window, and write him a new letter under the moon that appears to be red.

It's not ideal but I make do.

I strain my eyes and scratch my pen on the paper, telling him that I saw him last night. That it was such a shock, a wonderful surprise to see him. But I can't understand why he's not with Sarah.

I ask him what happened.

How could they have broken up when they love each other so much?

I urge him to tell me that it's all a lie.

I ask him about Ben. About how upset he must've been to hit someone like that.

I ask him about the fact that he's here.

At St. Mary's. At my school.

How did he become my soccer coach? How is it that he's going to be where I am?

How is it that I was running away from him but somehow, we ended up at the same place?

Somehow I'm going to see him every single day now.

And somehow I'm going to have to keep him safe from a witch called Salem.

CHAPTER FIVE

H e is standing at the edge of the soccer field.

His sparkling sun-struck hair is the first thing I notice about him. Again.

Back at the bar, he had his cap on and so I couldn't see it. But now I can.

Even though the September sky is gray, there's still enough afternoon sunlight that the strands are shining. They're fluttering in the slight breeze and I have to shove my hands down the pockets of my soccer shorts.

To curb the urge of running my fingers through them.

While his hair is sun-struck, the rest of him is all gray.

Gray trackpants, gray sneakers. And his signature gray gym t-shirt.

Back when I saw him for the first time in his kitchen, he wore the same style of t-shirt. It's not something that's very unique, the style, but on him it takes my breath away.

It's loose and it flutters against his body in the breeze. That's not the part I'm crazy about, however.

I'm crazy about the fact that his gym t-shirts sport non-existent sleeves. There are holes where his arms go and those holes are so big and sort of hanging that you can see patches of the side of his ribs and his obliques.

It's fascinating. And so sexy.

It hammers home the fact that this is real.

That Arrow is really here, at St. Mary's.

The secret love of my life, my sister's boyfriend.

Ex-boyfriend.

Ex.

God, it's still so weird to call him that.

I shake my head and continue toward the soccer field with Poe, Callie and Wyn, who have no interest in any kind of sports whatsoever. But picking a sport at St. Mary's is compulsory because it falls under team building exercises.

From the looks of it, we're kind of late because all the girls are already here, and they seem super excited and chatty.

Well, why wouldn't they be?

He's a soccer superstar and for the past two days, the campus has been buzzing with the news of him being the new soccer coach.

Which somehow, believe it or not, has made me even more infamous.

Some hate me because I lived in the same house as he did, which is a very weird reason to hate someone. Some offered to be my friends if I dished out dirt on him, which I absolutely refused to do. So basically, everyone hates me a little more than they did last week.

Yay me.

We reach the field just as someone asks the question, "Can we get your autograph?"

Before I can figure out who said that or Arrow can even respond to it, another one jumps in. "And a picture?"

"We don't have a phone, idiot," someone says.

"So what? We can just use Coach TJ's phone," the second girl throws out.

Coach TJ is the lady standing by Arrow with a clipboard. Like every other teacher at St. Mary's, she's stern – not as stern as Miller though – and has a tight bun. "Girls –"

Coach TJ doesn't get to talk because yet another girl speaks out. "I'm so sorry to hear about your injury," the third girl says, and the mood of the group quickly changes, becomes somber. "Galaxy was so close to winning the cup second year in a row."

The first girl who asked about the autograph jumps in then. "Yeah, we all thought you guys had it in the bag. It was such a sure-shot deal."

Several other girls murmur the same thing, but I'm more focused on watching him. Watching the new Arrow.

His reaction at the mention of his fake injury.

I watch as his jaw clamps and his summer-blue eyes narrow for a few seconds, before his folded arms flex and his stance widens. I watch as his anger sort of flows from one part of his body to another.

And I get this stupid urge again, to touch him.

To touch this newly formed anger.

"Yeah, it is," he says in a tight but polite voice. "You think you've got something in the bag but turns out that you haven't. You deal with it though."

I bite my lip as the urge grows.

It grows and grows.

I so wanna go to the front of the group and talk to him. I so wanna ask him about things.

But I *won't.*

I absolutely will not.

Because over the weekend, I've promised myself something.

Just because he's at St. Mary's now where I'll have to see him all the time, in the hallways, and on school grounds, the soccer field, doesn't mean that I get to bother him. That I get to let myself loose and do... wrong things.

Especially now.

When he's just broken up with my sister. When he's just coming out of an eight-year-old relationship. He doesn't need an overeager little sister to barge into his life and ask him questions like I did at the bar.

So I'm going to do what I've always done, keep him safe from my witchy ways.

"Can you teach me how to head the ball?" someone asks, breaking my thoughts.

Just like earlier, before Arrow can answer, someone else is ready with another question and it simply snowballs from there.

"I read somewhere that Real Madrid has been eyeing you. Will you be traded to play in the European League next season?"

"Have you met Messi? What about Beckham?"

"Yes! Have you met Ronaldo?"

"How much do you bench-press?"

"Can you bench-press me?"

This generates a lot of laughter until someone asks, "Do you have a girlfriend?"

At this, I stiffen.

My eyes go wide and my lips part as I once again watch anger move from his cheekbones to his shoulders. A shadowed look passes through his eyes and I remember my sister's words.

He was upset...

My witchy heart starts to pound and pound as his anger reaches his teeth and he clenches them once before throwing out a smile.

A practiced half-smile that I've seen so many times on TV.

"Soccer takes up most of my time right now," he replies, giving his standard answer. "So I'm not looking for a relationship."

Yeah, that's what he usually says.

Soccer is my life right now.

Or *I'd rather not talk about my personal life but I'm happy to talk about the game.*

He's always kept his love life under wraps.

Mostly because soccer really *is* his main focus and he wants to be known for only his game and nothing else. And secondly, because when Arrow joined the league, Sarah was still in college and he wanted to protect her from all the gossip and paparazzi.

See? It's so, *so* hard not to love him.

Why does he have to be so good and dependable and so fucking protective?

I've never seen anyone like that in my entire life.

No wonder my sister fell for him, and no wonder I fell for him too.

But anyway, that's his standard answer. However, a second later, he digresses and adds, "But who knows? Things can happen. I'm actually finding out that it's great to roll with the punches."

Then, he *smirks* at the end of his answer. At the end of 'roll with the punches.' And I fist my hands because when has he *ever* rolled with the punches? *When?*

He's such a fucking planner.

Such a fucking rule follower.

Not to mention, why's he smirking like that? I mean, as much as I hated that he smirked at that girl in the bar, I now understand that he did it because they were making out or whatnot.

He was smirking at *me* – I remember that very clearly as well – because he was playing with me, trying to distract me from the truth.

But why is he doing it here?

Is he freaking flirting?

I don't get to dwell on it because after he's given that bizarre answer, he goes on to answer all the other questions that the girls have asked him. With the same smirk on his face.

And I don't like that.

I don't like that at all.

He's flirting, isn't he?

He's freaking flirting with the girls and my legs are itching, *itching* to go and put a stop to it. And I can't because I promised myself that I'd stay away from him.

Besides, I have no right to be jealous, do I?

I didn't have any right to be jealous back at the bar and I don't have any right here, either.

In fact, I have even less of a right now.

He's not my sister's boyfriend anymore – for stupid fucking reasons, if you ask me – so it's not as if I can be jealous on her behalf.

Technically, he's free to flirt, to kiss, to do other things with whomever he wants and it's none of my business.

None of your business, Salem.

But Salem is stupid, okay?

Salem is a freaking idiot who has a super secret love for this flirting, smirking guy whose gym t-shirt is fluttering against his muscular body in the breeze and whose lips are so fucking gorgeous that I just want to die right here.

And before I can stop myself, I'm walking away from my friends and breaking off from the crowd. I walk around the huddle where the girls are still simpering, glaring first at Coach TJ because seriously, shouldn't she put a stop to this?

Are we here to play soccer or have an impromptu Q and A session?

The second target of my glare is Arrow himself, the coach. With sun-struck hair, glittering blue eyes and golden skin, he wears his title well.

The Blond Arrow.

"I thought we were here to play soccer," I say, loud and clear, effectively putting an end to all conversation and laughter.

My sudden appearance has jarred everyone. They weren't expecting me or my curt words. I can feel their astonished and antagonized stares at my back. I can even feel Coach TJ looking at me with a glare of her own.

But I don't pay them much mind because my eyes are glued to him, and his are glued to mine.

But then, he breaks our connection and his eyes move down.

They go to my nose first, then my lips, followed by my throat.

I swallow and he watches it.

I take a deep breath and he watches that too, studying my soccer uniform issued by the school. He studies my white t-shirt, my mustard-colored shorts. My knee-high socks and finally my soccer cleats.

He stares at them a beat like he did the other night when he gave me that hint, before lifting his eyes back up to my face and murmuring, "We are."

"So, why aren't we?" I ask, injecting all the fire in my tone even as my heart pounds under his thorough perusal.

From the corners of my eyes I see Coach TJ trying to say something, probably to set me straight, but Arrow beats her when he drawls, "Because we were waiting for everyone to arrive."

Okay, so I guess we were a little late arriving on the field.

I should probably acknowledge that. Especially after what he said the other night about being punctual.

But I don't.

Instead, I raise my chin. "Well, we're here now. All of us."

He runs his eyes – I swear, they've become dark, *darker* than they were a second ago – down my body once again and I have to fist my fingers.

"So I can see," he says finally after he's done studying me for a second time.

And for some reason I feel like...

I feel as if he was doing all this flirting on purpose. To provoke me and make me march up to him like I did in the bar the other night.

But that's stupid, right?

Why would he provoke *me* of all people?

So I try to be sensible, sort of, and ask, "Can we play now?" But for some reason, I can't stop myself from adding, "I thought punctuality was one of the cardinal rules around here."

And then, he does something that I swear I've *never* seen him do in the past eight years that I've known him. Not to the cameras, not to Sarah, not to that girl even.

He licks his lips.

It's not even a full lick or an obvious lick or anything. It's simply a slight peek of his tongue followed by a little swipe of his lower lip.

It makes him look so... wicked, so provocative.

So opposite of how I've known him that I have to actually do what he did. I have to *actually* lick my own lips like a moron to believe that it happened.

"Yeah, it is," he says, nodding slowly, his arms still folded across his chest. "Although I had no idea you cared about them. The rules."

I shift on my feet, trying not to think about his lip-licking. "I do."

"You do, huh?"

"Very much."

"Well then, this place is having a tremendous effect on you. Because I can't seem to remember a time when you were so enamored by them." He pauses and adds, somehow saying the words in italics, "*The rules.*"

Something about that makes me narrow my eyes at him. "That's because you never paid me any attention before. Since you've always been so busy with soccer and other things."

I don't know why I said that. There's no possible explanation for it, for why I'd goad him further like this.

But now I have and he takes the bait.

He takes it with his whole body in fact. He cocks his head to the side and widens his stance as the corners of his lips twitch. For some reason I think it's from both surprise and amusement.

"I didn't, did I?" he murmurs, shaking his head as if at himself.

"No, you didn't."

He hums, his eyes all sparkly and intense. "I am now though, and correct me if I'm wrong but didn't I see you at a bar recently? As recently as last week, around midnight. Blatantly ignoring all the rules you claim to care so much about."

Holy... What?

My eyes go so wide, so *fucking* wide at this, that I'm surprised they haven't popped out of my head.

Did he really, actually say that? *Loudly*, no less.

Yeah, he did because there's a sudden outbreak of gasps and murmurs around me.

That... that *jerk*.

I can't believe I'm using that word in context to him, to Arrow.

But God. *God*.

Does he have any idea how much trouble this can get me in? This is not a joke.

It looks like he does. He does know this isn't a joke and he has every idea about how much trouble this could get me in because the *jerk* is smiling.

Well, more like a lopsided, amused sort of smile that he's kind of trying to hide by scratching the side of his mouth with his thumb. And by ducking his head in a way that his stupid, sexy jaw catches the afternoon sun.

And his slight stubble glints.

Glints.

The jerk is glinting and I'm watching him like an idiot.

Say something.

I fist my hands at my sides and clear my throat. The whole crowd quiets down to listen to what I have to say and I swear to God, if I get out of this alive, I'm going to kill him.

I'm going to kill the guy I love.

But I let out a laugh first – nervous and completely fake, glancing at Coach TJ from the corners of my eyes; she's glaring at me. "You're kidding, right?"

I laugh again and his lopsided stretch of lips turns into a full one as he watches me grapple with the situation *he* created.

"Am I?"

"Yeah, you are," I continue. "But I'm afraid there's a problem in your stupid joke."

"Oh, is there?"

"Yes. Because I can't go anywhere off campus, let alone to a bar. I don't have the privilege yet. Besides…" I narrow my eyes at him and repeat his words from that night. "Lights out at nine-thirty, remember? That's the rule and even I wouldn't dare to break it my very first week at St. Mary's."

Something crackling passes through his eyes. "Is that what the rule is?"

"Yes. Maybe you should read the rule book."

"Maybe," he replies lazily. "Or maybe I should just ask you. Since you've become such a model student."

I purse my lips at his sarcastic comment. "So I was here. In bed. Where I belong."

I think I spoke too many words and gave too much of an explanation, and now they're going to catch me.

They're going to take away all my privileges – however basic they might be – and probably even shut me in a room so I never ever sneak out again.

All because this jerk is having his fun with me.

But then I hear him drawl, "Well, now that you mention it. It wasn't you." My body unclenches and he looks me up and down again. "The girl I saw had messier hair, I think. Poutier lips too. You're right."

It's a wonder I can talk after that 'poutier lips' comment but I do. "Apology accepted. Now you know."

"I didn't apologize." Then, "I would've loved to see that though."

"See what?"

"You." He dips his face and lowers his voice. "In bed."

I don't know what's happening. I don't know what he's doing or trying to do. I don't know why he's saying these things.

The most bizarre, breath-stealing things ever since he came back from LA.

"You want to see me in b-bed?" I ask with dried throat and swollen tongue.

He nods slowly, the strands of his hair falling over his smooth, unbothered forehead. "Very much. I would've loved to see you following the rules, being a good girl. Staying where you belong."

I swat my own hair off my forehead because my fingers are being impatient and unruly, whining to push aside his hair. My heart is being unruly too, whining to get close to him, whining to be laid at his feet.

"You're here now, aren't you?" *Somehow.* "You'll get to see that. Me, following all the rules."

"You have no idea how much I'm looking forward to it," he says, boring his eyes into mine, imparting a meaning, a secret meaning, that I don't understand and yet strangely, I understand in every way.

"Now, can we stop the soccer superstar ass-kissing and play?"

"Sure," he agrees magnanimously before tipping up his chin at me. "Just as soon as you stop acting like an overeager groupie who cuts the line and fall back into it. Like everyone else."

I open my mouth to retort because how dare he call me a groupie, even though whatever I've learned about soccer, I've learned from him.

But his words jar me. They remind me that we're not alone.

I mean, I knew that but now it really hits me that there's a group of girls standing behind me, glaring at me, including a teacher, Coach TJ. And I'm doing exactly what they thought I'd do.

I'm taking advantage of the fact that I lived with him and talking to him – who's also a teacher now – in such a brazen, familiar manner.

Under his challenging gaze, I duck my head and move back.

Once I'm standing in the line, I look up to catch Arrow – Coach Carlisle, sorry – still staring at me with an inscrutable look before he unfolds his arms and looks away. "One by one, I'd like you to come forward, introduce yourself and tell us what position you play. And then, we'll start with a thirty-minute warm-up game."

So that's what we do. We introduce ourselves. When my turn arrives, I try to look as demure as possible.

"Salem Salinger. I'm the wide midfielder."

My eyes are on my cleats so I don't know if I'm right or not. But I feel like he pauses on me. I feel like his eyes darken and his jaw tightens at my answer.

Mostly because I just named the position that he plays.

He's played that position majorly through high school and college, with a few exceptions here and there. But he shines the best as the wide midfielder. His free kicks and bends are legendary, or at least, on the way to becoming so. Like Beckham's were.

And that's why I'm a wide midfielder as well, because that's how I taught myself.

By watching his and Beckham's game tapes.

All in secret, all stolen by me, from him, from his room.

Aside from writing him secret letters, this was the only way I had to feel connected to him, by playing the game that he loved so much.

I've always been kind of athletic and interested in sports. I played soccer here and there. But when we moved to Leah's house, I really picked it up. I'd watch Arrow play in the backyard and when he'd be at school, I'd retrace his steps and play all by myself.

So yeah, I play soccer.

But I'm really nervous to play in front of him, in front of my soccer idol.

The Blond Arrow.

Once we're done with the introductions, Arrow divides us into two teams while Coach TJ takes notes of all players on the clipboard. He tells us to take positions and start. Coach TJ blows the whistle and there we go.

As one of the wide midfielders, I dominate the field at the center. I run and cover the most ground, tailing the opposing team's players in possession of the ball, and stealing it.

Which is my area of expertise, if I might add.

The stealing.

I always have trouble though, keeping the ball in possession. But today, I do everything that I can not to lose the ball.

I dribble it like I've never dribbled before, my feet flying across the field until the opportunity opens and I can shoot and score.

When I make the first goal within the first five minutes of the game, I feel like I'm on top of the world. But that's nothing compared to what I feel when I make a goal again ten minutes later from the center of the field and hit the net dead center.

It feels like euphoria.

Ecstasy.

I've never been this good before. Like, ever, and I'm not kidding.

I think it's him.

His new, dark eyes are having an effect on me. They're pouring all the adrenaline, all the fire into my veins, making me play the best game of my life.

I can *feel* his gaze tracking me around the field, watching me play for him.

It gives me such a high that when the whistle sounds at the thirty-minute mark, it takes me a few seconds to gather my bearings.

Suddenly, I feel three pairs of arms surrounding me and forcing me into a hug. It's the girls, Poe, Wyn and Callie. Callie was with me on the team so when she squeals we won, I can't believe it. Poe and Wyn squeal too, even though they were on the opposing team.

They tell me that I'm amazing and I think I'm going to cry because no one has ever said that I'm good at soccer.

No one has ever said that I'm good at anything actually.

"Salem."

That's his voice, loud and lashing, piercing through my happy bubble.

I actually draw back a few inches as soon as it hits me. The girls draw back too and our huddle breaks.

I spy his tall form at the edge of the field.

His muscled arms are folded, and his stance is wide. But instead of the deep admiration that I dared to imagine – because we won, didn't we? – there's a scowl on his features.

A dark scowl.

Before I can digest that, he dips his face and unfolds one arm. Then, he crooks a finger at me in a universal gesture of *come here*.

And it's so condescending that I'm stunned.

The way he's crooking his finger at me. Like he's really a soccer superstar – which he is – and I'm really his overeager groupie he can just order around by simple gestures.

Okay so, I might as well be. A groupie, I mean.

But still.

He doesn't know that.

But that's not the end of it.

When I don't move, he even arches his eyebrows at me, all arrogant and superior, before saying my name again in a voice that promises retribution. "Salem."

And like the stupid, idiotic, lovestruck girl that I am, I move.

Because he called out my name.

He didn't just call it out, I *saw* him call it out. I saw his tongue peek out at the 'le' of it, wedged between his teeth. I saw him hiss a little bit too, at 'Sa.'

Which is nothing new because I see it all the time when people say my name.

But I've never seen it from *him*.

Just like I've never said his name out loud in public, he's never said my name either. At least, in front of me.

So really, it's his fault that he's making me do this.

That he's making me forget my indignation – righteous indignation – and walk across the field to get to him.

"Arrow," I say when I reach him and flinch.

Damn it.

It just slipped out and at the worst time, no less. Almost the whole school is watching. I think I heard them gasp again.

But Arrow has no reaction to it whatsoever.

"How long have you been playing soccer?" he asks in a soft voice, studying my panting, sweaty form.

I blink up at him as I answer, "Since I was like, seven or eight."

"So you know the game pretty well, yeah?"

"Yeah."

"What position do you play again?"

"Wide midfielder."

"And what does a wide midfielder do?"

He asks the question as if he's asking a child and it makes me feel both embarrassed and angry.

But I can't do anything about it, can I?

He's my coach and I've already slipped up twice today.

I open my mouth to answer but I'm too late because he speaks again. This time loudly as if addressing the whole crowd but still keeping his blazing eyes on me.

"Actually, why don't you tell us *all* what the job of a wide midfielder is."

"I'm sorry?"

"Turn around," he explains slowly and clearly, again as if to a child. "And in a very clear and loud voice, explain to the whole team what you think a wide midfielder does."

I feel things happening inside my body then. Loud things, trembly things. All because he's trying to humiliate me.

All because he's standing so close to me while doing it that I can smell the musk of his skin.

Fisting my hands, I take a deep breath and purse my lips. Under his intense scrutiny, I turn around and say, "As a wide midfielder, my job is to cover the field at the center. That includes stealing the ball from the opposite team, passing it to the attackers and forwards of my team. Hopefully, so they'll make goals."

I don't know how the air can be so silent with so many people present, but it is. No one talks or whispers or murmurs. Everyone is simply waiting for things to unfold.

And everyone jumps, including me, when Arrow speaks. "Pass the ball and help forwards make the goal." I look away from the crowd and focus on him and his murmured voice. "Tell me, Salem, did you pass the ball to your forwards even once in the game?"

No.

I didn't.

My cheeks burn as he keeps staring down at me with harsh eyes. My whole body burns like he just lit fire to my soccer cleats.

But he's right.

I did commit the crime he's accusing me of.

I did not pass the ball.

Once I took possession of it, I didn't let it go. I took all the shots myself. If I wasn't open to take the shot, I dribbled and ran with the ball until I could. It was pure luck that the player from the opposite team didn't steal the ball from me and make the goal herself.

Swallowing again, I shake my head. "No."

"No, what?" he bites out and I flinch.

It burns me even more, his question, his *hint*, but I understand. "No, Coach."

He narrows his eyes for a second as if he's absorbing it too, me calling him Coach. It makes him even more menacing, meaner.

"Well, as your coach, allow me to educate you on the first rule of soccer. Soccer is a team sport. Meaning, you play as a *team*. Meaning, you don't steal your teammate's play. You don't let your forwards run up and down the field, looking like fools. Especially when they're trying to communicate with you, trying to tell you that they have a better chance of scoring if you just pass the ball. So next time, do your job, follow the rules and pass the fucking ball."

CHAPTER SIX

The Broken Arrow

Perfection.

Greatness. Being at the top. Being the best.

Those are the things that I grew up with.

Those are the things that have been drilled into my head ever since I was a kid and I'd see my soccer legend of a father, Atticus Carlisle, play.

Mostly on the television screen because he passed away when I was seven.

And how do you become the best? How do you achieve greatness and perfection?

You do it by working hard, harder than the others. You do it by being focused. You do it by making sacrifices that others won't.

You do it by following the rules.

Which is, again, something I grew up with because my mother is the principal of a reform school.

So I've always done my homework, eaten my vegetables. I've gone to bed at an appropriate time. I've gotten straight As. I've aced every practice.

In short, rules are how I've lived my life.

It doesn't make sense though that I'm here, back in my hometown of St. Mary's, for doing the exact opposite of that.

I'm not only back in my hometown but I'm also sitting on a pink couch with printed blue flowers on it. Because I broke the very first rule of soccer. The rule my dad taught me when I was only six or so.

"You never lose your temper, Arrow. That's the first rule. Soccer isn't about butting heads. It's about precision and accuracy. It comes from patience. You gauge the play of the other player before making yours."

I have to admit that I didn't understand it at the time but over the years, it became second nature.

Not losing my calm. Not losing my patience. Not losing my fucking temper.

But I did.

I lost my temper and beat up the assistant coach. It doesn't matter that he had it coming. It doesn't matter that I would've killed that motherfucker if they hadn't pulled me off. It doesn't matter that I fucking enjoyed it.

What matters is that I broke a rule – as impossible and otherworldly as it may seem right now – and got kicked off the team.

I got kicked out before I could win the cup and that's why I'm here.

In the pink and from what I can tell also purple office of the therapist that the team chose for me, Dr. Lola Bernstein.

She's a woman in her fifties, I think. She also wears glasses and a fuck-ton of jewelry. And she smiles. A lot.

I've probably been here five minutes and she's smiled at me at least ten times. So she smiles twice every minute. Once every thirty seconds, and I already want to punch her glass coffee table.

But I won't.

Because I don't lose my temper. I never lose it.

Besides, she's a Harvard graduate. She has about thirty years of experience and good credentials. I've been told that she's also worked at a very prestigious facility called Heartstone Psychiatric Hospital, before starting her own practice. If anyone can help me get rid of this anger inside of me, it's her.

So I'm going to follow the rules and not punch things around me like I strangely want to do these days.

"So, Arrow." She cocks her head to the side and her necklace tinkles. "Can I call you Arrow?"

I clench my teeth at her noisy jewelry. "People call me A but sure, yeah. Whatever."

"I can call you A. No worries."

She smiles. Again.

I don't know how to respond to it. Am I supposed to smile back? Am I supposed to ask her what she wants to be called? What, exactly.

Also, how does a Harvard graduate not know what the basic professional attire is? Why is she wearing a hobo-like skirt? How is that going to inspire confidence in her clients that she can fix their problems?

But again, I'm not going to get riled up. Because I never get riled up.

Besides, it's not like I've been to a therapist before. So I don't know what these people do.

"So," she begins when I simply keep looking at her. "This is the first time that you've had an anger problem, at least to this degree. Is that correct?"

I jerk out a nod. "This is the first time I've had an anger problem to any degree."

She raises her eyebrows. "Are you saying that you've never been angry?"

"Yes."

"But that's impossible."

"It's not. I don't lose my temper. It's detrimental to the game."

"Ah, soccer." She nods. "So you're very dedicated to soccer."

Something about that makes me tighten up my body. "Yes. Soccer is everything."

She hums and I don't like that. I don't know what that hum means. I'm about to say something to her when she asks me another question. "So what happened to make you this angry?"

"Excuse me?"

She shrugs. "You say that you never get angry because it's detrimental to the game. But something must have happened to make you so angry that you punched someone. So what happened?"

What happened.

She's joking, right?

Doesn't she know what happened? It's fucking plastered all over, what happened.

It's fucking plastered all over the team that I broke up with my girlfriend and lost my shit. And I lost it to such an extent that I got suspended because the douchebag I beat up was threatening to press charges against me. They even told me to get out of the city, work on my issues and come back when I have a doctor's note saying that I'm fit to play again.

The PR team had to step in and make up a lie about an injury.

All because I broke the first rule of soccer.

"I was under the impression," I begin, shifting on the pink couch – I cannot fucking get over the color – my body tighter than ever, "that you were hired by the team."

"I was."

"So shouldn't you already know what happened?"

She smiles again and I swear to God, I'm going to destroy her coffee table and that bookcase that she has by the wall, just to get myself to calm down and finish my very first therapy session.

My fingers are already tingling with the effort of keeping still and not curling into fists.

"I do know. But I want to hear it in your own words. So I'd love it if you'd humor me."

Right.

Okay.

Humor the goddamn doctor so she'll give me a note and I can go back to where I belong: with my team.

I clamp my jaw and count to three. Then, I count to five.

My gut is still churning but it's okay. I can do this.

I've done harder things on the soccer field. I can talk to a therapist and tell her in my own words what happened.

"I broke up with my girlfriend," I begin with clenched teeth. "And that made me angry. It made me so angry that I did what I never do: I broke a rule. And now I'm here sitting in front of you, talking about it."

She hums again and it's starting to grate on my nerves. "So about the breakup. Tell me about it. How did that happen?"

At this, everything in my body seizes up.

Every single thing.

My muscles strain and I have to clench my teeth as I feel something crawling over my skin. Something like a bug. A hundred bugs. A whole fucking army of them.

They crawl and slither even, getting me hot around the neck, getting my legs jittery and I lose the battle with my fingers and curl them into fists, digging the knuckles into my thighs.

Somehow, I manage to say, "How do you think breakups happen? We had a fight. We broke up."

Finally, she's lost her smile and there's a frown on her forehead. And I'm not sure if I like that better than her constant stretch of lips.

"Well, there must have been a reason, right? Breakups don't just happen."

That's the thing.

It happened. It fucking happened. And I didn't see it coming.

I didn't see the knife in her hand.

Not until she stabbed me with it.

I'm sorry, A. I didn't mean for it to happen...

That's what she said. After.

After she took eight years of our love and threw it away.

That she didn't mean for it to happen.

I dig the knuckles deeper into my jittery thighs and say, "Ours did. It happened."

"Yes. But what happened?"

The bugs have started to sting me now. They've started to bite at me. And I'm seriously considering smashing something.

"I don't see how that's relevant."

"I think it's extremely relevant," she insists. "You broke up and that's what has caused everything, so again, what happened to break you guys up?"

You know what, it's not going to be my fault.

If I do break her table, I mean.

It's not going to be my fault that Dr. Lola Bernstein is going to lose her glass coffee table and that little cactus she has sitting on it. Because she's the one asking stupid questions.

Questions that have no bearing on why I'm here.

"How much is that coffee table?" I ask, tipping my chin at it.

She frowns again but this one is lighter. "Why?"

I shrug, cracking my neck slightly. "It's extremely..." *Breakable.* "Attractive."

"You like it?"

I open and close my fists. "Yeah. As attractive as the rest of your office."

She looks around the office. "I thought you hated it. You didn't look too happy when you sat down on my couch."

"I don't hate your couch. I love your couch. And I love pink. Pink is my favorite."

She takes her smile one step further. She turns it into a low laugh. "Now I definitely know you're kidding. Pink cannot be your favorite. Because your mouth is saying one thing and your face is saying something else altogether."

"What is my face saying?"

"That you're angry."

I curl one side of my mouth into a tight smirk. "Huh. And here I thought your job was to not make me angry."

"My job isn't to *not* make you angry. My job is to fix the problem that's causing the anger."

"Well, then you should really think about redecorating your office. And not asking questions that have nothing to do with anything."

"So you don't like being asked questions?"

"Not particularly, no."

She nods. "What about them pisses you off, exactly?"

"The fact that they're stupid and irrelevant."

She hums and this time she writes something in her notebook.

"What the fuck are you writing?" I can't help but ask.

She parts her lips in an O. "Was that a question?"

"That's definitely not an answer."

She laughs again.

I just lose it then.

Because her laughter is loud. Her jewelry is even louder.

And I can't control my temper when my skin is crawling and my body is tight and I have this urge to break her furniture.

"I don't think this is going to work out," I clip.

"Why do you think that?"

Another stupid question.

"Because I don't think you understand what your job is."

"Why don't you explain it to me?"

"Your *job* is to give me tools to curb my anger. That's it. That's all. You tell me a few little tricks that I can use to get rid of this anger so I can go back to playing the game that I'm good at. That's your job description."

She purses her lips. "I don't think it works that way."

"Well then, you're no use to me." I spring up from my seat, my body all hot and tight, and glance around her office. I focus on the degree that's hanging on her wall. "You should take that down. And probably ask for a refund from Harvard. Given the circumstances, you should be eligible for one."

That's all I say to her before I storm out of her pink fucking office.

I'm going to have to call my manager and have him arrange my appointments with someone else. Someone more competent and professional.

Someone who doesn't ask stupid questions. Someone who doesn't talk about things I don't want to talk about.

Why does she want to know what happened anyway? It happened.

End of fucking story.

It happened and it almost destroyed my life and my career. And now I'm stuck here, teaching a bunch of schoolgirls who know nothing about soccer instead of being where I belong.

With the team, winning games.

So I need someone who can help me get there, rather than stoke my anger and make things worse.

After leaving the therapist's office, I ride over to the sports club that my dad used to go to. They have a private area where I can practice my drills and no one will bother me or talk to me about my disastrous injury.

I run. I do weights. I fucking run again.

I do everything I can to get rid of this violent streak that Dr. Lola Bernstein has evoked in me.

When exercising doesn't do me any good, I decide to ride to St. Mary's and work on my joke of a job. Maybe there are books that can make it easier, that can teach *me* how to teach girls who giggle at everything I say and bat their eyelashes at me like I've got any fucking interest in their schoolgirl antics.

So I go to the library in search of a textbook or something, anything to take my mind off what a shitshow my life has become.

But instead, I find someone else.

Someone I hadn't noticed before. Someone who's always been in the background.

The little sister.

Salem Salinger.

Eight years ago when my mom told me that two girls would be moving in with us, I didn't care. I had heard of the Salingers before but never took any interest in them. I had other concerns in life, bigger concerns like soccer and my grades, along with some smaller concerns like girls.

As long as the new arrivals didn't interfere with that, I didn't care who moved in or not.

But then Sarah happened.

She was hot. I was horny. I was supposed to take notice of her and I did.

I was popular at school, a star athlete, a straight-A student.

Even though I never had time for friends, people followed me around and I let them instead of wasting my energy and telling them to fuck off. Sarah was supposed to be interested in me like everyone else, and she was.

I thought it would be a fling because girls usually are flings. I don't want anyone disturbing my focus.

But turns out, Sarah was like me.

She was ambitious, focused, driven. It was like finding a perfect match.

An easy match.

It just made sense for us to be together. It made sense to date her, to make future plans with her. It made sense to convince my mother to let us be together when she found out that we had been going out behind her back for a couple of months. She had objections – namely, about my ability to handle soccer while I was also dating because my mom has always insisted that nothing at all should ever take my focus off the game – but when I won every game that year, we managed to put her mind at ease.

It also made sense to buy her a ring and propose to her.

What doesn't make sense is that I'm standing here, at the school library, and watching her little sister get up on the ladder to retrieve a book of her own.

I'm not only watching her, I'm studying the curve of her spine and the dip of her waist. I'm studying the tight globes of her ass.

To me, she's always been Sarah's little sister.

A kid in the background who hated the cold but loved ice cream. I always thought that was a pretty strange combination but whatever.

I also remember Mom lecturing her about her bad grades and her breaking curfew and whatnot. Sarah would bitch about her too, from time to time.

But honestly, I didn't care.

Nothing about Salem has ever affected me.

Not until now.

Not until I saw her at the bar with her wild hair, all loose and scattered about her shoulders, her eyes narrowed, her cheeks flushed – so flushed that it was visible in the darkened space – and her lips, parted and painted dark.

At first glance, she looked like Sarah.

Same golden eyes, same color hair, same pert nose. The same pale skin, standing there chewing me out for kissing someone else other than her sister; honestly, I don't even think I'd heard her talk before that night.

But then, I noticed the differences.

Like the shape of her eyes. They might be the same color as Sarah's, rare, but they arch up at the corners. They tilt up, making them look like she's always up to something bad, something mischievous.

Also her hair. Unlike Sarah's, her hair is curly. So much so that it bounces when she walks, independent of her body. As if it has a wild mind of its own. As do her lips. They're poutier, much poutier. Like her mouth likes to show off, be the star of every fantasy.

And her skin.

It's pale but it's marked by tiny dot-like freckles. They have spread on her skin like wildfire, again with a mind of their own, on her nose and under her arched-up eyes.

Thirteen.

I saw that on the soccer field yesterday.

Thirteen freckles on her nose and seven in total under her eyes.

They moved when I humiliated her in front of everyone. They trembled when she raised her chin defiantly and turned toward the crowd in front of which I crucified her.

I know I was being a little harsh but she deserved it.

She deserved my wrath for playing the way she did. So magnificently.

So fucking gloriously.

How did I not know this about her?

She lived with my family. She lived in my fucking house for years and I never knew this. I never knew that she shines brighter than any star that I've seen on the soccer field.

It was such a shock.

Such a... *betrayal* somehow, that I was never made aware of this. That's why I couldn't stop looking at her, watching her pumping her little legs up and down the field. That's why I couldn't look at anyone else.

She *forced* me, didn't she?

She forced me to look at her. She blindsided me, distracted me from other players and made me sloppy at my job.

What else don't I know about her? What else is she hiding?

So yeah, Salem Salinger deserves my wrath.

She deserves my anger for barging into my life like a storm.

For being a rulebreaker, and I absolutely fucking hate rulebreakers.

She deserves my wrath for affecting me the way she does.

CHAPTER SEVEN

Mrs. Miller, my guidance counselor, heard what happened on the soccer field yesterday.

During our first session, when she tells me that I need to clean her apartment for the next few weeks, I'm not surprised.

My new friends told me that this is what Miller does. She abuses her power in small ways and no one says anything to her. Because Leah is always busy with her conferences and so she has given Miller – who lives on campus by the way – the full rein of this place.

I should probably keep quiet and leave Miller's office now that we're done.

I'm not her favorite person and rightfully so.

I created a scene on the soccer field. And on top of that, I played wrong and got put in my place.

For which, I'm not at all mad at Arrow. I'm not.

I mean, he didn't have to be such a jerk but he was right. I wasn't trying to play for the team. I was trying to play for him and that was wrong.

So the best course of action is to leave. But I don't.

Because I want to say something first.

"You know, I know you hate me. I know you think I'm trouble and I don't blame you. I get it. I'm here, aren't I? But Leah and Arrow, they wouldn't treat me any differently just because I lived with them." I lick my lips. "I just thought you should at least know that."

Miller looks up from her desk. She already has a notebook open and an old-fashioned-looking ink pen poised in her hands.

"The fact that you called your principal and your coach by their first names tells me everything that I need to know." Her eyes are narrowed. "A lot of people here don't care about what the students did before they were sent to St. Mary's. They're ready to give these girls a second chance. But I'm not one of them. What you did and the reason you're here define you. And so I'll be watching you very, very carefully."

And then she goes back to her notebook and I get up from my wooden chair – she has special chairs for her sessions with the girls – and leave the room, with things even worse than they were before.

I should've kept my mouth shut.

I just wanted to make sure that she didn't blame the Carlisles for any of my bad behavior. But lesson learned. I'm not going to say unnecessary things now. Not in front of Mrs. Miller.

And I'm going to learn to call Leah and Arrow by their proper designations. I'm going to fucking remember that she's my principal now and he's my coach.

My coach. My coach. My coach.

Hours later, I'm still repeating that in my head as I climb up the ladder to retrieve a book, all the way in the back of the library.

And maybe because my focus is on my new coach, my foot slips on my way down and my book plunges, crashing down on the floor with a thump, and I know that I'm going to be next.

I *know* that in two seconds I'm going to fall and break my neck and I clench my eyes shut and grab the rung of the ladder hard, squealing and oh my God, I...

Out of the blue though, everything stops moving, and I feel a hand – a big, giant hand – on my lower back.

A warm hand.

No, wait. There are two hands.

Yes, two of them, one on the small of my back and the other on my front – my stomach, stabilizing me and the ladder.

With my chest jerking up and down, I pop my eyes open and dip my head to look at them, the arms grabbing my tiny body and keeping me from falling.

They are bronzed and dusted with dark hair, darker than the dirty blond hair on his head. There are taut veins lurking just under his sun-kissed flesh.

God, they're muscled and thick, his arms. And it only gets better from there.

His arms only get stronger and more curved and flexed the higher up I go, toward his shoulders, bursting out of his gray t-shirt.

And I realize he caught me. He caught my fall.

At the thought, my eyes whip up and land on his face to find him staring at me.

"You caught me," I repeat my thought on a broken, panting whisper.

His dark eyes flare. "You were falling."

I was going to thank him but something else slips out of my mouth. "I didn't..."

"You didn't what?" he rasps.

"I didn't know that your eyes could do that."

"Do what?"

I study them for a moment. I study their color, the dark flecks, his ever-expanding pupils, the thick, forest-like eyelashes surrounding them.

"Become dark like that. Navy blue. I-I always thought your eyes looked like the summer skies. Like lazy Sunday afternoons and bike rides and..." I trail off when his hold on my body flexes. And I realize something else.

That he's touching me.

I mean, that's obvious; he just stopped my fall, but I hadn't realized that his hands are splayed wide on my torso. And that his fingers are so big and large and so dominating in their presence that when he dips the pads of those fingers into my flesh, I feel it all over.

I feel it so much that I suck in a breath on parted lips.

"You like my eyes, huh?" he murmurs, watching my mouth for a second.

And I can't help but nod. "Yeah."

"Summer skies. Sunday afternoons and..." He pauses, a slight frown appearing between his brows. "And what was the last one?"

"Uh, bike rides," I say automatically.

Something about my answer makes him move his thumb on my belly, and if I wasn't already holding in my breath, I would swallow it down now.

I would swallow it and destroy it and never breathe again because he's moving his thumb, circling it. I know it's only through layers of cloth but I never thought the slight scrape of his digit against my body would be so hypnotizing.

"Bike rides, yeah," he rasps, nodding. "That's quite the list."

"I –"

Those eyes of his become heavy then, hooded, as he replies over me, "I mean, I'm used to my groupies screaming my name and all the things they want me to do to them but you're the first groupie to wax poetic about my eyes."

My spine straightens up at that.

Great.

He's mocking me again.

"I'm not your groupie."

"It's okay. It's not you, it's me. I'm just that charming. Girls can't stop thinking about me."

"Charming. Yeah, I don't think you need to worry about that with me. I can definitely resist your supposed charms."

He ignores me, his lips stretching into a smirk, his thumb drawing circles around my belly button. "What else do you like about me? My cheekbones, perhaps? That seems to have a devastating effect on the female population."

I tighten my fists around the rung of the ladder. "You know, you're such a jerk."

He leans closer, the heels of his palms pressing even further into my body. "Did you also have my wallpaper on your computer? Your phone maybe? Isn't that what schoolgirls do?"

"I don't know. Why don't you ask them?"

"I'm asking you. You're a schoolgirl too, aren't you?"

I glare at him and he chuckles.

"It's okay, you can tell me. And maybe I'll do that thing for you that every groupie wants me to do."

"What thing?"

His thumb tucks into my belly button. "Sign my name on your chest." He lowers his voice a little. "Right where your heart is."

My heart – my witchy, witchy heart – races and my *chest* tingles and I get up in his face before I do something like whip off my shirt and ask him to write on my body.

"You know what? Just let me go."

I don't know how it's possible but his beautiful, wretched eyes smirk at me as well. Before he lowers them. "You *do* know that you're wearing soccer cleats." He looks up. "Don't you?"

"Yes."

"And are you aware that you're not supposed to?"

I exhale sharply and I bet he can feel that. I bet he can feel every little twitch of my body because he hasn't let me go yet.

His hands are still holding me, causing my skin to heat up, causing my anger to spike up too. "Why, is that another one of your rules?"

He shakes his head slowly. "No. It's common sense. You don't wear them off the field. Because they make you fall."

I know, okay? I know. I know you're not supposed to wear them off the field. I don't need him to tell me that.

I don't need him to keep holding me like that either.

So I throw him a sweet mock-smile that again makes his lips tug up on one side. "Thank you for the impromptu lesson, Coach. Now, are you going to let me go or not?"

He nods his head in acknowledgment. "You're very welcome. And I will. Once you get down on the ground. *Safe.*"

So I do.

I climb down the ladder and get down on the ground. So I can get away from his hand, and him and all these rioting feelings inside of me.

Rioting and provoking and restless.

As soon as my feet are on the floor, his hands leave me, sending a rush of cold to the spots where he was touching me. But I don't pay attention to that. To how stupidly bereft I feel now that he's not holding me and saving me.

Instead, I bend down to retrieve my fallen book and clutch it to my chest, standing far away from him. "Where did you come from?"

My question is spoken with agitation, which is completely the opposite of how he appears.

Just like at the bar after he insulted the girl, he leans against the bookcase and folds his arms across his chest, bunching up his pecs.

"I was in here looking for a book," he replies, all calm and unruffled. "Lucky for you."

"A book on what?" I ask, again slightly agitated that he can look so collected when I'm all flustered.

"On soccer."

I frown. "You mean for coaching?"

"Yeah. For coaching."

He says *coaching* with clenched teeth and I hold the book to my chest even tighter. "Are you really my soccer coach now?"

"Looks that way."

"How?"

Like, I understand the breakup – as hard as that still is to believe – and his suspension from the team. But I don't get how all of that led to him becoming a coach at St. Mary's.

He clamps his jaw for a second before he says casually, "Because Mom thought teaching a bunch of schoolgirls would be a nice way for me to spend the time while I'm here. *Recovering* from injury. And what can I say, I can never refuse my mom anything."

"But that still doesn't..."

Oh, it makes sense.

It completely makes sense now.

Leah is doing to him what she did to me.

I tried to run away with stolen money and so she called the cops before sending me here.

She's doing the same with him. He punched his assistant coach and got suspended from the team, and so he's here, teaching a bunch of *schoolgirls* that he doesn't like.

"She's punishing you, isn't she?" I conclude while he watches me intently. "But that's so crazy. You just made a mistake. You were upset over the breakup and you punched him but –"

The muscle on his cheek starts ticking and I stop.

Oh shit.

I just spilled the beans, didn't I? I spilled that I know.

I know the real story about his fake injury.

And I did that even though my sister told me not to open my big mouth.

Damn it.

"So you know," he says softly, dangerously, and I swallow.

"I'm not gonna say anything," I say, lowering my voice because for the first time I realize how quiet the space is around us. How public.

We're in a library.

Of course, the space is quiet and public.

There are students sitting up front, studying. Thank God we're in the back, surrounded by thick, dusty volumes.

"How?" he asks.

"M-my sister. I called her and forced her into telling me."

"But you're not supposed to be making any calls."

Again, he's speaking in very soft tones, low tones, but I flinch, nonetheless. "Well, I break rules, don't I?" His face remains blank at my declaration and his eyes remain watching and for some reason, I keep explaining. "So that's what I did and called her. But only because you guys broke up and I was –"

"Worried," he speaks over me.

I jerk out a nod. "Yes, and she told me everything."

"She did."

"Yeah, and now I know your secret."

And that's when it hits me.

This is his secret.

The fact that his injury is fake and that he isn't recovering. He's here because he got kicked off his team for punching someone.

I'm his secret keeper.

I've been his secret keeper since I was ten and he asked me not to tell his mom about the juice carton and I breathe out what I wanted to say back then. "I won't tell anyone. Ever. Your secret, I mean."

"And what'd she tell you? What's my secret?" he asks, his arms still folded, but there's nothing casual about him now.

Not a single thing.

Not the way he's staring at me with dark eyes and not the way his shoulders have become rigid. Even his biceps are in permanent bunched-up mode.

"That you guys had a big fight the night before and you were upset. And you went into practice all drunk," I begin on a whisper, staring back at him, seeing how much tighter he gets with my every word. "And you took it out on the first guy you saw. Y-your assistant coach, Ben. You beat him so badly that they had to suspend you for the rest of the season and send you to anger management therapy. And... and they told a lie to cover it all up."

For a moment after I'm done, he only stares at me. He stares and stares and I feel like he'll never say anything.

But then, he does.

He says a clenched-out word. "Impressive."

And strangely, his one clipped reply makes me speak up, makes all the words gush out of my mouth. "But you're not like that. You're not angry. You're calm and disciplined and level-headed. You always have been. The reason you got angry was because you were upset. You were upset over the breakup. You were hurting. Because you loved Sarah. You still do. That's the reason you're angry. It's because you're in pain. And you took it out on the first person you saw."

I don't know what I was expecting after I finished my hurried, impassioned speech. Maybe I was expecting him to dismiss it or to make a joke or a sarcastic comment.

But I wasn't expecting him to move.

I didn't know that my words had the power to make him lean away from the shelf and unfold his arms. I didn't know that my words would expose his flayed knuckles when he lowers his strong arms.

They aren't as swollen and wounded as they looked last week, but there's still some redness there, still some bruising.

But I don't get the time to study them more because he's walking toward me, advancing, and his eyes have this intense look in them. So intense that it pushes my body. It pushes me to move back.

Back and back as he grows closer and closer, his footsteps thudding on the cement floor.

As soon as my spine hits the bookcase, he reaches me, trapping me effectively.

Between the wooden bookcase with large, thick books and his body that has a broad, muscular chest and a tapering, sleek waist. Not to mention powerful thighs, encased in a pair of jeans.

"You're right," he says, dipping his face toward me. "I am angry. And upset and fucked in the head. And I did take it out on him and I liked it. I would've killed him if they hadn't pulled me off. So yeah, I'm fucking furious and I'm furious all the time."

I swallow, hugging the book tighter, feeling the pain in his guttural words. "I'm so sorry."

But he completely ignores it and keeps going. "But I can't go around punching people, can I? I can't go around breaking things as much as I want to."

"No, you can't."

He leans even closer then.

In fact, he raises his arm and grabs the shelf just above my head. I swear, I feel the mountain-like bookcase wobble at his grip.

"So that's why I was at the bar that night," he whispers, his chain shifting against his V-neck t-shirt.

"The bar?"

He nods. "I was looking for a distraction."

It takes me a moment to understand what he's saying and when I do get it, I hug the book so tight that the binding hurts my chest and my arms.

"The girl you were kissing," I whisper. "You were looking for someone to..."

Have sex with.

That's what he means, doesn't he? He was looking for a one-night stand.

Someone to dull the pain, and I have to breathe slowly to let it digest.

To let the fact digest that the guy I'm in love with, my sister's ex-boyfriend, was looking for a girl to fuck.

"Yeah." His dark eyes squint for a second as he agrees with me. "I was looking for someone and I would've found her. But then you showed up."

I bite my lip. "I..."

"All messy hair and flushed cheeks." His gaze roves over my face before dropping to my mouth. "And darkly painted lips, and ruined everything."

I wince at his harsh tone.

But I don't think he notices because he keeps looking at them, my lips, and I have a feeling that he's thinking about them painted. He's thinking about the lipstick I wore and I can't stop myself from whispering, "I-it's called Teenage Decay."

He raises his eyes and does that lip-lick thingy that he did back at the soccer field. Where his tongue peeks out and takes a slight swipe of his plump lower lip and where I have to go ahead and do the same.

Because it's still so unbelievable to me. That sexy move of his.

"Teenage Decay," he repeats on a whisper, and I feel the bookcase wobble at my spine again as he grips it harder. "It suits you. Or at least, I think it does. Because that's the problem, see. I don't know."

"You don't know what?"

He tips his chin at me, studying me like I'm a puzzle or something. "You. I don't know a thing about you. Until now, I didn't know you played soccer. I didn't know you had a talent for lame poetry. I didn't know anything. About you. The girl who knows so much about me. You do, don't you? To draw all the conclusions about me. About my hurt."

Oh, he has no idea.

He has no idea all the things that I know about him, and I don't want to give him any idea either. So I try to act casual and shrug even though it comes out awkward.

"Uh, yeah. We lived in the same house. For years. A-and as I said before, you were busy with soccer and other things."

"Well, again lucky for you. I'm not busy now, am I?"

I look to the side. "I don't understand."

And as if in response to me averting my eyes, he raises his other arm as well, grabbing the same shelf by the side of my head, making a prison out of his limbs and chest. So I never look away from him again.

"Who taught you to play soccer like that?"

"Like what?"

From the corner of my eyes, I see his biceps bunch. "So magnificently."

"What?"

His jaw clamps as he keeps staring at me. "Yeah. I don't think I've ever seen a talent like that."

I press my back into the bookcase and crane my neck up. "B-but you said all those things and –"

The bookcase shifts again and if he keeps putting pressure on it like this, all the books will fall out.

And dig a hole on the floor and I'll fall.

I'll fall and keep falling.

Falling and falling. For him.

He frowns. "I said them because they were true. Talent alone doesn't mean anything. You have to hone it, make it better, channel it. I could teach you."

"I'm sorry, what?"

"I could."

I don't even have the time to bask in his compliment, bask in the fact that he used the word magnificently.

My favorite player said that I play *magnificently*.

Because then he says, "On one condition."

"What condition?"

He shifts closer then, bending his body even more.

With his arms raised and placed by my sides, it looks like he's doing a pull-up and his silver chain is swinging in a mesmerizing way.

He tips his razor-sharp jaw at me. "Just tell me if it's your thing."

"What's my thing?"

"Stealing." Before I can respond to that, he goes on. "Because that's mine, isn't it? That t-shirt you're wearing."

I freeze.

I practically freeze and combust all at the same time as I become aware – very uncomfortably aware – of what I'm wearing right now.

His old t-shirt.

The one that I stole after he left for California.

And he can see it, the whole world can see it because I don't have my chunky sweater on like I usually do.

Because ever since he humiliated me on the soccer field a day ago, I've been feeling so warm and heated that I haven't been wearing it. I even put up my hair and tied it into a top knot so as to let my neck breathe.

"I... I don't..."

"It *is* mine, isn't it?" He nails me with his eyes, pins me down like he did back at the bar, as if I'm a bird. "I remember throwing it away or something a long time ago. But maybe I didn't throw it far enough. Far enough away from your sticky fingers. So, is that your thing? Stealing? T-shirts. Money. I wonder, what else have you stolen? Not that I mind. I mean, it's an old t-shirt and some chump change. But I'm just trying to get to know you. We lived in the same house for years and I was busy with other things. Which is a shame, really, because I should've been paying attention to you. The little sister. You grew up kinda nice."

He said so many things just now.

So many, many things that I don't know which one to focus on. I don't know which deserves my attention the most: the fact that he basically called me a thief or the fact that he said I grew up nice, and now he's looking me up and down.

Because he is.

His gorgeous lips are turned up in a cold smirk and he's taking me in like... like I'm a doll or something. An object. That he's eyeing and I so want to get away from him.

But I'm frozen.

My feet are glued because despite the cold, calculating way that he's looking at me, my witchy heart is still beating like a drum.

My stupid belly is still fluttering and when he finally looks up to my face and licks his lips in that new way of his, I clench my thighs.

I curl my toes.

"So I have a proposition for you," he whispers with hooded eyes.

"What proposition?"

"I'll help you with your soccer, if you help me with mine."

"Help you how?"

"Be my distraction."

"Distraction."

He nods and somehow his scent has become thicker and the space around me has grown darker.

It's like he's blocking all the light with his big chest and dousing me in his musky, delicious scent.

He's dousing me in himself like he's gasoline and I have no choice but to drip, drip, drip with his scent.

"Yeah, distraction. My rebound girl. You know everything about me. You know I'm angry and I'm hurt and I'm upset. You know I can't play when I'm like this. So why not? Besides, you ruined it for me, the other night. It's only fair that you make it up to me now. What d'you say? Want to be my rebound girl, Salem?"

My belly clenches when he says my name on a whisper.

On a thick, rough whisper that rolls down my spine like the beads of sweat his heat is causing.

"I need to..."

Think. Leave. Get away. Throw myself at you.

My brain is short-circuiting right now.

All the wires, all the nerves in my body are coming loose and getting tangled up with each other, firing off like crazy.

And his next words do not help at all. "Come on, you looked pretty jealous back on the soccer field. You didn't think I'd notice? I saw the way you were all outraged. It was pretty funny actually. I'm not into schoolgirls but they're fun to play with. *You* are fun to play with. Plus as I said, girls have always found me irresistible and I know you're not immune. So if you have a little crush on me, no one would blame you. Especially not now. I'm not with your sister anymore. This could be your turn. Your golden fucking chance."

My turn.

This could be my turn.

He's right.

I *was* jealous. And now I know that he was flirting with those girls to provoke me.

I *do* have a crush on him, only my crush feels like love, big and doomed. All consuming.

It is love.

It has been love for years. For eight miserable years when I've cried in my pillow, written him secret letters, pined for him, longed for him, *watched* him.

Because he was in love with someone else. He was in love with my sister.

But he's not with her anymore, is he?

I know I promised myself that I'd stay away from him and keep him safe from my advances.

But he's the one suggesting it and he's in pain and...

And then, I'm not thinking anything at all because he's touching me again.

The thumb that he was moving back and forth on my belly is now on the corner of my mouth.

Arrow uses that rough thumb to trace the curve of my lower lip that's started to tremble. My whole body starts to tremble when he tugs my lip, making me part my mouth.

Making me arch my back and get pulled toward his body.

"Not to mention, this could be your revenge." He tugs harder at my lip and I go up on my tiptoes. "I know your relationship with your sister is complicated.

Has been for years. Maybe you could get even with her. We both could. All you have to do is say yes."

He's still swiping his thumb back and forth, still looking down at me with blazing eyes, and my body is still straining toward him like a lovesick fool.

Maybe that's why it takes me a second to understand his meaning.

Revenge on my sister. For having a complicated relationship with her.

Being a distraction for Arrow could be my revenge on my *own sister*.

As soon as I understand that, something flips inside of me.

Something that gives me so much strength that I raise my arm and knock his thumb away. Not only that, I use that palm to smack him, his harsh cheek.

And I don't do it just once. I do it twice. I do it so harshly that my palm burns with the impact.

But on him, there's hardly any effect.

Except for the flare of his nostrils and the tic of his jaw, he looks unaffected.

"You're a pig," I tell him with a vibrating voice. "You know that? You're an asshole. I can't believe you said that to me. I can't believe you would... I'll never do that to my sister, you understand? Ever. It hurt me, it *actually* hurt me that you guys broke up. Because you guys are being stupid and stubborn and I wanted you to get back together. I wanted to *help* you guys get back together. God, I'm an idiot, aren't I?" I shake my head. "Stay away from me. And stay away from my sister. She is better off without you."

CHAPTER EIGHT

My palm still burns.

It's been twenty-four hours and I think it still shines scarlet, the heel of my palm. With which I touched him.

For the very first time, no less.

Yeah, the first time I really touched the guy I love, I smacked him. Not once but twice. And he deserved it by the way, for saying those horrible things to me.

I'm not going to pretend that I'm some kind of a saint, a good girl. I have committed the crime of falling in love with my sister's boyfriend.

I have committed the crime of wanting him and craving him and watching him while he was with her. I've always considered myself dangerous, a ticking time bomb.

That's why I was running away that night. That's why I will run away when I get my chance again.

But not once, not in my entire life, have I thought despicable things about my sister.

If I'd blown up like a bomb that I am, I would've done it for love. I would've done it because my heart got so swollen with wrong cravings and secret longings that it burst out of my chest on its own.

Not for revenge. *Never* for revenge.

And I won't let *him* think such despicable thoughts either. I can't let him be that angry and hurt and miserable. So miserable that he's thinking of hurting someone else.

So, I've come to a decision. It has *two* parts.

The first part includes getting him to apologize to me.

Yes, I'm forcing him to apologize and be nice. Because I can't live in a world where Arrow Carlisle is a grade-A asshole.

I cannot accept the fact that the guy I've been in love with for eight years is mean and cruel. So I'm going to force him to be decent.

And the second part is ending his pain once and for all.

I know my sister has asked me to not interfere. I know that.

But I'm going to.

Because he's hurting and she must be hurting too.

Breakups are tough and if I can do something to curb their pain, then I will. Besides, this is the least I can do after betraying my sister in secret for years.

Although I'm not sure how I will accomplish this big feat. But I'm working on it. For now though, I need to make him apologize to me.

I look for him all day at school but I don't see him anywhere. He's not in his office either; I went and checked. I even wanted to ask Coach TJ about him but I stopped myself lest I appear overly familiar and step over any more of my boundaries.

When school is done and night falls, we sneak out again.

This time it's my idea.

Because like a fool, I think I might see him again at the bar like last week. I might find him there, looking for his next distraction.

My chest squeezes when I think that. When I think of him looking for a way to get rid of all his anger.

Will you be my rebound girl, Salem?

I wanted it, didn't I?

God, how badly did I want it.

I would've said yes. I was *going* to say yes. I was going to say yes to becoming his distraction, an object that he uses, just because I'm so crazy in love with him.

If only he hadn't said those words. If only he hadn't been a giant fucking asshole.

Anyway, we're at the bar now.

Like the last time, I have lipstick on. It's called Dream Broken Darling, a melancholic and dark shade of coral and brown, which suits my mood perfectly.

Just like the song that's playing overhead: "Sad Girl" by Lana Del Rey, the queen who makes music for doomed and heartbroken girls like me.

My mind is on the song and my hips are already swaying to it, and probably that's why I don't see the obstacle in front of me until I've crashed into its back.

It's Wyn.

Who in turn crashes into Poe, who bumps into Callie.

Coming out of my melancholy, I frown. "What's up? Why are we stopping?"

Wyn shrugs, rubbing her shoulder. "Because for some reason Callie has turned into a statue and won't move."

We're standing just a few feet inside the door almost in a line and Wyn is right; Callie, in the front, has stopped moving. The rest of us break away from our formation to go stand beside her.

"Callie, what's up?" I ask, touching her elbow tentatively.

"Nothing," she says, her eyes focused on something, her lips barely moving.

"Then why aren't you moving?" Poe asks.

Callie mumbles something indecipherable and I follow her gaze to find myself staring at a guy.

At a gorgeous guy, actually.

For the first time since yesterday, my mind is thinking about something else. And that something else is this guy that Callie is staring at.

He's got dark hair that's kind of spiky and messy at the top, as if he has a serious habit of running his fingers through it. And dark-colored eyes.

Gosh, those eyes are so sparkly and uncanny. Like black gems.

He stands directly opposite to us, among a group of people. From what I can see, this guy seems to be at the center of it.

Everyone – mostly guys and a couple of girls – is somehow talking to him at the same time. Everyone is looking up at him at the same time, as well.

Probably because first, he's taller than everyone in the group, and second, because he looks bored. Or maybe that's his resting face, looking arrogantly bored by everything around him.

Well, not everything.

Because in a matter of seconds, his dark-colored eyes have fallen onto the one thing that does interest him.

My friend, Callie.

His smooth features change. They buckle and morph to show slight surprise before a frown appears between his brows.

He clenches his smooth jaw too – much smoother as opposed to his messy hair – with what I can only describe as disdain.

Confused, I look away from him and back to Callie, and when I find the same expression on her face, things suddenly click.

"Is he... the guy because of whom you're at St. Mary's?" I ask her, remembering the story she told us about how she ended up at St. Mary's.

So one night, over dinner, they all shared their stories of how they ended up at St. Mary's.

Wyn, who lives in a rich neighboring town called Wuthering Garden, was sent here by her parents because she had a fight with them about applying to art programs when the time came. And she got so angry that she drew graffiti on her dad's car. Although, I can't imagine Wyn ever being angry with her silver eyes and soft voice. She's a pure artist. A girl who dreams.

Poe, who's from Middlemarch, another neighboring town, was sent here by her guardian because she'd prank him and he got really tired of slipping on banana peels and finding frogs in the middle of his bed. I can definitely see Poe doing something like that. She's a girl who loves trouble, and I say that with all the love in my own troublemaking heart.

Then came Callie's turn.

"Well, my oldest brother sent me here. Conrad. I've got four older brothers by the way and we live in Bardstown. No parents. Anyway, he sent me here because I stole a guy's car. And drove it into the lake," she said.

When I asked her why, all she said was, "Because he lied to me."

Then Wyn jumped in. "Don't waste your breath. She'll never tell the whole story. We've asked a million times."

Poe nodded. "Yup. All we've ever gotten is a name, a very sexy name: Reed Jackson."

So now at the bar, Callie stiffens at my question but jerks out a nod.

Poe is next to speak up. "*He* is Reed Jackson. Wow, I didn't realize how..."

"How gorgeous he is?" says Wyn, picking up Poe's trail.

"Exactly," Poe exclaims. "Gorgeous."

"That's the word, yes," I breathe out.

"Yeah. He's gorgeous," Callie says the first words since we all saw him, standing there acting like he owns the place.

Then she breaks the intense stare-down and looks at me. He, however, keeps the connection and friction in his gaze well and alive.

"And a liar and an asshole. So he's basically a villain. A gorgeous villain," she says with a tight smile. "Oh, and he's here. Fantastic. So I'm gonna need a drink before I go over there and drown *him* in the lake. Fuck Will, the bartender, I'm stealing his whiskey."

And then she marches away from us and toward the bar.

"What just happened?" Wyn asks.

"I think we might need to keep an eye on this guy," Poe says.

"Yeah. And on Callie too," I say and make to follow my friend.

But Poe stops me. "I don't think you should go after her."

"What?"

"Yup. You've got other things to worry about," Poe says, raising her eyebrows.

Wyn looks over my shoulder. "Yeah. Something like him."

Him.

They don't have to tell me anything more than that. I immediately know who *him* is.

In fact, I feel him.

I feel the skin on the back of my neck prickle and heat up. My entire *spine* prickles and heats up.

"You should go talk to him," Wyn continues. "We can take care of Callie."

"Yeah, give him hell," Poe says fiercely.

Again, I didn't tell them what happened. But they guessed that something awful had occurred back at the library, when I came out all red and shaky. And then he came out, a few minutes behind me with his jaw gritted, looking all arrogant and aloof as he left the building without sparing anyone a glance.

My friends asked me if they needed to do something about it. If they needed to prank him or if it was serious enough to go report it to someone. I told them I could handle it. That it was between me and him.

And I was right.

I am going to handle it because it *is* between me and him.

Still feeling him at my back, I exhale a breath. "Okay."

They both give me smiles before squeezing my shoulder and taking off after Callie.

At last, I turn around.

My palm stings as soon as I catch sight of him.

He's in the same corner as before. The one he was bursting out of. The same vintage jacket too that makes him look like a daredevil. A bad, rebellious boy. And the same cap, hiding the top of his face and his dirty blond hair.

Like the last time, he also has a girl by his side. This one is a brunette. She seems pretty interested in him, and why wouldn't she be? I bet she's counting her lucky stars that she gets to talk to a superstar athlete, The Blond Arrow.

Besides girls find him irresistible, don't they?

That's what he told me last night. And he's not even wrong about it because they do.

I do.

And I am crazy for him. Crazy and stupid and sad. All for him.

But I'm also going to give him a piece of my mind, and he probably knows that. Because it's all reflected on my face, my tipped-up chin and heaving chest. And unlike the last time when I found him engrossed in the girl, he is engrossed in *me*.

Yeah, he's watching me with his shining, flaming eyes.

The eyes that I stupidly waxed poetic about.

I fist my hands at my sides and strangely, those eyes shine even more. Like two beacons on his shadowed features.

A hot shiver runs down the length of my body and I move toward him.

He watches me make my way through the drunken throng with an inscrutable look while leaning casually against the brick wall.

I'm about to reach him when he bends down and whispers something in the girl's ear. He does it without taking his eyes off me and she leaves him with a nod.

I feel her pass me by but I don't pay her any mind. My eyes are still glued to him and his to me.

When I reach him, he drawls, "I thought we were staying away from each other."

Ignoring him, I ask, "Did you humiliate her too, like you did the last girl? To make her leave so quickly."

He flicks his bright eyes over my face. "No. After you showed me the error of my ways, I was nice."

"Oh, you were."

He nods slowly. "I just told her the truth."

"The truth. Really?"

"Yes."

"I can't wait to hear your truth."

He studies me a beat, something rippling through his sharp features. "I just told her that a crazy groupie is headed my way. And she's got a bad habit of getting jealous when I talk to other girls."

I clench my teeth and a few lines of amusement deepen around his mouth. "You wish, you asshole."

"You sure? Because you look a little..." He searches for the word. "Flustered."

"Oh, I'm sure. I'm very, very sure."

His eyelids flicker and go down to my darkly painted lips. "That's too bad then, because I was kind of looking forward to reminding you that you're just the little sister."

It takes me a few moments to gather my thoughts.

Mostly because I'm remembering the touch of his thumb on my lower lip. The roughness of it, the heat while he was flicking it back and forth, almost playing with my flesh.

And I was letting him.

I was letting him play with my lip, with my witchy heart. With me.

But not anymore.

"You can keep your reminders to yourself because I've got something to say to you," I snap.

Even though he hasn't moved away from the wall, I know he has lost all his casualness. It's in the way his eyes flash and his jaw clamps.

"And that is?"

I take a step closer to him and stab my finger in the air. "What you said to me last night was horrible. It was awful and completely uncalled for and you know it. You fucking *know* it. You treated me like shit and that's not cool. Actually, no." I pause and take a deep breath, and then say all the things that I didn't even know were bubbling up inside of me. "You've *been* treating me like shit since you arrived, when I've been nothing but nice to you. I don't deserve your assholishness and cruelty and your public humiliation and your stupid propositioning. So apologize to me. Right now."

When I'm done, I'm breathing hard and I'm sweating like crazy. My finger that still hovers in the air is trembling.

That could also be because he's looking at it.

He's staring at my finger and he does it for a second or two before looking up.

But even then, he doesn't look into my eyes, no. For some *insane* reason, he's staring at my nose. He's staring really hard at it and I don't know what to think.

I'm about to speak up when he finally looks away and up into my eyes, tipping his chin at me. "You're right."

"I'm right?"

"You didn't deserve it."

"I didn't?"

"That's what I said."

I stare up at him, my neck craned, my finger tired and shaking, still pointed at him. "So you're apologizing. You're saying you were wrong."

Was it that easy?

He straightens up then, his chest expanding on a sharp sigh. "You want to get your finger out of my face and move?"

I curl my finger into my hand and bring it down to my side. "Why?"

His cheekbones thrum with irritation. "You don't want to be my distraction, do you?"

I swallow as another shiver rolls down my spine. "No."

"Then stop wasting my time and get out of my way."

I do the opposite.

I plant myself in his way. I widen my feet and stand my ground.

Slowly, very slowly, Arrow glances down at my soccer cleats, and I tighten my muscles. I watch as he grits his teeth once, twice. Three times.

Before he raises his dark blue eyes. "I thought you didn't need me to remind you that you're just the little sister."

His words hit me somewhere in my chest but still, I don't budge. "I don't."

"So is there a reason why you're acting like a jealous little groupie again?"

That one hits me too, but I refuse to move.

I *refuse* to get out of his way so he can go to that girl and do things with her. Ask her to be his distraction for the night, touch her lip with his thumb and smirk at her.

"Yes." I raise my chin.

"I'm all ears," he clips, his bright eyes shooting fire.

"I'm not a thief," I tell him with a determined voice. "You called me a thief, didn't you? You asked if it was my thing, stealing? It's not. I don't steal things. For your information, I worked. I had a job at a restaurant. Ever heard of St. Mary's Date Diner? All the high school kids go there. You went there, remember? I worked there as a waitress. I *work*. For money. I only stole that money from your mom because I needed the cash. I'd just bought myself a new pair of soccer cleats and so I didn't have any savings left and I needed to get out of here as soon as possible, understand? And I was going to give it back to her. The entire one hundred and sixty-seven dollars. Once I was settled somewhere and had a job again, okay? And you'd know that if you'd bothered to ask me rather than throwing out accusations."

Okay, so I had a lot of anger inside of me tonight. More than I was anticipating.

But whatever.

It's not as if I'm lying. I did work at that restaurant. But I only started working there after he left for California with my sister. That I chose that restaurant in particular because he frequented it with his high school friends and my sister is a tidbit of information I'm not willing to give him.

Anyway.

There's an unfathomable look on his face as he stares down at me. A glint in his eyes that I don't understand.

But it makes me think that he wants to take a deeper look at me. Another look.

A second look.

I don't know. The point is that I should stop. I've said my piece. I've even gotten my apology now. Not that he was nice about it but still.

But the thing is, I don't wanna stop. I don't wanna walk away, because there's something else.

Something crazy and dramatic and drastic that I wanna do before I leave and go cry in a corner of this dark bar. Because as soon as I leave, he'll go find a girl and distract himself.

I shouldn't do it. I *shouldn't*.

I have to though.

I absolutely have to.

Because what I'm about to do will make my statement, 'I'm not a thief,' completely true. It will make me a borrower, at the worst.

So when it looks like he's about to break his intense scrutiny and open his mouth to say something – probably derogatory – I take half a step back and blurt out, "And there's something else too."

And then, I do it.

I grab the hem of my t-shirt – I'm not wearing a sweater tonight; I only have a t-shirt on, *his,* among other things – and tug it up.

I clench my eyes shut and pull it all the way up and take it off my body.

Yup, I take my t-shirt, or *his* t-shirt, off in a crowded bar. A bar full of drunken people, people who might have witnessed my shameful, slutty act.

At least I'm not naked underneath.

No, I'm wearing another t-shirt. My own.

Because I'd come prepared.

Like a fool, I not only thought that I'd run into him again, I even readied myself for it. All the while I was putting on my own top underneath, I told myself that I wouldn't do it. There is no chance in hell that I'd ever take my clothes off in a crowded bar.

I guess I underestimated myself.

And now his t-shirt is wadded up in my hand and I throw it at his chest.

"Here's your stupid t-shirt back," I tell him, ready to make my grand exit now.

Ready to go somewhere in a corner, curl into a ball and cry while he finds someone to curb his pain.

But all my thoughts about leaving and crying in a corner vanish when all of a sudden, he bends down toward me and snatches my wrist. He not only snatches it, he puts pressure on it and pulls me toward himself.

That's when I get a good look at his face.

I've been so agitated and embarrassed at what I did that I forgot to pay attention to him, but I'm paying attention now.

I'm paying attention to his rippling chest, going up and down with his harsh breaths. I'm paying attention to his chain that seems to be jerking up and down as well.

And his eyes.

God, his eyes are so narrowed with anger, they're almost slit-like.

"You're coming with me," he growls.

I swallow. "C-coming where?"

"Where you belong."

"What?"

He tightens his hold on my wrist, almost crushing my bones, and my eyes sting. "I told you not to let me catch you where you don't belong, remember? So I'm taking you back. To St. Mary's."

"I'm not –"

"You like making scenes, don't you?" he says with clenched teeth. "If you don't come with me right now, I'll make you such a star of your little striptease show that you'll be crying about it for days to come. So we're leaving, you and me."

I thought I'd seen him angry but he's furious right now. *Furious,* and I wonder if he was like this when he punched that guy.

If his cheekbones looked that sharp or if there was sweat dotting his forehead. If his shoulders looked as massive and mountainous as they appear right now, wrapped up in vintage leather.

"Okay. B-but..."

"But what?"

I don't know. I have no idea what I was going to say. I had no *idea* that he'd react this way either. So violently.

I mean, I knew he'd react and *maybe* get angry, but I never thought he'd be on the verge of blowing up.

"I came here with my friends and –"

He bends even closer, his swinging chain almost hitting my chin. "You better pray that I don't find out who your friends are or I'm going to bury them so deep in detention that they won't be able to get out for the entire year. And not because they broke the rules and came here. But because they brought you here, in that t-shirt, looking like that."

"L-looking like what?"

"Like a *goddamn* fuck doll."

"I'm sorry?"

"If you didn't want my attention, then you shouldn't have taken your clothes off in front of me. You shouldn't have worn that joke of a t-shirt." He grits his jaw and almost smashes the tendons of my wrist with his hold. "So walk before I make you."

My t-shirt got his attention?

Seriously?

It's a normal white crop top, baring my midriff. Well, it's off-shoulder too, but I always wear things like this. Usually underneath my chunky sweater, but tonight I wanted to make some asinine point that I can't even remember right now. So I went without it.

It definitely does not warrant a reaction like this.

My outrageous actions do, sure. But not what I'm wearing.

I look at his seething features before looking down at my t-shirt. "You have a problem with m-my t-shirt?"

"I have a problem with your *cocktease* of a t-shirt, yes."

I flinch. "But I wear this all the time."

He doesn't like that and the havoc he's wreaking on my wrist with his fingers increases. "Well, consider this your first and only warning. You're not wearing it anymore."

"But I... What's wrong with it?"

"What's wrong with it is that every drunk guy within ten feet of you is looking at you like you're a piece of meat. Like they wouldn't mind getting their hands on some of that." He jerks his chin at me and I'm starting to feel even more self-conscious than before. "Because you're taunting them, flashing them your pale-as-fuck belly and that swipe of a belly button. That's what you're doing, aren't you? Teasing them. Making them look at you. Stealing their attention. Don't tell me you thought there wouldn't be consequences."

"I wasn't taunting anyone. I was..."

Trying to make a point.

"Walk."

"You don't like that? Guys looking at me."

I don't know why I ask that but it simply comes out and his eyes narrow even more. He bends even further down until the rim of his cap is grazing my forehead. Until his lips are so close that when he opens his mouth to reply, I feel him writing those words on my skin. "No."

"Why?

"Because I want you to keep being who you are. Who you've always been."

"W-Who am I?"

"The little sister. The one who hangs out in the background and doesn't get seen. The one who keeps her head down and doesn't make a noise. And the one who definitely doesn't demand my attention. So are you going to walk or not?"

He's so freaking pissed off that I do as he says.

I walk.

I make my way out with him at my back as if he's my bodyguard and we take the hallway in the back that leads out to the parking lot. A few people are lingering outside, but no one pays us any attention as we make our way to his bike. He's still at my back, as if I need protection here as well.

By the time we reach it, I'm a panting mess. I have my arms wrapped around my waist and I don't know what to do.

How to make them go away, the past few minutes. How to make it better.

All I wanted to do was give him a little hell for being so awful to me this past week and then make peace with him.

"Arrow?" I say in a small voice.

Without responding, he leans over the seat of his motorcycle and grabs his helmet, offering it to me. "Put it on."

"Can we talk, please?"

His chest jerks up and down with a harsh breath. "Put it the fuck on."

My eyes sting. "Please. I didn't know you'd freak out like this. I was just... You were so mean to me last night and I just wanted to make a stupid freaking point and I know I got a little dramatic back there but I... I honestly didn't mean to make you mad."

His nostrils flare. "Salem."

I take a step closer to him.

My name from his lips, even curled up in anger, makes me want to touch him. Makes me wanna put a hand on his chest and fist his t-shirt and press close to him but I don't.

I don't want to make him even more angry.

I don't want him to reject my touch.

"Please? Don't be like this, okay? I don't like it. I don't like it that we're fighting and you're all angry. And we're acting like we're enemies. We're not. You're not my enemy, Arrow, and I'm not yours. Please, I'll do anything. Just... can't we be friends?"

As soon as I say it, my witchy heart starts pounding in my chest.

It's pounding and pounding, making my body vibrate.

With a certain need, a craving.

A desperate desire to be his friend.

A bone-deep desire. A desire that has burst forth from my soul and I can't ignore it.

Because for some very strange reason, we keep clashing, him and I.

For some crazy reason, we keep rubbing each other the wrong way. We keep creating sparks and friction. We keep creating fire.

And I'm done.

I'm done fighting with him.

I'm done arguing over stupid things.

I love him. He's the boy I've loved since I was ten. I don't wanna fight with him.

I never wanna fight with him.

So this is my peace offering.

I even offer him my outstretched hand. "Will you be my friend, Arrow?"

I know it's a childish question.

But I don't know how else to voice it. How else to tell him that this is an important moment in the history of my entire existence.

Asking him to be my friend.

Besides, I think he could use one, a friend.

He could use someone to just... be with. Maybe even to talk with, I don't know.

He could just use someone.

Although Arrow still hasn't looked at my hand. He still hasn't moved his gaze from my face to glance at my offering and I don't know how to stop the despair that's spreading through my body. Just when I think my arm won't stay up and will fall to my side, he takes it.

He takes my offered hand and catches me. This time from my fall into despair. Into sadness and melancholy.

I wouldn't have believed it, if I wasn't looking at it, our joined hands, with my own eyes. If I wasn't feeling the scrape of his large palm against mine.

So this is what he feels like. This is what his skin feels like against mine.

Hot and strong, and sand and velvet at the same time.

Finally.

I smile up at him and find him watching me, watching my smiling, painted lips. He does his lip-lick thing for a second before he squeezes my hand and pulls me forward.

He comes forward too and then he's hanging over me, his face dark but so beautiful.

"But I'm still taking you back," he growls.

I flex my fingers against his hand, trying to wrap my head around the fact that I'm finally touching him and that our fingers are threaded together. "Okay."

His grip increases even more. "And I'm keeping my eyes on you until I see you enter your dorm building."

"Yes."

"Then you're going to go into your room, climb into your bed and go to fucking sleep, you understand?"

I jerk out a nod.

"And you're never wearing a shirt like this. Ever again."

I bite my lip at the vehemence in his voice and nod again.

He narrows his eyes at my mouth. "Good."

"Arrow?" I whisper, blinking up at him, holding onto his hand like it's my lifeline.

"What?"

"Before we go back to St. Mary's, will you take me somewhere else first?"

He squeezes my hand to the point that I think he'll break my skin and crush my bones.

But I don't care.

He can do whatever he wants with me.

He can stab me with a knife and I'll be lying on the ground, dying, drawing little hearts in blood.

His eyes stay on my smiling lips for a second before he replies, "Fine."

CHAPTER NINE

I'm sitting on Arrow's motorcycle.

I'm riding with him, my inner thighs hugging his outer, my arms around his waist and my cheek stuck to his sweet-smelling t-shirt as it rests on his shoulder blades.

Before we took off, I told him, "So Friend, this is my first motorcycle ride and I have a feeling that I've got a thing for speed. Which means that you should really step on it."

I'm not even going to deny how much I loved saying *Friend*.

How much I'll always love saying it.

He's my friend. My Arrow.

Something moved over his features when I said that. A ripple of something that shone under the fat red moon.

He settled the helmet on my head. "Yeah, I'm not surprised."

"Why not?"

"Because, *Friend*," he buckled the helmet under my chin a little sharply, making me bite my lip. "I'm starting to realize that you've got a *thing* for everything that's dangerous and crazy."

I shouldn't have smiled at that. It wasn't a compliment.

Like it wasn't a compliment when he said I was worse than bad, but still, it felt like one.

Maybe because when he finished settling the helmet on my head, he stepped back and took off his vintage leather jacket.

I watched his shoulders rolling and his biceps bunching as they did the work of taking it off and then draping it over my shoulders. When I put my hands through the sleeves, he then proceeded to zip it up, right up to my chin like I'm a child or something.

When I said *thank you*, his jaw moved.

And then we took off and he did step on it, while I hung onto him.

Now we're here, at my favorite place ever.

My little darling place.

It's a bridge in Bardstown over the largest and bluest river that I've ever seen. It connects the main highway of the town to... nothing.

Well, okay. So it's old and rusty, this bridge, with a two-rod metal railing, stretching between an abandoned dirt road that's broken off the main highway to wild woods.

I'm not sure why they made it.

It's not really serving a purpose, connecting a dirt path that no one really knows about to savage, unnavigable woods. It simply sits here, taking up space, looking all dark and desolate and empty.

A lot like doomed love of eight years.

Which doesn't serve any purpose either. It's dismal and useless. Bleak.

And yet so fucking beautiful.

Just because the one you love is in love with someone else doesn't mean your love isn't gorgeous or real. It doesn't mean that your love should be killed or it should be torn out of your heart and thrown into a river or burnt down like an extinct piece of architecture.

No, it's still love. Like this is still a bridge.

"What the fuck is this place?" Arrow asks distractedly as he looks around, his bike parked on one side.

I watch him under the moon, all sparkly and glowy.

His hair's all messy and sticking up in places after he took off the helmet – he gave me his spare one – and his fingers are not helping things. He rakes them through the strands, messing them up even more, making him look the most stunning that I've ever seen him.

"Do you like it?" I ask, smiling, feeling warm and cozy in his jacket, that I unzipped during the ride because his proximity was hot enough, and loving it.

At my words, he focuses on me.

I'm by the railing, gripping the metal rod, using it to stretch back my spine.

He takes me in, my slightly swaying form, before settling his gaze on my hair. It's fluttering in the breeze and it's so long that if I stretch myself back even more and go parallel to the ground, it'll touch the dirt. I've tried it before; it's fun.

Finally, he looks up from his perusal of me. "Do I like it?"

I raise my eyebrows. "Yes."

"What's there to like?"

Straightening up, I gasp. "Are you serious?"

His lips twitch. "As a heart attack."

I shake my head at him and his amused lips. "God, you're so... unimaginative. This is my favorite place in the world. I used to come here all the time when I rode my pretty yellow bicycle, which I totally miss doing, but anyway. Look at the water." I stick my hand in the air and point to the water. I actually turn around myself to look at it. "It's shimmering under the moonlight. It's sparkling. And it's so vast. It's the only thing your eyes can see. And look at the moon." I point with my hand again. "It's so red. Like a fireball or something. I bet it's hot. Like the sun. And the woods." I turn to point to the woods as well. "So dense and mysterious and wild. Everything is so pretty here. Raw and natural and stunning."

It is.

The glinting dark water, the fat red moon and the thick bramble of woods.

Biting my lip, I turn to look at him again. Or at least try to, because somewhere in my twisting and turning, my feet slip and I stumble. My arms sort of flail and I manage to grab hold of the railing to stop my fall, but turns out I shouldn't have bothered.

Because he is here.

My Arrow. My friend.

He comes to my rescue, grabbing my bicep and pulling me up. He even sets me against the railing, all within three seconds.

"You have –"

I raise my finger and shake my head, cutting him off. "Uh-uh. You can't say anything mean to me now."

"Why?"

He looks really bothered about that and I want to laugh at his disgruntled expression. "Because you're my friend now. You have to be nice to me."

His eyes flick back and forth between mine. "Is that right?"

Nodding, I smile. "Yes. In fact, that's the first rule of friendship. Be nice." I go up on my tiptoes to get closer to his face. "And for a rule-follower such as yourself, it shouldn't be too hard, should it?"

He stares down at me, his hand still wrapped around my bicep. "If you think it's not hard then you're underestimating yourself." I narrow my eyes at him but he continues, "And for a girl who plays soccer so gloriously, it shouldn't be too hard to stay upright, should it?"

Gloriously.

I play soccer gloriously, he said. He said the same thing last night in the library but he was being such an asshole to me that it didn't make the impact that it should have.

But it does now.

That word drips down from my chest and settles somewhere low in my belly, like a warm dose of honey or sunshine.

My favorite soccer player in the whole world thinks I play *gloriously*.

Biting my lip, I say, "Well, I've got you now. To save me. Don't I? My friend."

Something dangerous and delicious flashes through his eyes. "What did you do before?"

"Before?"

He squeezes my bicep as if he's making sure that I don't fall again. "Before I came around to catch you."

I swallow at his question. At the inadvertent meaning of it.

What did I do before he came around to catch me?

What did I do when I didn't have his arms to break my fall and when I didn't have his gorgeous eyes looking at me like he wants to know all my secrets?

"I fell," I whisper.

His features become sharp for a second, snap taut, and I think I've said too much. I think he knows everything now. He hears everything now too, the loud drumming of my heart and the slight change in my breathing.

But I'm wrong.

He doesn't know and I'm never going to tell him.

This isn't even about that, about my witchy heart and my secret longing. This is about him, being his friend.

"You fell," he whispers back, his tone even lower than mine.

"Yeah."

"And hit your head?" he asks, his eyes grave.

"What?"

"Because that's the only explanation as to why you like this place."

It takes me a second to absorb his words and when I do, I push at his chest. As expected, he doesn't go anywhere; his chest is a solid, unmovable mass. My useless movements only make him chuckle and it's so adorable that I can't hold onto my anger.

"Just FYI, that is bordering on mean, *friend*."

His chuckle dies out. "It's harder than I thought, actually."

"Being nice to me?"

He shakes his head once. "Being nice to anyone."

I don't know where my boldness is coming from tonight – first taking off the t-shirt in a crowded bar, then asking him to be my friend.

But it's here, my boldness, and it's here to stay, at least for tonight.

So I stretch my neck to get even closer to him, where I can clearly see the pulse on his neck, thick and thrumming. Where I can map out his silvery features, the hills and dips of his cheekbones.

And then, I touch him.

I raise my hand and put it on his cheek and he stiffens.

Last night, everything happened so fast that I didn't get to feel it, feel the bones and the structure of his darling face. The face I see in my dreams.

But tonight, I feel everything.

His cheek is as hot and alive as his hand was, back when we shook hands at the parking lot. Slightly rougher though from the five o'clock shadow.

When I feel his jaw ripple, I whisper, "I'm sorry I hit you."

He stiffens even more, if possible. "Don't be."

I rub my thumb over the arch of his cheek. "I've never seen you like this."

"Like what?"

"So... uninhibited. So rough around the edges and sharp as broken glass." His jaw thrums again. "So cut open."

That's what he is, I realize.

He's cut open.

Like all these years, his emotions were under wraps, they were shoved somewhere deep inside of him. He was calm and collected and unruffled by anything and everything, always focused on his game. But now they're coming to the surface.

Now they're rushing through his veins and pooling under his skin, making him intense and hot and edgy.

Somehow, making him all the more irresistible to me.

He was right.

I do have a thing for everything crazy and dangerous.

"Cut open, yeah." His eyes glow as he stares down at me. "I'm that."

I'm compelled to say, "It won't help, you know. Hurting other people. Revenge."

His skin heats up just under my touch, becomes hotter than before, and my fingers skitter over his cheek, hitting all the sharp, stunning bumps of his face.

My sun.

"It feels fucking fantastic though," he says with a cold lopsided smile before moving away.

He settles himself at the railing and all I can do is stare at him and rub my heated fingers together. All I can do is think that I'm Icarus. The fool with wings made of wax.

They say it's arrogance that led Icarus to fly too close to the sun. They're crazy. It wasn't arrogance.

It was love.

He loved the sun too much. And that's why he couldn't stay away.

That's why I can't stay away either so I bridge the gap between us and stand where he's standing. He gives me a distracted glance before looking away and reaching back into his pocket, fishing something out.

A pack of cigarettes.

He gets one out with practiced ease, pops it in his mouth, almost clenching it between his teeth. Then he reaches back again and takes out a box of matchsticks. He lights one up with a deft flick of his wrist, and cupping his palm around the cigarette, he gets the tip burning.

He does it all with such smoothness, like he's been doing it for years, and I know he has.

I *know.*

I know about his smoking habit. His *secret* smoking habit.

But still, as he hollows out his cheeks and sends a gray puff of cloud skyward, I blurt out, "You're smoking."

He looks at the cigarette like he's seeing it for the first time and sort of sighs. "Yeah. Just don't tell my mom."

I know that he isn't serious but like the crazy girl I am, I can't help but say, "That's what you said to me. The first time we met."

He was about to pop it in his mouth again, but he stops midway and turns his head to look at me. "The first time we met."

"Yeah."

Then he turns his whole body toward me, forgoing the sight of the river. Not only that, he does it in a way that makes me think that I've arrested all his attention. "What'd I say?"

I never thought we'd have this conversation.

I never thought we'd have any conversation really, let alone a conversation about the first time we saw each other, while hanging out on a desolate bridge, in the middle of the night.

So I don't hesitate when I tell him, "It was early morning. You came in through the kitchen door after your run and you didn't see me there. You got the juice out from the fridge and you drank straight from the carton. And then you realized someone was watching. It was me. So you turned and said *don't tell my mom.*"

He also said something else.

He asked me if I was cold but I don't think he'd remember that. That's okay though. It's okay if only I remember the details of our first meeting.

It's not his burden anyway.

It's mine.

"And you were hidden between the wall and that old china cabinet. You had a blanket wrapped around you, didn't you?"

His words cut through the air between us and steal my breath away.

He remembers.

Gosh, he *remembers*.

But that's not the only thing he remembers because then, he goes ahead and says, "Because you were cold."

A stupid lump of emotion forms in my throat and I clear it away to nod and say, "Yeah. Because I was cold."

"Because you're always cold."

"I am," I whisper, grabbing the lapels of his vintage jacket.

I rub my nose in the collar and eat up his scent. And he watches me do that as he brings the cigarette up to his lips and takes a drag.

"I didn't, you know?" I whisper.

He tips up his face before exhaling and gray smoke fills the space between us. "You didn't what?"

"I didn't tell her about the juice thing. Ever," I tell him when the smoke clears and I can see his bright eyes again, on me. And then I tell him something else. "And neither did I tell her or anyone for that matter, that sometimes when everyone's asleep, you sneak out of the house. You go to the backyard and you stand under my window. And you smoke. Even though Leah told you not to."

In my knowledge, that was the only time Leah was ever mad at Arrow.

She'd caught him smoking one day and she really laid into him. Even Sarah was unhappy and by the end of it, they both made him promise that he wouldn't do it again.

But then weeks later, I saw smoke emerging from down below, thin gray tendrils of it, and when I went to investigate, I found him smoking.

And I found him again and again.

He doesn't smoke a lot, maybe once every couple of months or something, but he would always do it under my window in the middle of the night and I'd never tell anyone.

"Well, clearly not everyone. Was asleep, I mean," he tells me, puffing out another cloud of smoke.

"No. But I kept your secret. I'm the best secret keeper you'll ever have," I say proudly.

Oh, he has *no* idea.

Secrets are my jam.

Well, as long as I don't open my big mouth again like I did back at the library.

"Secret keeper, huh," he murmurs with a flicker at his lips.

"Yes."

"Well, then I'm glad."

"About what?"

"That you were the one who wasn't sleeping. And you're the one who found out about my injury. And you're the one I'm smoking in front of."

To emphasize, he pops the cigarette back in his mouth and takes a drag, letting it out slowly, all the while looking at me with an arched look.

I narrow my eyes at him. "And why is that?"

"Why is what?"

"Why would you smoke all those times when you promised you wouldn't?"

"Because I like it."

"But you don't break promises."

"I broke this one."

"*Why?*"

He throws me a flat look like I'm annoying him with my questions but I don't care. I need to know. And when it looks like he won't answer, I tell him in a curt voice, "Smoking is bad for your health, you know that, don't you? Especially when you're an athlete. It affects your lungs, which affects the way you breathe. Which in turn affects the game. And nothing should ever affect the game. Isn't that your motto? That's like the first rule you live by. So I don't know why –"

"You can stop talking now," he cuts me off and I bite the inside of my cheek to stop my smile.

Which of course he can tell, because his eyes narrow and a muscle jumps in his cheek. I blink up at him all innocently though. "I will if you tell me."

He sighs before turning away and looking at the river. "I smoke because it helps me relax. It's called de-stressing."

"De-stressing from what?" I ask, looking at his profile.

His shoulders tighten. "From a big game. A big test. Whatever."

"What?"

"The other option is that I get high or drunk. So this is no big deal, all right? It's a simple cigarette. Takes the edge off a little."

Is that really why he smokes?

I try to think of all the times I found him under my window, smoking. Was it always before a test or a game? Because he was stressed about it?

"And why are you smoking now?" I ask.

A breeze comes in and ruffles his hair further and I don't know if it's the fact that his hair is messy or if it's my question, but Arrow seems even more tense, the set of his jaw more strained.

"Because it helps me forget," he replies after a few moments.

I tighten my hands around the metal railing. "Forget what?"

"The fact that I'm here. Instead of where I should be, winning the fucking cup for my team."

"But you'll go back, right? You'll win the next cup."

His jaw pulses once. Twice.

"But not this one." A third pulse ripples through his jaw. "And it's on me. It's on my fucking stupidity. All because I broke the first rule of soccer."

"But you just made a mistake," I insist like I did back at the library. "One mistake should be allowed, right? You can't be perfect all the time."

I mean, I knew he worked hard. He still does.

I also knew that Leah expected him to be the best. She still does. Sometimes I thought that she was being a little too hard on him. But then again, his father was a great soccer player himself and with that, comes a tremendous responsibility.

I never knew this about him though. I never knew that he is so crazy intense about all of this.

"Yeah?" Arrow asks, studying my distressed face.

"Yes," I say vehemently. "You can't be. No one can be. You just slipped up a little, okay? And that's fine. You can't beat yourself up like this, Arrow. You can't kill yourself by smoking just because you have to sit out a season. It's crazy. Besides, you're already the best player they've got. You..."

My thoughts break when I notice his body move.

Like last night at the library, he advances on me. We were already so close though that it's hardly an advance. It's more like shifting, inching closer, but since he's so big and tall and he's got muscles for days, it feels like it.

It feels like he's advancing on me and arranging my tiny body as he likes with the metal railing digging into my ass.

And again like last night, when he puts his hands on either side of me to cage me in, it looks like he's doing a push-up, his chest dipped, his body curled, that silver chain swinging.

"The best," he drawls.

I raise my chin. "Yes. You are. Everything I learned about soccer, I learned from watching your tapes and YouTube clips. And Beckham's."

"Beckham."

"Yes."

He hums. "He's all right."

"He's amazing."

"He's okay."

"Are you kidding? He's a legend. They made a movie about him. But that's not even the point. The point is –"

"I thought you were my groupie."

There's a frown sitting between his brows. A few of his messy strands are dancing over that deep line and I'm so confused right now. "What?"

He flexes his grip on the railing, his frown growing deeper. "I don't like sharing."

"I... What?"

"I don't want you watching his clips."

I open my mouth to respond. Although honestly, I don't know what to say because this conversation is bizarre. But then suddenly, it makes sense.

Maybe he's jealous.

Which is so freaking ridiculous that I could laugh again. But his thick frown and that clamped jaw and dark eyes with which he's staring down at me, all irritated, makes me stop.

It makes me put my hands on the railing too, his fists touching mine. "Are you jealous?"

His brows snap even closer. "Are you going to stop watching his clips?"

"But he's an excellent player."

"Yeah, but he's got nothing on me."

Why is he so arrogant? Why do I like it?

And how did we go from talking about his smoking to this?

I arch my back and his eyes move. They stare at the pale patch of my belly and I wonder if he was one of the guys who wanted a piece of that, a piece of me.

I wonder if his jealousy extends from soccer to other things.

I know it's stupid but I still wonder.

"Isn't that a little arrogant?" I bite my lip.

He raises his eyes; his pupils look all burnt up and charred. "Not if it's the truth."

I feel something flutter in my bare stomach, something tugging and pulling just behind my naked navel.

Reaching up, I push back the messy strands of his hair because I know he doesn't like it. He doesn't like messy, wild things.

The Blond Arrow.

His jaw ticks at my action but I smile. "Okay, I won't watch him. I'll only watch you."

As soon as I say it, he grabs my wrist and takes it off his forehead. I fist my fingers when I see something flash across his face, something unfathomable but dark.

"So tell me something," he rasps, holding my wrist captive. "For a girl who works really hard for her money, a girl who had a job. Who'd take off her clothes to return the t-shirt she stole because she's clearly not a thief, why *did* you steal that money? Where were you going that was so urgent that it couldn't wait?"

My heart starts banging. "What? Why?"

"Was there a guy involved?"

"I'm sorry?"

Another flash of darkness passes through his features. "Was it a guy? Some loser like Beckham who you thought was so wonderful you had to run after him?"

The strands of his hair that I'd pushed away not five seconds ago have come out to play again. They graze over his lined forehead, making him look so unkempt and so wild.

So beautiful.

"Why?" I ask, twisting my hand in his grip but not to get free – I never wanna get free from his hold – but to feel his strength, his dominating fingers on me.

"I'm your friend, aren't I? A friend should know these things. So tell me. Were you running away for a guy?"

Yes.

I was running away for him. So I could get out of his life, leave him alone before my love makes me do something drastic. Before my secret love ruins *his* love.

I raise my chin and his necklace hits my jaw. "What if there is?"

His own jaw clenches as he says, "Then I'd like to ask him something."

"What?"

He runs his eyes over my body.

My wild, wind-whipped hair, the tingling tip of my nose, my parted and painted lips. My heaving chest under his vintage leather. My bare belly.

He stares at each part of me like it belongs to him. Like he can stare at those favorite little spots of his whenever and for however long he wants.

He can. He can.

But still.

It makes things happen inside my body. It makes me break out in goosebumps and it makes me bite my lip. It makes me arch my spine and makes my nipples bead.

He lifts his eyes, a flush covering his cheeks. "I'd like to ask him what the fuck is he doing, letting you run around town like this. Your friends, I understand. Maybe they're a bunch of clueless schoolgirls like you. But what the fuck is his problem?"

I draw back. "Excuse me?"

Instead of answering me, he touches me.

With his other hand, he touches my lip again. His broad thumb is probably smudging the lipstick at the corner, but I don't care.

I don't care about anything right now except him and his rough thumb.

"What's the name of this one?" he rasps.

"Dream Broken Darling."

"You're the darling?"

I shake my head, hypnotized. "No, he is." *You are.* "I-I like sweetheart."

"So what is he doing allowing his sweetheart to go where she doesn't belong, wearing something she shouldn't?"

I grab *his* wrist then and dig my nails in. "*My darling* doesn't control me. I can do whatever I want. I can..."

He licks his lip then and I trail off.

"Because if it was me." He presses that thumb in the middle of my lower lip, tugging at it. "You wouldn't be setting foot out of your room like this, let alone frolicking around town in the middle of the night."

"If it was y-you?"

He nods slowly. "If it was me, I'd keep you reined in. A girl like you needs that."

He'd keep me reined in.

If it was him.

If he was my boyfriend.

That's what he means.

He means that if we were together, he'd keep me on a leash.

He'd keep me bound like I'm an object or a pet. A fuck doll like he called me back at the bar.

A doll who's blinking up at him and whose lips he's playing with, whose wrist he's holding captive and whose nails are digging into *his* wrist.

"A girl like me?" I whisper.

"Raw, natural and stunning."

Did he just... Did he just describe me the same way I described this bridge?

He did, didn't he?

Something blooms in my chest. Something like flowers. Gardenias, the symbol of secret love.

"I... You..."

He puts pressure on my chin then. "If you were mine, I wouldn't let you ride around on that bike of yours in the middle of the night either."

"My bike?"

"Because you do that, don't you?" He swipes his thumb on my lip, an impatient movement. "When you think everyone is asleep, you sneak out of the house. You take out your bike and you go on rides. You ride for hours and come back at the break of dawn."

Yeah, I'd do that.

I'd take my bike out for a ride. I'd come here or go to my other favorite places and stay out for hours. But I'd be careful not to wake anyone up. Leah would've been furious.

But I didn't know that someone was awake. That someone knew about my nightly excursions.

"Y-you know about that?"

"Clearly, not everyone was asleep."

"But you never said anything."

"Maybe I was keeping your secret too," he whispers with grave and gorgeous eyes.

I don't see it coming – what I do next.

Maybe it's the fact that he called me stunning and he's been talking about me being his. Or the fact that he just told me he is my secret keeper.

He's been my secret keeper like I've been his.

Whatever the reason is, it makes me close the remaining distance and let go of his wrist. It makes me put my hand on his bicep and tilt up my neck and go in search of his mouth.

It makes me kiss him. Or try to.

Because he stops me at the last second.

He lets go of my hand, the one he had in his hold all this time, and grabs my hair in a fist, pulling me back.

With a low, dangerous tone, he tells me, "It's time to go back."

CHAPTER TEN

The Broken Arrow

I need a smoke.

Which is a surprise because I just smoked outside of Dr. Lola Bernstein's building before going in for my appointment.

My second appointment, to be precise.

Yes, I'm back. Unfortunately.

I talked to my manager and he said that the big shots on the team management won't change therapists. She's supposed to be the best at what she does so I have to stick with her.

And so I'm sitting on her pink couch again, watching her adjust herself in her armchair – purple armchair – as her tinkling bracelet bangs in my head like a gavel.

Hence, the need for my second smoke.

It's pretty rare, actually, for me to want to smoke again. I'm not a smoker, or at least not a regular one.

I only need it when I'm trying to relax before an important game or something.

I started back in high school, junior year. I had a big biology test and practice was brutal that week because we also had a big game coming up.

A few of the players were smoking outside of the school after practice and something about how they were standing, all relaxed and loose, smoke coming out of their mouths like they were expelling all their stress in the form of a gray cloud, made me want to try it too.

I was ready to dismiss it after one puff though.

Addiction of any kind is bad for the game. It had always been drilled into me, first by my mom and then by my coaches.

I would have too, dismissed it, I mean. If it hadn't led to a series of coughs, alerting everyone who was watching that this was the team captain's first drag. You can't have your reputation questioned or the players won't follow you.

So to shut up their derogatory laughter, I took another drag.

And another and another until it started to feel good.

Until the burn in my lungs turned into this high-speed rush that spread all throughout my body, making my shoulders relax and the base of my neck tingle. Making me feel like I was on top of the world.

Making me feel like I could do anything. Ace a fucking biology test and win the game against our rival school.

As I said though, I know my limits. I know the conventional wisdom. One smoke and that's it.

Besides I promised my mother that I wouldn't smoke. I'm breaking that promise so I can't have more than one anyway.

I'm an asshole for lying but I don't have to be a complete bastard too.

The days I smoke, I train harder. To punish myself for going back on my word.

But I would do anything, any-fucking-thing, for a smoke right now.

Because Dr. Bernstein has finished settling down and she's smiling at me. I look away from her and my eyes land on her coffee table.

The object of my fixation the last session.

It's not the same one though.

"You replaced your coffee table," I say, focusing on her.

Nodding happily, she leans forward and raps on the table. "Wood. Less of a chance that it could get broken. Accidentally."

She raises her eyebrows at me and I have to admit, my lips twitch a little. "Were you worried that it could get broken accidentally?"

"I don't know. You tell me."

I give in and chuckle. "It's a little early to say. But we'll see, Dr. Bernstein."

She chuckles as well. "You can call me Lola."

"I think I'll call you Dr. Bernstein," I reply. "Sounds more professional."

Still smiling, she nods. "Okay, let's be professional. So." She folds her hands on top of her notebook and I brace myself for her irrelevant questions. "Soccer."

I narrow my eyes, starting to feel my skin tighten up. "What about it?"

"Since you don't want to talk about your breakup, let's talk about soccer. How did you get into that? I mean, I know your father played for the New York club. So you were always interested in the sport?"

This I can handle.

I can handle questions about soccer. Although I still don't know what it has to do with my anger issues and how we're going to fix that so I can go back and play. But at least we're off the subject of the breakup.

"I was born into it," I reply. "My first memory is watching my dad play on TV."

"Were you ever interested in some other sport?"

"I played some basketball. Ran track. But it was always soccer. I'm my father's son."

I am.

My father – who was born and brought up in England – played soccer for the New York City FC, before he suddenly died in a plane crash. He met my mom when she was studying abroad and decided to follow her back to the States and get married.

If he hadn't died though, we would probably be living somewhere in Europe. It was my dad's dream to play for the European Soccer League.

I don't remember my father much. I don't remember how he was before he passed away. I've only seen pictures of him and he's always looked like such a distinguished man, my dad.

A great soccer player with a dream.

And now it's my dream.

To do what my dad wasn't able to. That's what I've been working toward all my life: to rise to the top and be traded to the European League. Real Madrid, if I have to be specific.

"So it must be painful, to sit out the season," my therapist comments.

"Very," I clip.

It's more than painful, it's fucking excruciating. To be sitting out when I should be on the field, playing.

Everything depended on me this season. I was their star player. I led them to victory last season and that was what was expected of me this season too.

But I went ahead and got suspended and now my entire team has to suffer because of me. Rodriguez is good but he's not me. He doesn't have my speed and my precision. And he's not going to win us the cup.

I know it. They know it. The whole media knows it.

So it's my fault that we're going to lose this season.

I'm sorry, A. I didn't mean for it to happen...

When the bugs start to crawl on my skin and my neck starts to feel hot, I fist my hands. I press them on my thighs to stop the jitters in my legs.

I'm not sure if my therapist is oblivious to my discomfort or if she's aware but simply choosing to ignore it, because her next question makes it even worse.

"So how you're feeling about your new job?"

"It's a joke of a job," I snap out before I can stop myself.

I didn't mean to say that.

I honestly didn't. I'm not one to complain when it comes to paying for my mistakes and I know the purpose of this job.

It's a punishment.

My mom's punishment.

But I guess my therapist caught me at a bad time.

Because I've had a shitty fucking day.

Four girls, on separate occasions, stopped me in the hallway to tell me about their love of soccer. To tell me how they've seen every one of my games and how I'm their favorite player.

It's fucking high school again.

At least back in high school, I had Sarah. Not that that stopped the overeager girls but still. There was some relief.

"Why do you say that?" Dr. Bernstein asks, breaking my thoughts.

I sigh and run my fingers through my hair. "Because it's not about the sport. It's just an activity to reform them. Teach them team building. That's why my mom put me up to this."

"Why would she do that?"

"Because she knew it would bug me. It would remind me of my mistake over and over. So I never make it again."

That's what my mother does.

She highlights my mistakes – which are very rare and far between – so I never make them again.

She knew I would hate coaching schoolgirls and that was the reason she gave me this job. To remind me of what I could be doing right this second as compared to what I have to do.

I remember one year my math score wasn't perfect. It was a shock to her and to me both. Because I'm good at math. I could do math in my sleep.

My mother went to the school with me to have a chat with the teacher and to find out if there was a mistake in my scores. Turns out there wasn't. I'd misread a number and hence, solved the equation wrong. She brought home my test, underlined that equation and stuck it up on the fridge.

So I'd see it every day. So I'd be reminded of my stupid mistake every time I went to get a glass of milk or juice.

Needless to say, I never misread a number again.

"Just because your dad is gone doesn't mean you can slack off. In fact, you have to work harder, Arrow. You have to work harder than everyone else. You have to do what he didn't have the time to do. You have to truly become your father's son."

So in order to do that, in order to become my father's son, she made me perfect.

She punished every single mistake of mine to the extent that I never made it again.

If I ate too many cookies before dinner and ruined my appetite, she forced me to eat every bite on the plate. It took me throwing up a couple of times from the stomachache before I learned not to do that.

If I ever fucked up a game or a test at school, she would make me stand in the dark until I learned to never ever screw up my passes or misspell a word on a test.

I think I was twelve or something by the time I was fully trained, by the time I became my father's true son.

Well, I truly became his son the day they drafted me to LA Galaxy and named me The Blond Arrow. But still.

"Well, that's a little intense."

My therapist's voice brings me back to the moment. "My mother's intense."

She is.

She's always been that way.

Sometimes I wonder though. If she was like this when Dad was alive. Or if his sudden death has made her even more stern.

Because it can get exhausting at times. It can get tiring, trying to meet her approval, trying to be perfect 24/7.

But it is what it is.

I have to pay the price if I want to be The Blond Arrow, don't I? Plus, she's my mother. She has brought me up herself, made sacrifices for me.

I owe her everything.

"I think we should talk about it, about your mother," Dr. Bernstein says.

"I think we shouldn't."

She stares at me a beat. "Can't you just quit? Your job, I mean."

"No, I can't."

"Why not?"

"Because I made a mistake and I have to pay for it."

"You know, it's okay to not beat yourself up like this."

As soon as Dr. Lola fucking Bernstein says this, I'm reminded of *her*.

The girl with thirteen freckles and a penchant for dangerous and desolate places.

My secret keeper friend.

My secret keeper *friend* who tried to kiss me.

She tried to put her mouth on me like some kind of a lovesick schoolgirl.

How naïve does she have to be to do that? How fucking reckless and careless to try to kiss someone as angry and as agitated as me.

How fucking stupid?

And so, my next words to my therapist come out clipped. "Maybe it's okay for you and for other people to not beat themselves up. But it's not okay for me. If I don't beat myself up, then I make mistakes. If I make mistakes, then I'm not perfect. If I'm not perfect, then I can't be who I am. I can't be The Blond Arrow. So maybe it's okay for other people to cut themselves some slack. But I don't get that luxury because I have to be my father's son. I have to make his dream come true."

Thirty minutes later when I leave my therapist's office, I get a text.

It's my mom.

I've been trying to avoid this, avoid having an actual conversation with my mother about everything. I've been making excuses, staying away from the house and living in a motel, but I guess I can't anymore.

Because she wants to have dinner Friday. And if I don't go to her, she'll come to me, and even though Friday is a couple of days away, my skin has already started to crawl.

My anger has already started to burn.

Because something that wasn't supposed to happen, happened and almost destroyed everything that I've worked for.

My father's dream.

I'm sorry, A. I didn't mean for it to happen...

CHAPTER ELEVEN

S omeone trips me up and my books fall to the floor.

I don't need to hear the snickering to know who it is. It's a group of four girls who've taken a special dislike to me.

My roommate, Elanor, is one of them.

She doesn't say anything to me, only glares with her big dark eyes when I enter our shared room. So I spend most of my time either with my girls in the common room, at the library or out on the grounds up until the last second before curfew.

"So riddle me this," one of the girls says with a snicker and a wiggle of her blonde eyebrows. "How much of a reject do you have to be that your own guardian sends you to the reform school she's the principal at?"

The second girl, who's also a blonde, joins in. "Yeah. What'd you do, Salem?"

Right.

Very funny.

A fuck-ton of snickering happens at this.

I don't want to cause any trouble. I'm not averse to making scenes – not me – but I don't want to fight right now. God forbid Miller sees us in the hallway – her office is only a few doors down – and gives me more things to do. My back has been killing me all week from cleaning her stupid apartment. I don't think it can take more abuse.

I'm not going to lie though. Scrubbing her toilet and bathtub is at least keeping me busy enough that I don't think about all the crazy, wretched things I've done. Namely on the night when we snuck out to the bar, which was four days ago.

And him.

Yeah, it is keeping me busy enough that I don't think about *him* either.

Well, who am I kidding? Of course I think about him.

I think about him all the time and maybe that's why when I hear his voice coming up from behind me, I think it's magic.

I think I conjured him up.

"Can I help you ladies with anything?" he says, and I freeze.

Ladies.

He said *ladies*.

All the girls have smiles on their faces because of that polite little word. Even I'm blushing and not slightly.

The first blonde girl who called me a reject begins, "No, we're just –"

"Are you going to pick that up?" Arrow cuts her off.

I fist my hands at his tone. I don't have to turn around and look at him to know that his jaw is ticking. Or that there must be a dark glint in his blue eyes.

I know all that. I can see it in my head. I can feel it all too.

He's like a wave of heat at my spine.

The second girl goes, "Well, these aren't our books, Coach."

The third girl in the group, who's a brunette like my roommate Elanor, says, "They're hers. She dropped them."

And I jump to say, still keeping my back to *Coach Carlisle*, "Yes. I'm just gonna –"

"No, you won't."

His curtly worded response directed at me makes all of us jump. The girls have their eyes wide and stuck on him and I'm fisting my skirt now, needing something to worry and crush between my fingers as his heat rolls down my spine in the form of sweat.

"You," he says and the girl who called me a reject stiffens. "You're the one who tripped her up, correct?"

No one says a word even though students all around us who were going about their business have come to a stop to witness what's going on. They're probably thinking that I'm at it again, the principal's ward who made a scene at the soccer field.

"It doesn't matter. I'll just get them," I say, ducking my head and making for the books again.

"Salem."

He says my name as a warning and I stop. Again, I don't have to look at him to know the state of his features, all tightened and bunched up, sharp as a blade.

"I'm giving you the courtesy of doing the right thing of your own volition," he says to the girls in a stern voice. "But if you can't, I can very easily order you to bend down and pick up the books. I can very easily order you to *stay* down for the rest of the day too." I feel him shifting on his feet. "Personally, I'd like to abuse my power a little bit. I'm stuck here anyway, right? Might as well have a little fun with it. So it's really up to you."

Everyone heard that and now they all have their mouths open in shock.

But not me.

I'm not shocked at what he said and how rudely he's behaving. I'm not shocked that he's being this new, cut-open Arrow.

Unfortunately, I like it.

Unfortunately, it excites me.

This excitement that I'm feeling has nothing on the excitement that I used to feel at the sight of the old Arrow, the one who would be all restrained and unruffled.

It's unreal, *this* excitement. It's the stuff they should bottle and sell on empty streets to bleak, miserable souls. So they can inject it in their veins and be forever high.

When the girl who called me a reject almost drops to the ground to do his bidding, I can't stop the tremble in my belly and my legs.

I can't stop the pounding of my heart. She hands me the books with a glare and I hug them to my chest.

"Good choice." Then to everyone else, "Show's over. You can resume your own lives now."

Afraid, they all jump to do his bidding too and I hear him mutter, "Fucking schoolgirls."

I spin around then.

And see him for the first time since he arrived on the scene.

He has his usual clothes on, his gym t-shirt and sweats, all gray, all freaking sexy. The barely-there sleeves of his shirt putting his biceps on display, tanned and strong, covered with dark hair, and I curse myself that I didn't explore the texture of his skin, the contours of his arms back when I had the chance.

The arms he uses to catch me when I fall.

I didn't touch them enough that one night when I was his friend.

Stupid Salem.

Because there's no way he'd want to be my friend anymore. *I* don't want to be *his* friend anymore.

What an awful idea that turned out to be.

I always knew I was dangerous. I always knew my love would drive me to do desperate, awful things.

Greedy things. Hungry things.

Things like attacking him with my mouth.

"You shouldn't have done that," I say in a hesitant voice.

He takes his time responding though.

He fills the silence with his heavy eyes, which he uses to survey me.

And he does it in such an intimate way that I'm surprised the world hasn't caught on yet.

That he's more than my coach.

That he's my Arrow.

I hug the books even tighter to my chest and shift on my feet.

"Done what?" he finally asks, lifting his eyes.

"Saved me like that."

"And why's that?"

"B-because they'll think you're giving me special treatment. Since I lived with you and all."

The tight set of his jaw says that he doesn't like that. "Has someone said something to you about that?"

I shake my head. "That's not the point."

"This isn't the first time this has happened to you, is it?" he concludes in a low tone, the silver chain around his neck glinting dangerously as he folds his arms across his chest.

I try not to look at the grooves of his sides that he's exposed by that movement. "It doesn't matter. It's –"

"Next time someone gives you trouble, you come to me," he orders.

"What?"

"I will take care of it."

His low-spoken command sends a rush of warmth through my body. A rush of goosebumps and thundering heartbeats.

He'll take care of me like he did just now.

But the thing is, I don't deserve his help.

I tried to make advances on him when I promised myself that I wouldn't. When I know he doesn't need those things since he's still coming out of the breakup.

Besides I'm not a rat.

So I tamp down all my shivers, take a deep breath and say, "You don't have to. I can handle it myself."

I stop when he unfolds his arms, and completely ignoring what I just said, states in the most professional voice ever, "And I'd like to see you in my office, please. After you're done with your dinner."

I look to the side, confused. "What?"

"I have something that I'd like to discuss with you."

"But –"

"And I've decided that you're done avoiding me now." Then he does the most coach-ly thing ever. He taps at his big leather-strapped wristwatch with his finger and tips his chin to get me moving. "See you in an hour."

With that, he walks away, leaving me all shocked.

Apparently, he can still shock me because I didn't think he would take matters into his own hands.

About the fact that I've been ignoring him.

I have actually.

I knew he'd noticed too. I mean, it's a little hard not to notice when every time I see him in the hallway, I duck my head or turn around and walk away, blushing like crazy for trying to kiss him.

But I didn't know he would summon me to his office for avoiding him.

It's a good thing though.

I've been acting like a coward. I need to apologize for what I did.

I made *him* apologize, didn't I? It's only fair.

Besides, I don't even think I'll get to talk to him much after this. Because remember part two of my grand plan? The one that was going to permanently put an end to his pain.

I put that plan into motion.

Well, it's more like Leah's plan, but there's a dinner on Friday and that dinner is going to change everything.

That dinner is going to make him happy and, well, everything will go back to how it was before. Arrow and Sarah, together, and me, the little sister, all alone, spending senior year at St. Mary's, waiting for an opportunity to run away.

Which is how it should be.

So yeah, I'm going to apologize because I won't get a chance after this.

With that determination, I go through my shower and dinner quickly and when I'm done, I walk to his office.

I have a new pair of cargo pants on, freshly laundered and ironed, and I've even tied up my hair with the mustard-colored ribbon in a neat ponytail.

All clean and tidy.

Just the way he likes.

I knock on the door and his voice travels through it to hit me in the gut and steal my breath. "Come in."

Swallowing, I turn the knob and open the door.

He's sitting at his desk. There's a book spread open on the table, a pen holder, a couple of Post-its, a stack of notebooks. Soccer balls are neatly arranged by the beige wall, along with a bookcase that has books on it arranged just so.

Everything has its place and order.

Even him.

Sitting in his high-backed chair, his shoulders broad and his back straight, he looks like he belongs here. He looks like he commands the room as much as he dominates the soccer field.

Maybe it's the way he's staring at me, with complete authority, complete possession. Or maybe it's the way his elbow rests on the arm of the chair and he's clicking this pen in his hand, waiting for me to step inside the room.

Step inside his lair.

So I do. I step inside and warmth grips me from every side. It grips the back of my neck, circles my waist and slides down to my thighs.

"Close the door," he commands, sounding every inch the coach that he is.

Every inch the famous The Blond Arrow.

Swallowing, I obey.

"Lock it," he orders again, clicking the pen.

"What?"

"Lock the door."

I hiccup a breath. "I... I don't think there –"

"Lock the fucking door, Salem."

"Okay."

I reach my arms back and turn the little thingy on the knob to lock it.

The instant my job is done, I do the craziest thing ever. I mean, I'm famous for crazy so why stop now.

I rush toward the desk, toward him.

Which might not be such a great idea given how aloof and mature he looks. How old and teacher-like.

But it's like ripping off a band-aid.

I need to apologize and I won't wait for even a single second to do it. I've already waited four whole days without making a well-deserved apology.

I stick my arms out. "Before you say anything, I've got something to say."

I'm aware that this is what I said to him at the bar, where I demanded he apologize, and the way he stares at me, without moving a muscle except to click the pen, I get the feeling that he's aware of it too.

That he was probably waiting for me to gush words like a river and create drama like the queen I am.

"Okay so." I wipe my hand on my thigh and lean against the edge of the desk to keep my shaking at bay. "I know I've been avoiding you and it's not cool. That's not fair to you, especially when I made you apologize to me in the bar. And made such a big deal out of it. So I'm sorry about that. For not apologizing sooner."

He studies me from his perch and even though I'm looking down at him slightly, I feel much, much smaller than him right now. "You're apologizing for not apologizing."

Well, when he puts it that way it sounds ridiculous.

"Yes. Sort of. But the point is that I shouldn't have done that. I should *never* have done that. I..." I try to gather my thoughts. "I'm sorry I tried to kiss you. It was completely uncalled for and a huge mistake. You're my sister's boy –"

Why can't I remember the correct terminology of anything?

"Ex-boyfriend and it's super tacky. And weird. And you don't need creepy advances by a stupid girl when you're going through so much. And the truth is that I really wanted to be your friend, you know? I really wanted to be someone you could talk to but I took advantage of that and I'm sorry."

I take a deep breath when I finish.

Although no amount of deep breaths will calm my heart. It's thundering inside my chest, lurching and writhing.

I'm not sure because of what though.

Is it because our friendship was so short-lived and the pain of it is intense? Or is it because he keeps staring at me in that intimate way of his?

Like he knows me. He knows every bone and every muscle and every cell in my body.

Every secret of my witchy heart.

Just when I think I can't take it anymore, his intense, dominating scrutiny, he leans forward and puts down the pen, shutting up the clicking, draping the room in complete silence.

Sitting back, both his elbows on the armrests now and his fingers tracing the curve of his lower lip, he asks, "Did anyone give you any trouble?"

"What?"

"After I talked to those girls in the hallway."

I press myself against his desk even more, trying to stop the trembling of my legs. Trying to stop this running thought that he looks so... mature and big.

Older.

When he's only about five years older than me.

Even so, I clasp my hands in front of me like a naïve little schoolgirl and shake my head. "No. It was fine."

Those girls only glared at me through dinner and nothing else. Besides, I was more engrossed in the fact that I had to go see him rather than pay attention to anything or anyone else.

His eyes drop to my clasped hands before nodding. "Good."

"I –"

"You never told me how you liked the motorcycle ride that night," he cuts me off in a soft, inquiring voice.

I open and close my mouth several times, unable to come up with anything.

"Did you enjoy it?" he continues with smooth, polished features, like him asking me all of this is completely normal.

And my chest heaves like wanting to answer him and tell him all the things about the ride and everything that happened to me since then is completely normal too.

I grab the edge of the desk and lick my lips. "It was great. Thank you. I-I have your jacket. Uh, that you gave me. I can bring it back to you if –"

"Keep it."

"But... it's yours."

He traces his thumb across his lip while studying me. "You like it, don't you?"

For some reason, my cheeks feel hot when he asks me that.

Maybe because ever since he gave me his jacket, I've been sleeping in it. I've been smelling it when I write him my nightly letter or when I really, really miss him.

I nod. "Yes."

"So it's yours now." Before I can argue more, he asks me something else. "It was your first, wasn't it? The ride, I mean."

I nod again. "Yes."

The first and probably the last, too.

Because I don't think I'll ever be able to sit on a motorcycle that doesn't belong to him. I don't think I'll even want to.

I don't...

Suddenly, he unlaces his fingers and pushes his chair back. The screech of the wheels and the squeak of the old chair cause me to part my lips and crane my neck as he comes to his feet.

Without taking his eyes off me, he rounds the desk with prowling steps.

"What are you doing?" I ask as I turn my body to keep him in sight.

Not that it's hard.

He's the biggest thing I've ever seen. The tallest and the largest.

The most glorious and the most stunning too, and he's walking toward me with a purpose.

He reaches me a second later and like at the bridge, he puts both his hands on the desk on either side of me, to come down to my level, his eyes all blue and serious.

But unlike at the bridge, he's doing it all in his well-lit office where I can see every flick of his eyelashes, every twitch of his jaw, every little sun-burnt strand of his hair.

"Arrow," I whisper, grabbing the desk with such ferocity that my knuckles are throbbing.

He still doesn't answer me though.

At least, not with words.

Still looking at me, his hand reaches up and pulls at the string of my ribbon.

I look down as the clumsy butterfly knot that I'd made before coming to his office unravels and my curls spill everywhere, mostly on his large fingers, my ribbon, falling and pooling down on the floor.

Goosebumps break out on my skin and looking back at him, I whisper again, "What are you doing?"

His eyes are on my hair. "Untying your ribbon."

"Why?"

"Because I don't like it."

My breath stutters. "B-but I thought you hated messy things."

"I do." He shifts his eyes away from my thick, scattered hair and focuses on me, my hastily breathing chest. "But strangely not on you. I like you messy."

I so want to say something, do something. Let go of the edge of the desk and grab his naked shoulders, dig my nails into his honey-colored muscles.

But I refrain.

Although a second later, the choice is taken away from me because he puts his hands on me.

He grabs me by the waist, picks me up and sits me down on his desk, all in a matter of seconds, and I have to put my hands on *him* because I feel so unmoored in this moment, so in the dark about his intentions that I grab onto him, his flexing biceps, to make sense of the world.

And when he just leaves his hands there, around my waist, I'm compelled to whisper, "What's happening? Why are you..." I lick my lip, my feet swaying, dangling off the desk. "Touching me like this."

Narrowing his eyes slightly, he digs his thumbs into my belly button. "Why, you don't like it?"

I do.

For some reason, I feel his words just behind my navel, where he's touching me.

So much so that I drag my nails along his biceps and pant, "I-I don't think you should."

"Why's that?"

"Because..." I swallow. "Because you're my coach and..."

And my sister's ex-boyfriend. And the secret love of my life and I'm so greedy...

"But I thought we were friends," he rasps. "You wanted to be my friend. Didn't you just say that?"

I shake my head. "I did. But we're not. Not anymore. It's better if we're not."

"Better for whom?"

I look at him with regret. "For you. I-I'm... dangerous."

He stares at me for a second. "I think I'll take my chances."

I let out a breath, looking at his gorgeous lips that just said that and if I were a better person, I would push him away and fight him more.

I'd tell him everything in my witchy heart so he never touches me again.

But God, it feels so good. That he's touching me. That he's holding me with his strong hands, so only a weak protest comes out of my mouth. "I don't think friends touch like this."

His nostrils flare as he swipes his thumb over my belly. "Well, you've never been friends with me." Before I can respond to that, his eyes drop to my lips as well and he asks, "So do you kiss all your friends, Salem?"

At the abrupt change of subject, I sort of jump.

Well, as much as I can with his hands on my waist, keeping me pinned to the desk. Blinking, I shake my head. "No."

"So just me then."

"I..." I duck my head, staring at the silver locket of his chain. "Yes."

"Like the ride, was that your first kiss too?"

I clench my eyes shut as a wave of embarrassment washes over me.

Not only that, like my swaying legs, my body sways too and somehow I end up on his hard chest. My forehead presses into the arch of his pectoral and I jerk out a nod. "Yes."

"Eighteen and never been kissed." He hums and I feel it against my cheek. "I figured."

I move away from him and look up. "How?"

He begins to massage my waist then. "You were so eager to take it. So eager for your first kiss. You had your pouty, dark lips all puckered up, eyes closed, tight body stretched up and neck tilted. Like some impatient little schoolgirl." He pauses for a beat to study me before saying, "I bet you're one of those."

"One of those what?" I ask and instead of answering, he proceeds to adjust me first.

His body has been curled over me like a blanket, his hands on my waist, kneading the flesh through my t-shirt, his shoulders blocking the view of the room around me.

But at my question, he slides me down the desk and shifts.

And I realize that he's in between my thighs as well. He's covering me from top to bottom.

Not only that, in the past however many minutes, my thighs have hiked up and made a home around his sleek waist and my feet are now dangling at the small of his back, instead of from the desk.

I should probably already know things like that but his drugging proximity has rendered me senseless.

When I'm all settled according to him, he answers, "One of those girls who have this really infamous syndrome."

My chest is sort of heaving from his maneuvers and now that I know I've got Arrow between my thighs, I squeeze them rhythmically to feel his strength.

"What syndrome?" I whisper.

"Needy girl syndrome."

"What?"

Amusement flickers in his eyes and around his mouth when he answers, "I bet you're one of those girls who call all the time. Who send a thousand texts, celebrate all anniversaries. Who have overly sweet nicknames for their boyfriends. Who make birthday and Valentine's Day cards. Show up unannounced to the guy's apartment with homemade dinner and a chick flick. You are, aren't you?"

I don't know how he can say these things the way he's saying them, all tender and velvet-like and still getting me to frown at him, still getting me to become all pliable and soft for him, all at the same time. "So what if I am?"

"And you make him watch that movie with you while you're draped all over him," he continues as his hands worry the flesh of my waist and caress it at the same time. "And he's thinking about maybe sliding his hand under your t-shirt, copping a feel, but he can't. Because you're crying at every romantic scene. And you cry the hardest at the end when the hero gets to the airport, right on time, and says all the right words and gets down on his knees. You do, don't you? Cry at a scene like that."

I push him away then or try to. All I end up doing I think is stroking his biceps and rubbing my thighs against his hips.

"No," I lie.

Which makes him chuckle somewhere low in his throat and loom over me like a shadow. "You're the girl every guy runs away from. You're every guy's nightmare, Salem. Because you're the girl with too much love inside you."

At this, I have to push him away.

I have to.

Because oh my God, he's such a giant asshole.

But when I go to do that, push him away, he tightens his hold on my waist. In fact, he draws me in closer and fuses our lower bodies together.

Fuses the place between my legs with his hard pelvis.

And all amusement vanishes from his face as he whispers roughly, "So you were right about the fact that it was a mistake, you trying to kiss me. But not for the reasons you think. Not because I'm your coach or your sister's ex-boyfriend. Or your friend."

"Then why?"

"Because I'm one of those guys too," he whispers against my lips, his eyes dark and penetrating. "I'm the guy who's a nightmare for a girl like you."

My thighs squeeze around him again and my arms creep up and I wind them around his neck. "Why?"

"Because I'm empty," he says with clenched teeth and punishing hands on my waist. "I'm hollow. Because whatever I had, I gave it to her. Whatever fucking love I had, she used it up and threw it away. She took it and flushed it down the toilet, understand?"

"Arrow..."

"And I don't have anything left now. Nothing but this deep-seated anger and a need to destroy something. *Hurt* something."

At this, his body shudders and I hold him tighter.

Tighter, tighter, tighter.

With my arms, with my legs.

And I decide that I should tell him.

I should tell him that he won't be feeling this way for long. That it's all coming to an end. All of this.

He just has to wait a few more days and then all of this will be over.

He'll have what he wants, her, and all his anger, his hurt will be gone.

"Arrow, listen to me, okay? I –"

But he's too far gone, his eyes dark and liquid, his body all heated up. "So if you think you're dangerous, I'm a wrecking ball. I'm a loose cannon. A wildfire. I can burn houses down. I can burn cities down too. So don't ever make the mistake of trying to kiss me again. Because I don't want a needy girl clinging to me and you don't want a guy giving you your first lesson in heartbreak."

I blink my eyes furiously, trying to keep my tears at bay, when he says, "A word of advice though: all this love, it's only going to bring you pain. It's only going to make you miserable. So maybe you should do something about that."

"Do what?"

"Find someone who can cure you. Someone who can fuck all the love out of you."

He abruptly lets go of me then.

He lets go of my waist and detaches himself from my body, and I have no choice but to slide down the desk and come down to the floor.

Panting and trembling, I look at him and he tips his chin at something. "That's for you."

It's a small rectangular box, a shoebox, the kind where I put my secret letters in, sitting on one of the chairs.

"It's soccer cleats. You're going to use them from now on. But only on the field. While I practice with you. Three times a week."

Still in a fog, I say, "What?"

He clenches his jaw, somehow looking all put together and confident, arms folded across his chest. "Now you don't have to watch old game tapes to learn."

I look at him, speechless.

"One more thing." He unfolds his arms and fishes something out of his pocket and sets it down on the shoebox.

I pick it up and unfold it; it's a permission slip.

For outings.

There's my name, the date and time along with his signature at the bottom.

"See you for dinner on Friday."

He's running late.

For the Friday dinner.

The dinner that Leah and I came up with.

Well, Leah came up with it when I went into her office and told her we needed to do something to get Sarah and Arrow back together. And that she had to be the one to do it because if it came from me, my sister would never follow through. She told me that she'd already arranged for it. And that Sarah was flying over this coming weekend.

Leah drove me home from school and Sarah got in a couple of hours ago. And now we're all waiting for him at the dining table, sitting at the edges of our seats, silent and tense. It's the same table at which I've sat for years. At which I've always kept my head down while at the same time, I've tried to catch a glimpse of him.

The guy I'm in love with.

Just then the door opens.

It makes a little noise, and suddenly the tension in the air spikes up. Suddenly, I'm flushed and squirmy and both anticipatory and fearful to see him.

Footsteps echo in the silent house and I clench my thighs, my eyes lowered at the table, my hands wringing in my lap.

And then, he's here. At the threshold.

I haven't seen him but I can smell him. I can feel his heat. I can feel my body starting to sweat.

A second later I have to look up because there's the screech of a chair against the hardwood floor.

My sister's chair.

She's standing up.

Just like that, I'm thrown back in time as I watch them together. As I watch them looking at each other.

As I watch *him* looking at her.

Like always, he looks at her like no one else exists. His features arrange themselves to be the most stunning they can be. His eyes become the most gorgeous that they can be as well.

And I fall in love with him again.

I fall in love with Arrow again while he's staring at my sister.

CHAPTER TWELVE

I think dinner was a bad idea.

Well, I knew he'd be shocked. I knew that.

But I thought that when he saw Sarah, he'd get over that shock or that initial burst of anger.

But none of that happened.

In fact, I think he got even angrier as the dinner progressed.

Not that he showed it.

He wasn't being rude or impolite or assholish to anyone like he gets these days.

He ate his food. In fact, he ate every bite and he was the only one. No one at that table finished everything. Not even Leah and Sarah.

But Arrow did and when he was done, he took a sip of his water and set down the glass gently. He even had dessert, and when dinner was officially done, he helped clear the plates.

He was every inch the Arrow that I'd known from before. And I didn't like it one bit.

I didn't like that he was keeping his anger in check. Even though I might've had a hand in bringing it out.

Now they're talking, Arrow and Sarah.

Or at least they're supposed to be talking, because right after dinner Leah asked me to go to my room and while I was leaving I overheard her saying that they needed to talk. That Arrow needed to act like a responsible adult and have a conversation and sort this thing out.

That was about fifteen minutes ago.

Since then, I've been pacing and pacing, listening to my own footsteps digging a hole in the floor and the loud beats of my witchy heart.

Until now.

Until I hear voices. Just under my window.

I rush to it then and drop down on the floor. Grabbing the edge of the windowsill, I peek my head out and see him.

My Arrow.

I see the top of his dirty blond hair and the broad line of his shoulders, propped against the wall.

The last time I saw him here, just under my window, was when he visited for Christmas with Sarah. I was so jacked up, so excited and shaky at seeing him in the flesh after months that I couldn't sleep. I was about to go out on my bike when I saw smoke rising past my window.

I did the exact same thing that I've done tonight.

I rushed to the window and peeked my head out. I opened my mouth and drank in the smoke he was letting out, filling my lungs with his cancer while loving him with all my heart.

However tonight there's no smoke.

He's simply standing there, casualness dripping from his body like river. But I know better. I know he's tense, I can tell by the rigid slope of his shoulders and how messy his hair looks. I bet some strands have come down to brush against his forehead.

I wish I could go to him and swipe them away. But I can't.

Because he's not alone and it's not my right, is it?

It's my sister's right and she's standing in front of him, matching him in every way. His looks, his confidence, his *height*. The way she's dressed in casual professional wear or whatever it's called: a pleated skirt and a silk blouse with her hair done up in a French twist. Or at least that's what she called it when Leah asked.

She only has to crane her neck a little when she says, "You didn't have to walk out like that."

"No, I had to," he says flippantly.

"I was talking."

"I know."

"So what, this is better? Standing out here. In this dark spot."

"It's my favorite spot, actually. I usually come out here when I want to escape. Like for example, when people are talking and I have no interest in what they're saying. But for some reason, they can't take the hint and shut the fuck up."

"You..." My sister exhales sharply. "That's so rude, A."

"Rude." He chuckles slightly. "Yeah, I'm that. Although, I believe the correct term is asshole."

"What?" It's kind of dark and they're both more or less silhouettes so I can't really know for sure but I know my sister is probably wrinkling her nose right now.

"Yeah, it's strangely satisfying," Arrow drawls. "It *does* get you slapped in the face sometimes. But I guess that comes with the territory."

"Excuse me?"

"It's worth it though."

My nails dig into the wood and I bite my lip, feeling a rush of electricity go through me.

It was me; I slapped him. And I call him asshole.

I call him that all the time.

And I'm filled with such need to go to him right now but I grind my knees on the floor.

Because I can't.

You can't, Salem. You absolutely cannot go to him now.

Once they get back together and the wedding is back on, I'm going to have to find a way to run and leave them alone.

"What are you talking about?" my sister asks, exasperated.

Arrow hums. "I don't think you'll understand. It's a little above your paygrade. So what do you want?"

My sister sighs. "A, we really need to talk."

"We don't really need to talk because nobody ever really *needs* to talk," he says. "People talk because they want to. And I find that I *really* don't want to."

"A, please," she says determinedly. "I don't know what's gotten into you but it's high time. You've been ignoring all my calls and texts."

"Again, that's usually a sign when someone really doesn't *want* to talk."

Sarah shakes her head, her hair shining under the meager light of the moon. "Look, I don't want to fight with you. I just want to have a conversation. I just want to figure this out."

"Funny. Because I was under the impression that there wasn't anything left to figure out."

"There is and we can do it. I know we can do it. We can do anything, you and me. We're a team." She moves closer to him. "I've been working very hard for you, A. You have no idea."

Even though it's dark, I still notice the stiffness in Arrow's body. It's not just limited to his shoulders now. It has gone on and clutched all his limbs and even his voice.

"Well, why don't you give me an idea then?"

"The whole team has been affected by your actions. We probably won't even make it to the semi-finals now. Rodriguez is not as good as you and you know that. The team is mad, A. They blame you. Their trust in you and your judgement has been shaken. I'm the only one on your side and I'm putting out fires everywhere," my sister replies eagerly. "People are still waiting for you to apologize. But I told them to give you time. I told them you'd do the right thing. Because I care about you. I love you. I want you back on the team. I want you back in my life."

There's silence for a few beats after that.

When my heart is pounding and pounding.

This is such a private moment.

I should move away. I should.

But God, my knees are glued to the floor and my nails have dug their way into the wood, and there's no way I can free them.

There's no way I can move and take my poisoned, encroaching presence away.

"How's Ben doing?" Arrow asks. "He know you're talking to me about getting back together?"

It's Sarah's turn to stiffen now.

Again, I can't see very clearly but I can feel it all. I can feel the tightness in her frame.

"Ben has nothing to do with this," she says in a low voice.

Arrow chuckles again. This time it's lacking in any humor though. "I beg to differ."

"A –"

"Because it didn't look like that when you were *fucking* him. Or maybe I'm wrong."

At this, I feel a pinch, a sting in my fingers. A sting that becomes a throb and takes over my whole hand.

Somehow that sting travels to my chest too, making a home there, squeezing my heart tightly. So *tightly* and painfully that I can't be sure if I'm hearing things or if this is real.

If he said what he said.

A second later, Arrow moves away from the wall and stands up straight. Not only that, he grabs Sarah's arm and gives it a jerk that I feel on my own body.

Bending closer to her, he growls, "Answer me, Sarah. Am I wrong?"

My sister is trying to free herself. "A, please. You're scaring me, okay? Stop acting like this. Stop being so –"

"What, angry?" He shakes her again. "The therapist you found me says the same thing. She asks me '*why are you so angry, Arrow? Describe in your own words what happened to make you so angry.*'" He laughs without humor. "Maybe I should tell her. Maybe I should tell her the truth. That one day I accidentally saw my girlfriend's phone. I accidentally read a message that said *I miss you. I miss your tight little body. Can we meet at the same place?* When I asked her about it, she lied. She said it was a one-time thing, but as it turns out, it wasn't. Because later that night I got into her phone again. She hadn't changed her password that she'd had since college days so it was pretty fucking easy. Maybe she's dumb or maybe she thought I wouldn't ever think of checking her phone, I don't know, but after an hour's worth of reading, I found out that my girlfriend, who I was planning on proposing to, had been having an affair. She'd been fucking my assistant coach for months. So I'm *angry*, Dr. Lola Bernstein, because the girl I loved lied to me, not once, not twice, not three times but for months. For *months*, she was sleeping with my best friend and not once did she think to tell me about it. Yeah, maybe I'll tell her that next time. Maybe we should tell my mother too. At least then she'll stop making these pathetic attempts to get us back together."

Sarah is crying now; I can hear her quiet sobs.

I don't have that luxury though. I can't cry.

My sobs have never been quiet. My sobs are howls. They're loud. They have the power to break eardrums and windowpanes.

So I'm biting the inside of my cheek to keep my tears from falling.

I'm biting it until I feel the blood pooling on my tongue, all metallic and warm.

"I'm sorry, okay? I'm sorry I made a mistake. I'm sorry I never told you. I thought I was protecting you from it. I thought I was doing it for your own good. I didn't want anything to affect your game, your focus. And I was going to stop, anyway."

"But I caught you first, didn't I?"

Sarah winces. "I love you, A. I was just trying to spare you the pain. I was trying to protect the life that we'd built. I was trying to protect your heart. I…"

"You were trying to protect my heart," Arrow says in a low, rough voice.

"Yes. Yes, I was. Please."

He stares at her for a few seconds before letting her go and stepping away. "I want you gone, understand? Make an excuse and leave before this night ends. And don't come back here for me."

He's ready to walk. He even takes a couple of steps away from her. But he stops just when he's about to pass her by.

"You said you were trying to protect my heart. But you killed it instead."

And then he walks away, his long steps lunging and determined, making him look somehow unstoppable.

Like he's the wrecking ball that he told me he was, back in his office. A force of nature.

My Arrow.

My sun on a warpath.

As soon as he disappears into the night, I let out my first sob. I turn away from the window and fall on my ass on the floor.

I sob and sob but have enough presence of mind to cover my mouth, to not alert the whole world that I'm crying.

That my witchy heart is breaking because someone killed the heart of the boy I love.

His big, precious, darling heart.

How could anyone do that to him?

How could my sister?

God, my own *sister*.

The girl who's perfect in every sense. How could she do that?

What was she thinking? I can't understand it.

I can't... believe it, even.

I hear her footsteps climbing up the stairs and I spring up from my crouched position. I don't even take the time to wipe off my tears that are still streaming down my face. I whip open the door.

Standing at the landing, Sarah frowns at the suddenness of it all. "What –"

"You cheated on him," I say in a strong voice.

I almost declare it to the empty, dark hallway.

She's taken aback, her frown deepening, and for the first time in my entire life, I don't like how smooth and flawless her skin is. She was crying a second ago, wasn't she? Why aren't there any track marks on her cheeks?

Why's she so perfect even in her misery? Why isn't her world falling apart like mine is?

"How did you... What?" she stalls.

"I overheard your conversation."

She loses her frown at this and her lips curl up in a sneer. "You had no right."

She's right.

I had no right to eavesdrop. It was wrong. But I did it anyway. And I don't care about right or wrong.

Not right now.

Not when my sister has so much explaining to do.

"You *cheated* on him," I repeat.

Her eyes widen and she marches closer to me. "Can you keep your voice down?"

"Why?"

I don't wanna keep my voice down.

I wanna scream and shout and kick and punch.

I'm so angry. I'm so fucking angry right now.

Fire roars in my gut. It roars and raises its head like some kind of an animal.

A dragon breathing fire.

Is this what he's been feeling all this time? This... heat and fury.

"Well, if you heard everything then you know why." Then she grabs my arm and digs her nails in my flesh, hissing in my face. "It was a mistake. I don't want my mistake plastered all over the world. I'm not like you. I don't revel in bad behavior. I don't take pride in it."

A flush overcomes my face, a flush different than the anger that I'm feeling.

A flush of embarrassment at my own betrayal against her.

But I won't let it overcome me right now.

I can't.

I can curse myself and punish myself later. Right now, I have to be strong. For him.

For my Arrow.

"Mistake? Cheating on your boyfriend is not a mistake," I snap at my sister for the first time.

I never thought I'd see the day. I never thought I'd be mad at her for anything.

But then, I never thought she'd betray Arrow like this.

"Oh, and you know a lot about boyfriends, don't you?" She grits her teeth.

"I know about lies. You *lied* to him. For months. You lied to me when I asked. You lied, Sarah."

"So? I don't owe you the truth, do I? I don't owe you anything. And I told you to stay out of it. I told you to stop asking questions because this is my life. And it has nothing to do with you but you wouldn't listen."

I suppress the pain in my chest at her callous words. I suppress the urge to scream, *I'm your sister. Doesn't that mean something to you?*

But again, this isn't about me. It's about him.

"What about him? You owed the truth to him, didn't you?" I ask, my arm going numb in her grip. "How could you do that to him? You slept with his best friend. Not once but for months and you lied about it."

"Listen, I don't need this from you, okay? I don't need you to tell me what's right and what's wrong. I did what I did because I was trying to save our love. I lied to him to spare him the hurt and I won't apologize for it. Once we were married, I would've stopped and none of this would've happened."

I fist my hands, seeing my sister in a new light. "God, are you listening to yourself? You were having an affair with another man. Behind Arrow's back. He loved you. He loved you so much, Sarah. And you loved him. God, I thought you loved him. I thought your love was this... epic, untouchable thing and I..."

I was wrong.

I was *so* wrong.

Because how can this be love?

How can months of lying be love? How can you hurt someone the way Sarah has hurt Arrow if you love them?

You can't hurt them.

That's the thing about love. You can't hurt the one you love, not deliberately. Not the way Sarah has done.

So I was wrong about everything. And Sarah was right. She told me not to meddle and yet, I didn't listen.

I meddled and brought them together and now he's gone somewhere and I'm having this argument with my sister. The sister I thought could do no wrong.

God, I've been so naïve.

I don't even know my own sister.

"You don't do that to a person you love. You don't hurt them like that. And he's hurting. Arrow's... *hurting.*"

You killed my heart...

My own heart writhes in pain and I have to let out a gasp.

No wonder he's been so angry and so *changed.*

No *wonder* he believes he's empty and that love brings nothing but pain.

"How do you know he's hurting?" she asks, her voice gone all thick and accusing.

"What?"

She jerks my arm, digs her manicured nails into my flesh. Even through my thick, chunky sweater, I feel like she'll break my skin.

"He's supposed to be just your soccer coach, right? How do you know what he's going through? Besides, aren't you a little too concerned about a guy you don't even like?" She narrows her perfect golden eyes at me. "You don't like him, isn't that correct? You'd leave the room every time he'd enter. You wouldn't even talk to him. Wouldn't go near him. So since when do you call A *Arrow*? Or maybe you've been lying too."

My heart, in all its witchy glory, jumps in my throat.

The tear tracks on my cheeks burn and blaze, under my sister's shrewd eyes.

"Maybe you're so concerned about Arrow because you like him yourself," she taunts. "I can see that. He has that appeal. Girls throw themselves at him all the time. Why wouldn't you? Do you like him, Salem?"

I shake my head. "I... I don't... It's not about that."

She bends down and grips my arm harder. "You do, don't you?"

I squirm in her grip, my body burning in shame. "Sarah, let me go."

Her eyes shine with maliciousness and her nails almost draw blood out of my skin. "I want you to listen to me, okay? If you have any ideas about *Arrow,* you should take them out of your stupid little head right now. He's mine. He's a little angry right now because the wound is fresh. But we have eight years together. That's what you told me, right? Eight years of love. Eight years of history. One mistake can't erase that. I won't let it. We belong together. He has to come back to LA sometime and when he does, I'll be waiting for him. And if that's not enough to make you understand and end your foolish fantasies, then let me tell you something else. He'll *never* be interested in someone like you. Someone so aimless and ambitionless. An embarrassment. That's what you are. Even Mom was embarrassed by you. She wouldn't show it but I knew. How could she not have been? You're an anomaly. Someone who shouldn't have been born in our family. A big, fat stain. And you'll be something else too, if you even *dare* to make a play for him, for *my* boyfriend. Something far worse. You'll be a whore, okay? Because that's what they call a girl who goes after someone else's man."

CHAPTER THIRTEEN

I wait for him under my window.

At the spot where he smokes and at the spot where they were talking, him and her.

Sarah left a little while ago. I don't know what she said to Leah, but she packed her bags and called a cab to the airport. Leah went to sleep then. She has to fly out for a conference early tomorrow morning and she said she'd take me back to St. Mary's before she leaves.

Meaning my time's almost up.

In the morning, I'll go back to all the rules and schedules and structure. I'll go back to detention and trigonometry and missing my bike.

I don't care about that though. I wasn't even expecting to get this much of a reprieve. Especially when I don't have the privilege yet.

But he got me out.

He sprung me out of that concrete fence like I was a bird trapped in a cage. So I can't sleep. I won't.

I'm waiting for him.

My emancipator.

It feels like he's been gone for ages. Chances are that he probably went back to his motel where he's staying.

So he won't be back.

But still, I wait.

Because for some reason, I think he'll come. He'll come back to the house. I'm not sure why I think that; there's nothing here to bring him back. Sarah's gone. He's upset with his mother.

But I'm here and I'm his friend. And something tells me he'll come back for me.

God, all this time. Why didn't he say anything? About what Sarah did.

Why didn't he...

A second later, I hear the roar of his motorcycle and my agitated thoughts disintegrate.

He's back.

He's *back!*

I've been sitting under the window on the cool autumn grass, my knees folded and hugged to my chest, my arms wrapped around them. I've been rocking back and forth with impatience but I freeze now.

I freeze at the sight of him in the driveway, sitting across his motorcycle.

His eyes on me. His brilliant blue eyes, that appear as dark as the night from this far, are glued to my curled-up form.

Like he knew I'd be here. I'd be waiting for him.

He's right.

No matter the time, the season, the weather, I'll always wait for him.

Without taking his eyes off me, he moves.

He leans forward, arcs his powerful thigh over the seat and gets off. As soon as he comes to stand, I spring up to my feet.

And when he starts to walk, I take off at a run.

My woolen-sock-covered feet thump on the ground as I race toward him and we meet somewhere in the middle of the backyard where I've watched him countless times from up above, through my window.

Although, meet is not how I'd describe the way I almost hurl my body at him.

Like I'm the bird zooming toward him that he let out of the cage, or maybe I'm not a bird at all. Maybe I'm a storm and he catches me with a wide stance and a solid body and I burrow myself in his chest.

I flatten my tiny body against his large one, my arms going around his waist and my cheek pressed against his ribs, right where his heart is.

His dead, darling heart.

I think I've shocked him. With my ferocity, with the strength I'm using to hug him, because he goes all stiff. But I don't let him go.

I'll never let him go. At least, not in my heart.

And maybe he knows that.

He knows that no matter what he can't escape my hug so his body loses its rigidity and his arms come around me and cover my spine.

I squeeze him then, and clench my eyes shut against the onslaught of fat, thick tears. I don't wanna cry. Not right now when I need to be strong.

When I need to be there for him.

"Where did you go?" I whisper.

His open palms move up and down my spine. "If I say I went to a bar, you're not going to start acting like a jealous little groupie, are you?"

Chuckling sadly, I say, "I called you. I even texted. You never replied back."

I did.

I dug up my old phone that Leah had given me when we moved in with her and Arrow. She'd also fed her and Arrow's numbers into our cell phones.

Needless to say, I never used it, his number. I'd stare at it though, several times a day.

But I used it tonight.

It kind of felt weird, texting the guy I've been writing secret letters to. A clash of modern, cold technology with how I've come to love him.

In an old-fashioned way.

"So acting like a jealous groupie it is," he murmurs.

"I was worried," I whisper.

As soon as I say it, I press my forehead on his chest and open my mouth. My lips are right where his heart is and I breathe out large puffs of air as if I'm trying to resuscitate it.

His dead heart.

As if I'm giving all my breaths to that precious organ of his. So it comes alive. So he doesn't feel empty.

But he doesn't let me revive his heart.

Instead, he grabs my hair and pulls my neck back. When I open my eyes, I find him staring down at me with a dark, intense gaze. "You know, I thought one of the advantages of *not* having a girlfriend would be that I wouldn't have to go through the whole 'I was worried' routine. Not that I ever went through it before. But still."

I fist his t-shirt at his back. "Too bad. You do have a girlfriend."

His frown is immediate and thunderous. "What the fuck?"

"I am a girl. And I'm your friend. So girl*friend*," I say, the most cliché thing in the history of all things.

He watches me a beat. "You learn that from a chick flick?"

I don't know how he can make me smile at a time like this, but he can and he is. "Yes. We should watch some together."

"Yeah, over my dead fucking body."

"Oh, I think you'll be alive."

His fingers pull at my hair as if emphasizing every word he's saying. "I think this friend thing isn't going to work out."

I shake my head in his hold and study his features, whispering, "Again, too bad. You're stuck with me."

The moon is red again tonight, a fireball, and it highlights the lithe lines of his body and lean angles of his face.

Bringing one hand to the front, I reach up and do what I wanted to do back when he was talking to my sister and smooth out the messy strands of his hair. I push them away now, and he clenches his jaw.

"What the hell are you doing out here?" he asks, irritated. "In the cold."

I huddle my shoulders and rub my cheek in his vintage leather jacket that I put on after Sarah left and Leah went to sleep. "You kept me warm."

His fingers squeeze my scalp, making me crane up my neck even more. "Shouldn't you be out there, haunting some bridge or empty street somewhere?"

My heart swells in my chest. It becomes so big that it's pressing against my ribs. It must be pressing against his too, I bet. He must be able to feel it.

Feel the size, the drumming rhythm of my heart.

When I'm done setting his hair in place for him, I bring my hand back once again and grip his t-shirt. "That's why you gave me that permission slip, didn't you? So I could be free."

Something passes through his face, clenching everything for a second. "It's Friday. Would you have snuck out to go dancing?"

I bite my lip and nod.

He bends down then, his chest pushing at mine, his fingers tightening in my hair to make a fist and his other hand pressing in the small of my back.

"So consider this, me reining you in," he growls. "Me putting a leash on you and making you follow the rules."

A current runs through me at his low, rough growl, at his dominating words. "I don't wanna go haunt a bridge or a street somewhere."

"So you decided to haunt me, instead?"

Something about that makes me bite my lip again. "Yes."

"And why's that?"

"Because I wanna talk to you."

"Talk to me about what?"

I swallow as my eyes sting with tears. "I know. I know why you beat him up. Ben."

His eyes grow bright then, violent even, his jaw clenching hard. "Why?"

"Because you wanted to," I whisper, pressing my knuckles on his back. "It wasn't because he was the first person you saw. It wasn't a bad coincidence. It was because you were looking for him. Because he betrayed you. Because my sister betrayed you."

There's no surprise on his face when I say that.

In fact for a second there's something very akin to a dark sort of amusement rippling through his stunning features. "You heard."

"You were standing under my window."

"I was."

Suddenly I understand. "You were... you knew I'd listen in."

His mouth curls up in a tight lopsided smile. "You looked pretty upset when you had to leave the room after dinner ended."

"Was this your way of putting a leash on me so I wouldn't go around breaking rules to find out what happened?"

"Yes."

My hands move then.

I let go of his shirt at the small of his back, and creep both my arms up and get them around his neck just to hold him closer, tighter.

Putting a leash of my own around him.

"I hated dinner," I tell him. "I hated everything about it."

His chest undulates on a slight chuckle. "Why?"

I tug at his hair. "Because you ate everything on your plate."

"And that's somehow objectionable to you."

"Yes," I insist. "You ate everything and you were so quiet. You even cleaned up after. When I knew, I could see how..." – I flick my eyes over his sharp, jutting features – "angry you were. Your shoulders were all tight and the way you'd clench your jaw every two seconds. But you never said a word. You were so nice, Arrow."

My tone sounds accusatory and he hears it too.

It thickens the lines of amusement around his mouth and eyes, and his own arms move, both his hands burying in my loose and wild hair. "I thought you wanted me to be nice."

I shift on my feet, restless. "Not like that. Never like that. I don't want you to hide your emotions, ever. I like you the way you are. All mean and rude. Completely impolite. And I promise I'll never hit you."

"What if I deserve it?"

I chew on my lips, thinking about it. "Well, maybe I'll hit you then. But only a little bit."

A smirk blooms on his mouth. "Very charitable of you."

"Stop making jokes. This isn't funny. This..." I grab his chain at the back of his neck. "Why didn't you say anything? All this time. All this time I thought... I thought I could do something to get you guys back together, and this dinner..." I take a deep breath. "I went to Leah, Arrow. I went to see your mom and I told her that we should do something to... to make you both see reason. And she'd already planned this dinner. But I want you to know that I knew about this. I knew about the dinner and that Sarah was going to be here. I hid it from you because I thought you wouldn't show up and... God, I'm so sorry, Arrow. I put you through this. I could've saved you. I could've spared you the pain and –"

"No one could've spared me the pain," he speaks over me with an almost lashing voice. "*No one* could've saved me."

I swallow painfully. "Why didn't you say anything, Arrow?"

His eyes flick back and forth between mine, a painful, tormented look flashing in them, and my witchy heart squeezes and squeezes.

"For months," he whispers, his rough words vibrating between us, "she lied to me. *He* lied to me. He was my closest friend. I trusted him. I trusted him with my game. He knew about my plans. He knew that I was going to propose to her. He knew that. He knew I had a ring. But I was stupid, wasn't I?

"I was blind. I was fucking dumb. Because for months, they went behind my back and I didn't suspect anything. I had no clue. I had no goddamn clue. I thought everything was fine. I thought everything was okay. Every *fucking* thing was perfect. But it wasn't. You hear stories about guys who get taken on a ride and you think, how fucking stupid do you have to be to miss that? How fucking stupid do *I* have to be to miss that? I'm The Blond Arrow. I'm supposed to win. I'm supposed to be perfect. Flawless. But I'm not, am I? I'm a failure. I failed in my relationship."

Oh God, no.

Please, please don't let him think that. Don't let him put this on himself.

Arrow puts so much pressure on himself as it is. He thinks everything is his fault and he beats himself up over it so much. I don't want him to think this is his fault too, his failure. When it's not.

This is absolutely not his fault and he's making me cry and I can't cry right now.

If I start, I won't stop and I can't do that. I have to be there for him. I have to tell him that he's not a failure.

I grab his face then. I grab it and I dig the pads of my fingers in the hollows of his sculpted cheeks.

"You didn't fail, Arrow. You were betrayed, okay? She betrayed you and I still can't believe that she did that. But it's not your fault. It's *not* your failure."

He grinds his teeth for exactly eight seconds – I counted – before saying, "Well, I got cheated on, didn't I? And I was the one who didn't know about it so whose failure is it, if not mine?"

I go to say something else, something that will make him understand.

Only I don't know what to say.

I don't know how to make him understand when he believes himself so wholeheartedly. When it's written all over his face, his tight and stubborn features.

His *pained* features.

God, there's so much pain. So much torment and I don't know what to do.

Except...

Except pull him closer and kiss his clenched jaw.

And his thrumming cheek.

I do it all lightly, simply a peck. But the effect of it on him is loud and jarring.

His brows snap together as his eyes focus on me. They lose their cloudy, pained look and a light flashes in them.

"What are you doing?" he growls, his fingers flexing in my hair.

"Giving you the answer to the question you asked me a long time ago."

Or at least it feels like it. That it was a long time ago. When in reality, probably only a couple of weeks have passed.

"What question?"

I rub my thumb in the hollows of his cheek and kiss him again.

I know he told me to not kiss him. He told me that he's a nightmare for girls like me. A walking talking heartbreak.

But he doesn't know that heartbreak is my friend.

That it's been my friend for years now. Since the day I saw him in the kitchen. That fifteen-year-old boy has grown into this tormented, betrayed, dangerous man and I'm more in doomed love with him now than I was eight years ago.

Arrow doesn't know that when your love is doomed, you're not afraid of a little heartbreak. You walk with it. You dance with it. You breathe it in.

So I ignore his rule and gather the courage to place a soft kiss on his gorgeous, exceptionally soft lips. "You asked me if I'd be your rebound girl. So I'm telling you that yes, I will be. I'll be that girl for you. The girl you come to, to fuck all your frustrations out. The girl who spreads her legs for you the moment she sees you're jacked up and you need it."

CHAPTER FOURTEEN

W hen I finish, I place one last kiss on his cheekbone.

It's like kissing the sharp edge of a knife, that cheekbone. That jaw. I always knew it would be though.

I did.

What I didn't know was what he would do when I did kiss him.

I didn't know that he'd slowly straighten up. That he'd slowly, with deliberate movements, let go of my hair and that when he does, I'd actually miss his tight grip. I'd miss the leash of his fingers, feeling unbalanced.

"Arrow, what –"

My words cut off when he puts both his hands on my waist and picks me up like he did back in his office.

But tonight, there's no desk where he can set me down.

Tonight, there's only his body and he makes me climb it.

My arms go to his working and corded shoulders as he boosts me up and causes me to wind my thighs around his waist before moving.

Without taking his eyes off me, he begins to walk with me in his arms.

He doesn't tell me where we are going and I don't ask him about it either.

Mostly because I'm panting and I'm busy adjusting my body in his lap and feeling all his hard and corrugated muscles.

But also because strangely, I know.

I know where he's taking me. And when my spine hits the wall, I'm proven correct.

We're standing under my window.

His favorite spot.

"You want to be my rebound girl?" he asks when I'm settled between him and the wall.

"Yes," I whisper, my hands sliding down from his shoulders to go to his chest and rub circles.

"You want to spread your legs for me when I need it?"

His chest moves, jerks up and down, and I feel it all under my palms, in my own chest even. "Yeah."

"You want me to use you to fuck all my frustrations out," he keeps repeating my own words to me and somehow, it ramps up my restlessness.

"Yes. All of them."

I even arch up against him to tell him that I really mean it.

And it's not a hardship, see. It's not hard to tighten my thighs around him and bow my back and rock against his athletic body.

It's not hard to let him know that I need him.

What is hard and *has been* hard was to hide it.

My need for him. My love. For eight whole years.

But not anymore.

I won't stop myself. I won't even feel embarrassed about my love for him.

Because I've realized something.

Something very important about myself.

My sister called me a whore. She said that if I ever made a play for him then I'd be a slut.

But that's the thing, isn't it? I'm not making a play for him. I'm not trying to steal him.

For the past eight years, I've been living in this fear that one day my love will make me do the unthinkable.

My doomed love will make me so desperate, so dangerous that I will try to get him, grab him, keep him for myself.

But now I know that I never would have done that.

Because in this moment when he's hurting, *I'm* hurting. When his pain makes his jaw clench, my insides clench. When anguish burns his eyes, my skin feels it.

In this moment, I can see everything clearly.

I can see that I never ever would've made a play for him. I never ever would've tried to wreck his relationship so he could be mine.

Even my attempt to kiss him on the bridge wasn't born out of malice or because I wanted to steal him away. It was born out of pure, overwhelming love.

A love I didn't want to fall in but I did anyway.

I didn't do it to hurt anyone. I didn't fall in love with my Arrow to hurt my sister.

I fell in love with him like dead leaves fall from the branch of a tree and rain falls from a swollen cloud. I fell in love with him like tears fall when you're sad and like blood oozes out of your skin when you step on broken glass.

It was natural.

So it's natural for me to heal his pain, or at least put a balm on it. Love him when he can't love himself and thinks he's a failure.

And when the time comes for him to leave, to go back to where he belongs, it will be natural for me to let him go.

Because his happiness is my happiness.

Until then, I'll be a girl in doomed love and I won't be ashamed of it.

Until then, I'll stay here and love him.

"And then what?" he bites out, his dark eyes glittering, his hands kneading the flesh on my waist where he's holding me. "Discard you? Fuck you and forget you? That's the job of a rebound girl. You know that, don't you? She's supposed to be a fuck doll. She's a girl who gets fucked and forgotten."

His words are his namesake.

Arrows.

They pierce my heart. The heart that's not so witchy after all. They make it holey. They make it bleed.

But still, I forge on. "Yes. I know."

He shakes me, my spine rubbing against the brick wall. "And do you remember what I told you? What I can do to you. What I'm *capable* of doing to you."

"I remember."

I remember every word he said. That he can burn everything down. That he can wreck things.

I know.

He shakes me again. In fact, he pulls me forward before shoving my spine into the wall, almost making me moan with his strength and dominance. "So what the fuck are you talking about?"

"I-I'm talking about being your rebound." I grab his chain and pull him closer to me. "This isn't going to be a relationship, is it? You're not going to be my boyfriend and I'm not going to be your girlfriend. So it doesn't matter what you said."

He exhales a sharp breath and I feel it pushing into me, his breath, his chest. His whole body.

We're in a more secluded spot now, I think. Darker and hotter. I feel sweat beading on my skin, his leather jacket drowning me.

I feel him drowning me too, the way he's staring at me, keeping me pinned to the wall with his large hands.

"I don't want your fucking pity," he snaps.

And I can't help but swat his chest. "This is not pity, you idiot. If I wanted to pity you, then I would've said yes to your stupid proposition days ago. You were pretty miserable back then too."

"So why?"

Because I love you.

Because you're my Arrow.

My broken Arrow.

"Because you're my friend," I tell him, a version of the truth.

At this, he comes even closer. So close that his hard abdomen moves and presses against that place between my thighs and I gasp.

His eyelids flicker and he notices my parted lips. "You fuck all your friends?"

"No."

He lifts his eyes then. "So, what, I'm special?"

"Yes. And because I have a right."

"What right is that?"

I get up in his face, grazing our noses together. "I lived with you for years, didn't I? Those girls that you pick up at a bar, they don't know you. You said it yourself. They don't know who you are. They don't care about you. But I do. I care about you. I know you. I know who you were and who you are now. So I'm going to be your rebound girl and no one else. Because *I* have the right. I dare anyone to even try."

So maybe I sound like a jealous little groupie but whatever.

Those girls don't love him. I do. They don't know how to take care of him. But I do.

He's my Arrow.

So if anyone's going to ease his pain, it's going to be me.

Arrow watches me, studies my face. My messy hair, my nose, my lips.

He even goes down to my heaving chest, my bow-shaped body. My thighs that are spread out around him.

It's both a lazy perusal and over so quickly that I'm left abandoned when he comes back to my face, my skin throbbing and tight.

"No," he clips.

"What?"

"I'm not going to fuck you."

"Why not?" I almost whine.

I mean, I'm willing and available and I want to.

It's my right.

And I'm ready to explain that to him again but I notice something.

A change in him. A change in the air, even.

It becomes heavier, darker. More heated.

Like him.

"Are you pouting at me?" he asks softly, his eyes on my lips.

At his low tone, a hot shiver skitters down my spine and I arch up even more.

I wasn't aware of it.

I wasn't aware that I was sticking my lower lip out in disappointment. Maybe because I've never done it before.

I've never pouted. I *do not* pout.

But somehow, I'm doing it right now.

Somehow, I'm doing it for him.

"You *are* pouting at me, aren't you," he concludes.

He is right. I am.

And it feels so... provocative, so seductive to be doing that. To be pouting at the guy I love because he won't fuck me.

Like he's the man of the house and I'm a naïve teenager.

He is the man of the house though, isn't he? He always has been.

Big and protective.

He even saved me from those girls and took me on my first motorcycle ride.

So I raise my eyebrows, feeling bold. "So what if I am?"

My boldness makes him sharper. It hollows out his cheeks and somehow juts out his jaw. It makes the blue in his eyes buzz and hum.

"Then I'd tell you to stop," he rumbles out a warning; his hands on my waist shift and get under the vintage leather jacket that I'm wearing.

"I don't want to."

"You think you'll get your way like this? You stick out your lip like a bad girl and I fuck you like a dying, desperate man."

A throb, big and pulsing, clutches my body and travels down my scalp all the way to my toes trapped in woolen socks, and I twist my hips. I undulate between him and the wall and I do something really bad.

I do something worse than inadvertently pouting at him.

Staring at him through my eyelashes, I put my hand on his, where he's gripping me at the waist and make him let go.

Well, make him is wrong; I can't *make* Arrow do anything if he doesn't want to.

But luckily, he wants to and he lets me.

Suspicion clouds his features but he lets me take his hand off my waist and bring it up. And then, he *lets* me put that large hand of his on my breast.

I don't know what I'm thinking or what I hope to accomplish by putting his hand there but as soon as I do that, as soon as I direct his hand onto my soft, bouncy flesh, his fingers move on their own.

They close over my mound and he squeezes it, making me whimper and causing me to clutch his wrist.

It also makes me spill a bad secret. "I'm not wearing a bra."

His eyes dip to my sunshine-yellow t-shirt and stay there. As if he can see. As if he can see my naked breasts and my hard nipples through the fabric.

"You're not," he rasps as he rubs his open palm on me, over the nipple.

Once. Just once.

And I jerk in his arms. "Yes. I never wear one. I... it makes me feel free and..."

He swipes his hand over my nipple again, still watching it, watching his fingers over my breast. "And what?"

"And no one has ever touched me there. Before."

All of it is true.

I don't wear a bra because mostly I've got my sweater on so I don't need it. Besides, my breasts are average B cups anyway. And yes, no one has ever touched me there before.

Finally, he raises his eyes, his fingers still insistent and still squeezing. "What about panties? Are you wearing any panties?"

"I am," I whisper, suddenly feeling how sticky they are, how wet and hot. "But it's only a little thong."

"Yeah? Why's that?"

"I-I like them. I have tons."

"Because I bet that feels free too, doesn't it?"

"Yes."

"And no one has touched you there either, have they?"

"No. No one."

At this, his fingers don't show any mercy on my breast.

He plumps it up and squeezes it and molds it however he wants. He even uses it to pull me closer, like this virgin piece of flesh belongs to him.

Even though he clearly doesn't want it. He clearly has aggression dripping out of his eyes and anger radiating off his fingers.

"So you put my hand on your tit and you tell me you're not wearing a bra," he growls, plucking at my nipple now. "You tell me you never wear one. And then you have the audacity to tell me that you love wearing a flimsy, useless string between your legs because it makes you feel free and no one has ever touched you there before. That no one has played with your nipples or squeezed your tits like this. No one has fingered that tight thing between your legs. Is that correct?"

That tight thing between my legs spasms at his rough, vibrating words.

"Yeah. No one."

"Is this your attempt at seducing me?" he asks me with another squeeze of my breast.

When he asks the question like this, with almost a mocking tone, my cheeks burn with embarrassment. They flush scarlet with my inexperience and how young I might seem to him.

The little sister.

But I have done it now, haven't I?

I have put his hand on my breast and I've told him all about my naïveté so even though every part of me is trembling, I raise my chin. "Yes."

He circles his eyes over my face, watches the shaking of my lips and notices my nervous swallow.

When he brings his eyes back up to me, he licks his lips. "It's tight, isn't it? Your virgin pussy."

"I-I think so."

His chest shudders with a tight, humorless chuckle. "Yeah, I bet it is. Girls like you always have a tight fucking pussy. A pussy that men fight over. Kill each other over."

Goosebumps break over my skin and I rock my hips again. "Girls like me?"

I ask the same question that I've asked several times before and he answers me on a raspy, choppy breath. "Yeah, girls like you. Bad girls. Bratty and spoiled. Girls who pout their lips when they don't get their way. You know there's a name for it."

"Name for what?"

"For the kind of pussy you have."

"What?"

He pulls at my nipple, making it all sore and achy. "Pouty pussy."

I feel it down there. That pull. That vicious pull of his fingers. The vicious whisper of his words.

I feel it in my pussy.

"What?" I whisper.

"Yeah. That's what they call it. Pouty and juicy. Bad girl pussy. And yours is going to be the juiciest. She pouts the hardest, doesn't she? She's the tightest too. Because you're worse. You're worse than bad, aren't you?"

Yes, I am.

I don't even care if I'm bad or desperate or whatever. I just want him closer. I want him to fix this ache in my belly, this current in my thighs.

This spasm in my bad girl pussy.

"Arrow, please..."

"But that's your downfall, Salem," he whispers, leaning his face closer and bumping our noses together. "Your bratty, pouty pussy. Because the more she pouts, the more she whines, the tinier she becomes. Tinier and smaller and you can't give her the very thing she wants."

"W-what does she want?" I ask, as if I don't know.

As if I'm so innocent that I don't know what he's talking about. But the thing is that I'm so far gone that I've got no brain power left.

I want him to tell things to me. I want him to do things to me too.

All the things. Bad and dirty and wonderful and glorious.

And he knows it – how can he not? I'm practically attacking him with my nails on his wrist and fisting his t-shirt with my other hand while I shift and rock against his stomach.

Arrow knows my predicament and he smirks. "A big fat cock. That's what you want, don't you? You want me to fuck you with it."

Oh God.

Yes.

I nod eagerly. "Yes."

He shifts his pelvis again and I don't know how he knows where my spot is but he hits it, and I twist between him and the wall, my eyes clenching shut.

"But you can't have it. You can't have the very thing that you want. Because your pussy is so tight and small that she can't handle it."

"Oh God, please," I sob, almost breaking his skin with my nails.

Almost making him bleed because I want him so much.

He squeezes my breast, pinching my nipple between his knuckles, making everything ache and ache. "Nah, you ruined your own chance. You should've thought of that before you pouted at me, Salem. Before you taunted me. You won't be able to handle my dick now. Because they don't make them any bigger than mine."

God, if he doesn't do *something* soon, I'll explode.

"You're such a –"

His laugh is both amused and pained as he cuts me off and *does* do something.

He leans over and kisses the corner of my mouth and I freeze.

My eyes go wide when he flicks his tongue out and licks that corner too before whispering, "Tell you what. You waited for me, didn't you? You worried over me. Not to mention, you're my *friend*. So maybe I can give you a little something."

"Something like what?"

He kisses the corner of my mouth again, a small, soft, soothing kiss.

"Your first kiss," he whispers, his hot breath fanning over my mouth. "I told you I wouldn't but maybe I can break my own rule."

"You can?"

"Uh-huh. For you."

"For me?"

"Yeah. Just to be nice."

Oh God.

Thank God.

And I open my mouth to say that to him, to thank him but he doesn't give me a chance because he's doing what he said he would.

After torturing me for ages, he's being nice to me.

With his mouth.

He closes his lips over mine and he gives me my first kiss – the kiss that I've waited for for eight years – and heat explodes in every part of my body.

Heat and lust and all the love that I have for him.

Which is good because I've been in the cold too long. I've been living in the harsh winter and finally, I've been touched by the sun.

More than touched, actually.

I've been consumed by him.

My sun has swallowed me and drunk me down before I can even draw a breath. Before I can comprehend anything, learn the texture of him and study the softness of his lips and the sharpness of his teeth in detail, he has put both his hands on my face and splayed them wide.

He has grasped my cheeks and grabbed my neck and he's arranged me in a way that will make him go deeper into my mouth.

That will make him eat at it and plunder it and violate it in the best, most glorious way possible. And he's doing all of that.

He's sucking on my mouth, tugging at the meaty flesh, biting at it, like he's been waiting to bite me for a long time now.

Like he's been so hot for me and his fire has burned so deep and so high and now he's purging it all.

Transferring it to me, and I take it happily.

I take it with gusto.

I even open my mouth so he can pour it inside me, push his tongue in. The tongue that's been driving me fucking crazy these past weeks. Because it makes his mouth so shiny and seductive when he does his lip-lick thing.

And tonight, I get to kiss that mouth.

I get to kiss my Arrow. I get to tug at his hair and pull him down on me. I get to moan inside his mouth and taste him with my tongue.

He tastes like fire, hot and tangy. Spicy.

I get to play with the silver chain around his neck and thrust my tits in his hard, *hard* chest. I get to rub them against his arched pecs and I get to rock against his stomach as well.

I get to hump it and that only drives him crazier.

That only causes his thumbs to dig on the pulse at my neck and his fingers to fist my hair and his mouth to turn up the intensity and the heat.

And before I know it, I'm moaning and rocking against him.

I'm taking something else from him too. Something more.

I'm so bad and greedy and spoiled that I'm taking an orgasm from him, as well. And it's not as if he minds it. No, not at all. In fact, he drives me to it. He urges me on with his teeth and his growls, and when that's not enough I feel him shift.

I feel him bending his knees slightly and still kissing me, I feel him letting go of my face and making for my ass.

He grabs the cheeks of my butt in his large, possessive hands and in a move that is so fucking sexy and arousing, he seats me on his powerful thigh. As soon as that place between my legs – that wet, hot and pulsing place – connects with his muscular limb, we both groan.

His chest shudders and so does his stomach. As if he can feel my wetness seeping through my pants and my measly thong and he likes that.

He likes making a throne for me to sit on. A throne for my bratty, bad girl pussy that pouts for him.

He also likes when I move on the throne he made for me.

I move and rock and shift. I drag my core up and down, chasing the delicious friction. I dance my hips in a figure eight while I knead his shoulders.

While he kisses me and kisses me, his mouth all wet and hot and soft, the complete opposite of his fingers on my ass.

They're tight and furious as they jiggle my flesh and flex it. He even delivers a tight slap to it, sharp and stinging, as he moves me like I'm his puppet, his fuck doll.

His fuck doll drowning in vintage leather.

As soon as I think that, I'm there.

He's taken me there. He's given me my first orgasm with him.

My sun. My Arrow.

The moan I let out is so, so loud and thick that Arrow takes a bite out of that too. He presses our mouths together hard and fast and eats it up. I even feel him gulp it down, his Adam's apple jerking with the swallow.

But I can't be sure because I'm breaking into a million pieces, twisting and writhing in his arms, all restless and sweaty and slippery, and he's still kissing me.

Although his kisses are softer now. They are sleepy and lazy and misty.

Drowsy.

Just like I am, and I would've lost my balance and fallen to the ground at his feet if he wasn't holding me.

If he wasn't clutching me tight to his heaving chest while winding my thighs around his hips again, making me hold on to him like a spider monkey.

I burrow my nose in his sweet smelling, sun-struck hair. "Thank you."

He rubs his chin on the top of my head, remaining silent.

"For breaking your rule for me," I continue.

He hums. "Maybe you're rubbing off on me."

I kiss his shoulder. "So I'm your rebound girl now?"

He flexes his grip and almost smashes me to his chest and I love that.

I love him.

"No." Before I can protest, he continues, "I'm not going to use you to get over your sister. Even I'm not that much of an asshole. Besides, you don't have what I'm looking for in a rebound girl anyway."

CHAPTER FIFTEEN

The Broken Arrow

"Y ou've disappointed me. I thought I raised you better than that."

My mother's voice stops me at the front door of my house.

I was about to leave after carrying a sleepy Salem inside and up to her room. Her *sunshine* yellow-painted room.

Which I noticed while I was depositing her on her bed.

"Is there a reason why everything is yellow in your room?" I asked, looking around her tiny space for the first time ever.

"Sunshine yellow," she corrected me sleepily. "It's my favorite color. Reminds me of the sun."

I draped her blanket over her. "You're a little too obsessed with the sun, you know that?"

She curled herself into a ball, still wearing my jacket that basically covers her from top to bottom. "I know. I love my sun."

But now I freeze at the door, my hand on the knob ready to turn it, wondering if my mother saw something.

If she saw me with her. If she saw what I did to her. How I vandalized her virgin mouth that's been taunting me ever since I saw her at the bar.

No one's ever touched me there. Before.

Jesus Christ.

"I thought my son wasn't a quitter," my mother continues, and I finally get enough sense gathered to understand what she's talking about.

She's talking about her sister, Sarah.

Not *her*.

She's talking about the girl I've been with for eight years. The girl who betrayed me. The girl who made a fool out of me. The girl because of whom I'm a failure.

As I turn to face my mother, my reckoning, all the peace, all the warmth from the past hour is gone.

Instead, I feel *them*.

I feel the bugs crawling and scratching at my skin. I feel hot under my collar. I feel the jitters.

I feel the shame.

That's what it is. This sensation is shame.

This is what my mother always reduces me to and that's why I didn't want to come to this house.

That's why I didn't want to talk to her.

Because I knew what I would find when I looked into her eyes.

Grave disappointment.

The woman who made me perfect. Who taught me to never make mistakes.

Who hauled me to practices, to all my games until I learned to drive myself. Who would stay up late at night to check on my homework, to make sure that I was prepared for a test, until I could handle it all by myself.

My mother.

"I'm not a quitter," I tell her with clenched teeth.

I'm not.

She's made sure that I'm not. It has been her life's work.

It has been *my* life's work.

"Aren't you? What do you call this then? What you did tonight." My mother comes forward, shaking her head. "I gave you everything. I gave you all that I could and it was hard, Arrow. After your father's death, raising a boy all alone was hard. Raising a boy who could walk in his shoes was harder. But I made sure that you did. I made sure that I kept your father alive in you. That I never let him die. I made sure you had every opportunity to succeed, to be the best.

To be the kind of son your father and I would be proud of. But look at you now.

"Your career is hanging in the balance. You're going to therapy for your issues. Issues I didn't even know you had. And you broke up with the girl you were going to marry. What do you call it, if not quitting?"

She cheated on me.

I want to shout at her.

I want to scream that she fucking cheated.

And she did it with my best friend, and she did it for months.

I trusted her.

I fucking trusted her but she betrayed me. She made a fool out of me and I was blind. I was blind to all of it.

I was going to marry her and I would have. I would have if not for those texts. I would've made her my wife and she would've made me a fool. I wonder if she would've carried on her affair after our marriage too. I know she says that she wouldn't have but I still wonder.

I still wonder if she would've taken advantage of my trust with my ring on her finger.

The ring I stomped on and broke, the day I left LA.

But I won't tell my mother that. I can't.

She already thinks I'm a quitter. She's already disappointed. How is she going to react when she finds out the truth?

That Sarah was fooling me and I didn't even know it. That her son was so blind and so fucking stupid that he had no clue about it. That her son got cheated on.

It will break her to know that her perfect son isn't so perfect after all. That her perfect son is a failure.

I didn't even want her – or anyone, for that matter – to know about the breakup. But I guess the news broke back in LA and my mother found out too.

But that is it.

That is all they're ever going to know.

It's better that my team hate me for punching Ben than they think I'm a fool.

Last season, our leftwing striker found out that his wife had been cheating on him and he had no clue. And I wondered how.

How the fuck did he not know?

Shouldn't a man know these things? It made me wonder about his ability to play on the field. If he's so clueless in his personal life, how the fuck do I know he's going to give one hundred percent on the field? And I wasn't the only one. A few pitied him, others thought that he was stupid.

I'm not going to be in the same position.

I'm The Blond fucking Arrow.

No one is going to question my judgement on the field.

I knew Sarah would never open her mouth because her reputation is everything to her. She won't have people thinking that she spread her legs for someone else while she was with me. I also knew Ben would never say anything either; it would make him look less of a victim.

Besides, my mother loves Sarah. She is the daughter my mom never had, and I can't break that illusion for her.

I can't hurt her that way.

I can't disappoint her any more than I have.

"Duly noted, Mom," I reply sardonically even though I can barely keep my eyes on her. "I think you should go back to sleep now or you'll be late for your flight tomorrow."

"I was against your relationship with her from the beginning. But you proved yourself. You proved your worth. But I guess I should've trusted my gut. I should've known that a girl would make you lose focus and screw up everything that we've worked for. I'm not going to let you kill your father again, do you hear me? He's not going to die again because you were foolish enough to lose your focus. Do you understand me? Do what you have to do so you can go back and fulfill your father's dream," she says and leaves me in darkness.

My father's dream.

To play in the European League. The dream that remained unfulfilled because he died.

As I step into the night, I fish out cigarettes from my jeans pocket. I light one up and puff out a huge cloud of smoke into the sky.

Sometimes I wonder if my father hadn't seen that dream with his own eyes, would it have become mine?

Sometimes I wonder if... if I could ever have other dreams. My dreams.

Or if every son inherits his father's dreams by default.

CHAPTER SIXTEEN

There's a little mailbox outside his office.

It has a thin slot where you can slide the letters and internal office documents and memos in. It also has a little lock on it, a shiny silver lock where he can put his key in to open the box and retrieve all the mail people have left him.

That's where I plan to leave him a note – a tiny little note – on Monday before classes start.

It's the first note in a long series of notes that I'm hoping to send him. Notes designed to weaken his resolve.

And seduce him.

Yes, I've never seduced anyone. Or at least I hadn't, not until the night we kissed.

The kiss that rocked my world and turned me into a horny, greedy girl who also humped his leg and came like a firecracker.

But that's beside the point.

The point is that I don't really know the art of seduction. Whatever I did that night was pure instinct.

That's what I'm going to do now too.

I'm going to follow my gut and seduce him by leaving him little notes. That seems like the obvious, most natural choice, right?

I've written him letters for years.

I'm used to telling him things on paper, and there are a few things that I'd like to tell him now as well.

Things like he can use me for whatever he wants and that won't make him an asshole. Or the fact that if he just tells me what he wants in a perfect rebound girl, I'll give it to him.

But there's a problem.

Which doesn't occur to me until I rush upstairs to the second floor where his office is, with the letter in my pocket.

The problem that I'm basically seducing my soccer coach.

The other problems, I was aware of. Problems like my sister would freak out if she knew. She'd call me names and she'd hate me. But she already hates me, doesn't she?

Or the fact that Leah might have an objection as well.

She loves Sarah and Arrow together, as evidenced by her dinner plan. So she's not going to like that I – the bad, rule-breaking sister – am planning to seduce her son. It was a miracle she didn't see us kiss in her backyard, for which I've been thanking my lucky stars for the past two days.

But somehow, it had escaped my mind that Arrow is on faculty here at St. Mary's – however temporarily, but faculty nonetheless – and I'm his student.

Seducing a teacher is definitely against the rules. And for a crime this big – even bigger than sneaking out and harboring secret cell phones – they might definitely lock me up somewhere.

Which makes me realize something else too.

The letters under my bed.

They're all addressed to Arrow and after years of writing them, suddenly they have become even more forbidden, haven't they?

As I walk toward his office, the tiny note sitting heavy in my pocket and people giving me more than a passing glance because I'm the principal's ward, I decide that I'll hide those letters. The old ones are locked up in my suitcase but the ones that I've been writing him now are under my bed. Maybe I can hide them all in the third-floor bathroom where Poe's cell phone is or something.

I'm not afraid of being punished but I can't have anyone looking at them.

Those letters are my biggest secret. My absolute most cherished possessions. They contain the longings and confessions of my not-so-witchy heart.

They contain the story of my doomed love and no one can ever know about them.

Least of all the guy I've written them for.

He hates love, doesn't he?

I can't have him know that I love him. I can never tell him.

So those letters are mine and mine alone and I need to hide them.

I hang around his office for a few seconds, waiting for the coast to clear, and when it does, I rush and slide the note in.

Five minutes later, I'm downstairs, getting my books out of my locker, my heart in my throat and my teeth making a mess of my lips.

I keep imagining the expression on his face when he reads it.

He will definitely frown, for one. He might also clench his jaw and that muscle on his cheek might make an appearance too.

And his eyes might darken.

Yeah, definitely.

I'm not sure what he's going to do when he sees it but...

Suddenly, I don't have to imagine his reaction or wonder about what he'll do because he's here.

I'm just shutting the door of my locker when he makes an appearance.

He's standing by the staircase.

The long, wide, concrete staircase with a beige-painted metal railing. It's located in the middle of the hallway that's busy with people walking up and down, going about their business.

But standing at the bottom of it, his eyes on me, Arrow is frozen.

And I was right.

His eyes do appear dark. They also appear flashing and bright at the same time, and the way he's staring at me, I don't have to guess that he's read the note.

His entire wonderful body is screaming with the knowledge.

His hands are fisted at his sides, the hands with which he rocked me over his muscular thigh and made me come. The hands with which he squeezed my breasts.

Which wake up, by the way.

My breasts, my nipples. The place between my thighs.

Everything wakes up and pulses. Becomes swollen.

I give him a slight smile and bite my lip.

When he narrows his eyes at me and clenches his jaw like I knew he would, I want to throw my books away and run to him.

I want to kiss his harsh jaw and sharp cheeks. I want to kiss his gorgeous, soft lips and writhe against his stomach in my school skirt while he kisses me back and mocks me for being greedy and bratty.

I want to say the words, whisper them in his ears, the ones I wrote for him.

My Darling Arrow,

Thanks for my very first kiss and my very first orgasm with a boy. It was glorious and hot. Clearly, my own fingers have not been doing the job your super amazing thigh did.

I want you to know that they kept me warm, your kiss and your orgasm, while I was sleeping all alone in my bed. So warm that I actually had to get up in the middle of the night to open the window of my room so I could let the cool air in.

I thought that it would be enough to get rid of this fever on my skin but it wasn't. Apparently, kissing you was like kissing the sun. And riding your thigh was like riding a fiery halo. So I had to take drastic measures.

I had to take off all my clothes and sleep naked, which was also a first. So thank you. It was oddly freeing.

Yours,

The Rebound Girl

PS: I'm not wearing a bra today either. And I've said goodbye to little thongs. They don't do much anyway. This is better. And more freeing. Have a great day!

I clench my thighs as I feel a throb in my pussy.

In my naked pussy.

I didn't lie in the letter; I'm really not wearing anything under the mustard-colored skirt. And somehow, he knows that my thighs are clenched.

Because his eyes drop to my skirt and I hug my books to my chest, my nipples so hard and sticking out that they poke through my white blouse and my chunky sweater.

I swear I see a thick vein in his arm pop. I even see him take a step forward, keeping his gaze pinned to my skirt as if he's coming at me.

As if he doesn't care that there are people loitering about and that they're starting to notice that the campus celebrity is staring really hard at the campus bad girl.

The bell rings then and he whips his eyes up, his cheeks flushed dark, the tendons on his neck standing taut.

Just to be naughty, I stick out my lower lip at him while he watches, before mouthing, *Bye.*

The whole day passes in a haze. I do all my classes in a haze. I talk to my girls and eat lunch and meet Miller for our weekly appointment in a haze.

But when I open my locker at the end of the day, my haze breaks. Because inside, I find a once-folded note. I'm so overjoyed that I don't even care how he got into my locker in the first place. Besides, who cares? I've got a note from him!

Is this another attempt at seducing me, Salem?

Because let me tell you that I was nice to you the first time. Very, very nice. But I'm running out of patience now. So think really carefully before you leave another note for me to find.

Also, you should know that I'm pretty used to girls passing me things secretly. Although I have to say that most of them have been articles of clothing rather than a clumsy sexy note written in the back of a trigonometry notebook.

PS: The equation you had on the back of your note was wrong. Find the correct solution below.

PPS: Do not be late for one-on-one soccer practice tomorrow after dinner.

I grin.

Even though I know I fucked up, writing him that letter on the back of a trigonometry equation, I can't stop my smile.

He wrote back.

He wrote *back!*

The guy I've been writing secret love letters to for the past eight years, wrote me back. Even though it's not a very encouraging letter per se. I mean, he's not falling on me like a dying, desperate man but it's something.

Something that makes my heart race and makes me write him another note that I leave in his mailbox the next day.

My Darling Arrow,

Are you challenging me? Are you saying that I can't sneak secret articles of clothing into your mailbox?

You should know better by now. You should know that I'm very well capable of leaving my tiny thongs and bras in your mailbox if you want me to.

The only problem is that I don't wear any, remember?

By the way, you should really stop glaring at me in the hallway. I'm not sure if you know this but it makes you look really sexy. Also it makes me wet. So fucking wet and horny and achy that yesterday, I had to excuse myself from my trig class and go to the bathroom so I could do something about it.

And I did.

I touched myself while thinking about the dark color of your eyes and that arousing clench of your jaw.

Yours,

The Rebound Girl

PS: Thanks for solving that trig problem. Miller was surprised at my fake math skills.

PPS: I'm really excited about our one-on-one session tonight.

PPPS: I want you to know that the orgasm I gave myself had nothing on the one you so very nicely gave me. Also, you were right. My pussy is swollen and tight and pouty. Perfect for a big, fat cock such as yours.

Again, I go through my day in a haze but when the time comes to get on the soccer field, I'm bursting at the seams.

I get there early even, hoping to impress him, but he's already there.

He stands at the edge of the field, watching me walk over to him, his expression smooth and his arms folded across his chest.

I open my mouth to say hi to him when he abruptly clips, "We'll work on your running."

"What?"

"Running," he says tersely. "We'll work on it."

"Why?"

"Because running involves knees. And we need to work on your knees."

I look at my pale knees. "What's wrong with my knees?"

He looks at them too but there's a certain absence of emotion. He does it all so clinically, so professionally that I'm... disappointed.

"You need to lift them up more when you run," he explains while raising his eyes back to my face. "It helps with the posture, and that helps with striking the ball and making goals. That's pretty much what soccer is all about."

He looks so coach-like right now. Like he did back in his office.

At least in his office there was a thrum of emotion sitting just under his skin. Here, he is completely emotionless.

There's even a whistle around his neck. Along with that big watch strapped to his wrist, he looks so freaking unapproachable and authoritative.

Mindful of a few lingering students around the field, I step closer to him. He barely shows any reaction to that but I don't get deterred. "Aren't we gonna, like, talk about things?"

His jaw moves then. "Does it involve soccer?"

"Well, no. But –"

"Then, no. We aren't going to talk about *things*."

The sun is setting, and the sky is all burnt orange, illuminating the golden strands of his hair. I rub my fingers together, remembering the velvety feel of them.

That gives me the encouragement to go on. "So what, I'm supposed to run around the field until you tell me to stop?"

He gives me an inscrutable look. "That's the idea."

"And you'll watch me."

"I'll watch you, yes." He taps his watch with his finger. "Now get moving. We're losing daylight."

I cock my head to the side and give him a small smile. "Fine. If you want me to run for you, I'll run for you. And if you want to watch, you can. But let me tell you something, *Coach*, I'm not afraid to make a show out of it." Then I lower my voice to a whisper. "For you."

And that's what I do. I give him a show.

I pump my bare legs and run around the field. I smile at him every time our eyes meet. And he watches me and that smile with a ticking jaw and narrowed eyes.

And when we're done, I untie my hair and shake it out. Because he likes me messy.

I even stretch out my muscles for a few minutes.

Once that's done, I bend down slowly to collect all my things. All in front of him, all part of a show.

I have no idea where I learned these things but I'm not going to stop myself now.

"Thanks for the lesson," I tell him when I walk over to his still-immobile and watching form all sweaty and flushed. "I think we really worked on my knees and my posture, don't you? Can't wait until you work on me more."

Okay, so maybe that last line was a little cheesy.

But whatever.

I never said I'm the goddess of seduction. I'm only Salem, a girl with witchy eyes and a witchy name. Not a witchy heart though.

I ride the high of that win – and I do think it's a win because his veins were bursting out of his tanned skin and his jugular was perpetually taut by the end of our session – until I find a note in my locker the next day.

That was quite a show you put on for me yesterday. I'll admit that I underestimated you. You looked really determined as you ran around the field, bouncing your little legs and working hard for me like you were interviewing for a job position.

As tempting a candidate as you are, I'm afraid I'll have to decline the offer of you spreading those legs for me and volunteering up your swollen and tight and pouty pussy for my pleasure.

At this time, I'm looking for someone more experienced. Someone who doesn't come just by riding my thigh and me playing with her nipples. Someone with an actual résumé of fucking. So I don't have to waste my time teaching her basic skills such as how to suck my big, fat cock or how to ride it.

Someone with whom I can skip to the part where I fuck all my frustrations out.

Good luck, next time.

I almost crumple his note when I finish it. I almost dash upstairs to his office and slap him in the face for being such an asshole.

Throughout the day, his words echo in my head and they're still echoing when I'm at the library with Poe, Callie and Wyn working on my trig homework. Maybe that's why I miss Arrow walking down the aisle. But my girls don't miss him.

In fact, Poe even calls him over. "Hey, Coach. Fancy seeing you here."

My head's bent and I was about to write something down on my notebook – though I can't remember what – when I feel him walking up to our table in the corner.

As soon as he reaches the desk, Callie bursts forth, "Are you looking for something in particular? A book, perhaps."

I am going to kill her, Callie and Poe both.

"Maybe we can help you look," Wyn says, and I add her to my list.

I thought they were my friends. I thought they cared about me.

In all fairness, they don't know anything. As in, they don't know his secrets – the fake injury and the cheating; and mine – that I'm in love with him.

All they know is that I blush really hard when he comes around and disappear in bars when I see him standing in a corner. And sometimes I stare off into the distance for long periods of time.

I still have my head down so I only have a view of his gray sneakers but I can imagine his expression, since that's my thing now, when he says drily, "That's a very kind offer. I never knew how helpful schoolgirls could be. But I think I can manage."

I'm afraid I'll have to decline your offer *of spreading your legs for me...*

Jerk. Asshole.

Poe leans forward then. "Okay, real talk. I have no interest in soccer whatsoever. But I like you."

"And what'd I do to deserve that?" he drawls.

"You helped our friend out last week," Callie replies. "With those evil girls."

"Yeah, I don't care about violence," Wyn goes. "Because why make war when you can make art? But we really appreciated that. So thanks."

Oh yeah, they heard about that. They were all in the dorm when it happened and they were really impressed when I told them about it.

He doesn't say anything but I can feel him jerking his chin at them in all his arrogant glory and it makes me squirm in my seat. I'm about to look up and put an end to this charade when Poe goes again. "Well, since you're so helpful, maybe you can help our girl out once again."

What?

"Yeah. She sucks at math. And Miller's starting to notice. Maybe you can talk to Miller about it?" Callie chirps sweetly.

"Oh, and can you also teach her a little bit of trig, if you have the time?" Poe asks in her typical troublemaker voice.

Wyn throws out a soft chuckle. "I second that."

I abandon all pretense of staring at the notebook then and look up. Only to find that his eyes are already on me.

Dark blue and hot.

But I ignore him for now and look at the girls. "I do not suck at trig."

Callie reaches forward and squeezes my hand in sympathy. "You so do."

"No," I lie. "I like trig."

It's Poe's turn to squeeze my shoulder. "No, you don't. Because nobody likes trig."

"You know –"

"Is Miller giving you trouble?" he cuts me off then.

Finally, I have to look at him and when I do I have to crumple the corner of my notebook because his eyes have gone completely black and he's staring at me intimately.

I glare at him. "No. She's not."

He doesn't like that, as evidenced by his sharp exhale. "I thought I told you to come to me if there was a problem."

God, he makes me so angry with his highhanded ways. Like he owns me or something. Like he wants to slay all my dragons and make all my problems go away.

I tamp down the flutters it causes in my belly and how I want to clench my thighs at his dominating tone. "And I told you that I can handle myself."

Arrow goes silent as he stares down at me, all tall and authoritative, the globes of his biceps and shoulders bunched up and on display in his gym t-shirt.

"Is that your trig homework?" He jerks his chin up.

I bring the notebook closer to me as if hiding it from his view. "Yeah."

"I can teach you," he offers.

"Excuse me?"

"They're right. You do suck at trig."

And oh my God, I lose my shit.

I completely lose it.

I shut my notebook with a loud snap, so loud that even I flinch. "Thanks for the offer. But I'm afraid I'm going to have to decline. I don't need your help." I even stand up under his fiery eyes. "I don't need you to *teach* me anything. I can learn everything by myself. In fact, I'm going to get started tonight. Learning things, I mean. The basic trigonometry skills. And by the time I'm done, I'm going to be so good at it that you'll cry and curse at your fate that you ever offered to teach me anything."

Ignoring him and the tightly coiled and dark form of my sun, I turn to my girls who're all looking at me with a mixture of amusement and awe. "I'm leaving. And you guys need to follow me so I can make a dramatic exit."

Which I do.

I make a dramatic exit and my girls, like the sisters I never had, follow me.

Hours later at midnight, they follow me to the bar too where I plan on getting educated, meaning I plan on finding a random guy and fucking him and getting rid of my stupid virginity.

I know it's an overly emotional reaction and I need to stop and think, which has all been said by my friends, but I'm too angry.

I'm too upset and I'm too hurt.

It hurts, okay?

It hurts.

It *hurts* that he'll fuck anyone, any random girl that he finds at a bar, but me. It hurts that after all these years he finally sees me but still, I won't hold his attention. He still doesn't find me attractive enough to fuck me.

I'm not asking him to love me, am I?

I'm only asking him to use me, use my body, and he won't even do that. And I'm too hurt and too much in love with him so I've lost my mind over it.

That's why I walk to the dance floor to find someone. Someone who'll take my virginity and make me perfect for the guy I love.

I don't know why I want to cry though. I don't know why I feel like throwing up.

The song that's playing is my favorite of all – "Born to Die" by Lana Del Rey – and my body is already writhing to it. I'm already twisting my hips, moving them in the shape of a figure eight, the way I did when I was chasing my orgasm on his thigh.

I throw my hands up and dance to the slow rhythm of the song, to the lyrics. I dance when my eyes cry pretty tears that flow down my cheeks. I dance when I want my legs to give up and make me fall.

At some point, a guy comes to dance next to me and my tears flow harder. He can't see them though. It's dark and he's drunk.

He's perfect.

He won't even know that I'm a virgin, completely unfit for the love of my life.

I'm about to ask him to take me somewhere equally dark, where he won't be able to see my tears, and fuck me, when I feel someone at my back.

Someone tall and strong and familiar.

Someone whose chest is moving, punching my back in a haphazard rhythm. I can even hear his breaths in my ears, noisy and loud, agitated.

He's so warm that he flows like liquid heat in my veins.

My Arrow.

I close my eyes in relief and Lana's voice explodes around me.

He grabs my waist, his fingers digging into my flesh.

A wave of heat grips me and I sigh.

I've been feeling cold and shivery, but he makes it all go away when he pulls me into his body. His hard, *hard* body and oh my God, I feel it.

I feel his erection at the small of my back and I can't help but arch up against it, rub up against the heat radiating from it.

He growls in my ear, his lips rubbing over my delicate shell, his hips shifting, pushing back. "Turn the fuck around."

I hiccup and do as he says.

His features are shadowed by the rim of his baseball cap but I see the movement of his jaw when he notices my tears. He wipes them with his rough thumbs, his digits lingering around the area of my parted lips.

"You're coming with me," he tells me.

"Where are you taking me?" I whisper.

"Where you belong."

My heart shrivels. "I'm not going back to St. Mary's."

His eyes flash. "No, you're not. Because you belong with me."

CHAPTER SEVENTEEN

His motel room is gray and dull.

That's the first thing I notice when I step in.

It's also very clean and made up. Generic. With a desk under the window, a slim-backed chair, a chest with drawers by its side. Tons of weights stacked up in one corner. A door that probably leads to the bathroom.

And a bed.

I'm not looking at the bed yet for some strange reason. But from what I can gather from the corners of my eyes, it has crisp white sheets with a dark gray blanket on the foot.

I walk in, my feet muffled on the gray carpet.

Unlike my heartbeats.

My heartbeats are loud. So very loud and I bet he can hear them.

My Arrow.

Who's just stepped in after me and closed the door with a click.

I feel that tiny click in my bare thighs.

Well, I'm wearing a plaid skirt tonight that I borrowed from Poe. Up until he showed up at the bar, I was feeling cold even in his jacket.

But not anymore.

My thighs don't feel cold at all. Not even when I was riding behind him and we were speeding down the highway, wind whipping against my flesh.

In fact, they were hot.

Like they are now.

When I reach the opposite wall, I turn around and lean against it.

Arrow is doing the same. He's leaning against the door, his arms folded across his chest, his eyes on me.

I press my thighs together. "There's a lot of gray in this room."

My first words to him ever since we left the bar.

He tips his chin, his stubbled, rough jaw catching the overhead light. "I like gray."

His first words to me after he said that I belonged with him.

Biting my lip at the memory, I tell him, "Gray's super dull."

"Unlike sunshine yellow."

I look at his hair then. It's all messed up, strands falling over his arched brows.

And I regret being so far away from him. Where I can't smooth them away.

I don't know why I chose this spot to stand against when all I want – all I've ever wanted – is to be close to him.

As it is, I dig my nails into my sweaty palms and shift on my feet, feeling the scrape of the wall on the backs of my thighs. "How'd you know I was at the bar?"

"You wanted to learn things, yeah?" When I hesitantly nod, he murmurs, "It wasn't hard to figure out where you'd go for that."

I clench my thighs again, getting sort of restless. "I thought you didn't wanna waste your time on teaching me."

"I don't," he clips. "But I don't want other guys teaching you either."

My breaths escalate.

It's such a guy thing to say – I don't want you but I don't want anyone else to have you either.

And maybe because I'm such a girl, it starts up a quickening in my lower stomach. "Why not?"

Something about what I said makes him move away from the door and I shiver in his jacket.

His footsteps should be muffled like mine were but they aren't. They're loud and thudding. They pulse and vibrate.

I feel all of that, the sound of his approach and the blazing look in his eyes, in between my legs. He pauses right before me and my lips part at how big he looks right now, big and tall and warm and I curl my toes in my soccer cleats, the old ones. Not the ones he bought me. I'm keeping those safe under my bed.

"Because you're my friend," he replies in a rough tone, his eyes flickering down to my heaving chest before moving back up to my face.

I don't know which word he has emphasized more, my or friend. Which word sends a shock of current running down my spine, and I don't even have the time for such nonsense because he leans over and puts a hand on the wall, just above my head, and whispers, "And only I get to teach things to you."

I swallow. "I'm –"

"What's this one called?"

He doesn't have to explain his question to me. I already know what he's referring to. He's looking at my painted lips.

"C-cherry Picker," I whisper.

I actually went rogue on my usual color choice – dark and different shades of coral – and went with something super red, Wyn's favorite.

Arrow brings his free hand up and traces the bottom of my lip with his thumb. "Cherry Picker."

"I thought it suited the miserable occasion."

His thumb digs into the center of my lip and he forces my mouth to part, narrowing his eyes. "Were you going to let him pick your cherry?"

I rake my nails up and down the wall as my pussy flutters at his possessive gesture. "I... I thought about it."

He almost mashes my lower lip with my teeth. "You did, huh."

"I mean, I –"

"You thought about letting him tear through that little piece of flesh between your legs." His hand moves down from my lips and he wraps his fingers around my throat. "You thought about bleeding on his cock. Is that what you're telling me?"

An intense spasm rolls through my channel at the graphic image he paints – my blood on his cock – and his possessive hold on me. "Arrow, please."

"Please what?" he whispers, his hand a hot brand on my throat. "Please don't say things like that, Arrow? Or please don't lose your *shit* thinking about that virgin pussy being violated by that drunk motherfucker? Or maybe..." He squeezes my throat and I'm almost off the ground, teetering on my tiptoes. "Or maybe don't lock me up in this motel room, Arrow, and go hunting for him. Don't think about beating the living shit out of that dumb fuck. Is that what you're pleading for, Salem? Don't kill him. The cherry picker you chose for yourself."

He can't beat him up, can he?

I mean, that's what he got suspended for, beating someone up.

Oh God, he can't do that and I can't let him.

But still, my whole body is buzzing with his violent reaction. My whole body is ablaze with his possessiveness, his raw domination over me.

This is bad, Salem. You can't revel in these things.

"You can't do that. You can't beat him up, Arrow," I blurt out, my heart jumping up to my throat and pounding against his palm. "Your team won't like that, you beating someone else up in a bar, in front of everyone."

It's like he doesn't even hear me as he whispers, "And this time, they won't be able to pull me off him until I finish the job."

I have to clench my teeth in order to tamp down the electric thrill his words fill my belly with and something really stupid and dangerous slips out of my mouth, but I stop myself at the last second. "Have you…"

"Have I what?"

I don't know what I hope to accomplish by asking this question but I can't help it. I have to know. Because God, he looks so angry and wild and so crazy possessive.

"Have you always been like this? B-before."

Stupid, stupid question.

Stupid, *stupid* Salem.

What would this accomplish anyway? Why do I care how he was before, when he was with my sister?

But the thing is, I don't think he was like this. I don't think he was this crazy dominating and crazy possessive. Sarah would have hated that.

Because Jesus Christ, I love every inch of this.

I love every fucking inch of his deep-seated need to control me.

When understanding breaks over his face like dawn, I fall in love with him even more. Because it only manages to darken his features. It only manages to make him wilder, more possessive, more… mine.

He leans forward, his grip on me still absolute. "No, I wasn't." His thumb digs into my fluttering pulse. "Maybe it's you. Maybe you bring out the worst in me. And you wanted me, didn't you? You wanted my fire. My heat. My fury."

I jerk out a nod.

He throws out a mean, tight smile. "Well, you got me. Every broken, cut-open piece of me."

Good.

I want him, however he comes. I want him to burn me, cut me, slice me open.

I don't care.

I'll still smile at him. I'll still love him. I'll still dive into the ocean and jump off an airplane for him.

He's my Arrow.

My darling Arrow.

I swallow, feeling as crazy as him, feeling as submissive and feminine as he feels dominating and masculine. "I just wanted to be... perfect. For you. I wanted him to take that piece of me away that made me unfit so you'd –"

He cuts off my words when he steps into me even more.

On top of that, he pushes my neck back, so I look him directly in the eyes.

"You wanted to be perfect for me," he rasps.

"Yes."

A harsh look ripples over his face, and I don't know if he wants to kiss me or kill me.

"Do you know what I've been doing all week? Ever since you started leaving your sexy fucking notes in my mailbox?"

"What?"

"I've been jerking off," he says with clenched teeth. "I've been jerking off like a goddamn teenager, here, in my room. At the school, in my fucking office. I've had to stop myself three times – three fucking times – from sending for you so I could see."

"See what?"

"Your virgin pussy," he rumbles. "So I could see if you're really not wearing any panties under those schoolgirl skirts of yours. If you're really walking around the school hallways with that tight piece between your legs, all bare and unprotected. So I could see if your pussy is really as swollen and pouty as I think it is."

Finally, I let go of the wall and clutch his t-shirt, my mouth all open and panting, my eyes all glazed over with lust.

But he's not done yet.

He delivers his final line as he almost kisses my lips. "If you got any more perfect for me than you already are, I'd fucking lose my mind. I'd bend you over and fuck you in front of the whole school while they watch and gasp and talk about rule-breaking."

Perfect.

He called me perfect for him.

Oh my God.

I don't... I don't know what to do. This is all I've ever wanted. To be perfect for him.

I don't know what to say except, "Arrow, I –"

But he cuts me off again, his lips pressing into mine so hard, his teeth digging into my plump flesh. "Do you remember the rules?"

I arch my spine, trying to get closer to him. "What rules?"

He watches my struggle but doesn't help me. He simply states, "My rules. Rules of being my fuck doll. You remember what I told you?"

I think about it. My mind is so foggy and drowning in lust and happiness at being called perfect for him that I have to really focus.

A second later, it comes to me. "Yeah, I do."

"What are they?"

I swallow as a stinging needle pierces my bubbling happiness. "Y-you fuck them and forget them."

His jaw clenches and something passes over his features, a shadow I don't have the brain power right now to understand.

"There's another rule," he clips, pushing our mouths together, and I peek out my tongue and lick his lips to get his taste.

Tangy and fiery.

"What is it?" I whisper, promising to follow all his rules even though it will hurt me.

His blue eyes catch fire at my question.

His entire body catches fire when he replies, his voice and words bathed in violence. "That absolutely no one, *no one at all*, gets to touch what's mine.

Because I don't share, remember? You don't let anyone put their hands on you. You don't dance with strange men. You don't talk to them. You don't look at them. You don't think about them. Is that clear?"

That's the easiest rule anyone has ever laid down for me.

The easiest rule in the whole world and I nod without hesitation. "Yes. I won't. I don't want anyone else."

A dark satisfaction washes over his face, his body, and I can't stop myself.

I *don't* stop myself from kissing him.

I bite into his lip and tug at it and kiss him the way I've been thinking about for the past week. And he picks me up off the floor probably in the way that *he's* been thinking about for the past week too.

As soon as my thighs cinch around his waist and my core rubs against his hard stomach, I let out a moan. He swallows it down with a grunt of his own.

"Where'd you get the skirt?" he asks, breaking the kiss, his palms kneading my ass in tight, sharp squeezes.

"My friends."

He delivers a stinging slap to it, even as his voice is amused. "The ones who made your exit dramatic?"

I writhe in his arms. "Yeah."

"Tell them I like them too. For looking out for you."

I kiss his jaw, all happy. "Okay."

"And tell them not to give you any more fucking skirts." Another punishing slap that makes me whimper. "Because you won't be wearing them after tonight."

I clutch at his hair. "Not even with you?"

"No. Because you won't be wearing much of anything when you're with me."

Before I can finish squeezing my thighs around him at his sexy words, I'm on his bed.

His kisses were so drugging and hot that I didn't even realize that he was walking, taking me somewhere.

Now I'm on my back and he's leaning over me, his silver chain dangling and hitting my chin.

But he moves away too soon.

With his cheeks flushed dark and mouth wet and parted, he stands at the foot of the bed, looking down at me while I clutch his sheets. They're cool and smooth under my burning body.

"Show it to me," he orders, his chest heaving.

Just like that, I know what he means.

I know.

His command flows inside my veins and fills me with so much lust and love and purpose that I can't believe I haven't exploded yet.

That I haven't broken apart in a million pieces.

But it's a good thing. Because I have to show him.

I have to show him my bare pussy and even though I didn't think I'd have it in me, the strength, I still scramble up to my knees and shed his jacket in under two seconds.

I see him swallowing, his eyes narrowed and focused on my skirt, right where my pulsing core is.

Like they were back in that hallway when I gave him my first note.

"I've been..." I whisper, tugging at the hem of my skirt, and his eyes snap up to mine. "I've been wanting to come to your office too. To show you. My pussy."

It's true.

I've been dying to lift up my school skirt and show it to him.

For some reason, just pulling up the skirt instead of taking it off altogether makes everything more erotic. More illicit. More of a rule-breaking kind of thing.

Like I'm not supposed to do it. I shouldn't want to show him that place between my thighs but I'm doing it anyway. I'm giving him a quick peek of what lies under my skirt because he makes me so horny and I can't stop myself.

He clamps his jaw, his eyes glittering. "Do it then. Be my bad girl. Flash me that pussy and make me go crazy for it."

If you got any more perfect for me, I'd lose my mind...

With his wonderful words echoing in my love-filled heart, I lift the fabric.

It goes up and up my trembling thighs, until it reaches my hips where I hold it. I move them, my hips, shifting on my knees, and at last, showing him the secret part of me.

I've got no panties on and he can see it all.

He can see the shape and the make of my core, all wet and naked for him. And he makes a sound.

He even jerks slightly at the sight of it.

Wiping his mouth with the back of his hand, he says, "She's bare."

I move again, undulating my hips, watching my sun turn dark and darker in front of my eyes. "I-I like how it feels."

I do. So I shave it and keep it all smooth and bare.

He looks me in the eyes then. "Free, yeah?"

My fists tremble, holding the skirt up. "Yeah."

He exhales a harsh breath at my answer before reaching back and snagging his t-shirt, pulling it up and off his body. His silver chain swings and comes to land between his muscular pecs with a slight thump.

God, he's so sexy. So fucking masculine and athletic.

I don't know where to look first.

I start at his collar bones, so beautiful and jutting, giving way to his tightly arched chest. The harsh planes dip down to build a corrugated stomach.

All tanned and smooth. So sleek and powerful.

Body of a sun-struck god.

I wanna go down further. I wanna follow the V of his pelvis and look at the bulge in his jeans but as soon as my eyes hit his belly button, he's upon me.

One of his knees is on the bed and his hand has clasped the back of my neck, making me look up and into his eyes.

"I was going to go easy on you," he tells me, his fingers squeezing my neck. "Because this is your first time. But you flashed me this cunt." His other hand comes to grab it and I jerk at the first contact of his fingers with my most intimate flesh.

With my most intimate and *horny* flesh.

"And I thought I could handle it. I thought I could handle looking at your pussy that pouts for me but I was wrong. I can't." He squeezes my neck again as he dips his finger in the center of my slit, making me bite back a moan. "I can't handle how ripe this feels." He stops at 'this' and slathers his palm with my wetness. "You feel that? You feel how juicy you are, Salem? So fucking hot and swollen, ready for me to take a bite." He bares his teeth at that and his thumb hits my clit as if pointing out *where* he'll bite me.

"And I'm going to, you understand? I'm going to eat that peach between your legs in a second. But I want you to know that I'm not myself. I'm not... *sane*. I need you to know that. I need you to know that I was going to go easy but I can't now. *Now*," he says, clenching his teeth, "I'm going to destroy your pussy. I'm going to fucking trash it and hurt her so good and in so many ways that you can't even begin to imagine. So if you want to back out, this is your last chance."

Is he crazy?

I'm not backing out. There's no way that I'll ever back out. In fact, I let go of my skirt and grab his naked shoulders, feminine pride bursting in me.

So, so much pride and love and lust.

"I don't wanna. Just..." I whisper.

"What?"

"Will you kiss me when you hurt my pussy?"

He grinds his jaw in response before he captures my mouth.

That's when I lose myself too. That's when I become insane like him.

That's when I lose my heart and my soul and I become his fuck doll.

So when he breaks off the kiss to take off my t-shirt, I simply raise my arms and let him. When he pushes me on the bed, I spread my legs to accommodate him, the girth of his shoulders. When he moves down my body, I fist his sun-struck hair and arch my back.

And when he licks me right at the center of my pussy, I moan.

I moan and moan as if I've been electrocuted.

By his hot, scorching tongue and his hands that hold my legs open for him.

For him to eat me.

To eat the pouty lips of my pussy, and that virgin hole that's never known anything other than my own fingers.

But now I know his tongue.

I know that his lips can suck on my flesh until I'm dying, and his tongue can circle the hole over and over until I'm screaming and writhing for him. I know that when he does all of that, he makes a sound.

A slurping sound.

A gulp as if he's drinking something delicious.

He's drinking *me* and he moves his head when he does it. He groans too as if I'm the tastiest thing he's ever swallowed, and he follows that groan with a lash on my clit.

He taps on it with his tongue and he bites it lightly with his teeth.

The bite is what does it.

That is what makes me break. A tiny little prick of his teeth on my clit and everything tight, tight, *tight* inside of me unravels.

The fist that was beginning to form in my lower belly opens up and I jerk and arch, coming into his mouth. My ass comes off the bed and he grabs my cheeks and tips me up.

He tilts up my pelvis and when I open my eyes, I find him drinking at my cunt.

I find him slurping and groaning, his dirty blond head buried and bent over my core, his hands plumping up my ass.

Just when I think I'll lose my mind even more at the erotic, hungry picture he makes, he lifts his head and I see that his jaw is covered in my cum and his eyes are bright with lust.

Licking his lips, he settles me down and I almost dissolve on the rumpled white sheets.

Especially when he climbs off the bed and begins to unbutton his jeans.

He does it all with tight, jerky movements, as if he's at the end of his rope and he hates everything that's keeping him away from me.

Even his jeans.

I can totally believe that. I can *totally* believe that he hates his jeans right now because God, the thing that they were confining was his dick.

And his dick is so. Fucking. Big.

And thick and dark-looking with a vein running on the underside of it. It curves slightly too, his shaft, at the end, the head fatter than the trunk.

Also, can I just say that it's so pretty? Like, I don't think I've ever seen anything prettier than his dick and I wonder if anything this big and capable of doing real damage can look pretty.

It does to me though and I go to tell him that.

I go to tell him that the way his thing curves and the way it's standing up straight, reaching his belly button, is so beautiful but the sound of crinkling distracts me.

He has a condom in his hands that I somehow missed, and now he's snapping it on his length. When he's done, he stands there, naked and gorgeous, staring at me, and my feet slide up and down his messy bed.

He looks at my hair that must be spilled all around his pillow, followed by my cheeks. He stays a beat longer on my nose, which he's always been so curious about, before going to my parted and painted lips. Then he looks at my heaving, flushed breasts and my trembling stomach. I still have my plaid skirt around my waist and my soccer cleats on, which I didn't realize that I hadn't taken off.

His eyes make me restless and I squirm on his bed, wanting him close. "Arrow."

He looks up then, and as soon as our eyes clash, I raise my arms up, calling him to me, beckoning him.

A tightness comes over his features, his body, for a second before he moves and comes to me. Into my arms and over my body, his hips settling between my thighs, his heavy cock rubbing against my lower stomach.

When his chain swings and grazes my lips, I suck it into my mouth and his eyes narrow with lust.

Pushing the metal out with my tongue, I tell him, "I love your chain. It makes you look sexy."

His latex-covered cock throbs on my stomach, his hands fisting the pillow on either side of me. "You mean, like my glares."

"Yeah, like that."

"You're a pain in my ass, you know that, don't you?"

He says it with such exasperation mixed in with a little bit of tenderness that I can't help but smile. "I know. But I think you like me anyway."

He hums, his lips twitching. "I think you shouldn't push your luck."

I grin and ask him something I've always wanted to ask. "Why do you always stare at my nose?"

He glances at it for a second before whispering, "Because you've got freckles on it. Thirteen, to be exact. And seven under your eyes."

Something about that makes a lump in my throat.

A big, huge, emotional lump and I swallow once, twice, and bury my fingers in his thick, rich hair.

"You've counted the freckles on my face?"

"They're a little hard to miss with how pale your skin is."

I swallow again and tighten my fists in his hair.

I love you.

My heart screams it but I know I can't say anything so I say something else. "I'm ready."

His chest moves and grazes the tips of my nipples before he comes closer. So much so that the strands of his hair brush against my forehead.

"It's going to hurt," he tells me in a guttural voice. "I don't know how much because I've never been with a virgin before. And –"

I cut him off with my wide eyes. Wide and questioning as my nails dig in his scalp.

I don't ask the question – the question that's suddenly blaring in my head – but he hears it anyway and it hollows out his stomach on a large exhale.

Stupid Salem.

What's wrong with me tonight? This is the second time I've fucked up.

"It's okay. You don't –"

But it's his turn to cut me off with a curt answer. "She wasn't."

Meaning my sister wasn't a virgin back when they got together, and for some reason I bring my thighs around his waist and squeeze him closer. My arms around his neck do the same.

Squeeze and hug.

His response is to stare at me for a harsh second as his cock becomes heavier, more swollen between our bodies, more ready to hurt me like he's never hurt anyone before.

"I want you to hold on to me," he orders.

I squeeze him with my limbs again. "Okay."

"Hold on tight, understand? Dig your nails in if you have to," he instructs and I nod, my heart filling up with so much love for him. "And if it hurts too much, tell me to stop."

I bite my lip, trying to keep the smile – despite the stupid moment a second ago – at bay. "Arrow?"

"What?"

I lean up and place a soft kiss on his lips. "Thanks for teaching me."

His eyes move over my face, all lustful and hot. "Pain in my ass."

Then he lifts himself up and positions his cock at my entrance. I suck in a breath and hold onto him like he told me. We stare at each other for a second before he twists his hips and enters me in one go.

Heat and stinging pain explode in my belly but instead of crying, I smile.

I smile even though I feel myself bleeding.

Even though I feel his big, fat cock throbbing inside of me, trying to stretch my body more than it's ever been stretched before.

Because he's inside of me.

My Arrow is inside my body and nothing will curb my happiness.

No amount of pain or burn will make my smile go away even as a tear rolls down from the corner of my eye.

Arrow sees it though and gets worried.

His sweaty forehead crinkles with a frown and he comes down at me. He gathers me in his arms and licks my tears away.

"Shh, it's okay. It's okay, baby. It'll go away, I promise," he whispers, all gently and tenderly.

Lovingly.

My smile at the ceiling becomes even brighter then.

At the way he then proceeds to rub his cheek against mine as if in affection.

I smile at the way he keeps shushing me, running his rough palms up and down the sides of my body, trying to loosen up the tension in me. At the way he blows hot breath on the side of my neck and my shoulders.

I smile at how he's my first and I'm his first too.

His very first virgin.

I smile at this unexpected gift.

I smile and smile at everything as his mouth begins to kiss me slowly and lazily like I asked him to. To kiss me while he hurts my pussy, and suddenly I can't stop touching him, touching his hot shoulders, his sweaty back, his bunched-up biceps.

And before I know it, we're moving.

We are rocking against each other and he breaks the kiss to raise himself over my body again, his palms on either side of my head.

His pumps are small and soft; they barely hurt. In fact, they produce a delicious friction that makes my thighs rise up and cinch around his waist, forcing him to move faster.

But he waits.

He stares down at me. To really make sure that I'm okay, and when he sees that I am, that I'm arching my back and digging my nails in his sides, he picks up the pace.

As soon as he does that, my pussy gushes cum for him, greasing up the way, and he takes advantage of that.

His strokes become short and jabbing and he's giving it to me now.

He's moving inside of me, pumping into me and I'm so tiny, so featherlight that my body is jiggling with his movements.

Moaning, I close my eyes when he hits a spot deep inside of me. It makes me sigh out his name. I bet it's that curved head of his pretty cock. It's rubbing up against something really crucial like my G spot, and I'm so close to coming.

My pussy is tightening up, spasming over his length and I feel him come back down to me, the sharp peaks of his body scraping against my soft ones.

He braces himself on his elbows and demands on a rough whisper, "Look at me."

I do.

I open my eyes against the erotic music of his flesh slapping mine.

"Who's fucking you?" he asks with clenched teeth.

I smell us in the air, the mixed scent of our bodies, musky and delicious, as I answer, "You."

"Yeah? What's my name?"

"A-Arrow."

"Say it."

Again he doesn't have to explain it. Somehow, I already know what he wants me to say.

"My Arrow's fucking me."

His eyes flare with possessiveness, with ownership, and his pumping graduates to pounding. "Who's inside of you, Salem?"

"My Arrow is inside of me."

"Who's making you bleed on his cock?"

"A-Arrow is making me bleed on his cock," I say, my thighs tangled around his waist, as the pressure in my stomach becomes an all-time high.

"And you'll remember that. You'll *remember* who this pussy belongs to," he growls.

I nod frantically, clenching my teeth. "Yes. Yes, this is my Arrow's pussy."

That's all I had to do. I had to call her his.

My Arrow's pussy.

And I come. I come on his cock.

I jerk under him, writhe and undulate like a wave and he tightens up.

He curses and strains, his cock expanding inside my channel. His head rears back, his spine bowing. I see his sweaty, hot body become tight and stone-like as his cock jerks inside of me and spurts the first dose of his cum in the latex.

We're both coming together then.

He's pulsing inside of me like I'm pulsing around him. I scratch his ridged abdomen and his hand fists my hair at the scalp.

I realize that's what he wanted to hear too – that I'm his.

That I'm my Arrow's, and I smile again.

CHAPTER EIGHTEEN

I'm still smiling about it the next morning.

Even though I didn't want to leave his side and that hot little cocoon of his dull gray room and rumpled sheets, I had to come back. So Arrow, after helping me shower, where he proceeded to lick me to another orgasm while soothing my sore pussy, and dressing me up in his t-shirt, dropped me off at the spot in the woods where I could sneak back in.

I didn't go to sleep though. Not right away.

Not until dawn broke in the sky, but still, I woke up at the designated time, got ready for classes, went to breakfast, and chatted with my friends, all of whom gave me knowing looks because I left with him in the middle of my dance with a smile on my face.

That's how I spend my entire day, smiling.

Even when Miller gives me extra homework – because I was smiling too much and daydreaming in her class – that I have to finish before next week, I still have a smile and that's how I enter the library, too.

Smiling.

I even greet the girl behind the reception desk with a friendly wave, which she obviously does not return but it's okay.

I'm happy.

I'm perfect. For him.

That's what he said, right? That I'm perfect.

I mean, yes it was only for sex but still. It was something.

I never had much interest in being perfect but ever since I was ten, I wanted to be perfect for *him*. I wanted to somehow bridge the gap between us and match him.

Turns out, I do.

I do match him and oh my God, I can't stop smiling.

And I thought this was the extent of my happiness, what I'm feeling right now. The bubbly, floaty sensation in my limbs and my stomach.

But I was wrong.

My happiness can be doubled. My happiness can be red hot. It can be bursting and pulsing and seeping out of my skin.

Because as soon as I turn around from the reception desk, my books against my chest, looking for an empty table where I can park myself and solve all the goddamn equations, I find him.

He's here and he's looking at me.

Like he was expecting me.

He's at a table in the corner, directly beneath the overhead light that brings out the gold in his hair. It brings out the gold in his skin too, especially in the curve of his bulging bicep when he raises his arm to rake his fingers through his strands.

My own fingers twitch when I see him do that, comb back the fallen strands, and my throat dries out at the sight of his beautiful face. At the hollows of his cheeks and the seam of his lips.

The blazing blue of his eyes.

It's wrong what they say. That when you die, your body turns cold and blue. No, blue doesn't mean winter and death.

Blue for me will always mean warm summer and life. Fire.

Blue for me will always mean him.

My Arrow.

He's sitting back in his chair, wearing his usual V-neck gray t-shirt, and when I simply keep standing in my spot, he folds his arms across his chest and raises his eyebrows, making him look all kinds of arrogant and sexy.

Then he does something even sexier, something that causes flutters to explode in my belly.

With his eyes on me, he nudges the chair by his side out with his foot. In a silent invitation to sit by him.

And I have to smile at that as well. I have to.

There's no way that I can't.

There's no way that I can't walk up to him now, my breaths and heartbeats a mess. My thighs a mess too. Of pulses and my wetness.

When I reach him and press the aching juncture between my legs against the table he's chosen, his gaze drops to it.

He licks his lips as if he knows that I'm wet down there and he's reliving my taste.

"You're here," I whisper.

He lifts his eyes. "I ran into your friends out in the courtyard. They told me you'd be here."

"So you came to see me?" I ask, breathless.

Resting his elbows on the arms of his chair, he commands, "Sit."

"What?"

"I heard you got extra homework."

"Uh, yeah."

"So I'm here to help you."

I press my books to my chest. "You're here to help me with my trig homework?"

Without answering me, he repeats, "Take a seat, Salem."

Confused and so totally floored because he came here to help me, I sit and put my books on the table. He straightens up and goes for them when I say, "Where were you all day? I was looking for you."

He pauses then, his hand in the process of opening my notebook. With his head bowed, I hear him sigh.

I'm not sure what that sigh means but I keep going, nonetheless. "I even came by your office but you weren't there."

I did go by his office during lunch.

Not sure for what. I mean, I wanted to see him but I wasn't sure what I'd do when I saw him.

Okay, I'm lying.

I knew exactly what I'd do when I saw him. I'd throw myself at him and climb his body and demand that he fuck me right then and there.

Again, he doesn't answer me and I frown.

He simply resumes flicking through my notebook until he comes upon a blank page. Then, he writes something on it.

I watch, mesmerized. Like I've never seen him write before. I have; we lived in the same house. I have seen him do his homework in the living room with my sister, but for some reason I can't stop watching.

I can't stop watching the way he grips the pen, so authoritatively, so *possessively* – like he gripped me last night – and how large and dominating his fist looks.

When he's done writing, he slides the notebook toward me.

In case you didn't realize it yet, we're at the library and the girls at the next table are watching us. They're watching every move you make. If they tell anyone and you get in trouble for flirting with the coach, I'm not going to like that. Personally when I don't like things, I choose to make it known. Very clearly. But I guess you don't want me to do that, do you? Since you're always telling me to be nice.

So unless you've changed your mind, I suggest you stop acting like an infatuated schoolgirl and let me help you with your homework, which you probably got because of me anyway.

There are so many things in this note that fill me with fluttery happiness. But then there are things that make me look up at him in outrage.

I even gasp before saying, "I'm not acting..."

Like an infatuated schoolgirl.

I don't say that but I think it, and of course he knows what I'm thinking. Because his lips twitch, amused at my reaction.

"Drama," he whispers, shaking his head slightly.

I gasp again. "I'm not..."

Damn it.

Taking a deep breath – because apparently some girls are *watching* and I can feel their stares now that he has mentioned it– I throw him a sweet smile. Then as calmly as possible, I go for the notebook and slide it toward myself so I can write him a very calm reply.

I'm not drama.

Okay, maybe I am. But in this instance, I'm righteously outraged. I'm not acting like an infatuated schoolgirl, you asshole. I was just happy to see you. And how do you know I got the extra homework because of you?

The minute that it takes me to finish the note, my dramatic antics are back, and I thrust the notebook at him.

He takes it with a slight smirk and his eyelids flicker and dip to read it. When he's done, he writes something back and inches the notebook toward me with his index finger.

Because I heard you were daydreaming about me while Miller was explaining the law of cosines.

What is the law of cosines, I wonder. But that's not important. There are other important things that we need to discuss.

How do you know that I was daydreaming about you?

To which he answers, *Because I fucked you into a coma last night. I've never seen a girl go straight to sleep after sex. I thought that's what guys did. So it's easy to deduce that you were dreaming about me and my legendary cock when you should've been focusing on the class.*

I peek at him through my eyelashes when I finish reading his note. His smirk is still in place but his eyes have become heavy.

Heavy with intensity and knowledge. With all the things he did to me last night, and whatever little outrage that I had melts away.

Jerk.

Why do I find him so adorable?

Why do I want to smack him and kiss him at the same time?

Biting my lip, I pretend to be irritated. *Oh please. *insert eye roll* I was not dreaming about you. And your cock isn't that legendary.*

It is. But he doesn't need to know that.

His answer is quick to come. *It is and you were. Because I was dreaming about you too.*

"You were?" I ask out loud and he sighs again, shaking his head once.

So I take to the notebook and pen another note. *What were you dreaming about?*

Eating a peach.

I read his note two times. Then, three.

By the time I'm done reading it the fourth time, my thighs are clenching and I'm squirming in my chair. I'm also crinkling and folding the corner of my page with sweaty, trembling fingers.

Do I really taste like that?

He does his lip-lick thing when he reads my note and when he's done reading, he shoots me a look. A hot blazing look, and I swallow.

Then he writes, pressing the tip of the pen really hard on the paper, *You mean do you really taste like a ripe fruit? All sweet and soft and made of sugar that when I take a bite, juices spill out of you and run down my chin? Fuck yeah, you do.*

I'm a mess down there.

A complete fucking mess. More than I was before. The wetness is seeping into my thong and going beyond it. Also I think I'm breathing too hard.

I'm breathing so loudly that the girls who are watching us still – I can feel their eyes – can hear me. They can tell that I'm on the verge of combusting and leaving my wetness in this chair.

My fruity, peachy, sugary wetness.

You have to stop talking like that, I write to him.

Then you should stop squirming like your peach is bursting to be eaten. You wet? he writes back.

My pen almost slips away from my grip when I answer, *Yes. So much.*

Yeah, I bet. I bet your pussy is all swollen and messy. Whining for me, isn't she?

Yes, she is. She wants you. I want you. Are you hard?

Like fuck. I ache. And you come here, looking so daisy fresh, so innocent and so soft in your schoolgirl uniform. So unlike the bad girl you are. Who wants to flip her skirt and flash me her pussy. You want to, don't you?

Yes, I want to.

That's why I'm squirming in my chair while those girls are watching us and the rest of the world is absorbed in their homework. That's why I want to tell him to meet me somewhere so I can show him how horny he makes me.

In fact, I'm even leaning against the table, searching for friction for my hard nipples as I reply, *Yes. I wanna. I so, so wanna. When can we do it again?*

I hear his pained chuckle and I notice that he's even more golden now, shinier and more glistening.

His note says, *I'm not going to have sex with you again right after I broke you in and made you bleed. I'm an asshole but I'm not a total bastard, Salem.*

Again, I read his note multiple times before I can gather enough sense to look up at him. I can't decide which I like more: him saying my name or writing it.

I guess I love it all. Just like I love him.

My darling, darling Arrow.

I pout at him, at his no-sex rule and his nostrils flare.

Then I pen him a request. *Okay, fine. But will you take me for a ride tonight?*

He reads my note and thinks about it for a second before answering, *Midnight tonight.*

It's a date. Yay!

I hear his sigh and when he passes me his reply, I hear him growl it in my ears, making me want to laugh.

Can we get back to trigonometry now?

I find him by his Ducati at midnight.

This is the first time I've snuck out all alone, without any help from my girls. I was a little nervous about it, but it turned out okay. What I should be more nervous about, or at least more anticipatory about, is the fact that I'm breaking one of his rules for the first time ever.

I'm wearing a skirt.

I borrowed it from Poe again, this one plaid too but with good-girl pleats and bad-girl length that barely covers my ass.

He's gonna freak, I know. But whatever. He can punish me if he likes. I have his jacket on though, which drowns me so it's not as if anyone can see anything.

Anyway, I'm here now.

I pause a moment to take him in. He's leaning against his motorcycle in his usual, familiar clothes that are already making me feel warm, smoking a cigarette.

His little bad habit.

A tiny rule that he breaks because it helps him relax and de-stress.

God, he's so hard on himself, isn't he?

So hard and critical. So tied up in severe knots.

That's why I came up with this idea. This ride at midnight. If I can't make him believe that he's not a failure, then at least I can help him let loose.

This broken boy.

This new Arrow.

The one who looks like a quintessential bad boy right now – seemingly dark hair, dark intentions, waiting for his teenage sweetheart that he's going to take away on his motorcycle. He's going to find a dark alley or a lonely corner under a rusty bridge somewhere and corrupt every little innocent part of her with those big hands and darling lips.

I begin walking toward him and the sound of my feet makes him look at me.

As soon as he does, he straightens up and lets out a puff of smoke and I start to run toward him like I did in our backyard.

Although I stumble just when I reach him, but he catches me, as usual. Panting, I hug him and close my eyes, pressing my cheek against his ribs, exactly where his heart is.

"If you don't stop doing that, I'll have to assume you're doing it on purpose," he drawls, his arms around me squeezing.

I rub my cheek on his chest. "Doing what on purpose?"

"Falling."

"Why would I do that on purpose?"

"So I could catch you."

I kiss his dead heart and look up. "Maybe I am."

He narrows his eyes at me as he squeezes me tighter and mutters, "Pain in the ass."

That I am and I'm going to become even more of a pain now.

"You're smoking," I tell him as I watch tendrils of smoke snake out of his gorgeous mouth.

"You're late."

"Why are you smoking?"

"Haven't we had this conversation before?"

We have and that's why I ask, my eyebrows raised, "So what are you trying to forget tonight?"

He stares down at me for a beat before growling, "We lost."

"The game?"

The clench of his jaw is my answer.

I raise my hand to cup his sharp cheek. "I'm sorry."

"We had it," he says, his eyes boring into mine. "We almost had it. It went into overtime and they had Rodriguez in the penalty shootout. It should've been me. I should've been there, taking that shot. And now we're out for the season. I –"

"Hey, hey," I cut him off, rising up on my tiptoes. "You will be there. You *will* do it. You just have to hold on for a little while." His jaw pulses under my palm and his eyes burn bright with anger, with self-hatred and I kiss his hot, smoking lips, trying to soften him up. "So will you please put out your cigarette so I can give you the gift I brought for you?"

Arrow simply watches me for a few seconds before the aggression leaches out of his body and he asks, "You brought me a gift?"

"Uh-huh."

"It's not a poem, is it?"

I swat his chest and a soft chuckle escapes him. "No, you idiot. Just help me up."

Again, he stares at me a beat before throwing his cigarette away and boosting me up and soon, I'm climbing over his body, my thighs around his slim waist and my arms clutching his shoulders.

But that's not the exciting part.

The exciting part is when he notices.

That I've broken his rule.

His hands grab my naked thighs, before inching up and covering the cheeks of my ass.

Bare cheeks.

"You're wearing a skirt," he growls, this time laced with sexual, dominating intent rather than anger.

Good.

At least he's not focusing on lost games.

I bite my lip and squirm in his lap, my bare pussy – I'm not wearing my thong tonight too – rubbing up against his t-shirt. "I know. I'm breaking one of your rules. So you can punish me if you like. But. Gift first!" I go fishing for his gift in my jacket pocket and produce it with a flourish. "That's why I was late. Because I stopped to bring this for you."

He doesn't look at it right away.

In fact, he stares into my eyes as he parts the cheeks of my ass with punishing fingers and when I bite my lip, only then does he glance down at my offering – a little flower, a gardenia, with a tiny green stem that I clipped for him from the garden.

"You brought me a flower," he rumbles, lifting his eyes.

I nod. "Yes. It's the official flower of St. Mary's, which you already know. But did you know that it also stands for purity and innocence?"

And secret love.

It also stands for secret love. But I'm not going to tell him that. Because this isn't about love, what we have. This is about making him feel better, even for a little while.

Instead of taking the flower, Arrow grabs a fistful of my ass and bounces me in his lap. "Purity and innocence."

I undulate against him shamelessly, trying to hold on to the flower with my trembling fingers. "Yes."

He bounces me again, causing an ache in my clit. "Yeah, I can see that. How innocent you look right now, giving me this flower. No bra. No panties. Nothing to cover up your perky, bouncing tits and your out-of-control pussy." He leans forward and bites my lower lip. "How innocent you looked last night, in my bed, when you gave up that flower between your legs."

I shudder. "Uh-huh. Totally. Innocent. But no one calls it a flower, Arrow."

"No? So what is it called then?"

His casual question is accompanied by a very *casual* flick of his thumb along the crease of my ass, making me moan.

But somehow, I manage to answer him demurely. "The p-word."

"Ah, the p-word." His thumb still moves up and down my crease. "Peach, you mean."

I shake my head and bite *his* lip. "You know what I mean, asshole. Stop teasing me and take my flower."

He chuckles then before snatching my mouth in a kiss and bringing his thumb down to my soppy pussy where he wreaks havoc on my clit. He doesn't let go until I climax.

Until I'm coming on his t-shirt.

Only then he slides me down his body with hooded eyes, takes my flower and takes me out on a date.

First stop is the ice cream parlor, all the way in the college town of Middlemarch. It's almost deserted, with only a handful of people inside the store. When he asks for a vanilla cone for himself, I chirp in and tell the guy behind the counter that *my* guy will take a chocolate cone with all the chips and sprinkles and trappings, just like me.

When Arrow gives me a look, I say, "You wanna be boring all your life or do you wanna be awesome like me?"

At which, Arrow grabs the back of my neck and lays a hard kiss on my lips, right in front of the counter guy.

Once we have our ice creams, we go outside and I straddle the Ducati that he parked on the empty street, and lick my cone.

At first he's simply leaning against the motorcycle, his face both lit up and shadowed under the insufficient street light as he watches me lick my ice cream. Then he throws away his cone and straddles the bike too.

Eyes heavy, he grabs my waist and yanks me over to him, my juices probably streaking a path across his leather seat. "I ruined your seat."

He drapes my bare legs over his powerful thighs, opening them up. "Not yet, you haven't."

Before I can say anything else, he sticks his hand under the jacket that I'm wearing and in turn, under the hem of my skirt and kisses me with ice-cream cold lips.

Shivering, I kiss him back, forgetting about the cone in my hand.

I jump when I feel something on my pussy.

Something other than his fingers.

Something like my flower.

The flower I gave him back at St. Mary's that he pocketed, right where his dead heart is.

Arrow is touching me with it.

I don't know when he got it out and when he snuck it under my skirt but he's sliding the flower along my slit, twirling it over my clit.

"Arrow..." I moan, my thighs trying to snap closed, but they can't because he has them trapped over his thighs and around his hips.

"Now there's a flower between your legs, isn't there?" he murmurs, chuckling, blowing hot, sweet breath over my lips as he plays with my core and again, doesn't let me go until I come.

Until I ruin his gift and his fingers with my juices.

Until I ruin my fingers too, with sticky, melted ice cream.

Then he takes me away again.

He takes me everywhere I want to go.

Until I tell him to find us a secluded spot because I wanna suck him off and lick him like my ice cream cone.

We stop under a rusty bridge in Bardstown, and in under five seconds, I have him against a brick pillar and me, on my knees, looking up at him.

I reach up and massage his hard cock through his jeans. I rub my cheek on the imprint of his dick, feeling his inferno-heat on my skin, as he looks down at me.

"I'm always so cold, Arrow," I tell him. "You're the only one who makes me feel warm. You're my sun."

His jaw becomes hard and cruel almost, his hands fisted at his sides. "So are you going to thank me for it?"

I reach up and kiss one, his fist I mean.

I kiss his knuckles, lick them, trying to soften them up, and it works.

His fingers open up.

They get hold of my jaw, forcing me to look up. "Unzip me."

Of course, I jump to do his bidding.

When I'm done, he pushes down his jeans and a second later, I'm looking at his cock, his beautiful cock with a pretty arch and that vein running underneath, all fat and juicy for me.

"Your dick is so pretty," I whisper as I stare at it with wide eyes, my knees grinding on the concrete, my nails raking up and down his partially-covered thighs.

His stomach tightens up and his pretty dick lurches. "Pretty."

"Uh-huh. So, *so* pretty."

He fists my hair and pulls at it, making me arch my neck, my back, making me lose my balance and fall against his thigh. "Pretty is not the word I'd call my dick, but I'll give you a pass tonight."

I clench my thighs. "Why?"

"Because you're going to put it in your mouth and suck it like your life depends on it. And because I'm going to fuck your pouty lips like I fucked your pouty pussy last night. And when you struggle to take me in, because I'm so big and fat for your innocent schoolgirl mouth, you'll make me blow. Right on your tongue, and when I do that, you're going to swallow it all, aren't you? You're going to swallow everything I give you like a good girl. So you can call it whatever the fuck you want, baby, because all I care about is sliding into your mouth and riding it to heaven," he says with clenched teeth and flushed cheeks, all dominating and large like the sun he is.

My breaths come out as a series of hiccups as I nod eagerly, my cheek bumping with the curve of his dick.

"I will, I will," I whisper, eagerly.

His eyes glow. "Then what are you waiting for?"

At this, I take him into my mouth.

I suck on his head with my pouty lips, his flavor exploding. Not only on my tongue but everywhere. My toes and my legs and my stomach and my chest.

Everywhere I feel his heat and his spice.

He pulls his t-shirt up and moves it out of the way to watch me pleasure him. His eyes bore into mine and it makes me both shy and bold at the same time. Or at least, it makes my mouth bold and I begin vacuuming him in.

But my eyes can't keep up. His stare is too much and I have to close them.

Even so, I feel his lustful stare.

I even see him in my head.

I see him, leaning against the wall like a god or a king, as I serve him like the overeager groupie I am. I dig my tongue into the tiny slit of his cock up top, curling it to scoop out his cum, and when he grunts above me, his hips arching off the wall, I feel that everywhere too.

Just like his taste, I feel his lusty, animal noises in every part of my body.

Especially in my hands when I wrap them around his beautiful dick, before enveloping it in my mouth as much as I can and fucking him.

God, his dick *is* beautiful. A piece of art on my tongue.

So heavy and meaty.

So flavorful.

His dick is my baby and I make love to it with my tongue and my lips.

It works because he grunts again.

Not only that, his hips are moving and arching and when I open my eyes to look up, I see that his head is thrown back, bunched up in a thick frown and he's got his t-shirt clenched between his teeth as he pumps his hips.

That clench. Holy fuck.

The strain in his jaw and those tight muscles on his abdomen. The sweat misting his hot flesh as he fists my hair.

Everything about him is so fucking beautiful that I redouble my efforts. I move my hands faster. I move my lips faster too. And he becomes harder, plumper, prettier and tastier in my mouth.

So much more aggressive and harsher until he simply explodes.

His cock jerks and shoots cum down my throat and I swallow it all like he told me to.

I drink up the liquid heat of his orgasm. It flows down my throat and settles in my stomach, warming me up.

I keep doing it until he's done.

Until he sighs out a big breath and his fists loosen up. Until he relaxes against the wall and looks down at me with slitted eyes.

When our gazes clash, I pant and wipe my mouth off with the back of my hand. "Thank you."

A big puff of air escapes him and, bending down, he puts his hands under my armpits and pulls me up, making me climb his body once again.

I rest my head against his shoulders. "You taste like fire, all hot and tangy."

His answer is to place a soft, silent kiss on my forehead and walk back to his motorcycle.

An hour later when he drops me off at St. Mary's and I sneak back into my room, I can still taste him on my lips.

I'm so high on it, so engrossed in his fiery taste, that my heart punches right out of my chest when I hear my roommate's first words to me. "Did you go somewhere?"

I'm almost all the way down on the bed, my blanket poised over me when she asks me this. And I don't know how but I answer her.

"Yes. Bathroom."

It comes out squeaky and high and all the things that should tell her that I'm lying.

I'm fucking lying.

But she accepts it and turns around in the bed to face away from me and promptly starts snoring.

CHAPTER NINETEEN

Elanor gives me weird looks the next day and the day after that, and the day after *that*.

Or maybe it's me.

Maybe I'm imagining things.

Because honestly, she always gives me weird looks, along with her other three friends. Although they don't harass me anymore.

Not since Arrow put them in their place.

So I don't know if I should be worried about what happened that night, the night I got back from my ride with Arrow.

I don't know if I should be worried that my roommate might know something. And if she knows then other people might come to know too.

People like the principal, my guardian, Leah.

She'll be super disappointed in me for sneaking out and breaking rules like this, when her main aim in sending me here was to learn to follow them. If she finds out that I go to see Arrow, then I don't know how severely she might react.

I'm not an ideal candidate for her son. Not that we're in any kind of a relationship but still.

And my sister.

She'll definitely think I'm a whore. Even though in my heart I know that I'm not.

Not to mention my letters.

I still need to hide them. But the thought of not having them close gives me so much anxiety that I haven't been able to move the shoeboxes.

But I will.

I promise myself that I'll be smart and I'll hide them as soon as I get a chance.

Meanwhile though, I should stop.

I know. I shouldn't take the risk.

If by some miracle Elanor doesn't know anything and I'm imagining everything, then I got really lucky that night.

I shouldn't tempt fate.

In fact, I'm not the only one who's tempting fate. There's someone else too.

Callie.

She sneaks out like me, all alone. I think she goes out to see Reed Jackson. The guy we saw at the bar a few weeks ago.

I've caught her a couple of times but never said anything because she's always given me my space. But I decide to say something after the Elanor incident.

"Is it him?" I ask her one day, pulling her aside in the library, and she flushes.

I don't have to explain to her who *him* is. Her gorgeous villain.

"Not really. But yeah." Then, "Is it him?"

And she doesn't have to elaborate on who my *him* is either. My darling Arrow.

"Yes." I nod. "Are you going to stop?"

She bites her lip for a second before shaking her head.

I smile sadly at her. "Yeah, me neither."

"You love him, don't you?" she asks, but when I clam up, she raises her hands. "It's okay. You don't have to tell me and I don't need an answer… to *know*."

I smile. "Do you? Love him, I mean."

She doesn't clam up but there's a sad smile on her lips. "Guys like that, you don't love them. You get consumed by them and then you wonder if there was ever a time you didn't think about them or feel them or hear them. Or see them in your dreams."

Yeah.

She's right. You don't love guys like that. You get eaten up by them and you love every bite they take out of you.

So we're both tempting fate. And the truth is that we probably will keep doing it.

Or at least, I will.

I will keep sneaking out of my room, scaling the fence and meeting Arrow at midnight. I will keep going out on rides with him where he speeds and I lean back and open my arms, letting my hair fly. I will keep going to his motel room with him too.

That dull gray room where I became his.

Because how can I not?

He needs me, doesn't he?

He needs me to distract him from all the things inside of him.

He needs me to be a giant pain in his ass and tell him to put out his stupid cigarette when he gets stressed over his supposed failures. Over the fact that he wasn't with the team, helping them win. When he doesn't listen to me and puts out his cancer stick, he needs me to put my mouth on his and kiss him, inhaling that smoke into my own lungs.

When he fists my hair and pulls my mouth back, looking all hot and angry, he needs me to tell him, "If you wanna kill yourself, then I'll die with you too."

And when he gets all jacked up by that, he needs me to spread my legs so he can fuck it all out of his system.

Oh, and he needs me to show him all the chick flicks so he doesn't keep watching the game tapes over and over, analyzing his team's every move.

And when he works out too hard, he needs me to wipe off his sweat.

Because Jesus Christ, he does.

He does work out too hard.

All those weights in his room that I saw the first night, they are for his training. Just because he's sitting this season out doesn't mean that he can slack off.

In fact, he's working harder than ever.

Every morning, he goes for a run. He works on his own drills at the local club house.

Every night when I go to sleep after the awesome sex – he was right; I do slip into a coma-like nap after sex – he works out again, a few feet away from the bed.

One night I wake up from my nap and catch him doing pushups on the floor. On one fucking hand. His other arm is up and folded at his lower back, and he's shirtless.

When I turn on my stomach to get a good look at him, Arrow's eyes snap up.

They're all dark and burning up with this aggression inside of him.

Sweat drips from his forehead as he watches me and does rep after rep. I see the planes on his back moving and shifting, like wings of some kind.

Tight muscles that bunch and release. Or maybe mountains, emerging from his back before disappearing within his body with every rep.

It's such an aggressive and masculine thing, the dance of his muscles and his harsh stare, that I rise up from the bed.

I let the sheet fall away from my shoulders and pool at my knees, leaving me naked, my hair swaying at my back.

Arrow's nostrils flare at the sight of me, but he doesn't falter.

He keeps going up and down, his breaths noisy and whooshing, his muscles in a state of constant making and unmaking.

When I'm on the floor, I come down on all fours and begin to crawl over to him.

He narrows his eyes at me, still going up and down, and I crawl and crawl until I reach him.

Until I'm so close to him that his sweat-drenched hair grazes my chest and my stomach. Until the puffs of his heaving breaths explode on my naked skin and his silver chain hits my ribs and my belly button.

I put my hand on his shoulder to find that he's burning.

"Stop," I whisper.

His muscles flex and he works harder, if at all possible.

"Stop, Arrow."

No effect.

"Please? For me?"

That does it.

He stops then.

But if I thought he'd go down on the floor in a heap of tired and burning muscles because God, they've got to be burning, then I'm wrong.

Because he comes up on his knees, sweat running like a river between his heaving pecs, and grabs my hair in a fist, making me look up at him.

"I had it," he bites out, glaring at me.

I put my hand on his sweat-shiny chest; his dead heart is thundering. "I know you did."

"Twenty more reps and I would've been done," he pants. "I would've broken my record."

See? I knew it.

I knew he was trying to break some kind of a record.

My *stupid*, darling Arrow, always trying to prove something. Always trying to be perfect when he already is so, so perfect.

"And probably killed yourself in the process."

He leans down on me and the droplets of his sweat plop down on my body like rain. "I. Had. It."

I study him for a beat, his panting, tight body, and I wind my arms around his neck. I go flush with his chest, his sweat slathering on my tits and stomach.

"Do you remember the time in your junior year?" I ask against his lips, my tongue peeking out to lick up the sweat and I can barely contain my moan at his musky taste. "You had a game. And you were playing your rival school and you guys were trying man-to-man marking for the first time?"

His eyes go back and forth between mine. "Yeah."

"And since it was new to you, you practiced like crazy, and the night before the game, you didn't even come home. Because you were practicing."

He didn't; I remember that.

I wonder if he was smoking then. If the stress of the game became too much for him and he almost killed himself for it, like he's doing now.

"What about it?"

I shake my head at him. "It was stupid then and it's stupid now."

His fist tightens in my hair and he finally puts his other hand on me. On my ass; he loves my ass. Or at least, he loves spanking it and worrying and plumping the flesh.

Arrow pulls at my cheek. Hard. "Excuse me?"

But I don't get deterred; I pull at his sweaty hair in response. "You were and you are."

"We won that game."

I know. I was there. He doesn't know it but still.

"So? Winning doesn't mean you kill yourself for it. If that's what you're doing all the time, all this stress and all this pressure, then how do you enjoy it? The game that you love so much."

"I don't play to enjoy the game. I play to win it."

"So what do you do when you want to have fun?"

"I fuck you."

I clench my thighs. "So are you going to?"

"Is that why you crawled over to me? All naked and pretty. Because you want to get fucked?"

My channel is pulsing at his rough tone. "Yes. But also to stop you."

"From killing myself."

"Yes." I pull at his hair again. "Because if you wanna kill yourself, I'll die with you too. Remember?"

His fingers on my body tighten and tighten to the point where it hurts so deliciously. "You're a goddamn pain in my ass."

"But will you still kiss me?" I ask, all shy and pretty like a good girl.

And he does.

He kisses me and then he fucks me on the floor and I spread my legs as far as they go and arch my back. I let him take out all his frustration on my body as he grinds into me with his big, fat cock.

But that's not all he needs me for.

He also needs me to slip sexy little notes into his mailbox at St. Mary's.

Because the other day, he ordered me to stop or I'm risking being caught flirting with the coach. Not to mention, it's his rule that he won't do anything on the school grounds.

Please.

Obviously, I break both his rules so he can break them too, and see that the world doesn't fall apart when he does.

So I send him little notes about how much I need him and I keep sending them until *he* sends for me. When I get there, wearing my mustard-colored skirt and my hair tied up in a braid, I find him sitting in his throne-like chair.

He tells me to lock the door first.

Then he tells me to untie my hair and when I do that, he commands, "Show me."

With my back against the door, I inch up my skirt. I slide my thong off my core and show him the peach between my legs.

He stares at it for a few seconds, his fingers gripping the arm of his chair in a harsh, violent grip before he commands me to play with my pussy.

I do that too until I make a mess of my fingers and my thighs, and until he's springing from his chair and coming at me. Picking me up, he brings me to his desk and spreads me out like a meal he's about to consume.

Flipping my skirt up, he enters me in one go and I arch my back.

"But I-I thought you had a rule," I tell him, scratching his abdomen under his t-shirt as he pounds into me.

"I changed my mind," he growls, fisting my messy hair. "You need my cock. So I can straighten out your bad girl pussy, bang her into shape."

Biting my lip, I smile and moan and scratch. "And see? The world is still well and alive around us even if you broke a rule to make me a good girl."

That makes him pause for a second, his lips parted and swollen from my kisses, his eyes lust-burnt.

"You think you're so smart, don't you?" he growls, punctuating those words with a harsh stab of his cock, making my entire body jiggle. "But that's not what you are, remember?"

I pant, my thighs trembling around his hips. "Arrow…"

Grabbing the edge of his desk over my head, he shoves his cock into me again, inching that heavy piece of furniture up with the force. "Tell me who you are."

I dig my nails into his stomach when he stops, waiting for my answer. "Your fuck doll."

"Yeah, so you don't make the rules, do you?"

"No."

"Who does then?"

"My Arrow makes the rules."

Still, he doesn't move, making me wait and wait and wait…

"Arrow, please…"

"It hurts, doesn't it?" he asks, his chain pooling on my throat, over my madly pulsing vein. "It hurts to wait. Is your pouty, bratty pussy hurting, Salem?"

I squirm my ass on his desk. "Yes."

His dick lurches inside of me, throbs like my soppy channel, and yet he's stubbornly stationary.

"Who's making it hurt, baby?" he whispers, going for my lip, nipping the fat curve of it.

"You," I reply. "My Arrow is making my pussy hurt."

As soon as I've said it, he gives me what I want.

He resumes his movements and I close my eyes in relief.

"And who's making your pussy feel good now?" He licks the spot on my lip that he's just nicked with his sharp teeth.

"My Arrow." I grab his sweaty hips, urging him to move faster. "My Arrow is making my pussy feel good."

When he makes me come a few minutes later and empties himself inside of me – or the condom actually – almost simultaneously, I wonder again.

How can I stop?

He needs me.

He needs me to love him.

Because if I don't, then his rage will eat him alive.

His rules and aggression. His pursuit for perfection.

His anger.

So yeah, I can't stop.

I have to tempt fate.

For him.

It's way past midnight and I've just woken up after my coma-like after-sex nap.

I'm at the foot of his bed and I blink my eyes open to find him directly opposite to me, propped up on the pillows, chest bare and one of his knees bent.

He's reading something on his iPad that's resting on his folded leg, a frown of concentration between his brows.

Well, at least he isn't killing himself down on the floor like he usually does.

I watch him for a second, absorbed in whatever he's reading, all lit up and sexy under the yellow light of his lamp.

This is exactly how he used to look back when we lived together while he did his homework or studied for a test. I'd watch him, hiding behind a wall or a piece of furniture, wishing I could go talk to him. I could tell him *good luck* or *I know you'll do great on the test* or something.

Which makes me realize that I can do that now. I can tell him things.

At least, some things.

So I move.

I get under the sheet and slither toward him in the yellowed darkness. I kiss his foot, the naked calf of his leg that's stretched out.

Getting on all fours, I shower kisses on his pretty dick. It was flaccid before, but now it's hard and radiating his signature heat.

Every time my lips touch his hot flesh, he tightens, his muscles strain and his dick becomes even harder.

I smell it and moan.

I suck his head into my mouth and hum, my body writhing on its own, reveling in his taste. I'm about to dig my tongue into the little slit up top to bring out more of his juices, but his hand creeps inside the sheet and fists my hair.

He jerks me away and forces me to crawl over his sexy, muscular body. Until I'm out of the sheets and straddling his tight abdomen, his cock in the crease of my ass.

"Hi," I whisper, smiling.

Arrow takes his time studying me, my naked form. His hooded eyes sweep over my face as he counts my freckles before moving down. He stares at my pointed dark berry-like nipples – he calls them pouty too – before twisting one with his fingers, making them harder and achier.

He smirks. "Hey."

I put my hands on his chest and play with his chain. "Why'd you make me stop?"

"Because we need to go in a little while."

"Can't I stay with you?" I pout.

Moving away from my breast, he brings both his hands to my ass and grabs the flesh. "No."

"Maybe a little longer?"

"No."

I pout harder. "Why not?"

"Because I don't need a needy girl clinging on my back."

I slap his chest and he swats my ass. Then, "And because I've got something to say."

At this, I completely sober up.

Arrow never has something to say. *Never.*

I'm the one with all the things to say.

So I frown and look into his eyes; they're slightly amused. "You've got something to say?"

"Yeah."

I lick my lips and his eyes take in the movement like they always do. He asked me what my lipstick was called as soon as I met him at his motorcycle. When I replied Good Bad Girl, he proceeded to wipe it off my lips with his mouth before spreading me open on his motorcycle and eating out my bad girl pussy.

I shiver at the memory but manage to control myself. "Well, what is it?"

He studies me a beat and I start to die with all the anticipation when he murmurs, "I think you should apply for the Galaxy's youth program for next summer."

"What?"

"Yeah." He nods thoughtfully. "They pick people from high schools and colleges and train them to go pro. And they have summer camps every year. I played with them, back in high school one summer. They're pretty good. Taught me a lot."

I know he did.

He was a junior when he went. That entire summer I missed him like crazy. I didn't feel the sunshine until he came back. As always, I wanted to run over to him but couldn't. So I watched him from afar, while he greeted his mother and hugged my sister.

"You want me to go there," I say.

"To the youth program, yes."

I open and close my mouth for a second before I manage to ask, "Are you saying that I... I play soccer. Like for real. On a team."

"Yes."

"But I've never played soccer for real. I-I mean, I don't even know how to play with a team. You said it yourself that first week. I'm not... I'm not good enough for that."

I mean, I have improved.

I do play with the team now and try to gauge their plays and assist them. Plus Arrow trains me three times a week.

We do all kinds of drills and God, the way he makes me run. It's only for an hour but I almost want to die by the end of it.

The other night, he taught me how to head the ball. He told me that you don't really use your head. You use your shoulders and your upper body. You get the strength from there and balance from your legs and then you shoot from your head, all the while poking and prodding at my body and positioning me.

"What happens if I don't follow these rules?" I asked, just to tease him because he was starting to look really serious.

He spun the ball on his finger before launching it in the air and kicking the shit out of it. It soared over the field and punched the net right in the center.

"Then you break your neck and you die. Or you break your neck and spend the rest of your life in a wheelchair. Now can we start?"

God, he's so sexy and authoritative, isn't he?

Plus we watch game tapes together. Well, when I'm not forcing him to watch chick flicks. He teaches me things from it. Like why he didn't go for that shot or why he went for the one he did go for. And sometimes, I argue.

"You know, you're so very careful about these things. You could've easily made that shot," I said about one of the plays that he deliberately missed.

"You see that?" He pointed to the screen. "That's a defender. He's right there. He would've stopped it."

"No, he wouldn't have. If you just bent your leg a little, got enough momentum in your body to kick the ball harder than you usually do, the ball would've flown right past him and hit the net."

"I knew what I was doing. You don't take chances like that at a championship game."

"*I* would've done it."

"That's because you're reckless."

I stuck my tongue out at him and said in a sing-songy voice, "And you're boring."

That did not go over well with him.

Or it did go over well, if you count him fucking me into submission while the game played in the background and he won the trophy.

So I don't know. I mean, I don't think I'm good enough to play on a team, you know?

I can kick around a ball with him and talk strategies, but an actual team?

Yikes.

"You're not good enough," he murmurs, bringing me back to the moment.

"I, uh, I mean I don't know. I'm not..."

"Did I say that?" he asks.

"No, Sarah..."

I trail off as soon as I say her name.

My sister's name.

His ex-girlfriend, the girl who cheated on him, while I'm sitting naked on his stomach, my wetness probably slathered on his skin.

His jaw clenches.

That muscle on his cheek jumps out as well.

I didn't mean to say that. I didn't mean to bring her up. And I haven't.

Ever since that night in our backyard where he told me about Sarah and Ben and how they've hurt him, I haven't said a word about it.

I haven't tried to talk to him further about what he feels.

I know he wouldn't talk. I *know* that.

I mean, he still hasn't told anyone about the cheating. He's so ashamed of it. Leah and everyone on his team still don't know.

So he wouldn't believe me even if I told him that he isn't a failure. That Sarah's mistakes and his breakup don't mean that *he* isn't perfect. That being kicked off the team because of it is only a minor hiccup and that it's okay to make mistakes and fall down.

It's *okay*.

But maybe, just *maybe* I should try again.

I should try to make him understand and...

Arrow chooses that moment to move away from the pillow and get up in my face. Not only that, his hands on my ass become brutalizing.

So deliciously brutalizing – despite the heaviness of the situation – that I have to arch up my back and hold onto his shoulders to keep myself balanced.

"Sarah," he bites out, staring so harshly into my eyes that it makes me catch my breath, "doesn't understand. She doesn't have the capability to understand how someone *not* like her can be so fucking magnificent. How someone not like her can fly on legs and flow through spaces and shine through cracks. She doesn't understand how someone *not* like her, someone who doesn't follow the rules, someone who makes her own rules, can bend the direction of a river when all she's done her entire life is trying to flow with it. And what she doesn't understand, scares the fuck out of her."

His fingers dig and dig into my flesh until I have to bite the inside of my cheek to keep my moan inside. Until I feel my eyes welling up.

But that could also be because... he's said something that I never thought before.

I never thought that about myself before.

I always knew that I wasn't perfect and I was okay with it, but I never thought that I could... do all those things that he just mentioned.

All those fantastical, magical things and...

God.

"Do *you* understand that?" he asks, his teeth gritted, the veins on his neck standing out.

I swallow, trying to control all my emotions.

All the raging, burning emotions.

I guess...

I guess I was wrong.

All this time I thought that he needed me. But I needed him too.

To tell me. To say wonderful things to me.

A thick stream of tears still spills out, which makes him go tight.

Tighter than before.

"What the fuck?" he asks, in total disbelief that I'm crying.

He's watching me with total disbelief too.

In fact, his hands are gone from my ass and have come up to my face, where he's wiping the tears and going, "What..."

Grabbing his wrists, I shake my head as more tears fall. "N-no. It's not..." I wave a hand in front of my face and take deep breaths. "I'm not... crying. Like, I'm not sad. I'm happy. These are happy tears."

He watches me for a beat, his hands still on my cheeks. "You cry when you're happy."

"Yeah." I nod and his expression is so bemused and adorable that I let out a broken laugh. "I also dance at sad songs."

He opens and closes his mouth, totally confused.

I lean over and kiss him on the lips. "My favorite is Lana Del Rey."

"Who the fuck is that?"

"I'll play you some songs. She's the goddess of sad love songs."

"I'll take your word for it."

I kiss his cheek while he's still wiping off my tears. "And I like empty ruined bridges."

"That I knew."

"And all the weird, lonely places in the world. And I like airport scenes in the movies and I love sprinkles on ice cream and I wear my soccer cleats everywhere," I whisper, beginning to rock against him anew. "And no one's ever been so nice to me before."

Finally, his lips tip up. "Isn't that the first rule of friendship?"

"Yeah."

"Well, I'm nothing if not a rule-follower."

I hum, our kisses growing salty.

I rise up on my knees and position myself over his hard cock. Looking into his eyes, I grab a condom from the nightstand and roll it over his length – something he taught his virgin fuck doll – before taking him inside my body.

Then I ride him.

All the while I tell him with my eyes, all the other things about me.

Things like I write letters. Love letters to him.

I put them in an envelope to never send them and then hide them in a shoebox.

I keep that shoebox under my bed.

Because I can't imagine sleeping without it.

I do all of that because I love him.

I've been in love with him since I was ten and he was fifteen.

I tell him that with my writhing, moving body because he's my Arrow.

He's my sun.

And like the sun he is, he gave me a gift.

He lit a fire inside of me, inside of my stomach. Of ambition. Like he lit a fire in my heart the day I fell in love with him.

That fire burns and burns until Monday comes and I find a note in my locker from him, after which all the fire dies out from my body and from this world.

By the time you find this, I'll be gone. I have to go to LA – something came up. But I'll be back in a week.

CHAPTER TWENTY

The Broken Arrow

W hen I left LA a couple of months ago, I was angry.

People were angry at me as well.

My teammates, my coaches. The PR team, the managers. *Everyone.*

They thought I'd lost my mind, coming to practice drunk and picking a fight with an important member of the staff, one who's been working for the team longer than I have. Especially when that member was a good friend of mine. The only friend.

Especially when I've never had a temper problem before.

I think for a second there when they found out that I did it because I'd just broken up with my girlfriend of eight years, they were sympathetic.

But when I refused to apologize after hitting him, their sympathy went away.

Overnight, I became a loose cannon. Who needed to calm down before he could be an asset to the team. Or at least, that's what Coach told me.

I don't remember much other than the usual jitters in my thighs and the crawling of my skin. The shame of failing.

The shame of making a mistake, breaking a rule.

Anyway, he also told me to attend this party that I'm at to look more like a team player, which has never been a problem before because I always played with the team. A good player – the best player – understands that you can't win a game alone. You *can* be the MVP but it's always a team effort.

Besides, I didn't think I'd be welcome here.

It's okay though.

If Coach wants me to show my face and prove to them that I'm a team player – even though they should already fucking know it – I'll do that.

Even if it means enduring their angry, suspicious looks. Accusatory looks.

They all think the same thing: we lost because of me.

I can see it in their eyes. I can feel it in the tightness of my skin, in the heat under my collar.

But it's the price I have to pay for breaking the rules and hitting that dickhead.

The party is a little thing one of my teammates has put together after the grueling promotional week we've had. Since we're out for the season now, PR team thought touring high schools and colleges to talk about the Galaxy's youth program and encouraging players to join next summer is a wise way to spend our unexpected free time.

I'm not much for touring or parties; I'd rather be home, either working out, resting my body or watching game tapes.

So it's not a surprise to anyone – in fact, I think they're all very relieved – when I choose to leave the room and stand out on the balcony, alone. Although tonight, instead of watching the waves – it's a beachfront property in Malibu – I'm watching my teammates.

I'm watching how well they mingle with each other. How much they enjoy each other. How they're laughing and thumping each other on the back.

This isn't the first time that I've seen all this but still.

It's so fucking strange to me.

I've always believed that nothing should take away from my focus.

Not friends, not parties. Nothing should stand between me and the game.

I don't think that I've ever thumped anyone on their back. Well, unless they've scored a goal on the field, but still.

As I look at them now, I wonder.

Maybe there's another way. Maybe I should try to... *enjoy* things more, for the lack of a better word.

But then all my thoughts vanish except for one.

Sarah.

She's just entered the room and I viciously take a gulp of beer from the forgotten bottle in my hand.

For a second there I thought it was *her*.

The girl with thirteen freckles and witchy eyes. That's what she calls them; she told me one night.

"See how they turn up." She pointed to the corners, sitting on my motorcycle, her legs dangling. "My eyes are witchy. Like my name. Salem. It's a witchy name, isn't it?"

She blinked up at me with such a wide, innocent look that I bit out, "Says who?"

"I don't know. People."

"Fuck people."

She smiled then. "So do you think you like it?"

"If I say yes, you won't make me write a poem about it, will you?"

"Shut up. Do you think you do?"

"*I* think I've never met a Salem before you."

"Yeah?" She grinned. "So I'm your first Salem?"

"Yes."

"Good. Because you're my first Arrow too."

She blew me a kiss then and I had to retaliate. I had to eat up her lips, painted with I Jinx U and her smile.

It's not her though.

It's not the girl with witchy eyes, it's her sister.

The girl who betrayed me. The girl who catches my eye a second later and begins to walk toward me.

I clench my fingers around the bottle as I see her approach.

Back when I first started dating her, she was pretty. Hot too.

But over the years, she's turned into a beauty. In a tight but tasteful black dress, she is easily the most beautiful woman in the room.

Someone I could have by my side while I focused on soccer. Someone who'd travel with me if she wanted to but have her own career, someone who knew how to handle the attention that being with an athlete brings.

Sarah was a perfect partner.

Well, until she wasn't.

Until she chose to fuck my friend behind my back.

"Hi," she says as soon as she slides the glass door open and steps outside.

I take a pull of the beer. "Wasn't expecting to see you here."

It's the truth.

She still lives in our apartment and so I chose to stay at a hotel for the duration of the week, which reminds me that I'll have to look for a different place before I move back.

Apart from that she has been scarce from all the events, which has been welcome but pretty strange. Given the fact that her team came up with this whole bullshit idea.

She tucks her hair behind her ear. "Bobby is my friend too. Plus it's business. Everyone from the team and management is here."

"Except your new boyfriend."

I was wondering if I'd finally see Ben.

Like Sarah, I haven't seen him all week and I'm guessing it's because everyone is trying to keep us apart.

Good thinking.

"I told him not to come," she replies. "I knew you wouldn't like that."

"Still taking care of me, huh?"

This time when I clench my fingers around the bottle, I almost feel the glass give under the force of my grip.

She sighs, a frown adorning her face. "I told you, A. I still care about you. That doesn't go away just because of what happened between us. We were together for eight years."

"Yeah, or maybe you're afraid that I'll break his jaw again."

Sarah steps closer to me and I'm hit by her familiar scent of lilies. "You wouldn't. I *know* you wouldn't. You care about the game. You care about your place on the team. You've worked so hard for it. You wouldn't do anything to jeopardize that. I know you."

Well, she does know me.

Because she is right.

I can't afford to lose my place on the team. I've worked very, very hard for it.

I've worked my *entire* life for it.

I've worked my entire life to be The Blond Arrow, my father's son.

And as angry as I am at the sight of my ex-girlfriend, I'm not going to wreck my life's work for her.

I *refuse* to break another rule.

Especially for my ex-girlfriend.

"You know, the therapist you found me?" I say, massaging the neck of the bottle. "I'm not sure she's as helpful as you think she is."

"What do you mean?"

"It means that I'm very close to stopping giving a shit and breaking something. So if you don't want to get caught in the middle of it, you should leave."

I take another bitter swallow of the beer – beer doesn't do anything for me; I need a smoke. Maybe I should call it a night and leave. We have one last school on the tour to visit tomorrow so I need my strength to endure that anyway.

And it's not as if I'm having any fun.

But a second later Sarah touches me, and I freeze at the feel of her small hand.

Her small, dainty hand that I always thought paired up really well with my large body.

She thought so too. Said it made us look like a perfect couple – her, fragile and feminine; me, dominating and masculine.

I bet she's never hit someone with that hand though.

Nah, Sarah would never do something violent like that.

She's not like *her*.

"I just wanted to say hello, A," Sarah whispers, breaking my thoughts about her sister. "And see how you're doing. Don't be mad."

I look at her a beat, at her beautiful face before replying with mock politeness, "I'm doing fine, thank you."

"Aren't you going to ask me how I'm doing?"

"I would but I don't care either way."

She smiles sadly and strokes my chest. "Well, I just... miss you."

My body tightens. "Is that right?"

"Yes. Don't you? I mean, despite what happened, don't you miss me a little, A?"

Her eyes drop to my lips and it doesn't come as a surprise.

I know she wants me.

She's wanted me back ever since I found out about her. And I have to admit that there's a certain satisfaction in denying her.

In making her squirm.

That's her classic move by the way, when she wants me to kiss her. Whispered words and sneaky glances to the lips. A subtle game of femininity that I've always found very hot.

What can I say? I like sex.

It's always been a natural relaxant. Something to take the edge off. Besides smoking, I mean.

And sex between us has always been pretty fucking hot. She's small in all the ways I like and I'm big in all the ways that makes things tight and interesting.

"You want to be kissed," I conclude in a low whisper that I know gets her going.

She glances at my lips again, her hand on my body growing urgent, grasping. "I don't know. I just... I want you."

Which means, yes, she wants to be kissed.

This is her way of appearing as feminine as possible.

Again, I'm not going to deny that it gets me hot; I like to dominate, and she doesn't mind.

She takes it all.

And for a second there it almost does get me going.

Until I realize that's all she ever does.

She takes it but she doesn't give it back.

She doesn't writhe under me, trying to fuck me back. She doesn't fist my hair and pull at it. She doesn't scratch me with her nails, goad me by breaking my rules.

She doesn't wear tiny little skirts or leave me sexy fucking notes.

She doesn't fan my aggression and provoke me into fucking her harder.

Into reining her in.

I look at Sarah, the perfect good girl, the girl I've been with for the last eight years, and I realize that... she's a little too perfect. A little too boring.

Kissing her feels boring too.

The same song and dance that we've been doing for eight long years.

"What do you think your new boyfriend would say to you kissing your old boyfriend? Or maybe you've done it so many times now to your *old boyfriend* – you know, going behind his back and all that – that you can't tell the difference between right or wrong anymore."

Sarah draws back as if I've slapped her.

Whatever.

I step away from her, ready to leave and get the fuck out of this party, but again, she stops me. This time with her words.

"This is not about Ben."

"But you're still fucking him, aren't you?"

"Why, are you jealous?"

I think about it and my answer automatically slips out, "Strangely, no."

Before I can analyze it, she says, "So what's the problem? Why can't you let this go?"

"Maybe because you cheated on me and lied to me. That tends to piss people off."

Scoffing, she shakes her head. "Do you have any idea how big of a mistake you're making right now?"

"Why don't you tell me?"

She exhales sharply. "Why do you think we were together, A? Why do you think we got together in the first place? It's because we matched in every way. I was ambitious and so were you. I was driven and so were you. We had this mutual attraction. You're as handsome as I am beautiful. We were together because being with each other made sense. Being with each other was easy. It was convenient."

I look into her eyes, her golden eyes that I found so rare. So fascinating and original. Something to be prized.

Something like perfection.

But now, like her, they seem boring. They don't tilt up at the corners. They don't shine as much.

So boring that a word comes out of my mouth in a flat, *bored* tone. "Convenient."

"Yes." Sarah smiles in triumph. "It was convenient. Somehow fate or whatever put us in the same house. Our thoughts matched. Our goals matched. We both brought something to the table. Do you know how hard that is to find? This level of perfection between two people?

"It's hard, A. But we have it. All these people, these ordinary people, they run after love and all those stupid things. But we have something greater. It was never about love between us. We have our perfection. We have our ambitions. Our plans. We're a team, you and me. We're the power couple, don't you see? I'm beautiful, educated, sophisticated; I look good on your arm. And you are my superstar athlete boyfriend. Why do you think I came up with the injury lie? Why do you think I appeased everyone while you were away? I didn't want you to lose everything you've worked for. *We* have worked for. Remember all the plans we made? Going to college together. You going pro. You getting traded to the European League. God, we were going to live in England or Ireland. Spain. We were going to do so many things together."

We were.

Going pro was always my dream.

Playing for the European League was always my dream too because it was my father's dream and my mother made sure that I saw it as well, when I closed my eyes.

But then Sarah came along, and she seemed so similar to me that all my plans and dreams became hers. She let me focus on the game. She let me completely disappear into myself when I was obsessed with a strategy. She let me watch the game tapes over and over.

She let me *be*.

It just made sense.

It was fucking *convenient*.

"And we can still have that," she continues, stepping closer and putting her hands on me again, on my rapidly heating body. "We can still be that couple, you and me. One mistake can't wash away eight years of togetherness, A. It can't. I won't let it. We can't be like other people and be bogged down with ordinary things. We're special. We have worked too hard for it, you and me."

She's right.

We're not ordinary, her and me.

We're perfect. We match.

We are destined for greater things. That's what I've been told ever since I was born. Greatness, perfection, being my father's son.

"You and me, huh," I murmur and her eyes shine with a hard glint of her ambitions.

"I know I hurt you with Ben. I know that but that wasn't my intention at all."

"So what was your intention then?"

"You were so involved in your game, the season, and I was new in town. I'd just started the new job. I was lonely. I didn't have a lot of friends back then. You kept bringing him around and yeah, I slipped up. I admit that. But I didn't want to distract you from the game because of something so inconsequential. I didn't want you to lose your focus. That's why I hid it for so long. I didn't want to hurt you. I was going to stop anyway once we were married. You are more important to me than some second-class coach. He's been on the team for four years, A, and he's still the assistant coach, can you believe it? You rose to the top within a year. He's got nothing on you. He's got nothing on *us*."

I have to bark out a harsh laugh.

I've been trying to keep it inside of me, this sharp piece of laughter, but it bursts out like a bullet. Like my body has been a loaded gun for so long and finally, finally the shot is fired.

Because *finally*, I understand.

Finally, things make sense.

They make *perfect* sense.

Convenience.

That's it. That's what our relationship has been all about.

We've been together because somehow our ambitions matched and everything came easy. We both brought something to the table – I was the popular jock and she was the good girl.

I gave her the status she craved and she was the perfect girlfriend who stood by me through the years while I achieved my dreams. Who encouraged me and never distracted me from my main goal.

My main focus – soccer.

In fact, when I graduated a semester earlier than her and was drafted, I didn't even think twice about leaving her behind. I was so fucking ecstatic about it. *She* was ecstatic about it.

Things were falling into place for us.

Our dreams were coming true.

But when she cheated, all that convenience went away, didn't it?

All the plans were broken.

Suddenly, all I could think about was her breaking my trust. All I could think about was her fucking my friend on our couch, in our bed, in hotel rooms. Her fucking him with my ring on her finger and me failing to figure it out.

Suddenly, my perfect girlfriend became a distraction, a failure. My perfect relationship turned out to be a lie.

I couldn't focus on my training. I couldn't focus on the game.

And I couldn't... win.

Yeah.

I lost a game, didn't I?

A week after I read those texts on Sarah's phone and found out about her betrayal, we had a big game. I was so shocked, so shaken up and out of it, that I wasn't at my one hundred percent. I missed a couple of goals and we lost.

I haven't forgotten that defeat, no. I remember it very clearly.

But what I did forget is the fact that that's when I hit Ben.

That's when my anger snapped and I broke the rule.

The day after we lost the game.

I hit him because I lost. Because they *made* me lose, Sarah and Ben and what they did. Because they distracted me from my one and only focus and because they stained my perfect relationship.

Jesus *fucking* Christ.

That's why.

That's why I've been so *angry*. I've been so tormented and fucking tortured.

Because I lost my focus. Because my relationship wasn't as perfect as I thought it was. *My girlfriend* wasn't as perfect as I thought she was.

I've been angry because I failed to hold onto perfection. Not because I failed to hold onto my *girlfriend* of eight years.

Isn't it?

It was never about love between us; she's right.

What we had was bigger than that.

What we had was convenience and an innate need for perfection, and I'm only now realizing this.

Eight years later.

Eight years and I finally get it.

Eight years and her jarring me out of my focus, to understand that it was always about being perfect in every aspect of my life.

It was always about being The Blond Arrow.

Even now I'm more broken up about the fact that I didn't get to play out the season than the fact that I don't get to live with her. I'm not even jealous, am I?

No, I'm not.

I don't even miss her.

In all this time that I've been angry over her betrayal, not once did I mourn the loss of her.

I laugh again, and this time it's more tired than sharp. More exhausted.

Unclenching my fingers from around the bottle, I set it down on the table.

"A?"

For a second, I'd completely forgotten that she was here. I'd completely forgotten that she was waiting for me to speak and when I still don't say anything, she grasps the lapels of my suit jacket – another reason why I hate going to these things, suit jackets.

"Are you leaving? Did you hear anything that I said to you? We are –"

I grab her wrists, her dainty feminine wrists that I can break very easily if I want to. But instead of it giving me a thrill like it used to, I find it... too convenient.

Too easy.

"I did. I heard every word."

"But –"

"You said it was convenient and you're right." I clench my jaw, flexing my fingers around her hands. "Everything about us was convenient and easy. We match each other on every level and we should get back together."

She smiles.

But her smile vanishes when I let go of her wrists and step back once again.

Once and for all.

"But look around you, Sarah. You're surrounded by ambitious people. This whole team is ambitious. I hear Rodney, one of the half backs? Is a real up and comer. Not to mention, he's single, and I overheard the guys saying that he likes brunettes. I think that's pretty convenient, don't you?"

Her face ripples with anger, with shock. "What has gotten into you? Why are you behaving this way?"

I chuckle humorlessly, feeling hollower, emptier than ever. "I believe the correct term is asshole."

She fists her hands at her sides. "So this is the end?"

End. Yeah.

End of an era.

An eight year long chapter of my life.

An eight year long relationship that never should've been and all I feel is relief.

"I think so, yeah." I jerk my chin at her then. "Good luck with Ben. Rodney. Whatever."

"And what are you going to do?" she asks with venom in her voice. "Find someone like me to love? Someone who doesn't distract you from your precious game and your goals?"

Love.

Is that what she said? That I'd find someone to *love*?

Something moves in my body. Something that eats up my short-lived relief. It's not the usual shame, this thing. It's not my skin crawling. It's not even anger.

It's something else.

Something more violent, more visceral.

Something fundamental.

Painful, even.

Something that's sitting on my chest, pressing down on my ribs.

I clench my teeth and tighten my body against it before replying. "No. You cured me of that, actually. Because you just made me realize something about myself."

"What?" She folds her arms across her chest, the very picture of perfect outrage.

"That a guy like me knows nothing about love."

A guy like me who measures his life with the goals he scores and the trophies he wins, who lives his life in the pursuit of perfection, who takes eight fucking years to realize the truth about his relationship, has no idea what love is.

The Blond Arrow has no fucking clue what love is.

The pain in my gut jacks up and I almost grab the railing to keep myself standing. I need to get out of here. I need to get away from her and I will, in a second.

Because I remember something.

Something that I want to say to her.

"Oh, and one last thing."

She goes alert.

"Your sister..." I pause and Sarah's eyes turn malicious, leaving me to wonder if this is the first time she's looked so ugly at the mention of her sister or has she always looked this way.

I wish I knew.

I wish I had *noticed*.

"What about her?"

"She's a hell of a soccer player."

"Excuse me?"

"I don't think I've seen her kind of talent in a long time. But she thinks that you don't appreciate it. You think that she's wasting her time."

"So?"

"So I suggest you watch your mouth when you talk about your sister. Because if you don't, then I'll have to give you a lesson on what being an asshole really means. And trust me, I'd love to do that. I'd love to make you understand what's gotten into me."

With that, I leave.

My chest burns with the pain, with something that I have no clue about.

I don't know what it is. I don't know how to curb it.

All I know is that I can't breathe. The whole world is closing in.

I need to get out of here.

I need to get out of this fucking city.

I need to go the fuck back.

CHAPTER TWENTY-ONE

E ver since he went away and left me with a note, I've been thinking about Sarah.

A lot.

She said she'd be waiting for him when he came back.

Was she?

I bet she was.

She said that eight years' worth of love is bigger than her one mistake. Honestly, I thought so too.

Until I found out about her mistake. About what she did to him.

To my Arrow.

I know he's not mine but still.

Still, I'm so mad at her.

I mean, I'm not in her position, okay? I don't know what went through her mind when she did what she did, when she slept with Ben.

But surely there was another way. A better way.

A better way than *lying* to the man you love and making him think that he failed, making him beat himself up like this.

So this past week I thought about it.

About the mistake she made and how angry I got over that, and how I still struggle to understand it and I wish I could call her.

I wish I could talk to her.

Because even though I never understood their relationship – I admit that now after that disastrous Friday dinner – I do understand something about making mistakes.

I'm in love with her ex-boyfriend.

I *fell* in love with him the exact same time she did.

Although I know now that I never would've done anything to hurt their relationship, it still wasn't right.

You don't do that to your own sister, and I'll always be regretful of that.

Not of my love for Arrow but what he was and still *is* to my sister.

So maybe we should talk and figure things out.

Maybe. I don't know.

I don't know anything except that he's gone and he might be getting back together with my sister.

Which is great because everything will be right in his world.

He won't feel like a failure. All his anger will go away. He will be like the old Arrow, calm and collected, unruffled by anything around him.

So why do I wanna cry?

Why do I wanna dissolve in my sheets at night?

Why do I wanna tell him to never ever change? To be like this forever.

But that's not all I want.

I also wanna tell him.

I wanna tell him that I love him, which is crazy. I went to great lengths to protect this secret. I was running away because of it.

I don't know what I hope to accomplish by telling him because we're completely opposite of each other.

He's this great perfectionist who hates making mistakes and I'm anything but perfect. He has all these rules and I love breaking them. He's a soccer superstar and up until recently, I hadn't even played on an actual team. And even though I have this little dream of applying to the youth program for next summer, I'm still not a fit girlfriend for a celebrity athlete.

Besides, for all I know, he's back together with Sarah and if my sister makes him happy, then so be it.

I'll never stand in the way of his happiness.

At least it's Friday and I'm out with the girls at Ballad of the Bards, and I don't have to think about all these things.

Plus Miller has been particularly nasty to me all week so I really need a little break.

I'm not dressed up or anything though. I have my regular clothes on, my cargo pants and a simple t-shirt with my chunky sweater over it.

I'm not wearing any lipstick either.

There's no use wearing it if I can't pout my lips at him and get punished for it.

Oh and tonight I've chosen to not dance as well.

So I'm sitting by the bar with Wyn, who has a sketchbook out, while Poe flirts with a guy at a nearby table and Callie is off somewhere.

With Reed Jackson.

He was already here when we all came in and since his dark eyes were pinned to the door, he spotted Callie right away. And since Callie already knew he was going to be here, she flirted with her bartender friend and danced with a few guys before disappearing.

As friends, we should be more worried about the fact that she completely vanished from sight.

But as friends, we also know that there's something between her and him. Something crazy and volatile and well, epic.

And then there are her nightly outings, which only she and I know about, but still.

So we're not as worried as we should be.

But anyway, my no-dancing-tonight rule breaks when Callie's bartender friend, who I've come to know by sitting close to him for the past hour is a great Lana Del Rey lover like me, asks me to dance while on a break.

He doesn't even give me the time to refuse him but picks me up and spins me around to the tune of one of the most depressing songs, which I happen to love, "Pretty When You Cry" by Lana.

Surprisingly, I laugh.

It's the first time I've laughed all week, I think. I can't believe I'm doing it to the song that I've most cried to while pining over the guy I love.

That's how he finds me a few minutes later.

The guy I love, I mean.

Out of nowhere he's here and he finds me laughing and dancing, swaying in the arms of another man.

For a moment, I think I'm imagining him, which can't be so far-fetched because while I was dancing with Will, who's burly and bearded, I was picturing him. My Arrow.

But then I get a good look at him.

He's wearing a suit jacket – a wrinkled thing now, something that I know he only wears during his events with the team. Plus his hair looks messy too, messier than I've ever seen before. All the sun-struck strands have fallen into disarray.

Not to mention, he doesn't have his baseball cap on, the one he usually wears to public places.

He looks so different than the usual and yet so familiar at the same time that I *know* he's here.

He's back from LA and somehow, he knew to find me at the bar. Well, it's Friday and I have a habit of sneaking out. So it's not really far-fetched.

But still.

He's *here*.

I stop dancing as soon as the knowledge sinks in and the heaviness and chill of the past week lift from my body.

I'm warm now. And happy and...

I realize something is very wrong when he begins to move toward me.

Because while my lips are stretched into a wonder-filled smile and my eyes are wide with happiness, Arrow looks the exact opposite.

He appears tight and unforgiving.

His lips are pinched and his eyes are slitted. And instead of them being pinned on me, they're glued on Will as he marches toward us with lunging, violent steps.

Holy fuck, I understand why.

Because I was *dancing* with him, with another man and because Arrow told me not to.

He told me to never let another man put his hands on me and I broke his rule, and now he looks like he's going to kill that man.

Oh God.

I'm an idiot. *He's* an idiot too because nothing was happening anyway and I have to go stop him before he does something crazy.

I break apart from Will, who looks at me with astonishment. But I don't have the time to explain. I have to stop the bulldozer of a guy who's very quickly coming upon us and who's sitting out the season because he did something similar. And if his words from the night he took my virginity hold any truth to them, no one will be able to pull him off Will until Arrow actually murders him.

So I rush over to intercept him and we meet a few feet away from the bar counter.

I put both my hands on his stomach, palms wide open, and I swear it's like stopping a giant boulder.

"Arrow, stop. No," I tell him, hoping and praying he listens to me before anyone else gets wind of the fact that The Blond Arrow is among them and he's very angry.

His jaw tics at my voice but he hasn't looked away from Will.

I fist the gray-colored dress shirt he's wearing. "Arrow. Please. He's just a friend."

At this, finally, he looks at me.

It feels like he does it in slow motion. His eyes shifting away from Will, his spiky eyelashes flicking down and his gaze, so dark and intense, coming to rest on me.

"Friend."

He says that word in a low growl and I flinch.

Oh shit.

That's the worst thing that I could've said.

I shake my head and dig my knuckles into his body. "I didn't mean it that way. You know I didn't. Arrow, he was just –"

My words get cut off when he steps away from me.

It happens so suddenly that I can't quite believe it. Wasn't I holding him tightly? Weren't my fingers fisting his shirt?

How did he break that hold so easily?

Like it meant nothing, me holding onto him.

Like *I* meant nothing.

And then he takes one last look at me before spinning around and leaving.

He's *leaving*.

He's just... walking away. He just came back from LA and somehow appeared at the bar and now he's leaving.

Because I was stupidly dancing with a guy who meant nothing.

Oh God.

I rush after him when I see him stepping out the front door. I come into the night and frantically, look around.

He's walking around the bar, probably headed to the alley that connects to the parking lot in the back.

"Arrow. Stop," I call out.

But he doesn't.

I didn't expect him to, honestly. So I pump my legs harder. He's taught me a lot about running in the past couple of weeks and I use that to my advantage now and reach him just as he gets past the row of big black dumpsters.

I go around him and put my hands on his stomach again.

"Arrow, please. I didn't... I didn't do anything," I tell him, getting close to him, fisting his shirt once more even though I know it won't make a difference.

But that's all the more reason to do *something* because he's just so harsh and sharp right now.

"You let him put his hands on you," he says, roughly, tightly.

The light in the alley is questionable.

There's a little bulb somewhere a few feet away from him, though his shoulders that seem to have grown overnight are hiding it.

And the moon is reddish as always in his presence but it's so far away tonight that it leaves Arrow in shadows and mystery.

Which I totally hate.

"Arrow, listen, okay? *Listen.*" I pull at his shirt, looking up at him. "I was just sitting there at the bar and this song came on. And Will, the guy you saw me dancing with, he told me he was a Lana Del Rey fan and he just pulled me up for a dance, okay? You know how much I love her and –"

He leans over me then, sort of coming out of the shadows where I can see him clearly.

I can see the tight peaks of his cheekbones. They jut out of his face, of his angular, *stunning* face, like pieces of cut glass.

"Did you like his hands on you?" he asks, his eyes alive and bright with darkness.

"No. Absolutely not."

"Did you like it when he spun you around and pulled you against his body?"

"No, Arrow. I didn't."

"No? So why the fuck were you laughing?"

"Because I was imagining you, you idiot." I shake his shirt. "Because I was picturing you in my head."

A mystery of an emotion passes over his face, quick and short-lived and I get closer to him.

The tip of my soccer cleats crashes with the tip of his polished boots and I blurt out the very first thing that comes into my head, "I will never do that to you. I will never *ever* do something like that to you, okay? I'm not..."

Her.

I'm not Sarah.

I don't say it but he hears it.

Because the mysterious emotion that passed over his face washes over his body too. His tight, hard body that sort of jerks slightly before he takes a step.

Toward me.

Or more like, pushes me back with those tips of his boots while he advances forward.

"Picturing me," he says, his voice gravelly, referring to my earlier statement about imagining him while dancing and ignoring what I said to him just now.

Ignoring my sort-of declaration about loyalty.

"Yeah." I nod, still clutching onto his shirt, almost tearing off the buttons with my forceful hold. "I was imagining it was you. That you were the one spinning me in circles and dancing with me."

"You were."

"Yes. And then you came in and I couldn't believe it."

"Why?"

"Because my wish came true."

"What wish?"

"You," I whisper with all the love in my eyes, while his are turbulent.

"I'm not anybody's wish."

You're mine. You're my wish.

You're my Arrow.

"I waited for you this whole week." I swallow, telling him the truth, letting it shine in my voice, on my face. "And I was... I missed you so much."

"You missed me," he repeats in a strange tone, as he keeps advancing on me, as he keeps pushing me back.

I whisper, "Yes. A-and I was worried."

"Worried about what?"

I was worried that you'd get back together with her.

That you'd become the old Arrow and that I'd lose you.

"I was worried that you..." *The new Arrow.* "Wouldn't come back."

"I told you I would," he growls. "I said I'd come back in a week."

I swallow and give him a tremulous smile that only manages to agitate him further, I think, if his big step toward me is any indication like he's restless to push me somewhere.

To a place I don't know about.

"But you came back early," I whisper.

"I did, didn't I?"

These words are clenched, forced out of him, and I open my fists and stroke his stomach. I let my hands roam and circle over the cotton of his dress shirt as I soothe him.

"Why?" I lick my lips and his eyes drop to my gesture.

It stays there, his gaze, over my lips for a few seconds before he flicks his eyes up.

They're burning. *Blazing.*

"Because of you," he rasps almost accusingly, and a breath jars out of me.

I blink.

And I stop moving.

Because at that very moment, we've reached our destination. Or rather *his* destination, the wall against which he can pin me.

He can cage me between his hard body and the bricks.

"You came back early for me?" I repeat, disbelieving, shocked, flabbergasted... happy.

He puts both his hands on either side of my head and I can't help it. I arch my back. I push my ass into the heated bricks and thrust my chest out.

"I came back early because you've got something I need."

"What?"

As soon as I ask the question, I understand what he means.

I understand what he needs from me.

The awareness hits me in the stomach, somewhere behind my navel before it tugs and pulls, making the thing he needs clench.

My pussy.

And God, my pussy needs him too.

Yes, it's not the most heartfelt declaration but it's something, isn't it? It's *something* – he was thinking about me while he was there, while he was maybe even with... her – and I bite my lip with both love and lust for him.

"You know what I mean, don't you?"

I nod. "Yes."

His eyes bore into mine then. "Tell me what I came back for."

I shiver at his command.

At his usual familiar command, and it makes my channel ripple. It somehow also squeezes my heart, expanding my love for him as I whisper, "My Arrow came back for my pussy."

His eyes flash when I obey him and maybe I'm pathetic but it makes my toes curl with pleasure.

"Yeah, that's right. I came back for your bad girl pussy," he rumbles, looming over my lips. "That's why I changed my flights, dealt with the most incompetent crew in the history of all airlines all day and flew out twenty four hours early. Because I haven't had her in a week."

He pushes his palm against the wall, his fingers flexing. "And because my fist is no good. My fist isn't tight enough, no matter how much I clench it. And my fist isn't wet enough, no matter how much I spit on my palm and grease up my cock, do you understand? So I'm going to need her."

The tendons on his neck vibrate, the silver chain glittering even more as he continues, "I'm going to need your pouty little snatch. I'm going to need your snatch to run like a river for me because I've missed that. I've *missed* you polishing my cock up, making it shine with your juices like it's some kind of a trophy. Some kind of a coveted prize that you want to buff and rub down between your legs. That's why I came back early. That's what I need from you."

By the time he finishes, he's rubbing our lips together. He's half kissing me and I'm half delirious with lust.

I'm half delirious with his heat and his scent and the way he's breathing in great gusts.

"I missed –"

"Shh, don't talk." He slowly shakes his head. "I've had a shitty fucking week, okay? And then I come to you for relief and find you dancing with someone else. It's a miracle that I haven't lost my shit yet. So don't say a word. Just let me fuck that pussy."

I grab his face then.

Somehow, in the midst of all the lust and love inside of me, I manage to break my hands away from his chest and put them on his harsh, ticking cheeks.

"Arrow, what happened? What are you –"

"Just let me feel good," he says and destroys all my words with his raspy ones.

With his guttural, *needy* ones.

So I slide my hands away from his face and into his thick, sun-struck, messy hair. Because all my questions and words can wait. They are inconsequential anyway. In the face of his need.

"Okay. Fuck me. Make yourself feel good," I whisper.

His chest expands on a long breath and I swear his eyelids become so heavy that his eyes are almost shut before he envelops my mouth in a kiss.

A hot and wet and desperate kiss.

The kind of a kiss that you give to someone when you see them after a year.

A decade, a century. A lifetime maybe.

This isn't the way you kiss someone when you've only been away for a week. You don't bite at each other's lips and you don't fill their mouths with needy noises and craving tongues.

You don't even pull at each other's clothes like this.

Like we're doing.

My hands pull at his suit jacket and his fingers fumble with the buttons of my cargo pants. I rip open his shirt, to try to get to his bare chest, his bare heat and he tugs at my chunky sweater, trying to get to my naked waist, my soft tits.

You definitely don't get so horny and needy, and almost naked in under ten seconds, in the back alley of a bar, hidden only partially by the dumpsters.

But maybe you do all of that, if you're me and him.

Arrow and Salem.

Arrow and his fuck doll; and Salem and the love of her life.

That's what we are, aren't we?

He fucks me and I love him.

But whatever we are, whoever we are to each other, in this moment, I know he needs me and I need him.

So when he breaks his kiss, I whine. I literally whine and pull at his hair, trying to bring him back.

But he doesn't listen.

He steps away from me, breaking my hold, and I stand there, panting. I stand there in only my thong and my t-shirt as I take in the damage that I've done to him.

I take in his half-open, wrinkled shirt, his dress pants unbuttoned and his belt dangling open, the silver buckle shining like the sun.

He is shining like the sun, his mouth glistening and swollen with my kisses, his eyes blazing as he does the same to me, takes me in, maybe to check the damage *he's* done to me.

"Arrow?" I whisper, my tits heaving, pouty nipples poking through the shirt.

He lifts his gaze, his expression hard and unfathomable before he grabs my waist and spins me around.

My hands stumble and slap on the wall while he grabs my hips and pulls me back. My spine arches on its own and my nails dig into the brick wall.

I turn around to catch him squatting down and I shiver.

But it's not from the chill of the night.

It's from the fact that as soon as Arrow goes down, his large hands grab the cheeks of my ass and pull.

He parts them.

He plucks the string of my thong from between my cheeks and snaps it aside. The elastic digs into the meat of my butt and I clench my eyes shut.

I rest my cheek on the brick wall as my body burns with arousal and embarrassment that he can see everything.

My pussy and my asshole.

But then, he goes in and smells it all.

He digs his nose in the crease of my ass and runs it up and down, taking in my musky, horny scent and groaning with it, and I forget about all the shame and embarrassment and push my hips back.

I push it into his mouth and he licks it.

He licks my pussy and I go up on tiptoes, parting my mouth so I can breathe.

But I don't think I *can*. Breathe, I mean.

Because he doesn't give me the time to do it.

Digging his fingers into my ass and keeping my cheeks apart and holes stretched, he goes in for another lick. This one covering the lips of my pussy, all the way back to my ass.

And he keeps doing that.

He keeps giving me licks all over, on both my holes and *Jesus Christ*, I've never felt hotter in my life.

Hotter and wetter and more turned on.

I even go so far as to pull at my t-shirt. I try to take it off because I'm sweating and shaking like crazy, all because he's eating not only my peach-like pussy, he's also tasting my ass.

But I think I overestimated my strength because I can only get my t-shirt up to my neck, to expose my tits to the night, before my hands give up.

Before I'm coming on his tongue and he's drinking everything like he always does. He's slurping and working his mouth on my pussy to get all of it, to not even miss a drop.

When he's done, I feel him take his mouth off and stand up.

I'm too weak to look back at him but still, I open my eyes and watch him emerge from the ground. I watch his shiny jaw and mouth, making him look even more like the sun. I watch him while he takes his dick out of his pants, his big, beautiful dick, and snaps the condom on.

I watch while he watches *me*, all silent and breathing hard as he grabs my naked hips and positions his cock at my still-pulsing entrance.

But when I see the muscles of his abdomen flex and his hips jerking forward, I can't anymore.

I can't watch because he's inside of me and I have to shut my eyes tightly.

Because oh my God, it's so big and good and fuck, it *hurts* that all I can do is grind my head into the wall and moan.

My pussy pulses over his massive length and he grunts loudly, louder than he's ever grunted before, and his forehead drops to my shoulder and my own head somehow comes back to rest on his.

When his other hand, the one not gripping my hip, settles on my bare stomach, I gasp out, "It's so big. Why does it feel so big? Like this..."

His dick jerks inside of me and I gasp again.

"Because you're still tight as fuck. Like a virgin. Even after I've stretched your hole a hundred times," he groans, rolling his forehead on my shoulder. "And because I've never had you like this."

"Like what?" I pant, my hands slipping on the wall.

He raises his head, his rough cheek brushing against mine, and whispers in my ear, "Like a dog in heat."

My channel pulses at his crass words – crass and delicious and somehow so erotic – and he has to pump into me. Once, twice, short and jerky motions.

And I have to put my hand over his where he's grabbing my belly. "I feel you in my..."

"Where?" he asks when I don't pick up the thread.

I was going to say stomach. That I feel him in my stomach but that's... wrong.

I don't feel him in my stomach.

I feel him somewhere deeper.

Much, much deeper.

I turn my head to look at him. "In my womb."

His chest shudders at my back and his face grows mean with lust. I think even his cock swells inside me, grows to insane, obscene proportions as it presses into my womb, my very femininity.

The very thing that makes me who I am.

The girl with all the feelings, all the emotions.

The girl in doomed love.

With the guy who's fucking her.

Who presses his hand on her stomach and strokes it, as if feeling for the ridge of his thick cock invading my body in such achy and wonderful ways.

"Am I hurting you?" he asks, his eyes narrowed, his hand massaging.

"In a good way."

He digs his fingers into my belly as his eyes go dark, darker than before. "Good." He moves his hips, his pelvis grazing against my bare ass, making me whimper with the pressure. "Because I want to fuck that womb too. I need to fuck that womb. I need everything you have. Every fucking thing, Salem. Everything you have belongs to me. It's mine. *All of it.*"

His words, possessive and growly, hit me in the very thing he wants to fuck, my womb, and I push my hips back.

I take him in further while moaning, "Yes, all of it. All of it belongs to you."

He takes me then.

He stretches me in new ways, making space for himself in the corners that I didn't even think existed before.

He presses his palm on my stomach, as if squeezing out my juices and greasing up his cock even more, and I moan again.

I squeeze his fingers on my stomach and bring my other hand away from the wall and over to the back of his neck as he moves inside of me. He's slowly picking up the rhythm and his body is pushing into me with every ram of his cock.

And I let him ride me as I hold onto him.

He pounds, pounds, *pounds* inside of me and I realize that he goes in so easily now. So wonderfully as if he's slicing through creamy, soft butter.

Every time he goes in, he jabs me in the womb and I scream. And every time I scream, he pushes harder inside of me, his hand digs deeper into my stomach, massages it in broad strokes as if soothing the hurt he's causing.

But the hurt is so good, so delicious that I only want more of it.

So I surrender.

I go flush with the wall, my nipples scraping against it as I writhe between the bricks and him.

All the while he keeps fucking me, practically bouncing me in his lap and I realize that the wall I'm stuck to is pulsing too.

Both with our violent, passionate fucking, and the music.

The sad love songs.

I can't be sure what song it is but I hear violins and melancholy and I let the years and years of love wash over my body.

I let the music – the one he's creating with his grunts and his slapping hips, and the one seeping through the walls – soak into my skin.

Letting go of my hip, he reaches his hand up and wraps it around my throat. Then he bends my neck to the side and for the first time ever, sinks his teeth over my pounding pulse and sucks on it.

And like a crazy girl I smile.

I smile because he's giving me a hickey.

He's taking a bite out of my pulse, my heart, the heart that's filled with all the love for him, and I come.

My womb contracts.

My pussy clenches over his ramming length and I have to give up the violins pulsing through the wall and arch up against his chest.

But it's okay.

I'll give up everything for him, all the sad love songs and all the bike rides. All the desolate bridges and lonely places.

I'll give up myself because I belong to him.

I belong to my darling Arrow.

As soon as I think that, he comes too.

He comes with a roar, his hands clenching and clenching my flesh and his hips stumbling and jerking against me.

His cock expands so much that I think the latex will burst and all the ropes of his cum will shower over my womb. And my greedy, lovesick womb will absorb it like I absorbed the violins and his violent fucking.

My entire body will absorb him.

Absorb everything he gives me.

The guy I'm in doomed love with.

My Arrow.

CHAPTER TWENTY-TWO

Something is wrong.

Very, very wrong.

I mean, of course I knew that. I knew that something was wrong because not only did he come back from LA feeling all mysterious and strangely restless, he also actually told me that he had a shitty week.

So I know things aren't all that great.

But then as soon as we were done back in the alley behind the bar and he dressed me up like I'm really his doll – without looking into my eyes though and with very tight, angry movements – it started to snow.

The very first snow of the season.

That's when I realize it's November now. Mid November.

I've been at St. Mary's for two and a half months. That's almost the same amount of time that Arrow – new Arrow – has been back.

Ever since he arrived, I've lost all sense of time. I've been living in a dream, walking on clouds and I don't like the reminder.

I don't like this reality check.

I don't like the snow either.

I know people think snow is pretty and auspicious and whatnot. But I'm the girl who loves summer and sunshine and open roads.

Snow interferes with all of that.

Now I have this foreboding in my chest that something awful is going to happen.

But I try to push it aside. I try to be rational and strong as I climb off his motorcycle when we reach St. Mary's.

As soon as my feet hit the ground, the wind brings the flakes of snow into my face and I huddle inside his vintage leather jacket that I'd worn to the bar. And I'm reminded of the first night that I saw him, kissing that girl.

He was so unapproachable back then, so deliberately tight-lipped.

And right now, he appears exactly like that first night. Tight and agitated. He hasn't even looked at me, actually.

He's staring straight ahead, into the darkness, his back all rigid. His fingers are clenched so tightly around the handlebars that I want to reach out and loosen them up.

I want to loosen *him* up.

Clutching the lapels of his jacket around my neck, I ask, "What happened?"

'In LA' is implied, I think.

I'm right when he clenches his jaw and says without looking at me, "You should go."

I take a step closer. "Arrow, tell me what happened?"

This time, the clench lasts longer. He even flexes his fists around the throttle. "I said you should go."

The longer he doesn't look at me, the louder my heartbeats become, and I have to grab the sleeve of his wrinkled suit jacket. "Arrow, please. Tell me. Did you see her? Did you see Sarah?"

I'm not sure if it's because I'm clutching onto the sleeve of his damp jacket or if it's the mention of her name, but he snaps his eyes over to me.

His dark, furious eyes.

And *God*, again, I think of the first night at the bar.

When the mention of my sister's name changed everything.

It changed everything that I believed in. Everything that I thought to be true.

That just makes me even more frantic, more desperate. Desperate enough to pull at his sleeve with not one but both hands.

"Arrow, tell me. Did you see her? What'd she say?"

"Leave," he says curtly.

But I don't listen. I can't listen.

How can I leave when he looks like this? When he looks... so furious and so flushed with anger. So scarlet, like his blood is rushing too close to the surface.

"Not until you tell me." I shake my head. "Just tell me what happened. Tell me what she said."

"Salem. Just leave."

His voice is quiet but it's dripping with warning. It's dripping with authority and a heavy threat. I should heed it.

I know that.

But the next question that bursts out of my mouth is so reckless, so fucking thoughtless and yet so urgent and important that I don't know how else I could have said it, if not in a squeaky, high voice, with my nails digging into his arm, my body trembling with dread.

"D-do you love her? Do you still love my sister?"

I think I screamed it. I think everyone heard it.

Everyone at St. Mary's heard that I asked the guy I love if he's still in love with my sister.

Or at least that's what I feel for a few seconds, because my eardrums are ringing.

My chest is vibrating.

The only thing silent and frigid, frozen over by the snow, is him.

The guy I asked this question to.

If I thought he was tight before, I was wrong. If I thought he was furious and hot before, I was wrong again.

He's burning up now, and I wouldn't be surprised if he melts all the snow on ground.

Especially, when he glances down – for the first time – at my fists in his jacket and I feel my hands sting.

Keeping his chin dipped, he lifts his eyes. "Get out of my face."

"What?"

"Just get the fuck out of my face before I lose it, okay?"

"But I –"

He jerks his arm then and my fists are shaken loose, making me stumble back a little.

But it's enough.

It's enough to give him the space he probably wanted because his foot goes to kickstart the motorcycle, and I know that as soon as he does that, he'll leave.

He'll leave me here, standing in the snow, with so many unanswered questions. With so many emotions and feelings that I will explode.

I won't make it through the night.

So I do the only thing that I can. The only thing that I can think of.

I hurl my heart at his feet, my beating, pulpy heart at his kicking feet, and hope that it's enough to make him stay.

"I love you."

I screamed that too, I think.

Everyone heard it.

Everyone heard my secret.

Holy. Shit.

Holy *fucking* shit.

I press a hand on my stomach because I can't breathe. Because all my organs are in disarray or at least it feels like it because I just told him.

I *told* him.

My secret of eight years.

My secret because of which I stole and lied and cried and lived in misery for eight long years. My secret because of which I was sent here, to St. Mary's.

I just told it to him and turns out, it was enough for him to stop.

It was enough for that foot to stop, the one resting on that lever. It was enough for him to stare back at me. Not only with his eyes but also with his body. He twists his torso in my direction as if he's completely attuned to me now.

Completely attuned to what I just said.

And maybe, *maybe* I would've taken that. I would've taken the way his body looks tight and coiled, turned toward me.

But then, he goes ahead and climbs off his Ducati.

He actually swings his thigh over and comes to a stand and I have to step back.

Because he's standing in front of me, his feet wide apart, his hands on his sides curled into fists and his chest moving up and down, all hot and snowy.

"What'd you just say?" he asks in a low voice.

In the most dangerous voice I've ever heard. A voice that causes my hickey – the very first love bite that he gave me – to burn and throb.

I swallow, pressing my hand further into my stomach, feeling chilled. "I-I..."

"You love me."

I swallow again. "I didn't mean it."

"So you don't love me."

"No, I do. I..."

His eyes narrow. "Well, which is it?"

Oh God.

Why does he have to look so intimidating right now? So tall and big and dark, his sun-struck hair all wet and brown.

I don't know how to handle this.

But I have to handle it, right?

I just said it. I can't take it back.

I *won't* take it back.

Just because it's scary doesn't mean I shouldn't do it.

Just because it was only a half-formed idea in my head to tell him, doesn't mean it's not true.

So I take a deep breath and say, "Okay, let me just start at the beginning. I write you letters. Not the ones we've been exchanging these past few weeks but others. Like, really long ones where I tell you about my day and I tell you what I did and who I talked to and who I saw and you know, where I just make general conversation with you. And I've been doing that for the past eight years."

I take a pause here to look him in the eyes; they've turned inscrutable now, his gaze along with his smooth, unruffled features as the snow falls around us.

"Since I was ten," I continue. "Since the day I saw you in the kitchen and you told me not to tell your mom about the juice thing and you asked me if I was cold. I... I wanted to answer you. I wanted to tell you that I wasn't. I mean, I *was*. But then you came in through the door, all sweaty and panting and the room was all yellow, you know? Because the sun was streaming through the windows and you appeared so... sun-struck. And as soon as I saw you, I felt this strange warmth flowing inside my body. And it made me feel so good and I wanted to tell you that. But then..."

I part my lips and my breath comes out all foggy and white and I bite my lip to compose myself. I bite my lip because he's all frozen now.

Frozen and smooth and listening.

He's *listening* to me, to my story. As if he's riveted.

Or maybe I'm imagining things because I wanna make it easier for myself.

"But then, I couldn't. I couldn't tell you that I wasn't cold. That you made my cold go away. And I couldn't talk to you like I wanted to. So I started writing you letters. Every night I'd write you a letter and I'd fold it and put it in an orange envelope, and then I'd put that in a shoebox that I hid under my bed. When I moved to St. Mary's, I brought that box with me. It's a couple, more than a couple of shoeboxes actually because I've written you a lot of letters. And I had them with me the night I was running away too."

I sniffle and rub my chilled nose with the back of my hand before straightening up my spine and beginning the awful, *awful* part of the story. "You asked me why I was running away that night and if there was a boy involved. There was and that boy is you."

My confession wrings out a tiny reaction on his part.

A very tiny, one-syllable word that he says in a flat tone.

"Me."

I jerk out a nod. "Yeah. I was running away because of you. Because you were gonna marry her. Because the day I saw you and you asked me if I was cold and I could never answer you? It was because Sarah came in that very moment and you looked at her and... you never looked away," I whisper, thinking about all the times I wanted him to look at me but he'd stare at Sarah.

"I think you forgot I was there. A tiny, messy, blanket-wrapped ten-year-old. And then you never remembered me after that. Never really paid any attention to me, even when I was there." I shake my head, wishing things could be different.

"Anyway, you used to be so fascinated with her, you know? I'd watch you watch her and I knew you were falling in love with her. And she was falling in love with you and I watched it all happen. And all the while... all the while *I* was falling in love with you too. With my sister's boyfriend. I've spent years feeling terrible and awful about it. That's why I kept myself away from you. That's why I'd never look at you or talk to you or just leave the room when you were there, because I loved you. Because you were Sarah's and what kind of a sister would I be if I did something to hurt your relationship. That's why I was running away. I didn't want to sully your wedding with my presence. I didn't want to be there, the girl with a witchy heart, in love with her sister's groom.

But back then, I didn't know something about myself. Something really important."

"What?"

I fist my hands at my side and raise my chin. "That I'd never do anything to jeopardize what you had with her. I'd never do anything to come between you two. No matter how desperate I got. Because your happiness is my happiness. When you smile, I smile. When you hurt, I hurt. So if you love her, then you should be with her."

When I stop, I make myself tight.

I clench my muscles and I flex my fists. I keep my eyes on him, unflinching.

If he wants to hate me for falling for him, for loving my sister's ex-boyfriend while he was still with her, then he can do that.

I'll take his hatred and whatever he has to say to me. Because as I said, I do regret it. I do regret that I fell in love with him when he was with Sarah.

But I refuse to regret the very act of loving him. I refuse to regret loving him to the point of misery and doom.

But all he does is blink and say, "And if I don't?"

I shift on my feet, more ready than ever. "If you don't what?"

"Love her."

It takes me a few seconds to put together what he meant.

If I don't love her...

That's what he meant, right?

If he doesn't love her then what?

Up until now, I felt like my breaths were frozen. I thought my body was chilled to the bone and I'd never be able to get any feeling back into it.

But everything comes rushing back. Everything comes *hurtling* back and punches me in the chest. It punches me in the gut, and I let out a shocked breath.

"Then I'd say..." I open my fists and loosen my body. "Choose me."

"You."

I nod. "Yeah, choose me."

"Why?"

This is the easiest thing for me to say, the easiest of all the things that I've ever said to him. "Because I love you, Arrow. I've loved you for years and if you give me a chance, I can make you happy."

"You can make me happy."

I swallow. "Yes."

"By loving me."

He's saying all these things in a flat tone but that's not the part I'm worried about, or at least not the only part.

The fact that he keeps repeating everything that I say is even more concerning to me.

"Y-yes," I reply.

He nods.

Then he ducks his head and shifts on his feet before looking up. "I just have one question though."

"What question?"

He cocks his head to the side and asks very casually, "Did I ask for love? From you."

"I..."

"Answer me!"

He yells out the words and it's such a shock after his curious tone that I flinch and whisper, "No."

"What did I ask for?"

"Arrow –"

"Answer the fucking question, Salem. *What* did I ask for?"

"My body."

He narrows his eyes. "Bingo. I asked for you to spread your legs for me. All I ever asked from you was your tight little pussy. That's it. I asked for a good fuck. Because you're supposed to be my fuck doll. Or did you forget that? Did you forget what your *job* is supposed to be? Your *job* is to shut the fuck up and take it. That is your job. Those are the rules." He scoffs then, shaking his head. "But then, who am I talking to? You can't follow a fucking rule to save your life, can you?"

I wring my snowy, cold hands and blurt out, "But I just thought if you could try..."

To love me...

"Try to do what?"

"T-to open your heart and maybe love –"

Something about that makes him laugh.

It not only makes him laugh, he even throws his head back and lets out that bark of a sound – a broken glass sound – up to the snowing sky.

The flakes settle on his harsh face and disappear. They settle on his agitated chest, his shoulders, his sun-struck hair and disappear.

I watch them, wishing I could be like that.

I wish I could be like snow. I wish I could touch him.

I wish I could disappear.

I wish...

A second later, he lowers his face and it's... agonized. The hollows of his cheeks, the arch of his brows, the line of his jaw, bathed in some kind of misery.

Some kind of torture.

"You wanted to know what happened in LA, yeah?" he says, his voice tight and heavy with both anger and something I don't understand right away except that it's hurting him. "You wanted to know if I still loved her. You wanted to know that, right?" He laughs again. "Yeah, okay. Okay. Let me tell you. Let me tell you that no, I don't still love her. I *never* loved her."

"What?"

He scoffs, looking at the sky again, running his fingers through his hair, fisting the strands almost, before looking back down at me with tormented, desolate eyes.

"All this time I thought our relationship was perfect and she was perfect and that she threw everything away. And I couldn't figure out why. I *couldn't* figure out why she would do that to me, why she'd break my trust like that, why she would cheat on me and destroy eight years of our love. I couldn't figure out how my *perfect* relationship, my perfect love fell to pieces. But the truth is that it wasn't love. There was no love between us. There never was.

"What I thought was love, what I thought love *looked like*, turned out to be convenience. Apparently, it was easy to be with her. It was easy to be with someone who was exactly like me. Ambitious, perfect, driven. Someone who didn't interfere with my precious fucking soccer. Someone who didn't distract me from my goals.

"Well, until she did. Until I read those goddamn messages and I lost my focus. Until my perfect girlfriend became a distraction and I lost a game. And last night in LA, I realized that I'm angrier about that lost game than I am over the fact that I lost my girlfriend. I'm angrier about the fact that my perfect relationship turned out to be a lie than I am about the fact that she slept with someone else.

"Last night in LA, I realized that I was never in love with her and she was never in love with me. We were just two perfect people in love with perfection. And I was so damn focused on my career and my game and my strikes and kicks and how much I can bench press, that I never noticed. We were together for eight years and I never fucking noticed. I never *noticed* that the girl I was going to marry was with me because she had high ambitions and I was with her because she never interfered with those ambitions."

He pauses here.

But I don't think it's to take a deep breath or gather his thoughts.

He pauses because he wants to let his words sink in. He pauses so he can stare at me, look me in the eyes and say, "The fact that I didn't see you wasn't because I was falling in love with your sister, it was because I was fucking blind. Because I've never noticed anything other than my soccer. So you didn't betray her because what you thought was love, what *I* thought was love, turned out to be a simple matter of convenience. That's what you thought, didn't you? That I loved her. That's why you wanted us to get back together. That's why you were so tormented over our breakup. Yeah, you should save yourself the heart attack. It wasn't love."

Yeah, that's what I thought.

That it was love.

That's what *he* thought too. I can see it on his face. I can see it on his rigid body. He thought he was in love.

He believed it.

He believed it with every fiber of his being but somehow, it turned out to be a lie.

Somehow, Arrow and Sarah were a lie.

They were a perfect lie.

And the pain of it is so visceral.

The pain of it is so big and huge that it almost feels like it's here. It's here with us. It's standing somewhere off to the side, casting its shadow on him and I have to go to him. I have to hug him and absorb him in my body.

I have to hide him from it.

But he doesn't give me a chance because he goes on. "So now you know what happened. Now you have all the answers, don't you? Now you know that I'm not only your nightmare, I'm worse than that. I'm worse because *she* didn't make me empty, I've been empty all along. She didn't kill my heart, my heart was dead all along. It was dead because *I* killed it myself. I killed it in my pursuit of perfection. I killed it because I wanted to be motherfucking perfect. I wanted to be the best of the best, to be on top. I wanted to be The Blond fucking Arrow.

"And so I destroyed every other emotion inside of me. And you know what? I'm glad. I'm glad because this is how it's supposed to be. This is how *I'm* supposed to be. I'm supposed to be my father's son. I'm supposed to be The Blond Arrow. That's my destiny. Being great. Being fucking legendary. *That* is why I was born. That is what I've been working for.

"So get out of my face, all right? Take your love and get the fuck away from me. I don't want it. I don't know *anything* about it and I don't care. All I care about, all I'm supposed to care about, is soccer. All I'm supposed to care about is being my father's son. And my father's son doesn't fall in love. He doesn't have emotions. He doesn't have time for emotions or love or fucking friendships. I almost destroyed my career, my dream, my father's dream over supposed love. I failed. But not anymore. So just leave."

"No."

I'm surprised that I said that.

I'm surprised that I said anything at all, that I have the strength to say anything after all the things he just said to me.

After all the things he said about himself and all the things he has realized about himself.

But I have to say something because I've been wanting to say *something* for a very long time and once I've said that, I'll go.

I'll take my love and I'll leave.

I'll get out of his face.

"You're wrong," I tell him, and his chest stops moving, or at least it looks like it. "You're not a failure. You never were. You don't fail because your relationship wasn't as perfect as you thought it was or because you punched a guy or because you got kicked off your team. Or because you missed a goal or didn't win a trophy. Falling down and making mistakes don't automatically mean failing. It means you're human. It means that along with being The Blond Arrow, the great soccer player, you're also Arrow. You're a human being and you bleed and you hurt and you stumble and hit the ground like the rest of us. So no, you're not a failure. You're only human.

"But that's not all. There's something else. Something else that you're wrong about. Something very important. Your heart isn't dead. You didn't kill it. Because when Sarah cheated, it hurt. When she broke your trust, it hurt. When she betrayed you, it *hurt*. And when something hurts, it means that you can feel. It means that your heart is not dead. That's the whole problem, isn't it? Because a heart never dies. You stomp on it; you stab it with a knife; pour gasoline on it and set it on fire; you ignore it and bury it in the pursuit of perfection. You do whatever the fuck you want to it, Arrow, but it doesn't die. It beats and beats and *feels*. It feels all the things, good or bad, like this crazy little maniac that doesn't know how to quit.

"And you know how I know that? Because a heart is the reason why a girl falls in love with a boy when she's ten and stays in love with him for years even though she knows he can never be hers. Heart is the reason why a girl cries for that boy every night and yet smiles at a single glimpse of him. Heart is the reason why she writes secret love letters to him and why she sneaks out at night to see the boy she writes them for. Heart is the reason why a girl like me falls in doomed love with a clueless fucking guy like you. So no, your heart is not dead, Arrow. You might be The Blond Arrow but even you don't have the power to kill it."

By the time I finish, I feel like an age has passed.

I feel like we've lived a thousand years, and in that time, the snow has thickened.

Instead of disappearing, it's sticking to the ground now. It's sticking to the leaves, the grass, the earth.

It's sticking to him.

The flakes are settling on his hair, on his eyelashes. They stay on the collar of his damp shirt. They wet the angle of his jaw, stick like droplets on his cheekbones and lips. I even see a few drops run down from his forehead and get into his eyes.

But instead of blinking, he keeps watching me. He keeps staring at me like he's... still so riveted. And yet furious at the same time.

The boy I love.

So cold with the snow but so hot with all the things inside of him.

I wish I could do something about it. I wish I could do more for him.

But I can't, can I?

I can't save him if he's unwilling to save himself. I can only love him.

Turns out though, he doesn't want that either.

So this is it then.

This is all I can do.

With one last look at him, at his tall dark form, I take in a deep breath and turn around.

I take my love and leave like he told me to.

I trudge through the snow. The beautiful, hateful snow.

God, I *hate* it.

I hate everything about this stunning, gorgeous thing. So much so that somewhere between scaling the fence and getting inside the back door of the dorm building, I've started to cry again.

I'm not outright sobbing though.

Not yet.

I don't know why. Maybe I need another push.

A bigger push. A more forceful push.

A push that will jar me back into reality that what just happened, really happened. I told him that I loved him and he told me to take my love and get lost.

I told him my biggest secret and he rejected me.

A few seconds later I get that, that last push that thaws this chill and numbness that I'm feeling, when I sneak back into my room, all wet and shivering, and stumble on something.

It's one of my soccer cleats. The ones he bought for me.

I usually stick them under the bed, but somehow I must've forgotten to and so now I trip and stumble because of them.

And then, I just can't stop crying into my pillow as the love bite he gave me throbs painfully on my neck.

CHAPTER TWENTY-THREE

The Broken Arrow

I *write you letters... I have shoeboxes full of them...*

That's the one thing echoing in my head as I ride back to my motel in the snow and tear through the door. I march over to my nightstand and snap it open.

And there they are.

Not the letters, no. Not the ones that she's been writing to me for eight years. These are the ones she's been leaving me these past weeks.

The ones I'm addicted to.

Every day I open my mailbox, that piece of shit junk that gets jammed and I have to shake it open, telling myself that I'm doing it because that's what's expected of me.

As a member of the faculty, I need to be apprised of what's happening at St. Mary's. The staff meetings, a memo about lunchroom cleanliness and all the bullshit that goes on at a high school.

But when I stick my hand in to collect those documents, the very first one that I open is her orange envelope.

I fold them over and put them in an orange envelope...

That's what she said, right?

That she puts them in an envelope like these, the ones that I have scattered around the gray carpeted floor as my body crashes on my knees.

As I go to fish them out of those envelopes though, I realize my fingers are wet and snowy. So I wipe them on my pants. I wipe them on the sheets of my bed, dry them before I touch those notes.

Before I read what I've already read a thousand times.

A thousand fucking times.

I actually like to read them when she's here. When she's sleeping because I tired her out after sex.

So I can look at her rosy cheeks while reading her words.

So her moans are fresh in my mind.

I read them and get jacked up.

Then, either I wake her up to fuck her again or I work out like a demon.

Because her written words flow in my veins, float through my chest like the nicotine smoke of a cigarette and I don't know what else to do.

She thinks I'm exercising, breaking my bones, tearing up my muscles because I have some kind of a death wish. Because I want to be at the top of my game when I get back.

I don't tell her that it's because of her.

Because I don't know what to do with her.

I don't understand her. I don't understand where she came from and how she affects me like this. I don't understand what to do with the words she leaves me.

I don't tell her that I'm obsessed with her letters.

Because what the fuck is that going to accomplish anyway?

I *am* going back.

I am going to be at the top once again.

That's my destiny, isn't it?

That's what I've always wanted. That's what they taught me to want, my parents. My mother.

Greatness and perfection.

So I don't understand why there's a pain in my chest. Why it hasn't gone away since yesterday, when it appeared at the party.

Why is it so intense, so fucking massive that my heart – the thing that I thought I'd killed a long time ago – almost rips out of my chest and thumps on the floor, sullying the notes spread out before me?

It's beating and beating. *Pounding*, my heart.

As if it's really a crazy little maniac, like she told me. The most alive thing in my body.

The most alive thing in the world.

The most alive it's ever been.

For the girl who writes me letters.

Hundreds and hundreds of letters. Thousands even. Because she's been writing them for the past eight years.

And *that's* because she's been in love with me for the past eight years.

She's in love with me.

With me.

She's *stupidly* in love with a man who knows nothing about love. Who knows even less about it and relationships than a fucking four-year-old.

Jesus Christ, Salem.

Baby, you've fucked up. You've fucked up so bad.

I bark out a laugh.

For some reason, I can't stop laughing tonight.

For some reason, it hurts every time I do.

It hurts to be hunched over her scattered notes.

It fucking hurts to read her words over and over, while rocking back and forth as my reborn heart bangs against my rib cage.

She loves me.

She. *Loves*. Me.

Why does she love me?

Why does it hurt that she does?

Why does it hurt that I can't be anything other than what I am?

Why can't I breathe? Why the world is still closing in at the thought that I'm The Blond Arrow?

The fucking perfectionist who can't love the girl who's in love with him.

CHAPTER TWENTY-FOUR

I once heard a song about a girl dancing on landmines.

Slow dancing.

Because she wanted to hold on to this boy she was in love with. And holding on to him was like holding an explosive in her hands. So she'd tiptoe around him all so she could love him. Until one day everything blows up in her face.

Things explode and she catches fire.

Well, what else do you expect when you fall in love with a grenade?

What else do you expect when you fall in love with the sun?

It's what the sun does.

It burns everything. Melts everything. Turns everything into dust.

That's why Icarus, the fool who flew too close to the sun with wings made of wax, was stupid.

That's why *I* am stupid.

And miserable and sad.

But what I'm not is angry.

I'm not angry at him. For being who he is. For being the sun he is.

I try though.

Especially the next day when I wake up and see, through the bars on my window, there's no snow on the ground. It's not that I love the snow or anything. It's just that I thought there would be some evidence of what transpired between us, me and him, only a few hours ago.

Some evidence of the chill, the wreckage.

Even his love bite is gone. I don't see it sitting on my neck, in the mirror.

As if I imagined everything. Imagined his teeth. Imagined the snow.

Again, I try to be angry at something.

At him.

But I can't be because it's not his fault.

It's not his fault that he doesn't want love. He doesn't need it. He doesn't even know what to do with it.

It's not his fault that he's The Blond Arrow.

He trained for it his entire life. He worked for it.

I have seen it with my own eyes. His dedication, his determination.

His single-minded focus.

So it's not his fault that in the pursuit of all that he forgot to be anything else.

To be anyone else.

It's not his fault that he's lost.

Because that's what he is, isn't he?

After what happened with my sister, what she did and how their relationship turned out to be. Even I'm lost because I, too, thought their relationship was perfect.

Arrow didn't *do* this to himself; it happened to him.

So I can't be angry at him.

But I *am* sad.

And turns out that it's also something I shouldn't be.

Because I already knew that there was very little chance that we'd ever get together. Very little chance that he'd ever love me.

Someone like me. Someone so opposite of him.

And I've known this ever since I was ten.

But my heart, my fucking heart, doesn't understand that. It doesn't understand logic and rationalizations and all the explanations I've been giving myself ever since I turned around and left him standing in the snow.

Because ever since I was ten, I've also wanted just one thing.

Him.

To be perfect for him. To be special to him.

Yeah, my heart is stupid and it hurts.

It hurts so bad that I walk around St. Mary's with perpetual water in my eyes.

My tears sit there as I work in the garden with the rest of the girls. When I secretly clip a gardenia and pocket it, one spills out and flows down to my trembling lips. Another spills when I do my trig homework later in the library and get all the questions wrong because he isn't here to teach me.

The girls are as supportive as they've ever been.

Especially when I tell them everything.

I tell them that I've loved him since I was ten and that I shouldn't have because he was with my sister. Then I tell them that last night when I yelled *I love you* to him, he told me to get lost.

I don't tell them about the breakup though, and all the other secrets that he has. Because I will never tell, not in a million years. I know that without filling in those gaps, I might come off as a girl with a witchy heart who goes after her sister's boyfriend.

But like him, they don't judge.

Like him, they absolve me, which is something I haven't really thought about, him absolving me, I mean. Because if I do, I might never get up from my bed. I might never stop crying for what he did for me.

Something wonderful.

Anyway, my friends listen and when I cry for the thousandth time, they wipe my tears. Then Poe says that we'll be going out tonight.

Because I could use a distraction.

Actually, I'm not the only one. Callie could use a distraction too.

Because her mood is like mine.

Her mood is blacker, actually.

Maybe because for the past two days, she's been kinda sick. I mean, it comes and goes. Like yesterday, she was throwing up in the morning but she was fine all day after that. Today too, she had a bout of vomiting before walking over for breakfast.

I don't know what's going on.

Maybe it's some kind of a stomach bug.

But whatever this is, we have decided that if it doesn't get better soon – as she keeps insisting – we'll drag her to the nurse ourselves.

So maybe going out is a good thing.

Although I don't think anything can cheer me up, not for a very long time. But if it helps Callie then I'm all for it.

That's why hours later, I stack my pillows on the bed and cover them with a blanket before tiptoeing out of the room. I walk down the darkened hallway and meet the girls at the exit.

However, instead of pushing the door open, they all give me grave looks.

Callie, who looks as healthy as ever, even after what happened in the morning, is the first to speak. "Okay so, don't freak out."

As soon as she says that my heart starts pounding and it must be visible on my face because Poe swats Callie's arm. "You're freaking her out by saying that."

Callie grimaces. "Yikes. Sorry. I honestly just wanted to curb the blow."

The blow.

My heart gets stuck in my throat at this and I slip and stutter with my words. "W-what..."

When I can't complete my sentence, Wyn steps in. "You're both freaking her out."

She grabs my arm and smiles. Although there's nothing happy about it as she says, "He's leaving."

"What?"

Poe touches my shoulder to get my attention. "I heard it through someone last night. Arrow's leaving. Coach TJ is gonna be the main coach until they can find a replacement. They'll probably make the announcement tomorrow."

Callie gives me a sympathetic look. "We didn't wanna say anything before. Because you wouldn't have been able to do anything about it."

"But you can now," Wyn says.

"Yeah, go to him." That's Poe.

They're all standing around me, holding some part of my body, my arms, my shoulders, as they tell me that I should go to him and do something about it.

Only I don't know what.

I don't know what I can do if he's leaving.

He's leaving.

Leaving.

I mean, I knew that he was gonna leave but I didn't know it was gonna be this soon. That it was gonna be just two days after I told him that I love him.

That's why he's leaving, isn't he?

Because I told him I loved him.

Because now he thinks that I'm gonna be declaring my love to him every two seconds. He probably thinks that I'm gonna throw myself at him like I've done countless times before.

Take your love and get out of my face...

And oh God, I have to tell him.

I have to tell him that I won't. That I won't bother him or make his life harder.

I won't go to him or talk to him or be all dramatic about it.

In fact, I promised myself that I won't even watch him around St. Mary's. I won't watch him in the hallways or in the dining room, in the library or on the soccer field.

So this is stupid, him leaving.

"I have to stop him," I burst out, finally coming to a conclusion.

I also do it loud.

Louder than I should have because the girls quiet down around me. They all give me startled looks and I shake my head. "I didn't... I didn't mean to be so –"

"No, it's okay. Go." Callie squeezes my shoulder.

"Yeah, I called you a cab. So you should be good," Poe tells me with a determined nod.

"But... what about us going out?"

Poe waves her hand. "That was just a hoax. Something we had to tell you so you'd be ready at midnight."

Wyn smiles proudly. "I came up with that."

Despite everything, I chuckle.

Gosh, they've thought of everything, haven't they?

My friends, and they don't even know the whole story yet.

Who would've thought that I'd make friends at a *reform* school? That I'd love them all to pieces.

And that they'd push me out the door when I just stand there, feeling over-whelmed and flabbergasted, so I could go and stop the love of my life.

But as soon as the night air hits me, I take off at a run.

I'm filled with determination and purpose.

I'm filled with calmness. Or as much calmness as I can be filled with at a time like this. At a time when he is leaving.

Because I declared my love to him.

God.

What an idiotic thing to do and what an idiotic way to react.

But it's okay. I'll stop him.

I don't remember giving the cabbie his address but somehow, I'm here.

I'm in front of his gray door and I'm knocking.

I realize I've never done that before, knock on his door I mean. Whenever I came here, to this L-shaped building with its gray railing, overlooking the highway, he was always with me.

So I think it's going to be a little shocking when he sees me on his doorstep.

And it is.

It *is* shocking when a second later, Arrow opens the door and finds me – the girl who loves him.

He actually draws back an inch and I fist my hands at my sides.

I'm probably the last person he was expecting to see and yet, here I am.

Complete with my love and all.

Complete with my messy hair and freckles and chunky sweater and soccer cleats. And out-of-control pounding heart.

In my defense, I do try to control my heart and not ogle him. Which is very difficult because he doesn't have a shirt on.

His hard muscles are on display and they're sweaty. Also, they are panting and heaving.

I try not to look at his expanding ribs and hollowing out stomach and the way he's frowning at me, mouth open, nostrils flaring.

Because he doesn't need that.

He doesn't need me to look at him with puppy dog eyes and his next words prove it. "What the fuck are you doing here?"

I try not to flinch, but I can only do so much in this moment. "I –"

"How did you get here?" he asks but then doesn't give me the time to answer him because he pokes his head out to glance up and down the sidewalk as if to check on things.

As if just by looking he can deduce how I came to be here.

I move back slightly while he does his inspection. While his musky scent fills my nose and his chest almost grazes mine.

Because again, he doesn't need that.

When he comes to stand straight, he warns, "Salem."

Breaking out of my stupor, I say, "I... You're leaving."

At my words, his jaw tics and he asks again, "How the fuck did you get here?"

"I took a cab."

He stares at me, immobile and frozen, his eyes dark. "Come in."

"I don't –"

"Just..." He sighs. "It's cold. You're shaking. Come inside."

As soon as he says it in his rough, gravelly tone, I feel the first shiver roll down my spine. The first tremble of my legs, my belly.

And I realize that he's right.

I *am* shaking. I have probably been shaking this whole time without my knowledge.

But it's not the cold.

It's him.

It's from the sight of him, all sweaty and so familiar in his dark gray sweatpants, hanging low on his pelvis, and his bare feet. His dirty blond hair that appears dark brown right now, matted across his forehead.

I bet he was trying to kill himself again, by working out too hard.

When I still don't move, he steps away from the door and holds it open, his biceps flexing. "Would you just get inside?"

"Right. Sorry," I mumble, trying again to act unemotional.

Just get your shit together, Salem.

Wiping my hands down my cargo pants, I duck my head and step inside, careful, *extremely* careful, not to touch him.

When he shuts the door, I turn around to face him and repeat, "You're leaving."

"I am."

"Why?"

His eyes go back and forth between mine for a second before he replies, "Because that was always the plan. Because I was always supposed to leave."

Plan.

Yeah, he's obsessed with planning.

"What about your therapist?" I ask, again all calm like.

"What about her?"

"Isn't she supposed to have a say in when you leave?"

He stares at me for a beat. "No one has a say in when I leave."

Right.

Not even me. Not that I ever had it but still.

He sighs again.

Although I don't think it helps with loosening him up at all. His body, his muscles are as tight as ever. They're almost straining from whatever is going on inside of him.

"Besides, I can find another therapist," he says, standing tall and straight. "In LA."

"And your team?" I swallow. "Are they fine with you coming back so soon?"

"I was always going to go back one day. So yeah."

I bite the inside of my cheek to keep my lips from trembling and my eyes from filling up. "But one day, right? Not right now."

"One day. Today. Right now. What's the difference?"

He asks the question calmly.

Very, very calmly and I bet he doesn't even have to go to all the lengths that I'm going to. To appear this way.

Because suddenly it hits me.

He's acting like the old Arrow. The one who used to be unruffled and determined.

Like the snow and the bite of his love that disappeared the next day, the new Arrow – *my* Arrow – is gone. In his place is the Arrow that I fell in love with but had no clue about who he was.

It leaves a bitter taste in my mouth.

A sour taste.

Like I'm drinking my own tears.

"Is it because of me?"

At this, I see a flinch.

I see the bare muscles of his stomach tightening and standing up in stark relief like I've punched him.

But his face shows no effect.

"What makes you think it's because of you?" he asks in a rough tone.

"Because I love you."

I suck in a breath at my declaration.

At my stupid, *stupid* declaration.

God.

No wonder he's leaving. I just can't stop saying it.

I just can't stop telling him how much I love him.

When I came here I thought that I'd simply imply it. But turns out it's super easy to say it now that the secret is out, and it's super hard for him to hear.

Because his abs tighten up again.

So I clear my throat and amend the statement. "I mean, because *I told you* that I love you."

"And?"

"And you're leaving two days later," I almost snap out at him, my hands fisted and my legs wide.

He notices it.

He notices my battle stance and something about that makes him sigh again.

This time though, the sigh works and he loosens up a little.

Making me wonder if this is what he wanted.

To provoke me so I'd lose my calm and become the crazy, dramatic Salem that he knows.

"Again, what difference does it make? I was going to leave anyway," he says.

It makes a difference because I don't want you to go, you asshole.

I wish I could say it to him.

I really, *really* wish that I could say it, scream it at his face and shake him.

But I can't.

"If you think," I begin, licking my lips, "that I'm going to throw myself at you again or declare my love to you randomly walking down the hallway or something then you're wrong. I got the message. I got it, okay? You don't want my love. You don't need it. You don't know what to do with it. So you don't have to leave town, the whole freaking state, just because I told you my feelings."

Okay, I didn't mean to go off there at the end. I shouldn't have raised my voice and bent my neck and clenched my teeth.

But I did.

Because how can he just stand there and be all unaffected when I'm going to pieces over here. When I'm shattering and there's this epic pain in my chest and I don't know if it will ever go away.

I don't know if it will ever stop hurting.

He swallows then and runs his fingers through his damp hair. "Look Salem, what happened that night –"

"Can't we just forget about it? Can't we just forget about that night? About what I said?"

"No."

"I –"

"I can't forget it." His voice rises up then. "I can't forget... what you said."

His jaw moves back and forth as if he's crushing my words – those three words that I said to him – between his teeth.

"So this is for the best," he continues. "This clean break. You go your way and I go mine. Besides, as I said, I was going to leave anyway. All of this was temporary."

Before I can say anything else, he moves.

I watch him walk across his dull gray room and retrieve an envelope that was sitting on his desk. He brings it back to me and my hand automatically reaches out to grab it.

Like I have to take everything he gives me.

Like I'm incapable of refusing him anything.

I'm pathetic, aren't I?

Shaking my head, I look at it. A nondescript beige envelope.

"I was going to leave it with Coach TJ, but since you're here, you can have it," he explains.

I frown. "What is it?"

"Application for the Galaxy's youth program next summer. I filled it out for you. And my recommendation letter."

My fingers spasm and I look down at it again.

My new dream, my ambition that he gave me a couple of weeks ago. Something that I never thought I could have: a goal.

A chance to play some real soccer because I never thought I was good enough.

Until him.

Until he told me that I was and made me realize that I could do it.

I'd forgotten about it actually.

Because of everything.

And I realize now that if he hadn't given me this, I never would've remembered.

"You filled out my application and gave me a recommendation letter?" I repeat when I look up, feeling... floored.

Overwhelmed.

And in so much pain.

"Yeah. I..." He clamps his jaw before swallowing. "I've never seen anyone like you – play like you do. You're talented, Salem. You're very fucking talented and no matter what you decide to do with it, I want you to know that you have my support. You have my belief." He swallows again, the blue in his eyes shining. "I believe in you. I believe that you can go places. Should you choose to."

I could drown in the blue of his eyes.

I could drown in the warmth he's causing in my body. I could drown in my love for him. In his belief. In *me*.

I could drown and die.

Not only that I could throw myself at him too.

I could throw myself at his feet, wrap my hands around his leg and let myself be dragged through the streets, trailing behind him as he leaves.

Just to slow him down. Just to stop him.

Just to *be* with him.

I could do all of that and I could do it all right this second.

The very things I promised that I wouldn't do.

All because he believes in me when no one else has ever done that.

That's why I hug the envelope to my chest and blink.

I also nod and whisper, "Thank you. Uh, can you call me a cab, please? I'd like to go back."

His eyes flare as if taken aback. "What?"

I hug the envelope tighter, dig my nails in my waist. "Please?"

At this, resignation washes over his face and he jerks out a nod. "I'll take you back."

I don't argue; the less time spent in his company, the better.

So I nod too and with a last look at me, he moves.

He goes into the bathroom, grabs a shirt and puts it on, even though he's sweaty from his workout. Grabbing his keys with tight movements, he strides to the door. He jerks it open for me and I walk through it.

And then, we're riding back to St. Mary's, me sitting behind his back, clutching his rigid frame and the envelope.

Hugging the love of my life and his belief in me.

His precious, immeasurable, invaluable belief.

Like the cab ride, I don't remember this ride either, which is a shame because this is my last ride on a motorcycle.

I always knew that if I can't ride with him, I wouldn't wanna ride at all.

Soon it comes to an end, my last ride.

Soon, I'm climbing off his bike and standing on the ground. I'm looking at his face, his beautiful, stunning face. Sharp, jutting features.

My Arrow.

Even though he had a helmet on, his hair's all messy, half damp from his workout and half falling over his brows, framing his navy eyes.

Eyes that have such intense, *intense* emotions.

Hugging the envelope to my chest, I say, "I..."

His hands on the handlebar flex and he says in a voice that sounds both eager and low, "You what?"

"I, uh, always thought, back when we lived together, that you were this perfect guy," I say, biting my lip and I notice another flex, this one on his jaw. "You were so calm and determined and focused, you know? So dedicated to the game, to your goals. I don't think I'd ever seen anyone with your focus. Not even my sister or my mom. I admired that about you. A lot. The Blond Arrow.

"But then years later, I got to know you. I actually got to know you. I mean, it's funny because I had all these plans of going away and you were somewhere else. But somehow we ended up in the same place. But anyway, I got to know a different side of you. A new side. This guy who smokes because he's stressed out. This guy who can get really angry when his trust is broken. Who can be so vulnerable and strong and tortured all at the same time. This guy who can be so mean and rude. Sometimes so much that I wanna smack him. But then sometimes he can be so sweet, you know?"

I chuckle brokenly. "I want to say that... I like that guy. That Arrow. And it hurts me that you think that guy is a failure. That he's a liability. That he should be ignored. That anything other than The Blond Arrow, any other instinct that you have, is wrong. It hurts me when you beat that guy up for his flaws. Because that guy has something to offer, you know? That guy has so much to offer. You know how I know that?"

His jaw is ticking and ticking.

And I know that the heart that he thinks is dead is pounding inside his chest. I can see the tight vein on his neck throbbing just like his jaw.

"How?" he rasps, his eyes somehow both molten and on fire.

"Because he's the guy who gave me this." I motion to the envelope stuck to my chest. "He's the guy who gave me a chance. *Me.* A girl who's never followed a rule. A girl who never ever wanted to be perfect. He gave *me* a chance. He inspired me to be more. Not only that, that guy forgave me. For something that I've been beating myself up for for years, for falling in love with my sister's boyfriend. He forgave me, Arrow. How can that guy be anything less than perfect when he gave me such a *perfect* gift?

"Please, please don't shut him out, Arrow. *Please.* He's inside of you and he's good. He deserves more. He deserves your acceptance. Don't shut that part of yourself out. Give it a chance, like you gave me. You told me that I could go places, right? That guy can go places too. That guy can do whatever he wants. That guy can be whoever he wants. Just... please give him a chance. Give *your-self* a chance. You can be *both.* The Blond Arrow and just Arrow. And do you know how I know *that*?"

This time, he doesn't say anything.

He simply stares at me with so much emotion that my knees get weak.

But I hold on.

Because I want to see him one last time, study him one last time.

I focus on his wicked jaw and sharp cheekbones. I focus on his tight broad shoulders. The sleek biceps, his muscular, powerful thighs.

The body built to be the best.

The Blond Arrow. Just Arrow.

My Arrow.

I reach my hand out and comb his sun-struck hair back for the last time. I lean in with my lips and kiss his cheek before whispering, "Because I believe in you too."

And then, I spin around and I run.

I run, clutching the envelope to my chest as tears stream down my face. As my heart pounds and pounds in my chest and my legs, making me run faster than ever.

I run even when I hear him call out my name. Not once but twice.

In fact, I run harder.

I don't wanna hear whatever he has to say to me because I know it won't be what I want to hear: that he'll stay.

So I keep going.

I scale the fence that I've done a thousand times before. I run through the grounds and race back to the dorm building and turn the knob again like I've done a thousand times before.

But when I get in, everything is different.

I haven't seen this before, everything bright and loud, instead of dark and silent. Crowded hallway instead of a sleepy, empty one.

Up ahead there are girls, a large group of them.

All in their night clothes, their hair rumpled, faces turned away from me because they're all looking at something.

A commotion of some kind.

There are voices and screaming and murmurs and gasps.

It takes me a moment to figure out that it's Callie's sweet high voice. "Can you just put that down? Is that really necessary?"

"Yeah, why are you being such a fucking bitch?" That's Poe in her husky troublemaking voice.

"She deserves some goddamn privacy," snaps Wyn, the soft and quiet one.

Crazily I think that it's weird how I can tell all of them apart by just their voices. It's a testament to the fact that I love them so much and I should go to them because they're in trouble.

I would've too, if not for the nasal voice that raises itself above all else. The one that I hear in trigonometry class every week and in our one-on-one sessions.

Mrs. Miller.

"I'm being a bitch, Poe, because a student is missing. And if a student is missing, Wyn, then she has no privacy and yes, Callie, this is absolutely necessary. Especially when we've just found boxes and boxes of letters addressed to whom I can only deduce is the principal's son. Who also happens to be the coach. And I know that you three definitely had something to do with her disappearance. Which means you'll all be getting detention along with her. The girl cops are looking for right now, Salem Salinger."

My name goes off in the corridor like a bomb. That grenade in the song that I've been humming for the past two days.

Maybe it should freeze me in my spot. Maybe it should chill me to my bones and make me pass out with shock.

But it doesn't.

Because they've got my letters.

Just then a gap opens up in the huddle and I see Miller. I see her with an orange envelope, and I see her retrieving a folded page before reading, out loud, "My Darling Arrow…"

And then, the envelope in my hand, his belief in me, slips out and falls to the floor and I'm running again.

I'm running down the hallway and I realize that the thump of my feet is the loudest in this space of chaos, even louder than Miller's nasally voice, reading out my letter.

The letter that belongs to me. The letter I wrote for him. And I need to get it back.

That's the only thought in my mind. Get that letter back.

I realize that girls have started to turn away from Miller and focus on me. They're gawking at me.

Gawking at the crazy girl who not only wrote these letters but was also missing. Who's now dashing toward a teacher with red eyes, screaming, "Stop. It's mine. It's mine. Mine. Mine."

But I don't care.

I need that letter back.

It's mine. It's fucking mine.

I'm so close to it. So close to that piece of paper, the only thing that I can see right now, but something jars my body.

Something binds itself around my stomach and stops me in my tracks and that gets me so enraged, so angry, so devastated that I kick my feet.

I claw at the band around my waist, all the while screaming and staring at that letter, clutched within foreign fingers. "Let me go. Let me go."

But they don't.

They don't let me go and that's when the explosion hits me, the explosion that happened two days ago and the one that occurred just now.

It all hits me like an earthquake and everything goes black.

CHAPTER TWENTY-FIVE

The Broken Arrow

I 'm not leaving.

I can't. I *can't* leave.

Because I have to tell her.

I have to tell her that the guy she was talking about, the guy who can be angry and mean and fucking sweet, the guy who inspired her, that guy didn't exist.

Not before her.

Not before seeing her at the bar, looking so luminous and stunning. Not before she marched up to me and changed my whole fucking life.

She brought him into existence.

Her.

She built that guy. She created his wildness, his temper, his needs, his wants.

She created his longing.

His cravings.

Such deep, great cravings that when I saw her walking away last night, I realized something.

I realized that the pain I'd been feeling, the hurt that wouldn't stop pressing into my body ever since that night in LA was want.

It was the result of my newly born cravings. Something that I'd never had before.

Something that made me call out her name, howl it out like a wounded, desperate animal but she didn't stop.

She kept running, filling me with such panic, such terror...

And I know now that I never would've been able to leave. I never would've been able to board that plane and leave her behind.

Because all my life I've only ever wanted one thing – soccer – but she made me want something else.

In the time she was with me, she taught me to want something other than a trophy, a goal or a game. She taught me to crave something more than cold and lonely perfection.

Something warm and cozy and sweet. Something wild and savage and provocative.

Her.

I crave her.

I crave her laughs, her voice, her challenges and dares. I crave how she breaks the rules, how she scales the fence to come see me. I crave seeing her drowning in my leather jacket and sitting on the back of my Ducati.

I crave taking her to the Lover's Lane that she'd talk about, but never got the chance to go. I crave teaching her all those moves I had made a list of: Elastico, Maradona, Forward Pull, V-Pull.

I crave her notes. Her letters.

All the things *she* inspires in me.

I crave them so much, so *fucking* much that my heart won't stop thundering.

It hasn't stopped ever since that night in the snow when she told me that it was alive, and I have to tell her all of this.

I have to tell her that I want her, I crave her but I don't know how to keep her. How to not fuck this up because this is the first time I want something.

Something other than soccer, and I'm fucking panicking.

I'm quaking in my boots.

But I'm willing to believe in myself.

Like she believes in me.

That's what she told me, right?

She told me that she believes in me and if *she* can believe in me, then I can learn to believe in myself too.

I can learn to *believe* that I can be whoever I want to be.

I always thought that if I accepted my flaws and forgave myself for my mistakes, if I didn't beat myself up or shame myself for screwing up, I wouldn't be my father's son. Or if I focused on something else even for a second, I wouldn't be my mother's son.

I wouldn't be The Blond Arrow.

But maybe there's another way.

Her way. My way.

A way that I can embrace all parts of me and be whole. Be *hers*.

Her Arrow.

So yeah, I have to tell her all of this.

In fact, I'm going to her now, right this second. I know it's Monday and school is in but fuck it.

I'm not waiting.

I'll pull her out of class if I have to but I'm talking to her and maybe she'll reject me.

After everything, I wouldn't blame her.

But I'll take it. I'll take it like a man and I'll keep trying.

I'll keep trying to be her Arrow.

But just as I'm about to kickstart my bike, my phone rings in my pocket. I almost ignore it but something makes me fish it out.

It's Mom.

I don't really want to talk to her right now but it could be important. It could be about Salem and her time at St. Mary's.

My mother is out of town for some conference or whatever but a day ago, I called her up and told her that she needs to get Salem out of that hellhole and bring her back home. My mother was reluctant – because every mistake has to be paid in full – but I was adamant. She can punish me all she wants and she can keep punishing me for the rest of my life but no one is touching Salem.

No one *ever* touches Salem.

Even my mother, the woman who raised me and the woman I owe everything to.

So I'm already expecting to shut her down but as soon as I pick up, she says, "Arrow."

Just my name.

And my fingers clutch the phone tightly. Forcefully.

I think she knows that she has my attention because she sighs. "It's about Salem."

Something grabs me by the gut. Something vicious and unrelenting. Something that makes me grip the phone even tighter.

"What about her?" I ask slowly.

"They found letters," Mom says. "They were addressed to you."

I write you letters...

"Someone alerted the warden that Salem was missing from her bed," she continues. "And the warden told Samantha Miller. And they found boxes and boxes of letters in her room and..."

I have shoeboxes full of them...

The thing in my gut spreads, slips into my veins and every corner of my body.

It's hot and savage and animalistic and it has claws. They're digging inside of me, in my muscles, making me growl into the phone, "What did they do to her?"

"People said that she freaked out when she saw Miller reading them out loud and she charged at her. The guards had to get involved. They had to restrain her; she passed out. She's at the hospital. She's fine though. She's fine. They think she got really hysterical and that's why she fainted."

"Which hospital?"

"The one in town. Listen, Arrow, did you know about the letters? Was she sneaking out to see you?"

The claws twist in my organs and I choke out, "Yes."

Because I was a stubborn, foolish asshole who was going to leave her.

"Is it because of her, then? Is that why you won't get back together with Sarah? Because you have a thing for her sister?"

I've heard that tone from my mom before.

It's a tone that brings a hot surge of shame. A surge of crawling bugs.

But I crush them now. This thing inside of me crushes the shame into a million pieces and that's when I realize what this savage thing is.

It's my heart.

It has turned into an animal. It has turned into an organ of fury. An organ of anger with claws and roars and it's pounding so fast, so ferociously that it's making me shake.

"No, Mom," I say with a voice that's shaking too. "I'm not with Sarah anymore because we shouldn't have gotten together in the first place. Our whole relationship was a mistake and the evidence of that is the fact that she cheated on me. And I didn't tell you because I was ashamed. Because I thought I'd failed and I wasn't perfect. Because I thought perfection was everything and I didn't want to disappoint you. But I'm glad it happened. I'm glad she cheated. I'm glad I'm not perfect because if I was then I wouldn't have noticed her. I wouldn't have noticed the girl for whom I'm going to fucking destroy this Samantha Miller. That's her name, isn't it? For her, I'm going to tear apart those guards because they dared to touch her. And I'm going to fucking crush every single person who stands in my way. And I'm going to do all of that because she's the girl I'll do anything for. She's the girl I'll *be* anything for. Do you understand? She's my girl and I'm going to her."

CHAPTER TWENTY-SIX

I forgot to hide my shoeboxes.

I forgot to put them in a safe place and now my letters are gone.

I kept telling myself that I would. That I would carry them all in my backpack and go across campus and hide them up in the third-floor bathroom or bury them by the gardenias or something.

I mean there are a lot of places where I could have hidden them.

But I didn't.

"I forgot."

I hear my own scratchy voice and I think I said it out loud.

But I can't be sure because things are a little hazy as well as a little loud. There are beeping sounds around me and I think that my eyes are closed too.

When I blink them open, I see a room I've never seen before but I immediately know what it is.

That stink of bleach and the white pristine ceiling can only belong to one place. Plus the beeping machine by my head and the drip that hangs by it and is connected to my arm are a clear indication.

I'm in a hospital.

Because they took my letters.

Because I forgot to hide them and they were reading one out loud and I didn't know how to make them stop.

"Hey, you're awake."

It's Callie.

I turn my head to look at her. "Hey. Yeah."

She's sitting on a chair beside my bed and she looks haggard. Her eyes are swollen and there are dark circles under them. Still she's smiling at me, her elbows on the bed. "How do you feel?"

I blink several times, trying to think.

I even try to move my body but everything feels so heavy and clunky. So lethargic and foggy.

"Dizzy. Lazy."

She chuckles. "It's okay. I think you're just weak. The doctor said that your sugar level was pretty low. And you just needed something to eat. So they gave you that." She points to the drip bag that's connected to my arm. "But it's fine. You're gonna be fine."

"What happened... to me?"

She sighs. "You were screaming and running toward Miller. We kept telling you to stop but you wouldn't listen so that stupid fucking bitch set the guards on you. And you completely..." Her fingers mimic explosion. "Blew up. And then just passed out."

I blink again, several times actually, as a lump settles itself in my throat. But somehow, I forge on. "What are you doing here?"

"They agreed to let us come see you. Not at first though. But we did some arguing. Plus Principal Carlisle called when she found out that Miller was holding us in her office. She kept us there for hours, interrogating us. Principal Carlisle got really mad about it. Said we should be with you until she gets back from New York. Poe and Wyn are here too, by the way. They're down at the cafeteria."

I lick my dry lips. "Thanks for having my back."

Callie squeezes my arm and I realize I'm in hospital clothes, a yellow paper-type gown. "Are you okay though?"

That lump of emotion gets bigger, clogging my throat again, and all I can do is whisper, "I forgot. To hide them."

Callie's eyes tear up. "I'm sorry. I'm so sorry, Salem. I feel like it's our fault. We asked you to go and –"

Somehow, I get enough energy to put my hand over hers. "No. It's not your fault. It's no one's fault. I should've hidden them somewhere and I knew..." I try to swallow again. "I knew I was taking a risk sneaking out. Especially after what happened with Elanor that night and..."

I trail off because suddenly I realize something.

Something that I ignored before in my grief.

The night it snowed and I came back, crying, I stumbled on my soccer shoe.

I know I chalked it up to me being untidy but I specifically remember stowing them under the bed, so when I ask my next question, I already know the answer to it.

"Was it her? Did she tell the warden?"

Callie nods. "Yeah. Just as soon as you left."

"She knew about the letters, didn't she?"

"She told the warden about them and all hell broke loose. Miller had every box taken up to her office." Callie squeezes my arm again. "We tried to stop them, I swear, Salem. God, I can't believe Miller was being so cruel. She's such a bitch."

"Hey, it's okay. It's fine. She always hated me. I should've hidden them but..." I look up at the ceiling again, my eyes stinging with tears. "I just couldn't, you know? I couldn't part with them and that was stupid. But then that's nothing new, really. I've always been stupid."

Stupid and hopeless and doomed.

That's what I am and I've always known that.

Always.

But I never knew that I'd lose my letters because of it. Because of my stupidity.

I thought they'd always be with me. That I'd always have them by my side.

They're my love story, see. I thought that as long as I had them, I wouldn't be lonely. That it wouldn't matter I don't have the one thing that I want so badly in my life.

It wouldn't matter that I'm doomed.

But they're gone now.

They're gone and God, I've never felt lonelier.

"You're not stupid, Salem," Callie says, breaking into my thoughts. "You're in love. You just love him."

I chuckle hollowly. "Yeah, I do. I love him."

And he's gone too, isn't he?

My Arrow.

The boy I wrote those letters for. He left too. He's probably on a plane right now, going to the place where he belongs.

Because he was always going to leave.

Because everything we had was temporary and it's for the best.

That's what he told me and he was right.

It *is* for the best.

I've always been alone in my love. So why should something change now?

Why should my love that has always been doomed suddenly get a new life? Why should he love *me* when he can't love anyone?

I'm not that special.

So I'm glad he's gone. I'm glad it's over and I'm glad that I can cry and sob and be all emotional without it being a bother to him.

Yeah, glad.

Glad is what I am.

"What happened with him?" Callie asks, hesitantly.

I shrug. "Nothing. He's leaving."

"Are you serious?" When I nod, her eyes flash with anger. "God, boys are so stupid, aren't they? What is wrong with him? Can't he see that you love him?"

I chuckle again. And again, it's hollow and it hurts my chest and my throat and my heart.

It hurts everything.

"He can. That's why he's leaving."

She scoffs, sitting back in her chair. "What a giant douchebag. I fucking hate boys."

And just like that, her dark circles become prominent.

They aren't even circles; they're pits, and her cheekbones are sunken and I realize that my friend needs me too.

Gathering whatever energy I have, I pull myself and sit up. "Callie, will you please tell me what's going on between you and him?" She stiffens and I grab her hand. "I know about keeping secrets, okay? I know. But please, let me help you. Please tell me what's going on with you?"

Tears shine in her eyes as she whispers, "Nothing." She sniffles. "Everything."

"Talk to me. Tell me, please. Maybe I can help."

"No one can help me."

"Callie, come on. What is it?"

She opens her mouth and breathes out. A teardrop streams down her cheek as she whispers, "I think... I think I'm pregnant."

My fingers tighten around her hand. "What?"

Ducking her head, she nods. "I'm pregnant. I haven't taken the test b-but I know."

"Is that why... Is that why you've been throwing up?"

Her shoulders slump and when they shake, I get my confirmation.

Gosh, I've been such an idiot.

We all have been.

Callie has been throwing up in the mornings, but she'd be okay all day. Isn't that like, the most obvious sign?

Leaning forward, I push back her soft blonde hair and urge her to look at me. "God, Callie. I'm so sorry. I'm..." My eyes fill up with tears too. "Why didn't you tell us?"

She whips her eyes up, all red-rimmed and angry. "Because I'm such an idiot, Salem. I'm the biggest idiot in the world. He broke my heart, okay? That asshole broke my heart and I promised myself that I'd never ever fall for him again. And he comes back into town and I do the exact thing I told myself I wouldn't. And now I'm pregnant. With that... villain's baby and..."

I rub her back in circles. "Hey, it's okay. It's okay. We'll figure things out. We'll –"

"There's nothing to figure out. Don't you see? It's not as if I can keep it a secret. People are gonna know and they'll expel me from St. Mary's and God, my brother is gonna be so mad at me." She covers her face, crying, and my tears start spilling too.

"Does he... Does Reed know?"

She shakes her head before lifting it, her watery eyes filled with determination, with a look that says she's a girl betrayed in love. "No, and I'm not going to tell him either."

"But shouldn't he know? I mean, he... he's the dad."

"Fuck him, okay? Fuck him. He lied to me all those years ago. I thought he loved me but he didn't. I was the only one in love, and apparently I still am because look at me, spreading my legs for him like a stupid slut. But that's it. That's all he's taking from me. I'm *not* giving him my baby."

"But Callie, I think you should really –"

My words die out when I hear a commotion outside.

Much like the one I heard last night when I entered the dorm building and found my love story exposed to everyone at the school.

But this one is much more violent.

This commotion has crashing sounds and thundering footsteps and a growly voice. "Where is she? Where the fuck is she?"

His voice.

It reaches me through the corridor and the glass windows of my room and raises itself above the beep, beep, beep of the machines and the thump, thump, thump of my heart.

It not only reaches me, it wraps itself around me like a pair of arms – his sleek, muscular arms – warming me up, making me realize that I was cold before.

But he's here and all cold is gone.

I can even see him through my window.

He's looking around, frantic, running his fingers through his sun-struck hair, his jaw unshaven and messy, the chain around his neck shining like always.

A second later, he finds me.

His eyes land on me and his whole body shudders. It's a visible spasm that rolls through his muscles. That I can feel in my own stomach.

We stare at each other through the space and I feel like he knows everything.

I feel like he *feels* what I'm feeling.

All the grief and all the sadness at losing those letters and I just want him to put those strong arms of his around me and hug me.

"Apparently, he didn't leave," Callie murmurs from beside me and the moment breaks.

Everything comes rushing back.

He was leaving, wasn't he?

Yeah, he was.

I don't know what he's doing here but my letters are gone and I'm lonelier than ever. And as soon as he starts striding toward me, I look away.

Callie gives me a tremulous smile. "I think I'm gonna go. I'll go find out what Wyn and Poe are up to."

I grab her wrist, suddenly feeling afraid.

I haven't looked but I know he's up to the threshold now. He'll enter the room any second and I don't wanna be alone with him.

Especially when I'm feeling so vulnerable.

"I don't... I..." I try to tell her but don't know what to say.

"Everything will be okay. Don't worry." She stands up from her seat.

"Are *you* going to be okay though?" I ask.

"Yeah." She smiles, grins actually. "I think for a douchebag who doesn't love you, he looks a little too worried about you."

I don't have the time to comment on her observation because he chooses that moment to burst inside the room.

After that I have no choice but to ignore everything else and look at him. At his navy-blue eyes, his heavily breathing chest, and I clutch the sheets of my bed.

Tightly.

"What..." I swallow. "What are you doing here?"

"You fainted," he says, his lips barely moving they're pulled so tight.

"Right." I shake my head. "It's nothing. I'm okay."

He clamps his jaw before saying in a rough voice, "They said your sugar level was low. And you were dehydrated."

I sigh. "Yeah, that. It's, uh, fine. I'm –"

"No, it's not," he snaps.

He does it so loudly and so viciously that I jump.

"What?" I ask, pulling at the sheet and curling my toes inside the blanket.

"It's not fine, Salem." He pushes the words out and I think they're costing him a lot because I swear he's vibrating. "It's not fucking fine. It means you weren't eating."

Oh God.

Him and his crazy obsession with what I eat.

It isn't a huge surprise that Arrow eats everything right and healthy. And back when... well, when I'd sneak out to see him, up until a few days ago, he'd make me eat all that weird healthy stuff too.

He'd even make me those disgusting green shakes.

I hated them but I loved how he'd take care of me and made me drink every drop.

Even now, even after everything, my chest overflows with warmth at the sharp concern in his tone.

"I was eating. I was –"

"You're not going back there."

I press my spine into the pillows. "What?"

"You're not going back to St. Mary's after this," he declares.

"I'm sorry?"

"I'm taking you home as soon as they discharge you. I –"

I raise my hand. "Hold on a second. What... What are you talking about?"

He flexes his fists, curls and uncurls them, at his sides for a second before growling, "I'm not leaving you in that bullshit place. That place with all those rules and bullies. You don't belong there. You..." He shoves his fingers into his hair and almost tears out a clump of his sun-struck strands. "You're there because of me. You got sent there because of me. And all of this, you not eating, you sneaking out, *happened* because of me too. Because I was being a stubborn fucking asshole. But not anymore. Not –"

"Stop."

This time, it's him who flinches because I was so loud.

So abrupt.

But I had to do it. I had to stop him.

Because look at him. He's... flooded with regret.

His features are pulsing with it. It drips from his body, from his glassy eyes, his agitated movements.

My fingers go limp in the sheets. My toes uncurl. I stop pressing my spine into the pillows as I watch him.

As I watch him doing exactly what I never wanted him to do.

Beat himself up.

He's beating himself up, isn't he?

That's why he's here.

Because he thinks it's his fault. Because he thinks it's an *obligation* to be here. Not because he wants to be.

And I've had it.

I've had it with him.

"Get out."

He goes rigid at my words.

"Get out," I say again.

"I'm –"

"No, you don't get to talk. You don't get to say anything. Just leave. I want you to leave."

He grits his jaw before shaking his head once. "Salem."

And God.

God.

I'm so fucking mad at him for saying my name like this, for turning it into a rough, sand-coated plea.

Like I'm putting him through such an ordeal by sending him away.

"Get out," I scream and before I can think it through, I throw a pillow at him. Hard.

Nothing happens though.

It simply hits his strong, massive chest and ruffles his hair a little bit before sliding down to the floor like a loser.

It doesn't even make him blink.

"I don't want you here, got it? I don't want your pity and your fucking, *'oh my God, it's my fault'* routine. I don't want that from you. I don't want you to stand there like your world has ended because you think you made a mistake. You *didn't*. All right, Arrow? You did not make a mistake. It was my fault. I snuck out. I wasn't eating. It has nothing to do with you. So leave. You're off the hook. You don't have to look so lost and tortured. You can go be the superstar of soccer like you always wanted."

I'm breathing hard and vibrating now.

And he's not breathing at all.

In fact, there's not a single movement in his body.

It's like I absorbed all his heat and all his air, and now he's left with nothing. Now he's devastated and he's grown holes under his eyes, dark holes, and his lips are pinched and his skin is all pale and leached of color.

It's like I've drained my sun.

It's evident in his hollow voice. "Salem, it's not... what you think. I've got so much to say and –"

"I don't wanna hear it," I snap out.

Because I have no other option but to scream at him and kick him out of the room.

Because the alternative is that I run to him.

I climb off this bed and run to him and cling to his shoulders because he looks so grief-stricken.

He looks as if he's mourning the loss of my letters as much as I am and that can't be true.

That can't be true at all.

"Salem –"

"God, stop saying my name. Stop saying my fucking name, all right?"

I throw another pillow at him, my second one, and another.

But apparently they only have three pillows and I've run out of them and he's still here so I just scream again.

I scream louder as tears fill my eyes and he gets blurry and everything that has happened since he came back from LA crushes me and suffocates me and almost kills me.

"Get out of my room. Just leave me alone. I don't want you here. Just go, please. Okay? Just go. I can't take it. I can't. They took my letters. Do you understand that? They were my letters, *my* love story and they took them and you look like you care. You look like you even know what that means. You don't know. You don't care. You have no idea what it means to care about anything other than soccer, isn't that what you told me? You told me that you have no use for love or emotions. You *told* me that you want nothing to do with it. So please just leave. You were leaving anyway, right? So for the love of God, leave now. I can't deal with this. I can't deal with you. Just get out of my face."

Apparently, I've run out of words too and I can't talk anymore.

I can't.

I'm crying and sobbing into my hands and I don't even know when I put them on my face. But they're there now, my hands, and I bring my knees up too so I grieve the death of my love.

So I can...

"You're wrong."

I whip my face up at his quiet words.

Quiet but determined, and a repetition of what I said to him on the night it snowed and I told him my secret.

I try to wipe my tears from my eyes so I can see him clearly. But I only get to glance at him for a second or two and notice that his face has whittled down to razor-like sharpness and his body is arranged in a battle stance, feet wide, chest broad, before my tears take over.

And I hear his voice again.

"Because I want."

What?

I don't know what that means and I don't get to ask him because as soon as he's said those three words, announced them almost, he turns around and leaves.

After that, all bets are off.

I can't stop crying as I hear his last words over and over.

Because I want...

Hours later, I wake up in partial darkness.

My eyes are gritty and heavy and this time I know why. It's because I couldn't stop crying after he left. I cried the entire day until they gave me a mild sedative and put me to sleep.

But I'm awake now.

When my eyes fall on the rows and rows of shoeboxes, I even scramble up in my bed. I don't feel dizzy or foggy at my sudden movements as I reach out and grab a box. I open the lid and there they are.

My little orange, sun-like envelopes.

My letters.

They're here.

I'm holding them in my hands and I don't understand...

Then my eyes fall on something else.

A lone envelope, sitting on top of one of the boxes.

It's gray.

And it has a letter inside it.

A reply to the very first letter I wrote for him, eight years ago.

CHAPTER TWENTY-SEVEN

Darling Arrow,

It's weird writing you a letter because we sort of live in the same house.

But I guess this is the safer option. I don't get why but it is.

Anyway, I wanted to answer your question from this morning. You know, when you asked me if I was cold?

I'm not.

I mean, I am right now because your house is really cold, dude. But I wasn't, back in the kitchen. Because as soon as you came in, you took the cold away, which again I don't get.

But anyway.

Maybe you have the sun in your pockets.

Do you?

Oh and I won't tell. About your juice drinking. I'm not a rat. Your secret is safe with me.

All right, then.

That's all I had to say.

Salem

PS: Oh! I have a question. Where'd you get that silver chain? It's so shiny and pretty. I'm not into jewelry at all. I'm more into riding my bicycle and maybe even a little bit of soccer (by the way, I know you're a huge soccer player. Like, super huge. I'd absolutely die if you ever taught me. Maybe one day you can? I'm not the best player but I can learn!)

Okay, sorry. I totally went off track. What I wanted to say was that I absolutely love it! Your chain.

PPS: I don't know why I started with 'darling' but it felt right. It felt like 'dear' is too ordinary for you and I don't think you're ordinary at all.

Salem,

I'm sorry it took me so long to get back to you.

Eight years.

That's quite a long time, isn't it?

But anyway, to answer your question: I don't know if I carry the sun in my pockets. But if I do, then I'm really fucking glad.

Really fucking glad.

And I don't think I ever thanked you for keeping my secret. The one with the juice and all the other secrets over the years.

So thank you.

For being my secret keeper.

To answer your other question: my dad gave me that chain. But I think you already know that.

He gave it to me because I scored the most goals in a game that believe it or not, I don't even remember.

I'm actually sitting here, trying to think about it. Think about what game it was but for the life of me, I don't remember. All I remember is that it was raining that day and I got to stay up late an extra hour that night because we'd won.

Find it inside the envelope. It's yours now.

Yours,

Arrow

PS: I found these boxes in Miller's office. I'm not sure if you'll like the fact that I had a hand in her being fired. But you'll just have to make your peace with it.

PPS: If you need anything, anything at all, I want you to tell my mom. I mean it, Salem. I want you to tell her and I'll take care of it.

PPPS: By now I hope you know that you are the best soccer player I've ever seen.

CHAPTER TWENTY-EIGHT

There's a mailbox outside of Leah's house.

That's where he leaves a letter for me.

Every morning.

And he's been doing it for the past two weeks, ever since I got discharged from the hospital.

Every morning I wake up and rush down the stairs to the front door. I run down the driveway in my pajamas to get to the mailbox and rip it open, and every day I find a gray envelope with my name on it.

Inside that gray envelope, there's always a white, crisp paper, folded once. On that paper, he writes me a reply.

To one of the letters that I wrote to him over the years.

Which makes me think that before returning those shoeboxes to me, he took the time to read my letters.

But more than that, I think he kept them.

He *kept* some of my letters so he could reply to them one by one.

Is that stealing, I wonder?

I mean, they were meant for him. They've always been meant for him.

So I don't know.

Neither do I know what his plan is.

Like, is he going to keep writing to me like this? Send a letter every day? Also, why hasn't he gone back yet?

Because he hasn't.

Two weeks ago when I sent him away after a dramatic display of rage, I thought he'd leave. He'd go back to California, the place where he belongs. The place he wanted to return to, earlier than planned.

But then he brought back my letters and gave me his pretty chain.

I didn't want to put it on, you know.

I didn't want anything to do with it; I was so mad at him. For beating himself up as always, for treating me as a mistake, as an obligation.

I was so, *so* mad.

But I guess I'm weak. I'm a sucker when it comes to him because I did put it on.

I did.

I have it around my neck right now. It sits on my chest – under all my layers of clothing – between the valley of my breasts, stuck to my skin.

Every time I touch it, I feel him.

I hear him too.

I hear his last words before he left.

You're wrong. Because I want...

Now, what does *that* mean? What does he want?

And then there's Leah.

She cut short her meeting in New York when she heard about what happened with me at St. Mary's. I was expecting her to lecture me, berate me about my sneaking out and, of course, the letters. Maybe even punish me but she didn't say anything.

Actually, she was... caring toward me.

Leah and I, we've always had a complicated relationship. She's always been a strict maternal figure who has tried her best to make me toe the line. Though she's never made me feel like I'm a burden to her, she's never made me feel particularly warm and fuzzy either.

So her sudden change was kind of surprising.

What was even more surprising was the fact that after I was discharged, she gave me two weeks off from St. Mary's. I would've understood her giving me a couple of days off, especially since the doctor said that I needed my rest, but two weeks was a lot. Even though that period included Thanksgiving break.

But that's not the most surprising thing.

The most epic surprise was when she came into my room one night and told me that if I didn't want to return to St. Mary's at all, she was okay with it. She even apologized about Miller and how it was her fault that she gave Miller free rein because she'd always been so busy with out-of-town meetings and conferences.

She continued, "I've always been hard on him, on Arrow. Extremely hard. Harder than necessary. Harder than... what's humane even. I told myself that I was trying to mold him into someone Atticus would be proud of. But now I think maybe I was doing it because I missed my husband. I missed him so much that I wanted to keep him alive. Through my son."

Before I could even attempt to respond to that, respond to her frank words about how she's treated Arrow, she ducked her head and cleared her throat.

"This came for you." She had a gray envelope in her hand that I'd somehow missed, and she put it on my dresser. "I'm glad he has you."

She left then, leaving me stunned.

That was the first letter from him, two weeks ago.

In which he told me that he'd leave a letter just like the one I was holding in the mailbox every day.

That's why I'm here tonight, in front of his motel door.

Because I want to know what it all means.

I want to know why he's doing these things. Why isn't he leaving? Why does Leah think he *has* me when he doesn't even want me?

If this is some crazy attempt to pay for what he thinks is his mistake, then I want him to stop.

I want him to stop torturing me, making me fall in love with him even more.

Before I can talk myself out of it because *holy fuck* I'm terrified and this feels exactly like the night I came over to stop him from leaving, I knock at his door.

Two loud sharp knocks that make my knuckles throb.

I rub them to chase the sting away and the door whips open before I've even finished the task.

And he's there.

Right in front of me. Only a few feet away.

The love of my life.

This is the first time I'm seeing him after that day at the hospital, and he looks... exactly the same.

Standing at the threshold, wearing a pair of washed out jeans and his gray V-neck t-shirt, he looks burned out, my sun.

He still has darkness under his brilliant blue eyes and his features are still all razor sharp and severe.

"Salem," he says in a rough voice.

In a voice that sounds unused.

My lips part. "Hey."

"What the fuck are you doing here?" he snaps, his brows pulled together in a frown.

It's the same question he asked me the other night too, and like that night, my nerves mount but I try to calm myself.

I try to seem unruffled.

"I came to see you," I say.

"How did you get here?" he asks – again the same question from the other night, which is not helping me stay calm but again, I try.

"I took a cab."

Something about that makes him clamp his jaw and stare at me severely. "What the fuck are you thinking? You just got out of the hospital. You're supposed to be resting. You're supposed to be getting better."

Despite all my attempts to stay unaffected, I fist my hands at my sides. "I got out of the hospital two weeks ago. It was a minor blood sugar thing. I *am* better."

"If you keep running around town like this, you won't be. You're not supposed to stress yourself out. That's what the doctor said, didn't he?"

"How do you know what the doctor said? You were never there."

At this, a resigned look comes over his face. "That's not the point."

"Did Leah tell you?"

He remains silent but I get my answer and then fuck being calm.

Fuck being collected.

"So you've been talking about me to Leah. But you haven't come to see me."

Because I'm mad about it.

I'm mad, okay?

Like, he'll leave me letters every day. He'll talk to me through them but he won't come to see me.

And I have waited.

Every. Day.

Every single day that he left me a letter in the mailbox, I actually waited for him to knock at the door. I waited for him to come see me, talk to me, tell me *why*.

So many times I wanted to catch him in the act myself. I wanted to set up camp at my window and intercept him when he came to deliver the letters.

But I stopped myself.

Because I've begged enough and I was giving *him* a chance to come clean.

To tell me.

Now I find out that he's talking about me to Leah.

How cruel of him to do that.

How unkind of him that he'd rather drive me crazy with all these emotions and questions than come talk to me himself.

He sighs then, plowing his fingers through his hair. "Come inside."

I glare at him for a few seconds and he returns it with a calm but somewhat heavy look. Then, I *do* go inside.

Because I need answers.

But unlike last time when I was careful to keep my distance from him while entering, I touch him.

Well actually, I bump his chest with my shoulder as I pass him by.

Because I'm angry and I want him to feel it.

His only reaction though is a soft inhale, like he's smelling me or something.

But I refuse to think about it.

I refuse to think about him taking a whiff of me or how heated his body felt or how long it's been since I touched him.

I absolutely refuse to wonder about anything related to him anymore.

But I break that promise a second later when I get my first look at his room.

I halt in my tracks and run my eyes across the space that I've been in so many times. The space that I remember every inch of.

It has always been so clean and organized and neat.

Right now though, it's the opposite of that.

Sheets are crumpled; pillows are strewn about. His gray blanket lies on the floor as if he's had a fight with it and threw it away in disgust. Discarded clothes make a tiny hill by the bathroom door.

And there are books. *Everywhere.*

On the bed; on the floor.

Some are wide open; some are closed. Some are stacked together in a large pile on the desk and in his slim-backed chair.

Since when does he read books?

Since when does he not clean his room?

"What happened?" I breathe out, looking around, my heart picking up speed.

"I just... didn't clean up. Wasn't expecting company," he says from behind me and I spin around to face him.

He's by the door, standing with his feet apart and his fists clenched, watching me.

"Since when do you not clean up?"

"Since my therapist said that I might have a mild case of OCD," he replies. "She wants me to embrace the chaos."

"Your therapist?" I breathe out, thinking of all the times he implied that he hated going to her. "The one... you don't like."

His eyes flick back and forth between mine. "I think I was a little hasty in my judgement."

"So you like her now?"

"I'm still deciding."

I look around the room again, feeling stunned. "Did she also tell you to read books?"

He narrows his eyes. "No, she told me to get a life." I frown and he continues, "Apparently, I don't have one. Well, if you don't count soccer. And having a life involves a thing called hobbies. She told me to pick one."

"So you picked reading?"

"It would appear so, yes."

He runs his fingers through his hair again and messes it up, making the strands fall on his forehead, making me clench my fists again so I don't accidentally run to him and smooth them away.

"I remembered," he begins with a slightly lost expression on his face, "that I liked to read. When I was a kid. Which isn't a surprise because I've always been a straight-A student. Given the choice though, I'd rather watch game tapes than sit and read, but..."

"But?"

He shrugs, his shoulders jerking up and down tightly. "But I guess I'm trying to see if it sticks, reading. Getting a hobby." He swallows tightly, audibly even. "Not sure how my dad would react to it though. I, uh, try to picture his expression. You know, if he knew that I was using my time to read, for pleasure. Something other than textbooks, instead of working on my game. But I can't. I can't picture it. I know what my mom would say. She'd tell me that while it was commendable I was taking an interest in books, I'm still wasting my time reading English literature. She'd probably throw them away."

My chest feels tight and I let out a breath as I watch him, watch how he stands, a little away from the door, how his toes dig into the carpet, how his fists are clenched.

How adrift and unmoored he looks.

"You're not. You're not wasting your time and I don't think your dad would mind," I tell him, wishing again that I could touch him.

I wish I could go to him and ask him how it was while he was growing up.

I only know bits and pieces of it from after I came to live with him, and I wish I could talk to him about all of it.

"Actually, I think that even if he did mind, I wouldn't care. Not so much. Not as much as I thought I would. I think I'd..." He pauses and licks his lips, pondering his next words. "I think I'd mind more if I didn't get to read. If I didn't get to find out what else I like. What else I can do. What else is hidden inside of me other than The Blond Arrow."

My knees tremble. They almost buckle at his words.

It's a mystery really how I'm able to stand up.

Actually, I'm lying.

I know how. It's him.

It's his eyes, the power and intensity in them. He's keeping me tethered and balanced.

"Is that what your therapist told you? To find out what's hidden inside of you?" I ask with choppy breaths.

He shakes his head slowly. "No. It was someone else."

I take a moment to just... breathe.

I take a moment to just stand on my feet and watch him. To absorb what he just said.

For the past two weeks, I've been going crazy.

I've been making up theories in my head. About why he's doing what he's doing.

Is it to punish himself and atone for his supposed mistakes when it comes to me? Or is there something else?

Something... wonderful.

Something that scares me. Something that steals my breath and gives me hope.

It's giving me hope right now and I'm petrified.

"It's been two weeks," I whisper after a while.

"I know."

"Why didn't you come see me?"

His nostrils flare and his chest undulates on a large breath. "I was going to come see you."

"You were?"

"Yes."

"When?"

"Tomorrow."

"I'm leaving for St. Mary's tomorrow."

I am.

That's why I came tonight looking for answers. That's why it's so imperative for me to know.

God, I just want to *know*.

"I know that too," he says. "I'm taking you."

"What?"

He nods in confirmation. But that's not the only thing he does.

He moves as well.

He takes a slow but deliberate step toward me and strangely, I move back.

"I thought two weeks would be enough time for you to rethink your decision of going back to that hellhole," he tells me as he comes closer. "But if you won't change your mind, then I'll be the one to take you."

My feet stumble slightly but I keep going. I keep moving back as I whisper, "It was you. You came up with two weeks."

"You needed your rest. But more than that, you needed some time away from that place. After everything that happened." A dark look ripples through his stunning features, a menacing look. "And I thought it would give you time to make the right decision. But I guess I should know better by now, shouldn't I? No one can control you. No one can bind you by rules or put you in a box or rein you in. You're Salem. You're probably why they name hurricanes and natural catastrophes after girls like you."

I swallow at the possessiveness in his tone, at the possessiveness in his eyes.

Actually, it's more than that.

It's more than possessiveness.

There's some tenderness as well. Some helplessness and torment. A hint of amusement.

All at the same time.

And it makes his eyes glow.

"I *have* to go back," I whisper, still moving back. "My friends are there. They need me."

"I know. That's why I'm going to take you. And I'm going to make sure no one, no one at all, dares to even look at you wrong, let alone says anything to you. And if they do, then it'll give me great fucking pleasure to take care of them. To take care of anyone who bothers you."

Finally, I come to a stop.

My butt hits something. It's the edge of his desk that's laden with his books.

His new hobby.

Despite the fact that I want to go back, that I want to see my friends and especially be there for Callie, I am really nervous.

I'm nervous about the gossip, the looks I'll get from the girls, from the teachers. By now everybody must know that I have a thing for him. By now everyone must hate me even more, if possible. So his promise to me, spoken in such an authoritative and possessive tone, makes my body all lazy and heavy.

Cozy.

But I can't give in to it. I can't.

It's dangerous.

He is dangerous.

Hope is dangerous. At least for a girl like me.

A girl in such hopeless love.

"And then what?" I ask hesitantly.

"What?"

"Once you've dropped me off, and made sure that I'm taken care of, will you leave then?"

That's when he reaches me, at my question.

And my heart jumps into my throat.

Especially when he dips his face and bends his body and cages me in like he always does.

"No," he rasps, looking me in the eyes, his hands on either side of me.

"Why not?"

"Because I've got other things on my mind."

"Other things than... soccer?" I ask, clutching the edge of his desk.

"Yeah. Soccer can wait."

"Y-you're kidding."

"No." He shakes his head. "Fuck soccer. There are other things that I'm thinking about."

God.

God, I'm so scared.

"Like what?"

Something happens to him then.

A strain comes over him and his arms flex, his fingers crinkling the pages of the open book that they're pressing on.

"Like a girl with witchy eyes and thirteen freckles," he replies.

"What?"

"Yeah, and how fucked up I am over her. So much that everything hurts."

"Everything hurts?" I whisper, digging my nails into the wood and clenching my stomach.

"Yeah. Everything."

"Why?"

"Because I was an asshole who didn't have his shit together when I met her and so I made her cry. And because even when I decided to stop being an asshole and *get* my shit together, I made her cry then as well." Then, "They had to sedate you, didn't they? The day I showed up. Because you wouldn't stop crying. That's why I stayed away. For two whole weeks. That's why I didn't see you. I didn't deserve to see you because they had to inject you with a drug to put you to sleep. Just because I was there. Just because I came to tell you."

"Arrow –"

"I wanted to tell you the night you snuck out to see me too," he continues, his words rough and guttural, cutting mine off, his fingers abusing the pages of the book. "But you ran away from me. So I thought, I'll tell her tomorrow. I'll go to her in the morning and pull her out of class. I was even making plans and thinking of scenarios where you'd refuse me and I'd make you listen. I'd beg you to listen." He swallows. "But then Mom called me. And I never got the chance. But I was going to take my chance tomorrow. I was going to tell you."

"Tell me what?"

"That you're that girl for me."

"What girl?"

He licks his lips before saying, "The girl who haunts me."

"I-I haunt you?"

He nods. "Yeah. You're the girl who keeps me awake at night. The girl who makes me look out the window and count the stars in the sky. I not only count them. I look for patterns. I look for shapes that match the freckles on your nose and under your eyes. You're the girl I wait for at midnight because she wants to go for a ride and she has a thing for speed. But she's always late and when she does show up, I complain about it because I'm an asshole. But the truth is that you're the girl I'd wait hours for. You're the girl I'd wait and wait for just to get a glimpse of you in my leather jacket. Just to see what color lipstick you're wearing and just to hear you say the weird fucking name of it in your sweet voice.

"You're the girl whose notes I waited for like a junkie back at St. Mary's. And some days you'd write me two notes and I'd be over the moon. But I'd hide it. I'd hide it because again, I'm an asshole. I'm an asshole addicted to your words. To your letters. That's why I stole them. I stole your letters just so I

332 SAFFRON A. KENT

could read them over and over and write you back. Just so I could write to you every night.

"You're the girl, Salem, who makes me want," he bites out, the tendons on his neck standing taut. "I *want*. So many things, you understand? And I don't know what it means. I don't fucking know. I don't understand and it terrifies me. It shakes me right down to my soul but still I want to find out. I want to know. I want to know why it hurts to see you cry. Why it hurts when you're in pain, when someone upsets you. Why the thought of you in that godforsaken place with barred windows makes me want to break something. Break the world. Why it makes me sick to my goddamn stomach, whenever I think of you walking away from me like you did that night. I want to know what it all means. Because I've never felt this way. I've never felt this... need. This craving. Not until you. Not until you walked up to me that night at the bar like a vision of some sort. A vision that haunts me. That haunts my body, my soul. My heart. So yeah, you haunt me, Salem."

His eyes are glassy and shiny by the time he finishes and I'm a mess too.

I think my eyes reflect the same glow. The same brightness.

I think my heart is beating just as fast as his when I blurt out on a thready whisper, "I know what it means. I know why."

His nostrils flare, his eyes sharp. "Why?"

I let go of the desk then.

I unclench my fingers from around the wood and bring my hands up. I put them both on his chest, flat and splayed.

And he shudders.

Violently.

I think he even rips the pages he was tormenting. I hear the sound and it echoes in my stomach.

In all the places that were left hollow in my body ever since the night when the cold and brutal snow came to the earth.

"The fact that you write letters to me every night. The fact that you stole and that you hurt when I hurt. The reason that I haunt you is because you haunt me too. You've been haunting me for eight years. And it only means one thing."

Finally, he brings his hands away from the desk too and puts them on my face. He cradles my cheeks and tilts my neck up. "*Say* it."

I blink.

I take a deep breath and fist his t-shirt, before I reply, "It means that you love me."

Again, a shudder goes through him.

But this one is even more violent. It's an earthquake.

His whole body shakes. His eyelids flutter. His grip flexes.

It's like an explosion inside his body.

The fall of a mountain inside his chest. The fall of a bridge, a building inside his gut.

The fall of him.

But it's okay because I'm here to catch him.

I'm here.

"I was wrong the first time," he whispers, his fingers burying themselves in my hair. "I was wrong. I didn't know for eight years. I didn't want to be wrong again. I didn't want –"

I shake my head, my heart writhing inside my chest. "You're not wrong. You're not. This is what it feels like."

His lips part and a breath escapes him, loosening up his body and fanning over my lips, hot and sweet. "This is what it feels like."

"Yeah. You love me."

"I love you," he whispers, as if testing the words in his mouth.

I think he likes them, the taste of them.

Because he says it again and he says it strongly, with his possessive, needy fingers twisting in my hair. "I fucking love you, Salem."

That's when it hits me.

It hits me right in the center of my chest.

He loves me.

Arrow *loves* me.

That's why he's been writing me letters. That's why he hasn't left. That's *why*.

Because he loves me.

Because I make him want.

Because I want...

Because I'm the girl for him.

"You love me," I whisper again, my eyes getting blurry, a smile trembling on my lips.

His jaw clenches for a second before he whispers gutturally, "I know I hurt you, Salem. I know that. I know I don't deserve you. You were right to send me away at the hospital. You were right to scream at me and hit me and... I'm rude and uptight. I have so many rules. I could be so focused and self-centered. So emotionally stunted. I have this sickness, this need to be perfect all the time and it can consume me. But I'll do everything in my power, every fucking thing in my power, to make you happy. You said that to me, remember?"

"Yes."

His eyes bore into mine. "Now, I'm saying it to you. I'll do everything I can to make you happy. I'll tear my heart out and throw it at your feet if I have to. Because it's yours. My heart that I thought I'd killed is yours. It beats for you, Salem. Like a crazy fucking maniac that doesn't know when to quit. And if you want, you can stomp on it and set it on fire and stab it with a knife. You can do whatever you want to it, it will still be alive. It will still beat for you. Just give me—"

"I won't," I whisper and he freezes.

It's okay though.

It's okay because I'm about to tell him as well.

All the things.

All the pretty, lovely things.

"I won't stomp on it." I lean my body against his, giving him my softness, and he grabs onto it. "I can't. Because you're that guy for me too. You've always been that guy for me, Arrow."

"What guy?" he rasps and I hear the sweet tinkling of hope in it.

"The one who makes me feel warm," I reply, hardly believing that I get to tell him, hardly believing that he loves me. "The one who protects me and takes me out on rides. Who buys me ice cream and complains about my chick flicks but still watches them with me, who makes all the rules that I love to break. You're the guy who gave me this." I fish out the chain from under my sweater and show it to him. "I put it on the day you gave it to me. I've had it on for two weeks now."

He licks his lips, his fingers fisting in my hair and his body pushing into mine. "I don't want you to take it off. Ever."

I suck in my stomach at his rough, commanding tone. "I won't. So you see? I know that you hurt me, and you made me cry." I raise my arms up and around his neck and he snakes his hands down to my waist. "And you'll probably make me cry in the future as well. But it's okay. Because you're the guy I'll cry for. Because you're also the guy who'll wipe off all my tears when I do. So we'll figure it out. Together."

"Together."

"Yeah. Together. That's what I've always wanted, you know? I've always wanted to be your girl, and when I came here tonight, I was so scared. I was terrified that I wasn't –"

"You are," he says fiercely. "You are that girl. My girl."

"Your girl."

"Yeah."

I smile at him and a rush of a breath escapes him then.

A huge gust of a breath.

It sways the loose hair on my forehead and warmth explodes in my chest.

Warmth and fire and flowers.

The whole world of emotions sprouts up just under my skin but then something occurs to me. "Oh my God, wait."

He goes alert. "What?"

I fist his hair. "I'm going to St. Mary's tomorrow."

Arrow slowly relaxes, his fingers resuming their kneading of the flesh on my waist, his nose bumping against mine. "I know. I'm taking you, remember?"

"But Arrow." I squeeze my thighs around his body because holy shit, how can he be so clueless? "They won't let me have any privileges, you idiot. After what I did, and I don't think I can sneak out anymore."

He throws me a lopsided smile. "So then, I'll call you every Saturday. We'll talk for ten whole minutes. And when they have visiting weekends, I'll be the first one at the gate."

"You will?"

"Fuck yeah."

"And when you go back? To LA?"

His jaw clamps shut, stubbornly. "I told you soccer can wait."

"But you have to go sometime. You have to –"

"I don't *have* to do anything."

"But –"

"Shh. I don't care about that right now," he whispers. "You said we'll figure things out, right?"

I bite my lip. "Yeah."

"So that's what we'll do. We'll figure it all out."

I look into his blue eyes.

Determined and burning and blazing.

There was a time when they reminded me of calm summers. But now they remind me of a hot flame.

Of wild, savage fire.

Fire that I love. Fire that made me believe in myself, inspired me to be more.

I know that fire, *his* fire, can burn down the world, if it comes to that.

So he's right.

We'll figure it out, me and him. All of it. All of the things that are uncertain but don't really matter if we wanna be together.

For now, I'll just revel in this moment.

I'll just revel in the fact that my love isn't doomed.

My love is flourishing. It has a life. It will grow. It will live. It will *become* something now.

With him.

"You love me, huh?" I whisper, playing with the sun-struck hair at the back of his neck.

Those eyes of his smile. "Yeah."

"And you stole my letters."

"I did."

"So you're a *thief*," I tease.

Slowly, a smirk stretches his lips. "Looks like it."

"It does."

"I'm not just a thief though."

I squeeze my thighs around his hips. "No?"

He shakes his head slowly. "No. I'm also a poet."

"What?"

He bends over me, curls his sleek, cut body all around me, making himself my world. Flicking his eyes all over my face, he whispers, "Dark curls; Golden eyes." He rubs our noses together. "Thirteen freckles; Flowers between her thighs." He skims his lips over mine. "Sweet; So sweet; My heart; My sweetheart."

My lips part on a shaky breath. "You wrote me a poem."

His lips part too to inhale the air from my lungs. "Well, you do have a thing for poetry, so."

"You called me your sweetheart."

I mean, he's called me 'baby' before, in the heat of the moment. But never this.

Never sweetheart.

"Because you're my sweetheart, aren't you?"

"I am." I nod, feeling like I'll burst. "And you are my darling."

"I am."

I blink, forcing my tears away. "I love it."

"Yeah?"

"I love you."

He stares at me for a second before whispering, "I love you too."

I kiss my darling then.

And my darling kisses his sweetheart.

EPILOGUE

Two years later

The baseball cap.

That's the first thing I see when I finish talking to a girl and turn around, the cap that he's had for years now, hiding his glorious sunstruck hair.

He's at the ice cream booth, placing our order.

With a happy smile on my face, I take him in.

I take in his wonderfully muscled shoulders draped in his vintage leather jacket. Not the original jacket that I've always loved and now belongs to me because he gave it to me back at St. Mary's – the one that I'm wearing right now over my usual t-shirt and cargo pants – but a different one. This one we bought together in LA.

He also has his typical V-neck gray t-shirt on along with a pair of washed out jeans. Usually, I tell him to wear other colors but today I didn't wanna bug him.

I wanted to be nice.

Because today's special.

Of course I don't think he remembers.

If the past two years have taught me anything, then it's the fact that the love of my life can be forgetful sometimes. He can remember all the plays and strategies. He can also remember the plot of a book, a tiny piece of a poem that he's read; yeah, his reading hobby? That definitely stuck. But he forgets important milestones and dates.

He definitely tries but it's a losing battle.

But hey, he's got me, right?

I always remind him. And then I make him pay a little. Just for fun.

I'll remind him today too.

But first, I wanna see how long it takes for him to find out that I've broken his rule.

Turns out, it's not so long.

Because once he's placed his order, he turns around to check on me. But when he doesn't find me at my original spot where he'd left me before going to get our ice creams, his jaw clenches. He runs his eyes, which I'm sure are dark right now, around until they land on me.

And I smile.

He frowns.

My lips part at his sexy glare and my fingers grip the silver chain sitting on my chest that he also gave me back at St. Mary's. He told me to never take it off and I haven't.

Not once in the past two years.

His gaze shifts to where I'm clutching his chain before coming back to my face. Just to play with him, I wink and pout my lips.

His eyes flash – dangerously, seductively – before his lips twitch.

Before leaving to get the ice cream that I told him I so desperately wanted, he told *me* to stay put because the place was crowded and he wanted to be able to see me from the booth. We're at a carnival-like thingy and I admit that the place *is* packed.

But come on.

I'm not a delicate flower or a child. I can go wherever I want.

It's just that my boyfriend – *boyfriend*; yay! – is kinda possessive and dominating and he thinks he owns me.

Which he totally does.

But still.

He likes to take care of me like I'm his most cherished possession – again, which I am – and so he tends to go overboard. But since I own him too, I put him in his place at times.

Like now.

By breaking his rule.

Once the ice cream guy hands him the cones, Arrow begins to walk back. His eyes are still flashing and gosh, the way he's walking, almost prowling, over to me, makes me clench my thighs.

Makes me shiver.

Two years, and still I'm not at all equipped to handle his sexiness.

I'm so not equipped, and I know that as soon as he reaches me, I'm going to throw myself at him like a lovesick schoolgirl, which I'm not. Not anymore.

I graduated from St. Mary's two summers ago.

But it's not a secret that I can be a little crazy and emotional.

A little reckless.

And in the time that we've been together, I've been both. A lot.

Maybe because it hasn't been easy, the past two years.

First, it was St. Mary's.

As Arrow promised that night – the night he confessed his feelings and said that we'd figure everything out – he dropped me off at St. Mary's the very next day. He wasn't allowed into the dorm building though, which he didn't like at all, so he kissed me goodbye at the door in front of everyone and told me that he'd call me Saturday.

He did, too.

He called me every Saturday until I graduated. He also came to see me on visiting weekends and took me out on dates. Again, as he had promised.

There was gossip as I'd feared and nobody at St. Mary's warmed up to me until the end – well, except for my awesome friends with whom I still keep in touch – but nothing I couldn't handle.

Anyway, the rest of the time, up until my graduation, we emailed.

Writing traditional letters to each other – which we did also – is fun but technology does have its perks. Especially when you're in a long-distance relationship with your boyfriend, who's also a very busy and bright athlete.

Arrow stayed in town for Christmas that year before leaving for LA.

I still remember how hard it was when he left.

Even though I wasn't sneaking out to see him like I used to do before they found my letters, the thought that he was close, in that gray motel room, had been a comfort.

But then he left because he had to.

So those first couple of months were not pretty.

I would cry a lot during our Saturday phone conversations and he'd try to console me. I'd write him long emails and he'd write me even longer ones. Sometimes he'd be the sad one instead of me, which he basically showed by being short and abrasive, always blaming soccer for our distance. I'd be the one to soothe him then and tell him that this separation was only for a few short months.

And I was right.

Because after I graduated, I joined the Galaxy's youth summer program all the way in California.

Honestly, I did that more to be close to him than for soccer.

But whatever.

It was a happy time because I could see him and talk to him without all the million freaking rules and restrictions.

Well, overall happy. Because that was also when I broke the news to my sister.

I hadn't been looking forward to it but it had to be done.

I had to tell her. And I had to do it in person.

So I'd asked Arrow – and also Leah – to keep our relationship a secret until I could get a chance to see Sarah. Arrow wasn't happy about it but he did it for me. He also wanted to be there when I told her, but I refused.

I had to do it alone and I did.

We met for coffee – she wouldn't agree to lunch – and I told her.

And she told me that I was a whore. That I broke her trust and betrayed her in the worst possible way.

I mean, it wasn't unexpected.

I had always known that she'd say those things. I always knew she would never forgive me for loving Arrow.

But still, it hurt. It made me cry for a few days when I got back from our little coffee date.

Now my sister and I, we don't talk.

We haven't talked in ages. She doesn't return any of my phone calls or emails. She even quit her job with the team and moved to New York a few weeks after I'd broken the news to her.

As much as it still hurts, I get it.

I get her anger.

It's the same anger that I have for her, for doing what she did to Arrow. For betraying the guy I love.

But Arrow doesn't get that. He is mad. At Sarah, I mean.

Not because of what she did to him. I think he lost all his anger the night he realized the truth about their relationship. I don't think he even considers what he had with Sarah a relationship.

He's mad on my behalf.

He's mad because Sarah has never treated me like a sister and he doesn't like that.

I try to put him at ease though.

I try to tell him that it's okay. That I have him and he's the only one I need to be happy.

But he's adamant in his hatred and fury.

Honestly, I get that as well.

I know how he feels. Because that's exactly what *I* feel for Leah.

What I've been feeling for Leah for the past two years, ever since I found out the whole truth of what she did when Arrow was a child.

After Arrow decided that he was going to stay in St. Mary's awhile, he also started seeing Dr. Lola Bernstein regularly. It took him some time to open up, but slowly, he told her things from his childhood.

He told me things too.

Things that I had no idea about.

Horrifying things. Things that made me cry for the little boy he was, scared and trying to be perfect for a mother who was never happy with anything.

Things that I now call abuse, and rightfully so.

It *was* abuse.

The way Leah would make him work harder than any other kid. The way she always dangled his father's death as the reason to be the best.

I always knew she could be very strict and exacting. Always expecting the best from Arrow. I also knew – after he came back into my life – that he could be very self-critical and intense about perfection.

But gosh, it's worse than I thought.

Much worse.

I only moved in with them when he was fifteen. By then, Leah had successfully trained him into a perfect freaking son.

So I hadn't really known about it – the depths of damage that Leah had caused – until he opened up to me last year about the things he'd gone through when he was just a kid.

His mom was cruel to him. Beyond cruel.

And I don't think I can ever forgive her. I can be civil to her for Arrow's sake but my loyalties lie with my deeply damaged and dark sun.

So that's the second thing that has been hard for us: Leah and how her actions have affected Arrow.

But we said that we'd figure it out and that's what we have done.

And that's what we're doing.

I come back to the moment when he reaches me, tall and handsome, his large fingers curled around the delicate ice cream cones.

"Hi, boyfriend," I say, before taking one of the cones from his hand. "Thank you."

I lick the chocolate ice cream with sprinkles while peeking at him through my eyelashes and he grumbles, "You can't follow a rule to save your life, can you?"

I pout. "Sorry."

"Are you?"

Biting my lip, I shake my head before leaning up to kiss his cheek with ice cream lips. "No."

I go to move away but he grabs the back of my neck and keeps me pinned to his hard body as he growls, "Maybe I should make you."

I raise my eyebrows. "Maybe you should."

"There was a reason I told you to stay put. You could've been lost."

"I was perfectly safe. I just wanted to say hi to Cleo."

"Who's Cleo?"

Seriously?

God, my boyfriend.

He doesn't remember anything, does he?

I've talked about Cleo a thousand times before. I've talked about her husband, Zach, a thousand times before too. We're at his show, for God's sake.

Zachariah Prince, aka The Dark Prince, is a performer who does amazing things with his motorcycle. He flies it over holes. He circles the wall of death – like he did at the show that we just saw. He jumps off ramps and does all sorts of daring and dangerous things.

Cleo Prince, his wife, handles all his social media and that's where we became friends. Because I wouldn't stop fangirling on Zach's Instagram and somehow, she found out that I'm Arrow's girlfriend and she's a huge fan of The Blond Arrow aaaand yeah.

Today was the first time I met her in person and I totally loved her.

We're planning on going out to dinner together, all four of us. I just have to convince Arrow and she has to convince Zach because Zach gets a little jealous when Cleo fangirls over Arrow.

And well, we all know how Arrow gets when I fangirl over someone else other than him.

But come on, The Blond Arrow and The Dark Prince together? It's so happening.

Anyway I remember telling Arrow about meeting Cleo at the carnival thingy.

I sigh.

I shouldn't find this so adorable, but I do.

So much so that I kiss his jaw again.

"She's the wife of the guy we came to see." I explain further when he doesn't seem to grasp it, "The Dark Prince. Zach. The amazing guy who does wonderful things while riding a motorcycle, remember? We just saw him."

Finally, the bell rings and a thick frown appears between his brows. "I wouldn't say wonderful."

"You're kidding, right? It's beyond wonderful. Above and beyond."

His grip on my neck contracts and goes tighter. "I thought you were *my* groupie."

Warmth blooms in my chest at his possessive tone. "Are you jealous?"

"Keep it up and you'll find out."

I shake my head at his irritated tone. "You're so cute."

"Cute."

I wish his cap was off so I could grip his hair. His wonderful, rich, sun-struck hair, and mess it all up.

Because he looks a little too uptight, a little too irritated for such a wonderful occasion.

"Yes. You're the only one who gets to write his name on my chest. Don't you know that by now?"

His beautiful eyes move to my chest and my breaths start to come out in soft gasps. My bra-less breasts tingle and my nipples get all hard and achy.

Maybe because he did write his name there, last night. He also wrote his name on my stomach and way high up on my thighs.

He likes to do that.

Write his name everywhere on my body.

And then, he likes to fuck me really, really hard while he stares at me, at the girl who belongs to him.

At the girl who has his name on her skin. Because he put it there. Because he wants to declare to the world that I'm his. He has claimed me.

I think I'll have it tattooed one day, his name, on my ribs, where my heart is.

A flush comes over his gorgeous high cheekbones when he lifts his eyes. I'm so busy staring into his dark gaze that I don't even notice when he's crept his hand forward and grasped the chain sitting between my heaving breasts.

He tugs at it, pulling me forward and making me arch my back. "I do, don't I?"

"Yeah."

His eyes sweep over my face in the usual way. My hair, my nose.

My lips.

He tips his chin. "What's this one called?"

"Sweet Little Sweetheart."

"Sweet Little Sweetheart," he repeats on a whisper.

"There's a reason I chose it," I tell him.

"I know."

"You do?"

His gaze comes back up and arrests all my breaths and heartbeats. "Because it's been two years since I called you that and you like to celebrate every little thing like the needy girlfriend you are."

I gasp, dropping my ice cream – because who the fuck cares about ice cream when your boyfriend just said he remembers – and clutch his t-shirt with both hands. "You remember?"

It *has* been two years since then.

Since the night I went to see him in his motel room.

Two years since I became his and he became mine.

Our anniversary.

Dropping his cone as well, he tugs at the chain again. "Why do you think we're here?"

"B-because I was bugging you to go see the show."

I *have* been bugging him. As soon as I knew Zach was going to be doing a show in California, so close to LA, I started begging Arrow to go.

Not only because I'm a huge fan but also because Zach and Cleo belong to my hometown, Princetown, where I lived before moving to St. Mary's.

Arrow never showed any interest in going at all though.

Not until one day he surprised me with the tickets.

But I honestly didn't think he had done it for our anniversary.

"I thought the dates were a coincidence. You never said anything," I say in a breathy, awed voice.

"It's called a surprise."

Tears sting my eyes. "You surprised me. For our anniversary."

A lopsided smile appears on his lips even as a grave emotion takes hold of his features. "Well, we haven't spent much time together in the past couple of months. Because of my practices and things."

That's true.

The season is still on – they have the last championship game next week – and so he's been really busy with soccer practice. Another reason why I thought he wouldn't remember.

Plus I've been busy with my own stuff.

Yeah, I've got stuff now. Namely, college.

It's a little weird. I never thought I'd go to college. But then I never thought that I'd play on an actual soccer team at that school and I do that as well.

After the summer program at the youth academy, I decided to stay in California with Arrow. Obviously.

We got a great apartment and I worked for a while at a nearby café while I decided what to do with my life. College wasn't on my radar until my friends from St. Mary's told me to give it a shot.

Arrow was supportive as well and I was like, why not.

My mother had left me with a college fund and I had the best guy in the world to tutor me if I ever needed it, and so I started college earlier this year.

It's a lot of work and along with Arrow's practices and hectic travel schedule, sometimes it's hard to find any free time.

But I understand.

Even though we get busy at times, I know we love each other.

I know it when I leave him sexy notes all over the apartment and he always replies back. I know it when *he* writes me sweet little poems and sticks them in my textbooks for me to find later.

When we have impromptu picnics on our living room floor because we don't have the time to go out to a restaurant or to the movies. When he comes home exhausted and we simply cuddle on the couch in silence before falling asleep.

I *know*.

"But it's okay. I don't –"

"And I forgot," he cuts me off. "Last year. But I didn't want to forget again. I didn't..."

I cradle his jaw. "Hey, it's okay. I know you're busy. I know you forget things. But I don't mind. I don't, Arrow. It's okay. You're just trying to figure things out. We both are."

He is.

God, is he trying.

Just because he's accepted that he wants more from life doesn't mean it has been a fun change.

Some days are easy for him. Some days Arrow remembers that he doesn't have to be perfect all the time. He doesn't need to constantly prove himself.

But there are hard days too.

When he's on edge, on the warpath. When he gets this urge, this anxious, jittery feeling to work himself to the ground.

On those days, I remind him that he's my Arrow now. The guy I'm in love with, and he's perfect the way he is. I remind him that he doesn't need to be what they told him that he should be.

He should be himself.

Dr. Lola Bernstein helps as well. He still sees her but mostly they have Skype sessions since she lives in the east and we're here in California.

He also talks to his mom, trying to build a new relationship if possible. They talk about his dad a lot, about how he was before he died. I think he's just trying to figure out his father, whose dream he was pursuing with such focus. He's trying to figure out if his dad was really the man that his mother portrayed or was there more to him than the wish to play for the European League.

In the meantime, European League is on hold for Arrow.

He's only focusing on his game here and trying to take it easy.

"Things with us, with *me*, haven't been easy," he says, the lines of his features harsh and tight. "I never thought I could... live like this. That I could *be* someone. Someone else. Myself. I never thought I could feel so much. And for the past two years, that's what I've done. I've felt. And *felt* and Jesus Christ, it's fucking fantastic. My heart, I can hear it. I can feel the rush in my blood when you touch me. I can feel my breaths stopping and jacking up when I look at you. And when you smile..." He takes in my lips again and a puff of breath escapes him. "My chest hurts. It aches and I know that I have to kiss you or I'll explode."

"Yeah?"

He licks his lips and raises his eyes, open and shining. "Yeah and I'm scared that I'll fuck it up. I'll fuck it all up and you'll realize that you're better off and... I'd be lost all over again and –"

I put a finger on his lips. "You won't be. You won't be lost, Arrow. Because I'm not going anywhere."

He swallows. "No?"

"No. I'm Arrow's girl, remember? The girl you kissed in front of the whole world."

He did.

Last year at the championship game.

When Arrow shot the winning goal, I was so freaking happy that I actually ran out onto the field to hug him.

I'd always wanted to do that, you see. I always wanted to attend all his games and cheer for him from the stands and last year when he made his comeback after sitting out half the season before, I could.

Only security stopped me.

But I shouldn't have worried because through all the chaos, Arrow somehow noticed my attempts to get to him and abandoning everything, he started toward me.

He came to me panting and sweaty and freed me from the guards, from where they were trying to hold me off like a trapped bird. Then he picked me up and made me climb his body like he usually does and kissed the fuck out of me.

In front of the whole world, the media gave me a new name: Arrow's girl; his teammates still give him a hard time but he doesn't mind because they're his friends now.

So yeah, I'm Arrow's girl.

Arrow's eyes shine anew, this time with a possessive light. "Yeah, to tell them."

"That I'm yours?"

"Fuck yeah, you're mine."

This guy is crazy, isn't he?

And I love him so much.

So, so much.

"See? You won't have to be without me. I'm your girl. Now and forever. Your needy, crazy girlfriend and you're my perfect, idiot boyfriend."

A slight smile flickers on the side of his mouth. "That you are. Needy. And crazy and perfect. My perfect."

I wind my arms around his neck and stretch up my body. "Say it."

His chest moves with a long breath, a long sweet breath, before he grabs my face and rasps, "My heart. My sweetheart."

---

rrow

All my life I've been taught to chase perfection.

I've been taught to chase greatness and reject my flaws, my emotions. My heart. My very soul.

But I'm starting to understand that our flaws, the design of our hearts, the fabric of our souls, are the very things that make us unique.

That make us, *us*.

That's why some people study science while others study art. That's why some people dance and others sing. Some people write poetry and others don't understand the meaning of it.

That's why the world is big and vast and different. Because we all have something to offer.

Because we're all perfect in our own way.

And I'm perfect too.

Not in the conventional sense, no. But for her.

At least, that's what she tells me.

She tells me that I'm perfect for her and these days, that's the only kind of perfection I care about.

Becoming her perfect.

Her Arrow.

The girl with thirteen freckles and witchy eyes.

The girl who changed my life and taught me things about myself.

The girl I'm in love with.

My Sweet Salem.

THE END
(For Arrow & Salem)

C allie
When: A couple of months ago; First sighting of Reed Jackson

Where: Ballad of the Bards

I don't like whiskey.

At all.

It burns and it's a masculine drink. Or at least, that's what I've grown up believing because I've got four brothers – all older than me – and their choice of drink is whiskey.

Me? I like cosmos or pina coladas or mimosas. Drinks that are purple and pink and orange and taste sweet and wake up your tongue and sizzle between your teeth. Not that I'm legally allowed to drink yet but still.

Tonight though, I'm choosing to drink whiskey. And Jesus Christ, it's awful.

Awful.

I hate it. But I hate *him* more. The guy because of whom I'm drinking this terrible creation.

Reed Jackson.

The liar. The guy who betrayed me and broke my heart.

He is here. Somehow. At my favorite bar.

I saw him standing in the middle of the crowded room, looking well and alive, not ten minutes ago. Looking like a dream.

What the fuck – *fudge* – is he doing here?

Okay, so I don't curse. Well, at least I try not to. Because again, I've got four brothers who curse enough for the rest of the humanity. So I try to be a lady when I can.

But it's okay. I'm drinking whiskey straight from the bottle, aren't I? So I can curse like a sailor too.

I can curse and call him names, all the bad fucking names that I can think of because how the fuck is he here tonight?

How. The. Fuck?

Shouldn't he be away, at college?

He goes to college in New York City because that's where all the rich kids from our town go, apparently. And it's not even holiday season. It's fucking September. People have classes in September.

What the fuck is he doing here in fucking September? That fucking asshole bastard.

That motherfucking asshole bastard.

That motherfucking asshole *douchebag* bastard.

I try to think of other bad words that I can call him as I take another pull of this terrible whiskey when a shadow falls on me, long and pervasive.

Pitch black.

I'm standing outside the bar, my spine propped against the brick wall, the liquor bottle clutched between my fingers.

As soon as I saw him in the bar, I froze for a few seconds. I thought I was dreaming until my friends started asking me questions about him. And well, it wasn't hard for them to deduce that he is the guy. He's the reason I'm at St. Mary's.

And as soon as they realized that, I made a beeline for the whiskey, which I basically forced Will, the bartender and my brother's friend, into giving me and got the heck out of there. Because I couldn't be in the same room as Reed.

So this shadow that's rapidly growing closer could belong to anyone. A stranger. And since there's no one else around except a row of trashcans on my left, I should be afraid.

I'm not though.

My heart isn't pounding out of fear. It's pounding out of anger. And knowledge. My breaths are spasming and breaking because I know that shadow.

Even though I haven't felt it in two years, I know it.

I know the guy walking toward me, prowling even, in lazy, languid steps.

Somehow I knew that he'd seek me out. I knew he'd come for me because just when I saw him, he saw me as well. And when he reaches me, I realize that maybe I shouldn't have left the confines of the bar.

I shouldn't have come outside, all alone.

Because in this moment, as he stands before me, I also realize that I was wrong before.

I said that my heart wasn't pounding out of fear. I lied.

There is fear.

Oh yeah, there is – among other things – and because of it, I'm not looking at him.

I can't.

Maybe because as long as I don't look at him, I can pretend that he isn't here. That I *didn't* see him at the bar and I'm not drinking whiskey because of him.

It's stupid logic but I think I'm allowed that because God, he *is* here.

But anyway, I chicken out and avert my eyes from his large, dark frame and look at something else. Something over his shoulders, a bright white thing that practically demands all my attention.

His white mustang.

His baby. That's what he used to call it when I knew him.

It's parked in the lot behind us and it's so freaking shiny and posh and so out of place in this area of Bardstown that even if I wanted to look at something else, I wouldn't be able to.

So I look at his car.

But no matter how hard I stare at it, trying to deny that he's here, I can't tune out the fact that he's staring at *me*.

I can't tune out the fact that it's been two years since I last saw him and I'd almost forgotten how powerful, how enticing, how *bad* his stare can be.

How it could make me do anything.

So despite all my silly logic and denial, I break down first because I want him to take his dangerous eyes off me and say, "Your baby looks good."

There. I said the first words and they totally sounded casual and breezy.

I mean, it's not as if I'm an expert at all things breakup. But I do know that when you encounter your ex-boyfriend, let's say for the first time in two years after a super ugly breakup, the first thing is to look casual.

And I think I did that.

I did it, didn't I?

I sounded casual. Right?

Oh my God, what if I didn't sound casual? What if...

"She does."

That's all he says and I get my answer.

I get that I did sound breezy. I did.

Because he didn't sound breezy at all. He sounded intense. His two words sounded heavy and laden with things. Things that make me think that he wasn't talking about his stupid shiny car at all.

He was talking about something else. *Someone* else...

Like me.

And then I have to look at him to confirm and I do and well, my friends were right. He is gorgeous.

Damn him.

He *is* shiny. Even shinier than his expensive car.

It took me a lot of time to figure out why, back when I was naïve and in love. Why does he shine more than any other person that I've met? What's the secret?

It's his very skin actually.

It's kinda pale. Almost silvery. Moon-like.

You'd think that his pale, winter-like skin would make him look sickly or pasty. But no.

God, no.

It makes him look like one of those ancient statues made with marble by the Greeks or the Romans. Those statues, they are beautiful and resilient. Immortal. Awe-inspiring. They have withstood time and years and they still look the same, untouched and untarnished.

That's how he looks.

He looks immortal. An otherworldly being with his gunmetal gray eyes and dark hair. A creature of the night and snow.

Maybe even a Vampire. Corrupted and seductive. And yet, thrumming with life and energy, an inner sort of glow that comes from within.

If only he was a noble vampire like Edward Cullen or something. A hero disguised as villain.

But he's not.

He's the opposite.

And he's staring at me like he wants to eat me.

So I stop checking him out like a lovesick Bella and say, "Are you sure she's safe though? Your baby. In this neighborhood." I shake my head in mock concern. "People can be very dangerous."

My words only amuse him and his lips – soft and red in contrast to his marble-skin – stretch up slightly. "Can they?"

"Yeah."

"What do you think they'll do?"

Drown it in the lake again.

But I don't say it.

For one, I can't believe my plan to ruin his baby forever didn't work. Maybe I should've thought of something else, something more damaging than driving it into the lake. But then I wasn't thinking at all when I decided to destroy it.

I was fucking furious and in pain.

"I don't know, steal it? Again." I clench my fingers around the neck of the whiskey bottle. "Slash your tires. Steal your rims. Spray paint your hood. Smash your windows. Douse the whole thing with liquor and burn it down once and for all."

His amusement only grows. "That's... quite a creative list."

"I'm creative."

"And definitely dangerous."

"Oh, you're in for such a surprise, trust me."

"Does it come with a little bow tied around it? Your surprise."

His eyes aren't on my face when he says it or purrs it actually. They are somewhere down below. On my stomach, to be exact. And after a second, I realize why.

It's because my dress has a bow wrapped around my waist.

It's a lacy thing, my dress. White and covered in embroidered blue flowers that ends mid-thigh, paired with matching blue ballet flats. When I put this on earlier tonight, I thought it was girly and cute and perfect for a secret night out with my friends.

But right now, with the way he's staring at my bow and the ruffled hem that skims my bare thighs, my cute dress turns into something indecent.

Something that you wear behind closed doors. Something that's meant to be stared at and devoured and ripped to shreds by a guy whose intentions are as dark as his skin is glittering.

Perv.

"No, it comes with long nails and sharp teeth," I tell him with a sweet, mocking smile and a chirpy voice.

He lifts his eyes and drawls, "Well then I'll be over here, sitting on the edge of my seat, waiting to unwrap it."

Okay, I lied. Again.

I can't do this. I can't sound casual and breezy and unaffected. When he is being so purposefully intense.

I don't know what his game is, but I want him gone. And the only way to make it happen is to find out what he wants. Why he sought me out.

Knowing him, he came here to ruffle my feathers, make me squirm. Which is fine. Really.

Let him do what he came here to do.

Because the sooner he does all of that to his satisfaction, he can leave and I can move forward to forgetting this terrible coincidence.

"As much as I'm enjoying talking to you," I burst out as my nails scrape against the liquor bottle. "I don't have time for this. So let's do it."

"Let's do it," he says flatly.

I widen my stance, shift on my feet like a fighter, getting ready to throw in punches. "Yeah. Let's do this thing so you can leave me alone."

He watches my feet for a second, notices my stance before asking in a low voice, "Are you sure?"

I raise my chin and wave my hands. "Yes. Come on. I'm ready."

"Okay." He nods, his eyes hooded. "Where do you want it?"

"What?"

At my question, the air turns hot.

I don't know how he does that, turn the air around us so dense and opaque with just one look. But it's always been this way.

He always makes it harder for me to breathe.

Like he's suffocating me and I love it because he does it so sweetly.

He gestures toward the wall that I'm standing against. "Yeah, where do you want it? Here, up against the wall? Or in the backseat of my car." He doesn't give me the time to respond to his statement. "It's been two years but I remember how much you seemed to love writhing on my leather seats. And if I'm being honest, I'd love to see that again. But lady's choice, of course."

"What... I..."

My mouth is in the process of forming confused, dumbfounded words when I get his meaning. His stupid innuendo.

He's talking about sex.

The fucking asshole is talking about sex because I stupidly said, *let's do it.* That's it, isn't it?

Ugh. I'm an idiot.

But! The motherfucking nerve of him!

"You're funny," I snap. "*And* delusional. If you think I'm letting you touch me ever again, you need your head examined."

"Is that so?"

"Yes. Because it's never happening. So say what you came here to say and leave."

He looks at me thoughtfully. "Hmm. I'm not so sure you want me to leave though. Because this feels like a dare and you know how much I like those."

I clench my teeth while I debate throwing this bottle at him. "It's not a dare, it's reality. Touch me and lose your teeth. So you really need to leave now."

Instead, he smiles, his ruby red, cruel and gorgeous lips, stretch up in a curve as he takes a step closer and I press my back into the wall. "You're not making it easy though."

"Not making what easy?"

He takes another step toward me as if to act out his next word. "Leaving."

"Get away from me or I'll punch you, okay? I'm not kidding."

He dips his face toward me, his voice going even lower while I'm over here, squeaking. "If you keep talking like that, I'll start getting ideas."

"What ideas?"

"That you're flirting with me."

I swallow as my skin starts to feel tight, restless. Swollen.

God, why? *Why* does he have to be like this?

Seductive and stunning and so freaking consuming.

Why does my body have to react to it?

He broke our heart, you stupid body. He betrayed us, remember? We were in pain for days. Weeks.

We still are...

"Oh my God, you *are* delusional," I tell him, fisting my hands.

Reed shakes his head slowly, his eyes glittering with challenge. "You know you don't have to try so hard with me. You want me to touch you, Fae, just say the word."

Fae.

And just like that, I stop breathing.

I stop shaking. My restlessness evaporates and I freeze.

I freeze in a time two years ago. When he used to call me that.

His white mustang was his baby and I was his Fae, short for Fairy. It's because of my blonde hair, blue eyes and a pocket-sized body but with long, graceful, dancer's limbs.

His words, not mine.

I'm not pocket-sized. I'm an average 5' 4 ½". But like a foolish girl that I was, it used to make me happy. It used to make me smile that he had a special name for me. I had a special name for him too but I'm not going there.

I'm never going there.

I take a deep breath, clutch my whiskey bottle and look him in the eyes.

"Hey, *Reed*." Deliberately emphasizing his name, I smile with my mouth but my eyes are lethal; I can feel it. "I know it's been two years and all but my name is Calliope Thorne. People also call me Callie. And if I'm being honest, I'd rather you not call me anything at all. But asshole's choice, of course."

He smiles too. Not the full-blown smile from a few seconds ago but a fraction of it. And like me, his mouth might be smiling but his eyes are grave, intense, heavy with our shared past.

"Calliope Juliet Thorne," he murmurs. "I know what your name is, Fae. I also know what my name is. Do you?"

My breaths escalate.

They swell and crash inside my lungs when I think of his name, his full name.

Reed Roman Jackson.

This time when I go back in time, I can hear my own voice, my sixteen-year-old smiling voice, telling him, *I'm Juliet and you're Roman. And everybody knows that Roman is just a different version of Romeo. So that means we're Romeo and Juliet. Which also means that we should probably stay away from each other. Since they both die and all...*

If only I had taken my own advice and stayed away from him.

It's in our very names, our fate. Our catastrophe. Our destruction.

"You said that our names made us Shakespearean, star-crossed lovers," he says, bringing me back to the moment. "A teenage tragedy. And I told you that they didn't. Because what did fucking Shakespeare know? To me, you'll always be Fae. And to you, I'll always be Roman."

That's what I used to call him, Roman. Not Reed.

Because back then I was a fool. I thought he belonged to me like I belonged to him.

So like arrogant, defiant lovers, we gave each other secret names, names only meant for us: Roman and Fae.

What a stupid idea to call each other by different names.

What a stupid fucking thing: first love.

One minute it's life and the next, it's death.

That's what it felt like when he broke my heart. That I'd died and so in this moment, I pull myself together and straighten my spine.

It's hard but it needs to be done.

When you fall in love with a quicksand of a guy like him, you need to be strong.

Your heart needs to be made of iron and your spine needs to be forged out of steel so you can look him in the eyes and tell him, "I remember. I remember everything. I remember everything I said to you and everything you said to me. And that's why I know that we *are* a teenage tragedy. Because you made sure of that, didn't you?" I clench my teeth for a second because I feel a pain starting up in my chest, traveling up to my jaw, my temples, stinging my eyes. "So get away from me because I wasn't kidding about you losing your teeth. *Reed.*"

For a few seconds after I'm done, it feels like I haven't spoken at all.

Because he doesn't move. In fact, he bends down toward me even more.

Our eyes are connected, his gaze calm and scrutinizing while mine is wide and fearful of his intentions. A microsecond later, I feel something happening, something slipping from my fingers before he straightens back up.

It's my bottle. He stole my whiskey from me.

I fist my empty hands. "Give it back."

Again instead of obeying me, he throws his head back and swallows down a huge gulp of my whiskey. Asshole.

When he's done, his red lips glisten and his face sparkles like the moon. "See you around, Fae."

And then he's gone and I can breathe.

But it's not as glorious, to be able to breathe, as I thought it would be.

Because with every breath that I take, I think of him.

I think of how beautiful he is, how gorgeous. How he looks like a prince. A hero. And how it's all a façade.

Because he's anything but a hero. He's a villain.

A gorgeous villain.

To be continued in "A Gorgeous Villain"
(St. Mary's Rebels Book 2)

Two years ago, Reed Jackson betrayed Calliope Thorne and broke her heart.
So she stole his most prized possession – a white mustang – and drove it into
the lake for revenge.
Now, Callie is stuck at a reform school while Reed is off at college, living his
life without repercussions.
Until he comes back.
With him comes back all the feelings that Callie has been trying to bury:
anger and heartbreak.
But most of all, desire. At the sight of his beautiful but lying lips and his
gunmetal gray eyes that still taunt and smolder when he looks at her.
Whatever though. It's not as if Callie is ever going to fall for her ex-boyfriend
again. Or let him corner her in a bar one night and touch her, kiss her...
Neither is she going to kiss him back. Or worse, sleep with him.
Because that would make her naïve and foolish.
Oh, and also *pregnant*.
And there's no way Callie is ever going to get pregnant at eighteen and with
Reed's baby, no less. The guy she hates.
The guy who taught her all about heartbreak. Who might look like a gorgeous
hero but really is the villain of her story.
Buy NOW

EXTENDED EPILOGUE

If you enjoyed Arrow and Salem's love story, I'd be eternally grateful if you considered leaving a review.

Want more Salem and Arrow? Click here to get an Extended Epilogue.

Would you like to be notified when Saffron releases another book or if there's a sale happening? Sign up for her mailing list here!

BAD BOYS OF BARDSTOWN

St. Mary's Rebels Spinoff series
Coming soon!

You Beautiful Thing, You (Bad Boys of Bardstown 1)
Releasing June 6th, 2023
Pre-order now!

Nineteen-year-old Tempest Jackson wants a baby.

No, her biological clock isn't ticking, but she's desperate for unconditional love. Rejected by all except her brother and soon to be married off by her father for financial gain, she aches for someone to hold close and call hers.

Enter Ledger Thorne. Soccer god, devastatingly handsome and her brother's rival.

Once upon a time they had a thing. A beautiful thing. But while Tempest thought she was madly in love, Ledger was only using her for petty revenge.

So Tempest has a plan: seduce the sexy jerk who broke her heart, use him to get pregnant and then leave him in the dust like he left her, to marry a stranger.

Only the problem with making babies is that it doesn't feel like revenge. It feels a lot like that thing they used to have: Hot and stormy, and intense and intimate.

But Tempest isn't a fool. She'll stick to the plan.

Because wasn't it Ledger who turned their beautiful thing into something ugly?

Now it's her turn...

NOTE: This is a STANDALONE set in the world of Bardstown, a St. Mary's Rebels spin-off.

Oh, You're So Cold (Bad Boys of Bardstown 2)
Stellan Thorne's story!
Releasing December 12th, 2023
Pre-order now!

A Wreck, You Make Me
(Bad Boys of Bardstown 3)
Shepard Thorne's story

Bad Kind of Butterflies
(Bad Boys of Bardstown 4)
Ark Reinhardt's story

For you, I fall to Pieces
(Bad Boys of Bardstown 5)

I'm Hopeless, You're Heartless
(Bad Boys of Bardstown 6)

Add the series to your TBR

"OUR ATLAS OF ATTITUDE"

Soccer Nation

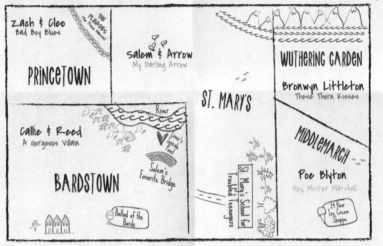

Zach & Cleo
Bad Boy Blues

THE PLAYERS
(No Time Now)

PRINCETOWN

Salem & Arrow
My Darling Arrow

WUTHERING GARDEN

Bronwyn Littleton
These Thorn Kisses

ST. MARY'S

Callie & Reed
A Gorgeous Villain

River

Lover's Suicide point

Salem's Favorite Bridge

MIDDLEMARCH

Poe Blyton
Hey, Mister Marshall

BARDSTOWN

Ballad of the Bards

St. Mary's School for Troubled Teenagers

24 Hour Ice Cream Shoppe

ACKNOWLEDGMENTS

Thank you so much for reading Arrow and Salem's story. I hope you enjoyed it and maybe you saw a little bit of yourself in it somewhere. At least, that has always been my hope with the stories that I create.

I can't believe that it's almost been a year since I wrote one of these things, acknowledgement, I mean. I never thought it would take me so much time to finish this story but it did. There were times when I thought I probably wouldn't see the end of it because things were so hectic and my creativity was burned out.

I'm glad I stuck to it though. I'm glad I could see Arrow and Salem and myself grow with every draft I wrote and every revision I made.

Since 2020 has been such a weird year, I didn't want to do a standard acknowledgment that I've always done. The following people deserve more – much more – than a mention. If it hadn't been for them, I wouldn't be writing this section at all.

First and foremost, my husband. I always say that he's the reason I'm doing this. He's the reason I'm in this industry and that I have stayed so far. If it were up to me, I would've quit and moved on. And this book literally wouldn't be possible without his support.

It was the height of COVID when I was writing this and New York was the epicenter. I was scared and anxious and my juices weren't flowing at all. But I had a deadline (at least, mentally) and I had to deliver. If it were not for Mr. Kent listening to this story over and over, chapter by chapter, conflict by conflict, I would never have figure out why Arrow was being so difficult. I never would've figured out why the hell he doesn't just kiss her and be done with it. It was him who figured out Arrow's character for me. Heroines I understand, heroes give me a lot more trouble. And stuck together in our apartment, Mr. Kent was the one who got the brunt of my crazy creativity. So THANK YOU. Thank you for listening to me, for being my sounding board, for helping me figure out why some things in the story were slow and why some things needed to shine more than the others. Thank you for telling me that what I do is magical – even though I always have trouble believing you –

and that you love me more because I'm such a tortured artist. Haha! This book is both my baby and yours. I love you more than I can ever say.

The next person I want to thank is a fellow writer and my friend, Bella Love. When I finished the story, I told her that I wanted to scrap it and tell everyone that this story isn't happening after all. But she told me to send her the manuscript and once she was done, she told me that I was crazy. That Salem was the sweetest bad girl I'd written so far and reading this book was the highlight of her day. Thank you so much for pulling me off the edge. I adore you.

Melissa Panio-Peterson, for being the other half of my brain. It's spooky how similar we are in our thoughts and how you can read me and what I envision creatively. Thank you for being an expert in all things SAK. After publishing a handful of books, I have realized that one of my biggest concern is always to deliver on my brand, on what readers expect of me and MPP is my SAK brand checker. Haha! Thank you so much for supporting me and believing in me and understanding what I do with my work.

The next on the list are these lovely people that I've found through accident and now are a part of my team:

1. Dani Sanchez of Wildfire Marketing Solutions, thank you for not freaking out on me when I kept telling you that this book won't be out for a while and when that while turned into almost a year.
2. Leanne Rabesa, my editor and fact checker, the one who tells me when I've fucked seasons up and when I have impossible character ages. Thank you for telling me that Salem's age was wrong and that Arrow needed to be older than what I'd originally made him.
3. Najla Qamber, my cover designer, thank you for not ditching me when I kept changing my vision of the cover on you. Thank you for putting those gorgeous lips on the cover. If anyone could do it and portray the sexiness and angst of the book, it was you.
4. Virginia Tesi Carey, my proofreader, thank you so much for being so flexible when I kept changing dates on you. I was so embarrassed to be doing that; a deadline is a deadline even if self-made and I never break it. But man, this year was such a crazy ride. Thank you for sticking with me always.

ABOUT THE AUTHOR

Writer of bad romances. Aspiring Lana Del Rey of the Book World.

Saffron A. Kent is a USA Today Bestselling Author of Contemporary and New Adult romance.

She has an MFA in Creative Writing and she lives in New York City with her nerdy and supportive husband, along with a million and one books.

She also blogs. Her musings related to life, writing, books and everything in between can be found in her JOURNAL on her website (www. thesaffronkent.com)

Made in United States
Troutdale, OR
04/11/2024

19115720R00239